The woman stood in the interior shadows. He could barely see her. She waved him inside.

He got out of the car and walked up to the door. She didn't say anything, just opened the door wider so that he could walk inside.

She hadn't turned on any lights in the bedroom area. Light from the bathroom spilled into the shabby room, enough that Coffey had no trouble seeing the man. He wore only a pair of briefs. He was sprawled on his back across the bed. Hairy and thin, he looked no more than twenty-five. His arms were covered with tattoos. One of them was iridescent and seemed to glow in the faint light from the bathroom. It depicted a woman's skull.

But nothing about the man was more compelling than the knife that had been stabbed deep into his chest. From here, the knife appeared to be nothing more exotic than an inexpensive butcher knife. But inexpensive or not, it had done its job. His chest hair glistened with blood.

Coffey said, "Close the door."

She did so and then came over and stood by him.

"Ever seen him before?"

She looked at him. Her voice was shaking. "I don't know. But why would I pick this motel and this room if I didn't know what I'd find here?"

Her implication was clear. As soon as he'd seen the man on the bed, he'd had the same thought. Murderers came in all shapes and sizes. Even lovely women committed murder sometimes. And sometimes they were so shocked by their actions that they suffered from temporary amnesia. . . .

DAUGHTER OF DARKNESS

THE DOOR TO ROOM 127 OPENED...

DAUGHTER OF DARKNESS

ED GORMAN

DAW BOOKS, INC.
DONALD A. WOLLHEIM, FOUNDER
375 Hudson Street New York NY 10014
ELIZABETH R. WOLLHEIM
SHEILA E. GILBERT
PUBLISHERS

Copyright © 1998 by ED GORMAN.

All Rights Reserved.

Cover art by Don Brautigam.

DAW Book Collectors No. 1106.

DAW Books are distributed by Penguin Putnam Inc.

All characters and events in this book are fictitious.
Any resemblance to persons living or dead is strictly coincidental.

If you purchase this book without a cover you should be aware that this book may have been stolen property and reported as "unsold and destroyed" to the publisher. In such case neither the author nor the publisher has received any payment for this "stripped book."

First Printing, December 1998
1 2 3 4 5 6 7 8 9

DAW TRADEMARK REGISTERED
U.S. PAT. OFF. AND FOREIGN COUNTRIES
—MARCA REGISTRADA
HECHO EN U.S.A.

PRINTED IN THE U.S.A.

To Sheila Gilbert,
for her skill, her patience, and her generosity.

ACKNOWLEDGMENTS

I'd like to thank Sue Reider, John Helfers, and Tracy Knight for their help with this book.

"Who love too much hate in like extreme."
—Homer

PART ONE

Chapter One

A week earlier, a *Tribune* columnist had noted that Chicago was becoming "an exciting city of shopping malls."

The columnist had no way of knowing that only six days after her column appeared, life in one particular Chicago mall would get exciting indeed.

The date was Sunday, April 8th, the first truly springlike day of the year. The mall was packed. There were serious shoppers, browsers, shoplifters, loafers, and lovers of various kinds, especially those in junior high and high school, for whom the mall was a mini universe of fast food stands, a six-screen theater, three record stores, and a huge Gap outlet. Nirvana comes to suburbia.

Judith Carney was easily overlooked in such a crowd. At five feet, six inches, one hundred and twenty-two pounds, and thirty-seven years of age, there was nothing remarkable about her at all. Her short hair had recently been tinted a darker color to hide stubborn streaks of gray. She wore a demure white blouse, blue slacks, blue hose, and a pair of blue flats. She carried a hand-tooled leather purse, one she'd bought from the Pueblo Indians when she and her husband and the kids had traveled the Old West last summer. She was plain but not unappealingly so. When she smiled, she was very nearly pretty.

She had been at the mall for more than an hour. Thus far, she'd bought two small items, a Sue Grafton paperback at B. Dalton's, and an umbrella at Penney's. She'd needed a new umbrella for some time and just hadn't gotten around to getting it.

In her hour at the mall, she'd gone to the ladies' room three times, each time to run cold water and swallow aspirin. She was suffering a very strange headache, one that also seemed to radiate pain in her ears as well. If the last few aspirin didn't do the trick, Judith would go home. She couldn't fight the pain much longer.

Shortly after leaving the ladies' room this last time, Judith decided that what she really needed was a little time off her feet. She went to the food court and bought herself a Coke and an oatmeal-and-raisin cookie. She didn't really have much of a sweet tooth but oatmeal cookies had pleasant associations for her. Her mother used to bake oatmeal cookies on cold winter afternoons when Judith had to stay in (she had a predisposition to head colds) and read her Nancy Drews. It was funny all the memories that a cookie could bring tumbling back.

She had just finished her cookie when the headache suddenly got much, much worse. She was well beyond the curative powers of aspirin—or any other over-the-counter medicine. She needed to go home.

She was sitting at a small table watching the people fanned out across the food court. Sunlight streamed through the long skylight on the roof. Everybody looked so healthy and Midwestern and happy on such a fine, lazy Sunday afternoon.

For instance, the woman sitting right across from her. A grandmother, had to be. A grandmother and her little granddaughter out shopping for the day. And now Grandma was giving her little granddaughter her treat for the day. The cute, pigtailed girl was shoveling a chocolate ice cream sundae into her mouth with great vital enthusiasm. Every few moments, Grandma would dip a white paper napkin into her glass of water and then daub the napkin on the girl's sweet, sticky mouth.

These were the two Judith decided to kill. She had nothing against them personally. Had never seen them before. It was probably because they were sitting so close to Judith. No other good reason, really.

She set her purse on the small food court table. Opened it up. Reached inside. Brought out the .45 that belonged to her husband.

And opened fire.

She killed Grandma first, a crown of blood-soaked white hair flying off the top of the older woman's skull. Then the little girl. Judith put two bullets straight into the little girl's forehead.

Screams. Shouts. A black man in a short-sleeved white shirt, yellow bow tie, and jaunty summer straw hat grabbed Judith around the shoulder and neck and seized the gun. But Judith offered no resistance, really. To her, this was all like a dream. In fact, all the shrieking, sobbing faces seemed to recede behind a thickening white mist. Even their voices began to recede.

She would go home and tell her two little girls to play quietly so Mommy could get some sleep. And then she would lie down on the sunny bed, lazy as a cat, and read a few pages of her new Sue Grafton book. And then she would drift lazily off to sleep. And when she woke up, everything would be fine, just fine.

That was when the cops showed up.

Chapter Two

A homeless man found her in the alley and brought her inside to Sister Mary Agnes.

In the Downtown South area of Chicago, Sister Mary Agnes' shelter was legendary. Not the Downtown South of trendy restaurants and festivals of fine arts, but the dark and neglected part where men still sleep in gutters and women sell themselves for the price of their next fix.

Sister Mary Agnes had fixed up an infirmary of sorts and this was where the woman was taken. The white room contained a cot, a tall glass case filled with medicines, and a toilet. The air smelled tartly of antiseptics used earlier in the evening.

The woman was gently placed upon the cot and covered with a white sheet. Sister Mary Agnes got the lights on and started to examine her.

The first thing that struck the nun was the woman's face. She had the classical beauty of a statue. Her body was as slender and supple as that of a dancer. You did not often see women like this in a homeless shelter, especially not dressed in a Ralph Lauren Western shirt and jeans. Sister Mary Agnes guessed the young woman's age at twenty-five or so. One thing, though, the woman wore too much garish makeup. The nun, being a nun, wiped the makeup off when she cleaned the woman's face with a washcloth and hot water.

The woman was just now beginning to stir. She opened lovely, dark eyes and asked, "Is this a dream?"

"No, I'm afraid not," Sister Mary Agnes said. "You're in a homeless shelter."

The woman sat up. "A homeless shelter? What'm I doing here?"

Sister Mary Agnes put a steadying hand on the woman's shoulder. Like a drunk who was going through delirium tremens, the young woman was now overwhelmed by panic.

"Everything's fine. You need to lie back and relax."

"Who're you?" the woman said suspiciously.

"My name is Sister Mary Agnes. I run the homeless shelter here. Now why don't you lie back down? I want to shine a flashlight in your eyes."

"For what?"

"To see if you have a concussion."

"Are you a doctor?"

"No, but I've picked up a few medical pointers over the years." She smiled. "And I play one on TV."

She gently eased the woman back down on the cot. From the folds of her black habit, the nun took a small silver penlight. For a short, stout woman, the nun moved with surprising grace and economy. Her rimless glasses, which usually slid down her pugged nose, reflected the fluorescent overhead.

"What happened to me?" the woman said. She was somewhat sweaty and disheveled, but she bore no outward signs of injury, no bruises or cuts.

"I don't know."

"How did I get here?"

The nun shone the penlight first into one eye then the other. "No sign of a concussion."

"How did I get here?"

"One of our residents found you in the alley."

"The alley?"

"Umm-hmm. You were propped up against the wall. He thought you were sleeping off a drunk."

"Oh, God," the woman said. Panic had been replaced by quiet fear. "You know what?"

"What?"

"I don't even know who I am." Before the nun could say anything, the woman said, "I don't even know what my name is."

"Maybe we should get you to the hospital."

The woman seized the nun's arm. "No. No hospital." Fear was now terror.

"Why not?"

"I'm—not sure. Just—I don't want to go."

"But you need a real doctor to examine you. Amnesia is serious."

"Maybe it's just a momentary thing."

"Maybe," the nun said. "But I'm still not equipped to handle it."

There was a knock on the door. "Yes?" Sister Mary Agnes said.

A middle-aged man wearing a faded blue T-shirt and a pair of loose gray work pants came into the infirmary. He walked with small, careful steps, as if he was afraid his knees might give out at any moment. He looked painfully sober. He raised his right hand. A woman's leather wallet rode in the middle of his palm.

"I went out and looked in the alley like you said, Sister," the man said. "I found this." He handed her the wallet.

The nun eyed the cowhide wallet quickly. "Thanks, Ron. I appreciate it."

He said, "Harrigan's up in the TV room watching some old movie. You want me to tell him to go to bed?"

Sister Mary Agnes combined compassion with a drill sergeant's tenacity. She had strict rules for the men who stayed here and God forbid you broke any of them.

"Just tell him to keep it low," she said. "He's having a bad time."

"He fell off the wagon, huh?"

The nun nodded. "Yeah. So now he's got to dry out all over again. You know the insomnia you get when you're drying out."

"You give him any sleeping pills?"

"Three of them. But obviously, they didn't do much good. So let's let him watch TV." She turned to the woman on the cot. "This is the man who found you."

Ron grinned shyly, obviously intimidated by the woman's beauty.

"Thank you, Ron," the woman said.

"My pleasure, ma'am." Then, to Sister Mary Agnes, "Maybe I should put a time limit on him. Two or three hours, say."

Sister Mary Agnes fought back a smile. The men loved to boss each other around, to act as her lieutenant. The men were harder on each other than she could ever be.

"Just get some sleep, Ron," Sister Mary Agnes said gently, "and let Harrigan worry about himself."

"Okay," Ron said, obviously disappointed, obviously eager to go up to the TV room and boss Harrigan around a little. "If you say so, Sister."

He nodded to the young woman and walked carefully out of the infirmary.

"Is that mine?" the woman said, staring at the billfold.

"I assume so. I asked Ron to go check the alley. See if he could find anything you might have dropped."

The wallet was a good one. Fine leather, hand sewn. The nun opened it up. "Well," she said, "Whoever you are, you seem to be doing pretty well for yourself."

"Why do you say that?"

"There's over a thousand dollars in your wallet."

"Why would I carry that much money?"

Sister Mary Agnes shrugged. "I don't know. But your clothes are expensive, too."

"They are?"

"Ralph Lauren."

"Is there any ID in the wallet?"

"No. Just the money."

The woman closed her eyes, rested the back of her hand on her forehead, as if she had a terrible headache. "This doesn't make any sense. Any of it."

"The big thing right now is to just take it easy," the nun said. "Don't get any more worked up than necessary. You're safe, that's the important thing. How about a Diet Pepsi or something?"

"I am pretty dry."

"Good, I'll be right back, then."

Sister Mary Agnes walked through the empty first floor. Fifteen picnic tables were spread out over the wide concrete floor. In the back was the kitchen. The shelter fed up to two hundred men and women a day. The Archbishop saw to it that Sister Mary Agnes' shelter never ran out of food. It was said that the nun intimidated the Archbishop and that he would do anything to avoid a confrontation with her. Sister Mary Agnes had heard this same story many times. She didn't believe it but it was amusing to think about.

She passed the steps that led to the second floor. Up there, forty cots covered a large room. In the winter, men slept on blankets on the floor, anything to get out of the cold. The Archbishop saw to it that Sister Mary Agnes was also kept in sheets and blankets.

Sister Mary Agnes walked more slowly than she had earlier in the day. At her age, a certain melancholy came over her at day's end. She had gone to the convent straight from the farm, back when she was sixteen years old. She'd served as a nurse in World War II, and had gone into the concentration camps with the American armies. She still had screaming nightmares about the camps. The camps changed her. She hadn't believed in true evil until she saw them. She'd believed, up until then, that virtually all men and women could be redeemed if only they would submit to God's wisdom. But the camps showed her otherwise. The camps showed her that there were men and women who were truly evil and could never be redeemed. Years later, when she found out that the Vatican and the Pope had helped key Nazis escape to South America, she knew that true evil had even claimed the souls of her own clerics. This had engendered in her a profound and long-lasting crisis of faith. She came back to Chicago in 1949 and went to work in the ghettos of the city. Only through working with the poor and the outcasts was she able to find Christ again.

In the dark kitchen, the nun went to one of the two super-size refrigerators a local merchant had donated to the shelter after the good sister had given him an hour-and-a-half lecture (right in his own store) on the true meaning of charity. She was used to being in the kitchen at this time of night. Her old friend Michael Coffey often stopped in for a diet soda about now.

Coffey . . . she smiled when she thought of him. All the guilt he felt for the death of his wife and daughter. She'd been able to help him at least a little bit. And for that she thanked God.

She wondered where Coffey was now. . . .

Chapter Three

THERE were three kinds of cab drivers at the Windy City Cab Company. The first was the lease driver, who paid the company daily for the cab he drove. The second was the owner-operator, who paid a weekly leasing fee and who would own the cab when the lease had been paid. The third was what they called the medallion driver. This meant that you bought and owned your own cab.

Three years ago, Michael Coffey had been a Chicago homicide detective. His police career ended on a snowy November night when an escaped killer surprised Coffey in a dark apartment. Coffey killed him. Two years earlier, the man had murdered Coffey's wife and daughter. What made the situation even worse was that while the shooting was taking place, Coffey was out with some of his cop buddies bowling and drinking beer. If only he'd been home. . . .

Her maiden name had been Janice Cooperman. She'd lived down the block from him as they were growing up, this in a neighborhood over by DePaul University. He was Catholic, she was Jewish. Both his people and hers said it would never work. They said this when he started walking her home in fourth grade; they said this when he took her to their very first eighth grade dance; they said this when he gave her his class ring in eleventh grade; they said this when they took a junior-year apartment near Northwestern, which they both attended; and they whispered it at their wedding, where a priest *and* a rabbi conducted the ceremony. Little Janice Cooperman with the long, dark bangs and the big, dark eyes and the devastatingly sweet smile. He'd fallen in love with her that very first day her folks moved in down the block; and he loved her still. And would always love her.

Soon after his confrontation with their murderer, Coffey took early retirement and bought himself a new Ford and, after getting his chauffeur's license, became a cab driver. He no longer felt he could be a reliable cop. There were too many emotions surging through him to remain completely rational. Despite the fact that all his friends thought he was crazy, he liked the city at night. Yes, there was violence, but there was glamour and excitement, too. The job also let him do something else he had a passion for. He was able to sleep late in the morning, usually hitting the sack around two a.m., and then get up and spend some time at the typewriter. He had sold his first novel last year, a paperback original about a rookie cop. The book had won him decent if not remarkable reviews and a contract for a sequel, which he was halfway through. He had framed reproductions of his first cover hanging up in no less than four rooms in his house. His sister Jan had suggested that maybe he could hang one on the front door. That was one thing about the kid sister he'd always loved so much. She was a true Coffey, a smart-ass from the get-go.

There were a number of conventions going on in the city, so Coffey had spent a good deal of the night in the Loop ferrying guys back and forth between expensive hotels, past Blooomingdale's and Brooks Brothers and Neiman Marcus, and out to the North Pier where a number of yacht parties were going on. The new night spots were especially popular tonight: the Hard Rock Café and Michael Jordan's and Rainforest and the House of Blues. Conventioneers were apparently getting hipper, no longer settling for the same old same old. Nobody had barfed, nobody had picked a fight with him, nobody had asked him to find them hookers. Coffey felt blessed. He'd drive over and have a soda with Sister Mary Agnes, and then call it a night.

He kept the window rolled down. It was one of those smoky-smelling autumn nights in the city. Hot and ripe. Indian summer.

The front of the shelter was dark. Coffey had a key, so that was no problem. He usually let himself in anyway. This time of night, you could generally find Sister Mary Agnes in her tiny office going over the books, or in the infirmary trying to calm somebody who had delirium tremens or was experiencing some bad drugs. If the person looked to be in serious trouble, Sister Mary Agnes always called an ambulance right away, then phoned ahead to a nearby ER to let them know who was coming and what the trouble was. Coffey was amazed at how little the nun slept. Partly this was due to her nightmares. The nun had told him all about going into the concentration camps. She'd brought the Holocaust home to him in a way that he'd never experienced before. No wonder she had nightmares. . . .

The front part of the ground floor was in shadow. In fact, the only light Coffey could see anywhere came from the infirmary. Coffey, a slender, intense-looking man with unruly black hair, made his way to the light.

He peeked in and was stunned by what he saw. The woman was startlingly gorgeous. Classically so. He just stood there in the doorway, looking at her as she lay there, apparently sleeping. Her face suggested so many things, beauty, intelligence, eroticism, humor, and yet—great sorrow.

And then he realized *why* the sleeping woman appealed to him so much. Because she resembled *Janice* so much. . . .

The resemblance was almost chilling.

But what was anybody so lovely and so well-dressed doing in a homeless shelter? And where was Sister Agnes?

The woman said, "Have you seen the Sister?" Her eyes were open now. They were as beautiful as the rest of her.

"I was going to ask you the same thing."

"She went to get me a soda. But she's been gone a long time."

"She'll be along, then." He couldn't take his eyes off her.

"You . . . you look as if you've seen me before," the woman said quietly. "Do you know who I am?"

What a strange question to ask—almost as if *she* didn't know who she was. "No, I'm afraid I don't." Then, "My name's Michael Coffey, by the way."

The woman made a hapless face. "That's one of the things the Sister and I are trying to figure out."

"Oh?"

"My name. I can't remember it. She thinks it may be amnesia of some kind." The woman looked absolutely terrified. And he didn't blame her.

* * *

The woman was sitting up on the cot when Sister Mary Agnes reached the infirmary.

The woman put her lovely face in her long, shapely hands. "This is such a nightmare. I can't remember anything."

Sister Mary Agnes stepped forward and handed her a can of Diet Pepsi. "Here, sweetheart, you said you were dry."

The woman looked up, took the can, and quietly thanked the nun.

Sister Mary Agnes said, "Coffey drives a cab now, but he used to be a homicide detective. Maybe he can help us."

"The first thing we need to do, is get you to a hospital," Coffey said. "You need to be examined by a doctor or two. Then you need to go to the police. They can help you find out who you are."

"Maybe by that time," Sister Mary Agnes said, "your memory will've come back. Most amnesia goes away pretty quickly."

"I'll be happy to drive you in my cab," Coffey said. "Free."

"That's an offer he only makes to pretty women," Sister Mary Agnes said. "The 'free' I mean."

The woman suddenly clutched her head, a whimpering sound coming from her throat.

"What's wrong?" Coffey said.

"Headache," the woman said, a moaning tone in her voice now. "Motel room."

Coffey and the nun looked at each other. Motel room? Was the woman having some kind of breakdown?

"We really need to get you to an ER," Coffey said.

Coffey and the nun went over to the woman and helped her to her feet. Her slender hands still clung to her head and her face was a portrait of near-intolerable pain. Sister Mary Agnes hurried to her medicine supply and grabbed a large bottle of aspirin. She dumped three into the palm of her hand and then rushed over and fed them to the woman one at a time, who chased them down with Diet Pepsi.

***

"How's your head?"
"Better. Amazingly so."

"You stick with Sister Mary Agnes, and you can't go wrong."

The woman smiled. "Apparently."

There was a sadness to the empty streets at this time of night. Coffey had once seen an Edward Hopper exhibit at the Art Museum. Ever since, empty midnight streets had always reminded him of Hopper's paintings, the lonesome sitting alone in diners while darkness prowled around them, hungry, relentless, and sometimes fatal. They always looked so small and scared, Hopper's people. This part of Downtown South was Hopper country, the neon burning in the windows of ancient taverns, the ancient rusted cars, and the occasional sad winos shambling down the streets.

"She sure is nice," the woman said.

"Sister Mary Agnes?"

"Yes."

"Yeah. She sure is."

"How do you know her?"

"She was my shrink for a while."

"Your shrink?"

He looked over at her. "I started drinking more than I should." He told her what happened to his wife and daughter. And he told her about his novel, his new life. "The liquor started to affect my work. I tried AA. I even tried a detox clinic. Neither one worked for me. So one night I found this homeless guy crawling around in the street—he was in really bad shape—and since I was near Sister Mary Agnes' place, I decided to take him there. That's how I met her. After she cleaned up the poor guy and got him into bed, she asked me if I wanted a cup of coffee. I said yes, and I've been seeing her ever since."

"So you've quit drinking completely?"

"Completely. Eleven months dry."

"That's impressive." Then, "It's so terrible, what happened to your wife and daughter."

"Yeah," he said. Then, almost to himself, "I was out bowling with the boys when it happened."

Even from a few blocks away, Coffey could see the blazing red neon sign EMERGENCY ROOM glowing in the night. He had no experience with amnesia except in mystery novels. But right now, the woman's headaches bothered him a lot more than the amnesia did. She could be seriously injured. He pressed the gas pedal a little closer to the floor.

The woman cried out and once again seized both sides of her head. The pain was so intense it lifted her up off the seat and then quickly slammed her back against it. He hit the brakes and pulled over to the curb.

She was crying softly.

He took her in his arms, and just held her tightly. Her body was damp from sweat and trembling from pain and anxiety.

"There's somewhere I need to go," she said, gently slipping out of his arms.

"Yeah," he said, starting to take the emergency brake off, "the ER."

"No. We can do that later."

"Listen," he said. "I'm not trying to scare you, but you could be seriously hurt. The ER is just a couple of blocks away. And that's where we're going."

"No," she said, reaching over and setting her hand on his. "Please do what I'm asking. Please. There's something I—I need to find out."

He wanted to argue the point, but what was the use? He saw how determined she was.

"How's your headache?"

"It comes and goes. The last time—it really hurt."

He studied her a moment. He still saw Janice. "Yeah, I kind've got that impression." Then, "Care to tell me where we're going?"

She gave an area to look for. She wasn't sure of the exact address.

Dark streets. Empty spaces where houses had once been. Roaming dogs. Streetlights like lonely sentries swaying in the wind. These sights filled the windshield.

"Around here," she said suddenly. And then pressed her fingers to her forehead.

"The headache again?"

"Yes."

"We could always go to the ER."

"No, please."

They drove on. Wind was kicking up small dust storms in

the gutters, pushing along pieces of paper like urban tumbleweed. Coffey always felt snug at such times. The cab was new and safe. The dashboard glowed a restful blue. He liked the cab especially now, with the woman sitting near him.

"You like driving a cab?"

"Yeah. Except for the drunks. Which I suppose is a little hypocritical of me since I have the same problem."

"But at least you've done something about it." Then, "It feels so weird."

"What does?"

"Having this perfectly normal conversation with you—and I don't know who I am. Or how I got here."

She jerked again, her whole body, and her head dropped back against the seat. It was as if she'd been shot.

What the hell was going on with her, anyway? What was this mysterious mission?

"Around here." She touched her fingers to her forehead. Her eyes were closed, squinting, as if she were desperately trying to visualize something.

"You said that before. What's supposed to be 'around here?'"

"There's a motel somewhere around here."

"We're coming into a section where there are a *lot* of motels."

He noticed that she kept her eyes closed. She sat perfectly rigid. "Is there one named the Econo-Nite?"

"Yes. About three blocks from here."

"I need to go there."

"You mind if I ask why?"

She opened her eyes. Sat up. Looked at him. "I'm not sure why. I just—had this image of it suddenly. I felt this pain in my head, and there was a picture of the motel. It was strange. You know, that the pain would trigger an image like that."

"Maybe you're starting to remember something."

"Maybe. But I don't like it."

"Why not?"

"Because I also saw a door in the motel. Room 127. And it scares me."

"But you don't know why?"

"No. I just have this—terrible feeling."

He did something he'd been wanting to do for some time. He

reached out and touched her hand. "Maybe I should get you to the ER first. You could be starting to hallucinate."

"I don't think it was a hallucination."

"Sometimes, they can be very real. I had the d.t.s once. I dreamed there was a giant lizard in my closet waiting to pounce on me."

"No, please. Let's go to the motel first. Then the ER."

"You sure?"

The woman nodded. She looked lost and terrified.

Chapter Four

WAS there anything sexier than watching a strange woman undress?

A few years ago, Quinlan had persuaded a department store friend of his to put a surveillance camera in one of the women's dressing rooms. He did this in the spring, when there was the usual bikini frenzy among young women.

Quinlan had watched the tapes over and over. They were far better than commercial porno because that was staged, with very predictable responses by the actors and actresses. Watching unsuspecting women undress was a much bigger turn-on. . . .

As now.

Quinlan sat in front of a bank of three color TV monitors in a small, dark room. A console of buttons and switches sat before him.

The monitor screens were filled with identical images—the tall, slender dark-haired woman just now stepping out of her panties, her ample breasts swinging bountifully as she bent over.

He pushed a red button on the console and said, "Sandra, you're feeling very sexy now. Very sexy now. You feel a need for an orgasm." Microwave technology being what it was these days, the signal went out just as a radio signal. Microwave signaling no longer took a couple hundred pounds of clumsy gear.

Quinlan's suggestion worked very quickly. Sandra began to touch herself in slow, gentle but singularly erotic ways. Her fingers found the lovely baby-pink nipples of her uptilted breasts, and then the gentle slope of her belly, which showed the faint red banding of where her panties had been. From there, she found her sex, and the moment she touched it her entire body shuddered and exploded. She became wanton with herself. Quinlan smiled. Just as the dressing room had been superior to XXX-porno, just so was this superior to the dressing room.

He was in complete control of a beautiful woman.

He wondered what the district attorney would say if he knew what his wife was doing this afternoon. Quinlan and the DA were golfing buddies. Quite innocently, at dinner at the DA's house one night, Quinlan wondered if Sandra, the DA's wife, would like to be a guinea pig in some experiments at Quinlan's clinic some time. Sandra, a very jaded suburban housewife, volunteered on the spot. She said it sounded exciting. If she only knew the things she'd done at the clinic, the things that Quinlan had totally erased from her memory. . . .

When she was finished with herself, Sandra (on command) put her blue sweater and gray skirt and gray suede pumps back on. She had an elegant, slightly spoiled face, the face of a beautiful woman who was used to being kept happy. It gave Quinlan great satisfaction to use women like this, the wives and daughters of gentry and society.

Then Quinlan said, again depressing the red button, "Now, I want you to go over to the table in the corner, Sandra. And pick up the gun."

She did so without hesitation.

Her fingers had barely touched the weapon when the door of the room opened and a man shuffled in.

His face was grimy with dirt and dried sweat. His hair was a bird's nest of filth and weeds and grass. His workshirt and trousers had once been a real color. Now they were simply the color of his face, the color of poverty and a kind of despair that could only be alleviated with the succor of cheap wine. The wine would bring a red tint back to his cheeks and a crazed sad private giggle to his lips. The eyes reflected nothing. He was too drugged out to feel anything. The man was one of Chicago's homeless. One of Quinlan's employees had snatched him off the streets last night and brought him out here to the clinic. The way Quinlan saw it, he was doing the poor bastard a favor.

The man came into the room and closed the door behind him. Just as he'd been instructed to. Now, he stood staring at the far wall, the dead eyes seeming to comprehend nothing. He

DAUGHTER OF DARKNESS 31

paid no attention whatsoever to the beautiful woman standing before him.

Now came the test.

He'd see how far along Sandra had come over the past three months.

He depressed the red button again. "Sandra, I have to warn you. He's going to rape you and then he's going to kill you. But he'll kill you slowly. He's HIV-positive. Remember the photos of the AIDS patient we showed you? How horrible he looked? You'll die later on with AIDS. Your only chance is to kill him, Sandra. Raise the gun and point it at him and kill him. You don't have much time, Sandra. And you're the only one who can stop him. You have the gun. You have to kill him, Sandra. You have to kill him now."

But could she do it?

Quinlan sat there, fascinated by what he was doing. Could she actually do it? God, he hoped so. As a man of science, and a man who loved controlling women, he sincerely hoped so.

She started to raise the gun, point it at the homeless man. . . .

***

Robert James Quinlan was probably the only man to ever appear in both *Psychiatric America* and *Cosmopolitan*. At least in the same month.

The psychiatric magazine was honoring him for doing the most important work in behavior modification since the controversial Russian, Maslow.

The women's magazine was honoring him as one of the country's most handsome and most eligible bachelors. They went positively orgasmic over his "Robert Wagner-like good looks."

Shortly after the articles appeared, Quinlan left behind the snows (and the nubile and willing daughters of rich and powerful people) of Harvard and went to the sunny shores of California, up the coast near Malibu, where he was CEO of the Sigma Corporation, a company that was rather mysterious once you looked into it. (Not to worry; he immediately found nubile and willing young women here, too.) Sigma was mysterious on purpose. It was a CIA front. Quinlan had signed on with the Agency to expand his work with behavior modification, angling it more toward mind control. At the time, the Agency was trying to take certain control secrets it had learned in its MK-Ultra program (years later it was called the Artichoke program when it was exposed by a senate investigating committee) and combine them with the results of his own work. Simply put, the Agency wanted to know if there really *was* such a thing as mind control. While the public (thanks to hours of sloppy and scaremongering reporting done by the networks) just assumed that there *was* such a process, the Agency had great doubts about the results the Russians, the Chinese, and the Koreans had reported. During the Korean War, for instance, it was widely reported that the Koreans had "brainwashed" many American troops. But what "brainwashing" meant in this context was simply that, through the use of torture, drugs, and sleep deprivation, the Koreans had succeeded in turning American soldiers into mental basket cases. They suffered from depression, terrible paranoia, and anxiety, and even certain levels of schizophrenia. But as to "secret soldiers" controlled from afar—that was all crapola. The poor bastards were utterly useless. Most of them died not long after being returned home; and the majority of them died in psychiatric hospitals.

Enter Robert James Quinlan, MD.

The first thing he did for the Agency was to thoroughly appraise MK-Ultra. He found it howlingly bogus, the handiwork of various Agency Dr. Strangeloves who spent most of their time telling each other what geniuses they were. They had focused on introducing massive amounts of barbiturate drugs into their test subjects. Sodium amytal seemed to be the drug of choice. The reports were hilarious. According to these reports, when these drugs were combined with sleep deprivation and "subliminal messaging," the subjects were virtual robots at the beck and call of their masters. But as Quinlan said to an Agency man in Menlo Park (Quinlan wondered if the man received two paychecks, one from Stanford where he was a professor, and one from the Agency), all the Strangeloves had managed to produce were totally exhausted people who couldn't sleep because they had so many anxiety-producing drugs in them, not least of which were several caffeine-derived uppers. He succeeded in convincing the folks at McLean that the program had to be completely rethought and started all over again. His plan won begrudging acceptance. None of his superiors wanted to look as if they'd been taken in by the first bogus experiments of Project Artichoke. They denounced it dramatically, and blamed it all on departed bosses.

Working with the CIA gave Quinlan two things: virtually unlimited funds and complete freedom to experiment as he chose to. No questions asked.

He brought three elements to his experiments: LSD (even though it had been perceived as both dangerous and useless following the infamous Canadian Government-CIA joint experiments of the early seventies), electroshock therapy, and what he called "pulsed microwave audiograms."

The LSD allowed him to break down the subject's defenses; the electroshock therapy allowed him to override the subject's real memory and to implant new, false memories concocted by Quinlan himself; and the microwave audiograms allowed Quinlan to "shoot" commands into the subject's mind on a subliminal level. Radio signals were a perfect way to reach the mind subliminally.

As was his wont, Quinlan—in his arrogance—overstepped the bounds. He asked the friendly folks at McLean to start feeding him agents that they would like to get rid of. He said they would be perfect subjects. He could scramble their brains and leave them little more than empty human shells. He'd have perfect test subjects, and they'd pension out men they'd come to distrust or despise. Fine. The plan sounded great.

But Quinlan's experiments with mind control—this was in his fourth year of enjoying the sunny climes of Southern California—went too far. He locked two unpopular agents in a room. He gave each a World War II German Luger (Quinlan had an eye for fashion even in guns) and then started pulsing microwave orders to each of them. He had been preparing them for weeks with electroshock and LSD. Now, he needed a practical demonstration that the microwave audiograms would produce their desired effect.

He had a relentless heart, Quinlan did, and a ruthless imagination.

***

Sandra raised the gun, but she didn't fire.

The homeless man stood unmoving, a zombielike deadness covering his face.

She kept the gun up in the air, pointed directly at the homeless man's chest.

But she didn't fire.

Quinlan flipped a switch, activating the audio microwave command. Back in his CIA days, there'd been a lot of staff jokes about how he was trying to make up for being such a prick by using a microwave to make lunch for his staffers. He'd overheard the joke. He wasn't offended. He'd merely found it stupid. He was using microwaves because it was a short radio wave and therefore a perfect means of transmitting subliminal commands to his subjects. Microwaves could pass through the elements (fog, smoke, rain) that block light waves. The Russians had quite successfully used microwave spying devices in Moscow's American Embassy. He was using microwaves as one means of controlling his subjects.

Quinlan pressed the red button and said, "You don't have long, Sandra. He's going to move on you suddenly—and then it'll be too late. He'll be too quick and strong for you. Remember the other day, when the three men raped you and beat you? He'll do even worse, Sandra. He has a knife in his pocket." The rape Quinlan referred to had been "imaged" into her head with a combination of drugs and virtual reality. It had apparently been quite convincing. It had taken several injections of Paxil to calm her down. She was one of those people who were almost immune to the magic of proactive psychiatric drugs. You had to dose her heavily.

She fired three shots.

Bam bam bam.

No hesitation.

The heavily-drugged man did not scream or even clutch his chest. He simply dropped to the tiled floor.

There was no reaction from Sandra, either. She was now as immobile as the man had been. She hadn't even lowered the gun yet. It was held straight out in front of her, as if she were about to embark on firing target practice.

"Very good, Sandra," Quinlan said. "Very, very good."

Now it was time to reward both of them. He would lead her

to the elevator and take her up to the top floor of his clinic where they would make love in his handsomely appointed apartment.

Sandra had been a very good girl, and she deserved his gratitude.

Chapter Five

THE Econo-Nite was a V-shaped stucco place with twenty-six rooms and an office with a severely cracked front window. The crack came from a bullet the last man to rob the place had left behind. The Econo-Nite was stuck up almost as often as the Cubs lost ball games, which was to say a lot. Coffey had brought numerous fares here. They all ran to lower-echelon salesmen on the arms of lower-echelon hookers.

Room 127 was around back, next to a row of bright thrumming soda machines. Moths kept hurling themselves at the dirty yellow light above the exterior stairway. There were only four cars parked on this side of the motel. Two of them were shiny and new. Maybe the Econo-Nite was moving up in the world.

Coffey pulled into the slot and turned off the motor.

She said, "Mind if we just sit here a minute?" Her voice was trembling.

He smiled and tapped the cab meter. "This is going to cost you a lot of money."

"Do you ever hug strangers?"

"Every chance I get."

"I'm not coming on or anything. I—it'd just be nice if somebody'd hold me a minute."

"That's another service that goes with the cab ride. Free hugs."

He took inordinate pleasure in holding her. She was woman-child, dear and precious and fragile. It had been so damned long since he'd held anybody he'd cared about. He'd tried a few women, but they'd been blind dates and they hadn't been any more interested in him than he'd been in them. He made sure that he held her chastely. That's what she wanted and needed right now, a nonsexual hug. Hell, maybe that was what *he* needed, too. And the fact that she looked so much like Janice. . . .

"Thanks," she said after a time, pulling away. "And thanks for not coming on."

He nodded.

She looked at the door of Room 127. "I'm afraid to go in there."

"Then let me go in."

She shook her head. "No. I appreciate the offer. But I'm the one who needs to go in. Will you wait for me?"

"Of course."

She opened the door and got out. The night smelled of autumn. It was a good smell, actually; clean and fresh. At least to Coffey.

She leaned back in and said, "How about one more hug?"

"Well, I suppose," he said with a mock sigh. "If you twist my arm." He scooted over to the passenger window.

She clung even tighter than she had previously. He lost himself in the fragrance of her hair. The softness of her breasts pressed against him. His groin started to send out unmistakable signals. He eased himself out of the hug before he ruined the moment.

"I'll go in with you if you want me to," he said. "I don't mind."

"Thanks again. But I'd better do this alone." She peeked back in. Though she was an elegant and very adult woman, there was still some girl left in her, and he liked that very much. "Wish me luck."

He gave her the thumbs up.

She closed the car door quietly and then started walking slowly—reluctantly—toward Room 127.

She paused at the door and knocked. The knock was so soft, he couldn't hear it, just see it. She knocked again.

After a time, she pushed the door inward. Apparently, it had not been locked.

While he waited, he looked up at the sky. Rain was still on its way. The moon drifted behind thunderheads. It felt as if the temperature had dropped five degrees since they'd left the shelter.

The door to Room 127 opened. The woman stood in the interior shadows. He could barely see her. She waved him inside.

He got out of the car and walked up to the door. She didn't say anything, just opened the door wider so that he could walk inside.

She hadn't turned on any lights in the bedroom area. Light from the bathroom spilled into the shabby room, enough that Coffey had no trouble seeing the man. He wore only a pair of briefs. He was sprawled on his back across the bed. Hairy and thin, he looked no more than twenty-five. His arms were covered with tattoos. One of them was iridescent and seemed to glow in the faint light from the bathroom. It depicted a woman's skull.

But nothing about the man was more compelling than the knife that had been stabbed deep into his chest. From here, the knife appeared to be nothing more exotic than an inexpensive butcher knife. But inexpensive or not, it had done its job. His chest hair glistened with blood.

Coffey said, "Close the door."

She did so and then came over and stood by him.

"Ever seen him before?"

She looked at him. Her voice was shaking. "I don't know. But why would I pick this motel and this room if I didn't know what I'd find here?"

Her implication was clear. As soon as he'd seen the man on the bed, he'd had the same thought. Murderers came in all shapes and sizes. Even lovely women committed murder sometimes. And sometimes they were so shocked by their actions that they suffered from temporary amnesia. He'd seen it happen more than a few times in his cop years.

Coffey walked over to the open clothes rack. The man had hung everything up neatly. He left everything the way it was. He didn't want to disturb the crime scene any more than absolutely necessary.

He went over and clicked on the table lamp on the right side of the bed. The woman jerked as if he'd shot her with something. She obviously didn't want to see the dead man any more clearly than she already had.

She went over to the stained armchair and sat down. She put her face in her hands, the way she might have at the scary part of a horror movie. He could see her eyes gleaming between her fingers. She was afraid to look but *had* to.

Coffey spent a few minutes checking the bed and the area around it. People dropped things sometimes. But not this time. He found nothing.

He went into the bathroom. The tiles were coming off the shower wall and the toilet bowl was stained with rust. The hot water handle on the sink was missing. Fun place.

He spent a full three minutes examining the sink more carefully. The sink was white. Only close inspection yielded what he was looking for.

He called out to the woman to come into the bathroom.

When she stood next to him, he said, "I'd like to see your hands."

"My hands?"

"Yes."

She put her hands in his. He brought her closer to the light bar over the medicine cabinet. It took him a while but he found it.

"What're you looking for?" she said.

"Blood."

"Blood?"

"You washed up very carefully. But there're still some traces of blood in your fingernails. The same with the sink. Traces of blood."

"Then that means—"

He shook his head. "Right now, we don't *know* what that means. We need to keep looking around this room."

He went back to the room with the bed and started searching again. He tried desk drawers, the closet, and the space atop the window air-conditioning unit. He kept a handkerchief wrapped around his fingers. No prints. He crawled under the bed and felt around, and then he went back to the bathroom and looked in the cabinet under the sink. He lifted the toilet lid and peeked in there. And then he opened the narrow three-shelf towel closet.

That was where he found the dress. It was rolled up and stuffed in the back behind a stack of towels. His hand got wet and sticky just touching it.

On the next shelf he found the small overnight bag. It was smeared with blood.

He carried both the dress and the overnight bag into the other room. He put them down on the edge of the bed.

The woman looked stunned when she saw the dress. "I—recognize that somehow. I think it's—mine."

"You or someone got the dress bloody and then changed clothes."

She looked at him, tears filling her eyes. "Does this mean I killed him?"

"I don't know."

"Oh, God. You have to help me."

She slipped her arms around him and clung to him with life-and-death desperation.

He held her for a time, and then she said quietly, "Can we wait for them out in the car?"

"Wait for who?"

"For the police."

"I'm not calling the police. At least not yet."

"You're not?"

He took her hand gently. "Look. We need to talk about some things. Maybe we can figure a few things out before we contact a lawyer. The lawyer comes before the police."

"Where'll we go?"

"I've got an extra bedroom. You can stay there tonight. We'll be fresh in the morning and we can figure out what we need to do."

She touched her hand to his cheek. "You're taking a chance. I could be a murderer."

"Yes," he said. "I know. Now let's get out of here."

It was misting when they got back outside. They walked to the car. Just before he got in, Coffey scanned the parking lot. Police training.

A Ford van was parked next to a dumpster. There was a small black box of some kind on the roof of the van. Next to the Ford was a battered ten-year-old Pontiac with Rebel license plates. And next to that was a newer model Chevrolet station wagon.

Then he noticed the silver Jaguar. It was cruising down toward them, a classic of design and engineering, altogether the wrong context for such a vehicle. The driver was a young blond man in a blue blazer, white shirt, and yellow necktie. He watched them with obvious interest, staring at them openly until he passed them. Then he disappeared around the corner.

Coffey was wondering about the Jag when a carload of people whipped into the spot next to him. They were all dressed up in square dancing costumes. They were well into their sixties and looked as if they were having a great time. One of the older ladies, who looked sweet and cute in her cowgirl duds, said, "We won the dance contest tonight!"

"Here we are."

He pulled into the alley leading to his garage. He edged the car inside and then shut off the lights. The garage smelled of motor oil and dead grass clinging to the power mower bag.

There was a narrow walk leading to the back door. The misting had stopped, and it was actually kind of pretty now, chilly but in an invigorating way, the sky starry and the grass dewy.

Inside, he got the lights on and showed her the guest bedroom. He got an extra blanket from a closet and put it on her bed. It would be very cold toward dawn.

While she spent fifteen minutes in the bathroom cleaning up, he put on some decaf in the Mr. Coffee.

"The coffee smells good," the woman said as she came into the kitchen.

"Help yourself."

She went over and poured herself a cup and brought it back to the table. She sat across from him.

"I can't get it out of my mind," she said.

"The motel room?"

She nodded, sipped her coffee. "I keep trying to tell myself that I couldn't possibly have killed anybody. That I'm not that sort of person." She set her cup down. "The trouble is, since I don't know who I am, I don't really know what I'm like either."

"That's why we need to get you to the hospital and the lawyer," he said. "Between them, they'll be able to help you."

She studied him a moment. "What if the police charge me with murder?"

Her long neck was graceful, lovely, and looking at it was like hearing an especially moving fragment of music. "I'll help you all I can."

She smiled sadly. "I've decided to call myself Amy."

"Oh?"

"The towel you have in your bathroom. On the little tag, it says, Design by Amy."

He smiled. "Amy it is, then."

"At least for now." She reached over and touched his hand. "Thanks for helping me."

"My pleasure."

"You're a nice guy."

He shrugged. "Occasionally I am."

"I'd like to hear more about your wife and daughter. Sometime."

"Sometime," he said. Then, "We need some sleep. Morning's going to come early."

She tightened her grip on his hand. The desperation was back in her eyes. "I just hope I didn't kill anybody."

He stroked her fingers gently and said, "You need sleep. That's the only thing to worry about now."

"You really don't think I killed him?"

"No, I really don't think you did."

This was what she wanted to hear, of course, and he didn't mind saying it. But he wasn't sure if it was true. He wasn't sure at all.

He felt as if he was reliving his life with Janice in some strange way—he'd once considered writing a novel with a reincarnation plot that bore an eerie likeness to tonight—but what if she was a murderer?

Chapter Six

EVEN by the standards of the Chicago elite, the Stafford mansion was something to behold. A house and garden reporter had once noted that the place would probably intimidate the Queen of England. Tudor in design, the mansion sat on four acres of impossibly expensive land. Firs and pines kept the place from the eyes of commoners. Inside, there was a wood-burning fireplace nearly as tall as a college basketball player; patterned hardwood flooring imported from Norway; nine bathrooms, eight bedrooms, and a huge library. There was also, if one was inclined to keep score of such things, a gymnasium, a dance floor, and an art gallery that included two original Van Goghs and four original Monets. Both Tom and Molly Stafford loved the French impressionists.

At the moment, Molly Stafford wasn't thinking about art. She'd awakened a minute ago in the vast, shadowy master bedroom of the mansion. As she sat up, she realized that her husband was gone from bed. Then she saw him over by the window, staring out at the fog and drizzle. She wished she could immerse herself in her charity work, as she sometimes could. Both she and her husband knew how fortunate they were, and they spent inordinate amounts of time and money helping out with various charities, especially the Salvation Army and St. Jude's, two groups that were known to be honest and forthright (hungry, ambitious yuppies were now heading up most charities, and there was something about charity workers in Gucci shoes that thoroughly turned off Molly). She put in as much as twenty-five hours a week on her charity projects.

But there was only one thing on her mind tonight. There *could* be only one thing on her mind tonight.

She slipped from bed and went silently to him, sliding her arms around his shoulders and kissing him tenderly on the right side of his face. Tom was movie-star handsome; he'd been Robert Redford blond until he reached his mid-fifties. Now he was Paul Newman gray. He sat in blue silk, monogrammed pajamas. She could almost feel his weariness. He hadn't been able to sleep well for many nights.

Jenny, their twenty-five-year-old daughter, had disappeared eight days ago. There'd been no word from her or about her. At twenty-five, most young women are adults quite able to fend for themselves. But Jenny had only recently been released from a ten-month stay in a psychiatric hospital following a horrible depression. "We'll find her," Molly whispered softly. Tom patted her hand. He had been born wealthy and powerful and had spent his working years vastly expanding that wealth and power through an investment firm he'd bought as a young man. She was used to seeing him in control of virtually every situation. He was rarely rude or nasty, though he was known to explode sometimes. But not now. She could almost *feel* his weariness. All these sleepless nights. And the long, slowly grinding wait to hear from her—to no avail. He was as broken now as an old and enfeebled man. Three or four times, she'd heard him crying softly in the den.

"Come back to bed, honey," Molly said. "At least *try* and get some sleep."

He patted her hand again and wearily stood up. "I guess I'll go down to the den and try to get some work done. I may as well."

He was probably right, she thought. Lying awake, unable to sleep, was a special kind of hell. Might as well get up and get something accomplished. Work would at least briefly take his mind off his missing daughter.

He came into her arms then, and she held him with a mixture of sexual need and maternal solace. But it was only the latter he was interested in tonight. It had been this way for some time. Sex had always been cathartic for her; for him it was a deep and abiding pleasure but seemed to offer no particular psychological harbor.

"Go back to bed, sweetheart," he said quietly. "I'll see you in the morning."

Soon, he was nothing more than the sound of soft footsteps on the grand staircase.

***

The man in the silver Jag, the man Coffey had seen cruising past the room in the motel, was David Foster.

Until he was fourteen years old, Foster was fat. Very fat. So fat that when he played sandlot baseball, the boys used to say, "If you pick David for your team, he counts for two!" Real hilarious. Unless you were poor David, who was actually a hell of a nice kid.

Or unless you were his parents. They were just-so kind of people. To the manor they were born and in the manor there was—just so—no room for fatties. There were no fatties on either side of the family, so what exactly was the *deal* with David, anyway? They went to all the chic doctors in both Chicago and New York but not even the smartest or the chicest seemed able to do anything about David. He took injections of animal serums, he went to several different fat camps, he hung from gravity boots upside down, he jogged till he literally dropped, he sobbed, he prayed, he cursed, he pasted magazine photos (at his mother's suggestion) of teen idols (*skinny* teen idols) on his mirror ... but not jack shit worked. He still counted for two whenever anybody chose him for sports.

And then he became a freshman in high school, and it was enough to make you believe in all those sappy TV movies where there's a miracle cure in the third act and little blind, deaf, and lame Suzie becomes a singing and dancing Broadway child prodigy overnight. He, David Alan Foster, lost all his weight.

His parents, who loved him in their icy moneyed way, now had something else to worry about. Cancer. It had to be cancer. Cancer was the only possible explanation for suddenly losing this kind of weight. They'd been selfish and vain and superficial as always and so the dark forces of the universe said, *You want a skinny kid, you got a skinny kid.* And zapped him with the big C. But it wasn't the big C. God knows the doctors *looked.* But all that had happened was that lucky David had just inexplicably lost all his weight.

And he was more than thin. He was *handsome* and thin.

Handsome and thin. And, boy, did he make the most of it. He slept with short girls, tall girls, white girls, black girls, yellow girls, red girls, nice girls, bad girls, sweet girls, girls who giggled, girls who wept, girls who smelled bad, girls who smelled good, girl, girls, girls—And despite this, the Age of AIDS, the worst he got for all his activity was a quick case of the crabs, which horrified his mother ("I just hope Grandma Clark never finds out about this!") and secretly amused his father, who took to talking about it with the other middle-aged men at his private club (they were past bragging about their own sexual prowess, so now they boasted of their sons'). And then he met Jenny Stafford. And meeting her, after a long circuitous chain of circumstances, was what had led him to be in the parking lot of the Econo-Nite Motel tonight.

He pulled the silver Jag over to the curb and punched in a number on his cell phone. It took six rings before there was an answer.

When a voice came on, David snapped, "The kind of money I pay you, I expect better service."

"I don't take this kind of crap, David. I've got too much business."

David said, "We've got to make our move on her. It's time."

"That's all you needed to say."

"And there's somebody I want you to check out." He gave the man the particulars on the cab and the cabbie. "Find out as soon as you can and get back to me."

"You'll be hearing from me," the man said. And hung up.

***

The scene in the motel invaded her sleep and woke her up. She lay awake in Coffey's guest bed yearning for the days when she was a little girl. Her life had been happy then, and not just because she was rich. She'd felt satisfied and safe with her life. That was what had made her happy. She was something of a loner, true, but that was all right. She loved to read and play music and watch adventure shows. She was a huge *Star Trek* fan back then. Somewhere there was a family photo of her at age six with her three front teeth missing and a big grin splitting her face as two huge Spock ears sat stop her head. Then she thought: *but how do I know that I was rich? That I was happy? That I liked* Star Trek*?* The headache again. So strong she felt as if she wanted to vomit. A cold sweat all over her body. And trembling. Arms and legs. Trembling. Like a junkie.

Unfamiliar room. And this miserable headache. And could she really trust Coffey? He seemed to be innocent. But was he? But if he *wasn't* innocent, then who was he and what did he want?

And where did memories of a rich little girl with stupid Spock ears come from? She felt as if she were trying to give birth to another full-grown person inside her . . . as if she were *two* people and not one.

She no longer felt safe here.

She no longer trusted Coffey.

Had to get dressed. Had to get out of here.

***

The street was dark, shadow-haunted. She was hurrying, her footsteps unnaturally loud in the early-morning silence. It had rained some more, so all the buildings gleamed wetly. And emptily.

Block after block of dusty store windows, used furniture places, laundromats, pawnshops, bail bondsmen. The farther she got from Coffey's, the worse the neighborhood got.

She needed to find a cab.

All she had was the address. That was the strange thing. She'd slept a few hours in Coffey's guest bedroom and then suddenly awakened, a voice in her head. Well, not just a *voice,* a *presence.* It was as if something were pushing against her brain, hoping to dislodge it, take over the same space. There was no other way to explain it.

The presence gave her the address.

She had no idea where the address was, or what its significance might be. All she knew for sure was that the address was somehow important to her. Very important.

She walked on.

A yellow cab went around a corner two blocks down. She cursed, feeling forlorn, deserted.

Six more blocks. Long ones. Wet ones. It had started raining again.

She saw a convenience store, an oasis of light in the oppressive darkness. And parked right in front of the door of the convenience store was a taxi cab.

She hurried, before it could get away.

. . . she was not aware of the dark Ford van following from a distance of half a block, creeping slowly along the rain-glazed, neon-splattered streets. . . .

The cabbie had left his car running. A brave and foolish man. The back door of the cab was unlocked. She quickly crawled inside, sat back in the darkness of the corner. The cab smelled of barf and disinfectant and cigarette smoke and dampness. A two-way radio crackled forth words up front but uselessly, like signals sent deep into empty outer space.

The cabbie took his time. He didn't come back for another five minutes or so. When he got in the cab, the entire vehicle heaved to the left and the springs sighed deeply. He was a big man, this one.

He put the cab in gear and backed out of the parking lot, the reverse gear whining all the time he used it.

He turned up the volume on the radio. An all-night talk show. A woman was talking about being raped and violated by aliens.

The cabbie didn't seem to know she was there in the back seat. She sat up and said, "I have money."

Two things happened at once: the cab driver let out an ear-shattering shout and the cab itself shot briefly to the right, into the oncoming lane. He quickly righted the vehicle.

He turned around and looked at her and said, "You just scared the shit out of me, lady!"

He had a nice face, kind of a baby face. He was probably in his late twenties and overweight by as much as fifty pounds. He wore a brown zipper jacket and a Cubs baseball cap. There was a vulnerability to him that she liked and trusted immediately.

"I'm sorry," she said.

"So now the gals are taking over, huh?"

"Taking over?"

"Yeah. You know, robbing cabbies."

"Oh, no," she said, "that's not why I'm here."

He watched her in his rearview mirror. She could see he was studying her, trying to decide for himself what she was really all about. He probably carted around a lot of really strange people in his cab. He probably knew a lot *about* really strange people.

"I just need a ride," she said. "As I said, I have money." She held up a fistful of dollars, the same dollars the nun had found in her wallet tonight. "I'm sorry I scared you."

"I guess I just didn't see you was all. All the cabbies gettin' killed lately, I'm just a little jumpy. So where's the address?"

She told him.

"Yeah, right, lady."

"What? Is something wrong with the address?"

"Not if you believe in fairy tales."

"Fairy tales?" she said, baffled by his words.

But before he could answer, his two-way radio began crackling. The dispatcher wanted to know if he could pick somebody up. He said that he already had a fare.

After breaking the connection, the cab driver turned up the radio a little. A caller was saying that he found it strange that an alien race would travel all the way across the galaxy just to get laid. Especially with a different species. The cab driver chuckled.

She sat back and stared out the window. They were on the Crosstown now. The rain was coming down harder. She had a bad headache. She couldn't remember her name. She felt utterly isolated. Maybe she shouldn't have left Coffey's. She liked him and he was certainly protective of her. She wanted to scream at the cab driver to turn off the nonsense radio program. She didn't want to be part of that world. She wanted to be part of Coffey's world again. His nice, warm smile. His nice, warm kitchen. His nice, warm guest bed. Why had the *presence* in her mind awakened her? Why had it given her this address? Where was she going anyway?

She slumped back in her seat, cold and alone, and trying to block out the inane words coming from the radio show.

She was trying very hard not to think about the man in the motel room. The dead man.

Chapter Seven

COFFEY wasn't sure why he woke up. A dream, perhaps. Or a nightmare.

He lay in his dark bed, listening to fat, noisy raindrops fall from the eaves to puddles below.

He did all the usual things when he awakened at this time of night. Scratched his chest, his groin, used left leg to scratch right leg. Thought of getting up to take a pee. Thought maybe he could hold it till his *official* waking up a few hours later.

He wondered how the woman was doing. He felt good about her being under the same roof. He realized that this was a testament to his general loneliness. Here was a woman who might well turn out to be a murderer, but he was so taken with her that he didn't care. He didn't ever want her to leave.

His bladder got insistent. He swung his legs out from under the cover and then off the bed. The hardwood floor was cold on his bare feet. Dressed only in pajama bottoms, he padded out of the room.

He remembered so many middle of the nights when his daughter was an infant. He and Janice had taken turns getting up in the middle of the night to answer her cries. He could still recall the warm feel of her baby flesh against him and the sweet smell of her bottle formula and all her assorted belches, farts, and hiccups as he'd walked her around the kitchen, trying to get her back to sleep. Memory made him smile. Sometimes, when he was at work, he'd suddenly be overwhelmed by his feelings for her—how much he loved her and how much he feared for her. Life, especially infant life, was vulnerable to so many things—accident, disease—and even crazed ex-convicts. He wanted to hold her again in the middle of the night, love her, and protect her—as he had failed to protect her the night of her death.

He went down the hall to the john. On the way, he passed the guest bedroom.

He went into the john and did his business. Washed his hands. Dried them. And then started walking back down the hall.

When he got to the guest bedroom, he paused. Listened. What did he expect to hear? It was unlikely that she snored like a truck driver. She was probably enjoying a nice, quiet, and exhausted sleep. With the things that had apparently happened to her, of course she'd be exhausted.

But he had this feeling. Maybe it was his cop instinct. She was gone. That's what the instinct told him. He imagined the blond man he'd spotted at the motel breaking in and kidnapping her. But, no, Coffey had a good alarm system. No matter how good the blond man might be, Coffey would have heard something.

She was gone. He knew that now. Knew it absolutely.

But what if he was wrong? What if he opened the door and she was lying there awake? It might look like he was trying to put the moves on her. He wanted to her trust him, respect him. He didn't want to look like a sexual opportunist.

There was only one way to find out if his instinct was correct. Open the door and peek in.

He opened the door. Peeked in.

In the shadowy room, he could see that the bed was made and that she was gone. He walked in, flipping on the overhead light, blinking in the sudden brightness.

No sign of turmoil. Or forced entry of any kind. The windows were solidly in place. None of the furnishings had been pushed around.

She had clearly walked out of his house of her own volition.

He hurried to the front window, to see if there was any sign of her on the street. And that was when he saw the van. He recognized it immediately—the same dark Ford van that had been in the motel parking lot. With the strange small box on the roof. Now, with him clearly visible through the window, it suddenly swept away from the curb and moved on down the block into the gloom.

Why would a van be following him? It obviously had something to do with the woman he'd found tonight. But what?

Chapter Eight

SHE began dozing off and then waking up and then dozing off. Once, she woke up disoriented—not sure where she was—but the grinding idiocy of the call-in show soon fixed her location.

This time, she woke up because the cab had turned off the expressway and come to a stop.

She opened her eyes and realized that they were no longer in the city proper. Long stretches of grass and trees filled the windshield. As the cab began to move again, she saw, hidden in the gloom, vast houses set far back from the road and, for the most part, surrounded by imposing fences. Mansions. The majority of them were barred by gates.

She said, "Are you sure this is the right place?"

"It's the address you gave me," he said. "I just take orders, lady." There was no sarcasm in his voice.

"But these are mansions." She was confused. Then she thought of her dream. And being a rich little girl. With Spock ears.

"That's right. And so is the place you want to go to. In fact, it's the biggest mansion out here."

She looked out the window. She was like a child overwhelmed by a spectacular sight. "I just don't see how this is possible." Why would she come here?

"Well," he said, "we'll know soon enough."

"Oh? How will we know?"

"When we pull up to the gate, we'll have to identify ourselves. I don't look forward to waking these people up at this time of night, believe me."

"Then if it's the right address—"

"If it's the right address, they'll let you in."

"And if it's not?" Her voice shook.

He shrugged. "If it's not, we'll go somewhere else, I guess." More mansions. Endless fencing. The rain had let up. A quarter moon rode the tops of fir trees that seemed to be on all the estates. Silvered shadows.

He slowed down, taking a right up a driveway that abruptly ended at a formidable gate.

"Here we are," he said, nodding to the gate.

She felt fear. She wasn't sure why. Did this place have something to do with the dead man in the motel room? Was this where he might have lived?

"Don't drive off," she said.

"Don't worry. I'll be right here."

The night had gotten very chilly. She huddled inside her clothes. The air smelled cold and damp. She walked up to the gates. She could see the security camera peering down at her from its perch in an oak tree. There was an intercom to press.

She thumbed the black button and said, "I need to know who lives here. I'm lost."

There was no response.

She looked back at the cabbie. The cab's engine throbbed. Needed a tune-up. It smelled of gas and oil, and the headlights were dirty.

Then a woman's voice was saying, "Jenny! Jenny, it's you! It's me, Eileen!"

She wondered who Eileen was.

***

Eileen the maid knocked loudly, anxiously on the door of the master bedroom. She had to knock twice before there was any response.

"Yes?" Tom Stafford called. He had come back to bed after an hour's work in his den. He was exhausted.

"Something's—come up, sir."

Stafford got up immediately and grabbed his blue silk robe, which he always left on the back of the antique Edwardian chair that sat on the far side of the ornate nightstand.

"What is it, honey?" Molly said from the bed.

"I'm not sure."

"It's Jenny!" she said anxiously. "It's about Jenny!"

By the time he reached the door, she was right beside him.

Eileen was in a buff blue terrycloth robe. Her hair was in curlers. "Jenny's at the front gate! A cab brought her!"

"Jenny!" Tom Stafford said, as excited now as his wife.

"Just let them in," Stafford said. "We'll put some clothes on and meet them on the porch."

"Yessir."

Tom and Molly pulled on robes and slippers. They took the steps of the grand staircase like children, two at a time.

Molly hurried around the large room with its divans and grand piano and empire curtains imported from Paris. She turned on every light in the room. The shadows fled.

They tried waiting patiently on the porch for the taxi to appear. But they paced frantically and had to restrain themselves from running down the drive.

They heard the cab work its way up the drive. And then she was there, getting out of the back seat of the cab. Their daughter Jenny. Molly wasn't sure whether to laugh or cry. So she did both.

At first, the young woman wasn't sure who they were, the two people coming at her. But as they took her in their arms, and as the man whispered something to her and the woman laughed almost hysterically—

She knew. Her name was Jenny Stafford. She lived here in the mansion. As her mother and father hugged her, her real identity came to her. It was almost like a divine message.

She was Jenny Stafford. She was home.

She was unaware of the dark Ford van parked just outside the gates of her estate. . . .

Chapter Nine

GRETCHEN Olson was seventeen the first time she escaped. She had been reading a crime novel (she loved crime novels, the gorier the better) about a prisoner escaping by crawling under a truck and hanging on to the grid system while the truck drove right through the gates.

It worked perfectly for Gretchen. There was one difference. Gretchen wasn't escaping a prison, she was escaping a mental hospital. She had stabbed and hacked to death both her parents while they were sleeping. She was eleven years old at the time. The press marveled how such a sweet-faced little girl with white-blonde Dutch-boy hair (and who then weighed sixty-one pounds) could possibly inflict all the crazed damage she had.

Anyway, her escape. After six years in the maximum-security psychiatric hospital, there were three things that Gretchen wanted to do: lose her virginity, get drunk, and drive a car very, very fast.

Aunt Gwen secretly brought her money every monthly visit, Gretchen having convinced her that there were many ways to spend money in here, so she had more than four thousand dollars in cash when she rolled out from under the laundry truck one mile from the gates of the hospital.

She had a ball in Chicago. She bought herself a discreetly sexy dress and started cruising the bars over near Wicker Park. She'd studied the Chicago papers and knew where the twenty-something crowds hung out.

She learned to dance that night, and it was fun. The fact that she was a clumsy and awkward dancer didn't matter. She was gorgeous in her little lost-kitten way and nobody *cared* how bad a dancer she was.

She got drunk, too. Rum was the culprit. You mix rum with Coca Cola and it tasted like a confection and not liquor at all. She didn't realize how *much* it was liquor until it was too late.

By then, though, she'd found Brad. He was a handsome, twenty-nine-year-old surgeon. He said he wasn't married but she could see the lingering red ring indentation on his finger. Not that she cared. She found it pretty funny, actually.

There was another nice thing about Brad. He had a Porsche. An itty-bitty red one. Brad let her drive it. They went on the Dan Ryan and raised hell for an hour. She was a much better driver (she'd practiced on a hospital tractor mower, the operative principles being pretty much the same) than she had expected herself to be.

Then they ended up out in the boonies, parked near the lake. It was a clear summer night. The lake surface was painted gold with moonlight, and the night was a wild perfume of various fragrances.

She was quite methodical about what she wanted to do. First, she wanted to make out for a while. Then she wanted him to slowly begin to seduce her. She wanted to give *and* get oral sex, and then she wanted to make love. At one point, so dizzy, she was afraid the rum was going to come back up on her and she'd do something really insane like vomit in his mouth. But she managed to keep it down.

He wasn't much of a lover. He made a lot of noise but that was mostly about *all* he did. He pinched her nipples so hard, they hurt. And when he had his finger in her, he just kind of waggled it around was all. Maybe the way they had state maps (Your Guide to Iowa), they should have body part maps (Your Clitoral Vacation). She couldn't *believe* he was a doctor. How could a *doctor* know so little about the female anatomy?

The thing was, he wasn't a doctor. And his name wasn't Brad. And he didn't own the Porsche.

He was an escaped forger from Joliet Prison, his name was Rick, and he'd stolen the Porsche from the Saks Fifth Avenue parking garage in the Loop.

Gretchen learned all this after the cops stopped them on

the Dan Ryan going 132 mph and then took them both into custody.

She never saw Brad-Rick again. Nor did she know what kind of punishment he received. He'd obviously put some years on his sentence.

During her interrogation, both cops left the room for a time. When one of them came back, he found her crying. "What's wrong?" he said.

"All that time I was with Brad," she said, "I didn't have a single orgasm."

He smiled a cold cop smile. "Things're tough all over, kiddo."

She was returned to the psychiatric hospital. But not for long. A certain Dr. Quinlan had seen her story on the news and asked if she could be transferred to *his* psychiatric hospital. Being very well-regarded by the state psychiatric board, and being a major contributor to the campaigns of both the mayor and the governor, the transfer was made.

***

Oh, shit. Gretchen was just sneaking out of Building Four when Roy Barcroft caught her. Building Four was set far away from the other three. It was Quinlan's private domain.

Barcroft was head of security here at the compound, as the staffers called Quinlan's psychiatric hospital. The official name was Windcross, but nobody on staff ever called it that.

Four large new brick buildings. Quinlan made it look as much like a college campus as possible, down to the ivy that had begun to climb the walls. There were three large tennis courts, Olympic-size outdoor *and* indoor swimming pools, and a nine-hole golf course. There was a guest dining room where gourmet cuisine was served on weekends, the room having the appointments and the ambience of a four-star restaurant. It was expensive to spend your time at Windcross, but wealthy people who were in legal trouble—or who had loved ones who were in legal trouble—generally found a way to be placed here. Quinlan was not apologetic about the fact that Windcross had made him rich. He always pointed to the research he was doing here on the vagaries of the criminal mind. His research had been applauded worldwide; liberals and conservatives alike felt his published papers brought real wisdom to America's ever-escalating crime problems (forget about the highly questionable FBI stats that showed violent crime on the decline). If he liked women, expensive cars, and even more expensive airplanes, so be it.

"Oh, shit," Gretchen said.

Barcroft was closing fast on her as she darted from the side door of Building Four to the grass that edged on the asphalt road that ran through the compound.

He was a big man, Barcroft, the kind little girls had nightmares about in boogeyman dreams. He had a wide, tanned face lined on the jaw with a long scar. He had midnight-black hair and dark eyes that seemed jack-o'-lantern luminous when he was angry. And, boy, was he angry now.

"Hey!" he shouted.

But she kept on running. She kept the mini video camera tucked into her chest like a quarterback suddenly deciding to run for glory. She was already out of breath. Despite her tiny size, her diet consisted largely of Three Musketeers, popcorn, Diet Coke (she was just a teensy-weensy bit bulimic) and Hot Tamales. She never exercised and rarely lifted anything heavier than the *TV Guide*.

And right now it was all catching up to her.

She headed straight for the asphalt. Maybe she could run faster on a flat, hard surface. This particular area had only been sodded a few years ago and it was still lumpy in places.

But she didn't make it to the asphalt. Not erect, anyway.

The toe of her Reebok caught on the edge of the curb and she went sprawling face first. She remembered to keep the Minicam pressed tight to her chest, with her arms over it to cushion the fall.

Then Barcroft was standing over her. At the moment all she could see was one neatly creased khaki trouser leg and a spit-shined black boot. She looked up, her sweet erotic little face breaking into a gamine grin. Now seemed the right time to try the old Gretchen charm.

"Hi, Barcroft."

"Hi."

"I bet you're really pissed, huh?"

"Stand up, Gretchen. I want to see what you've got there."

She became aware of her circumstances suddenly: lying on the asphalt; a dark train rushing and rumbling through the prairie night in the distance; the half-moon almost unnaturally bright in the navy blue sky; the scent of her own perfume; Barcroft's black-booted foot tapping impatiently.

But he was beyond the range of her charm at the moment. Sometimes, he was mildly flirtatious. Not tonight.

"Stand up."

"I'll tell Quinlan if you hit me."

"Stand up, Gretchen. Now."

So she stood up. He could have helped her, lent a hand, but he didn't.

"What the hell's this?" he snapped.

He jerked the camera from her arms and held it out in front of him. He looked at the camera for a long moment and then looked over at Building Four. "What the hell were you taping in Building Four?"

"Nothing. Honest. I was just carrying it around."

But he already had his cell phone out. "Let me talk to Quinlan." He would be asking the twenty-four-hour operator to clear his call directly up to Quinlan's apartment. "Well, tell him I'm *ordering* you to clear this call through." Another pause. "I'm sorry to disturb you, Dr. Quinlan. But we may have a major problem on our hands."

He glared at Gretchen. "Something we need to discuss in private." Beat. "Fifteen minutes, then."

"You really are pissed, aren't you, Barcroft?" she said, smiling, after he put his cell phone away. She was still trying, uselessly, to flirt with him.

But he didn't say anything. He just grabbed her elbow and marched her along the grass back to Building Four. This was like being taken to the principal's office. Only much, *much* worse.

Chapter Ten

THE first person the Staffords called was their family physician, Doctor Grainger. He advised them to give Jenny one of the sleeping pills he'd prescribed long ago, and told them to let her sleep as long as possible. He'd see her tomorrow afternoon. Then he told them how happy he was that she'd come home.

Molly said, "Do you think we should call Priscilla?"

"It's pretty late, hon," Tom said.

"Well, we called Dr. Grainger."

"Yes, but he's an MD. Priscilla is her psychiatrist. There's a difference." He took her in his arms. Held her. "God, I still can't quite believe she's home."

"Neither can I." She looked up into her husband's face and gave him a long kiss. Then, "Please, can't I call her? She's been worried sick."

He grinned. "You just want to share the good news."

She laughed. "That's right."

"Well, then call her. I'm going up to bed. I think I'm actually going to be able to sleep now."

Unspoken was the fact that they had no idea where their daughter had been the past eight days. Unspoken was the fact that Priscilla might well want Jenny sent back to a sanitarium.

Tom swatted Molly affectionately on the bottom and then climbed the stairs to the second floor. Molly went eagerly to the phone.

***

"She was taping you," Barcroft said.

"Taping me?" Quinlan said. "Where?"

"Building Four. The Tower."

"How the hell did she get up to the Tower?"

Barcroft had been dreading the moment when this was brought up. In theory, Building Four was the most secure of all the compound buildings. Even more secure, again in theory, was what they called the Tower. This was a large addition that had been built on to the roof. Nobody got in there except Quinlan and the people he authorized. Barcroft had never been in there. Not once.

But somehow little Gretchen had snuck in.

"If you want me to quit," Barcroft said, "I'll have a letter of resignation on your desk tomorrow morning."

"I don't want you to quit, Roy," Quinlan said evenly, obviously fighting to keep his legendary temper under control. "I want you to explain to me how the hell she got into the building and then into the Tower."

They were in the living room of Quinlan's apartment, which was a study in blacks, whites, grays, and chromes. Imposing as it was, it was also comfortable, with the built-in bookcases and the large open-hearth fireplace and the deep white shag carpeting. The west window offered a spectacular view of the distant Chicago skyline, a menagerie of lights and skyscrapers and giant planes descending toward O'Hare, a panorama that you never got tired of looking at.

Barcroft was now wondering what secret the Tower held. He'd always been curious. Especially since he'd learned that the entire construction was sound-baffled—completely soundproofed. A security man was a nosy man, and he'd love to see what Gretchen had gotten on her tape tonight.

But the Minicam was in Quinlan's hands, and Quinlan wasn't about to share his secrets with Barcroft.

"Where is she now?" Quinlan asked. In his dark blue silk pajamas and holding a pipe, he reminded Barcroft of Hugh Hefner. Quinlan spent a lot of time entertaining various female patients in his pajamas. And "entertaining" was a word open to wide interpretation.

"Down the hall. In a secure room."

"As 'secure' as the Tower?" Quinlan said, smiling coldly.

Barcroft felt his cheeks turn hot.

"Keep her down there for a while. I want to go over this tape in private."

"Yes, sir."

Barcroft turned and started to walk back to the electronically keyed door. The correct thumbprint was the only way in or out.

"Barcroft?"

Roy turned, faced Quinlan.

"I'm sorry about the cheap shot. You know, at the last there."

"I had it coming."

The cold Quinlan smile. "Yes, you did. But that didn't mean I had to say it."

Barcroft stared at Quinlan a moment, then turned and pressed his thumbprint to the ID pad.

***

About an hour after she got to sleep, Jenny had to urinate. She hiked up her sleeping gown and sat down. The toilet seat was cold on her backside. When she started peeing, the sound seemed unnaturally loud to her in the shadowy bathroom, the only light being the moon through the window.

She was just getting up, just turning around to flush the toilet when she saw—

—an image of a motel . . . an image of a dead man in a room in that motel . . . an image of her own long, slender hands . . . bloody—

A searing headache burst inside her head. She cradled her head in her hands, trying to stop the pain.

And then they were gone—the images *and* the headache.

Some sort of nightmare, she thought, as she slipped through the shadows in her bare feet, headed back to bed.

Some sort of nightmare.

Chapter Eleven

QUINLAN stood at his window, with his wonderful view of Chicago spread out before him. He had his pajamas, his pipe, and his handsome self.

This was the first thing Gretchen saw when Barcroft brought her into the apartment.

Barcroft knew he wasn't wanted. Quinlan didn't even turn around to see him.

"I'll talk to you tomorrow," Barcroft said, and then went away again, leaving the two alone.

Gretchen was scared. She was also pissed off, depressed, and very, very horny. Two years ago, when he'd requested that she be transferred here, he'd introduced her to real sex. He had no idea (at least to her mind) what he was doing because he'd created a sex machine. But for all her masturbation, all her compound sexual flings, only one person brought her true satisfaction, her lord and master—Quinlan.

She said, "I know I shouldn't have done what I did, okay? If you want to yell at me and shit, then just get it over with, all right?"

He didn't say anything. He still didn't turn around.

She went on: "The only reason I did it was because I couldn't think of any other way to get back in your life. I mean, you've completely shut me out. And I mean completely."

Quinlan eventually slept with most of his female patients in the compound. This usually took place after he had stabilized them with therapy and drugs and perhaps electro-convulsive treatments. He always told them the same thing, that having sex with them was part of the bonding process. After the intimacy of sex, he would say, they would feel free to say anything to him. And who was to argue with such a polished and handsome man, especially one who had helped them find at least a semblance of mental peace and order? Most of the women knew when their time with him was finished. This varied. Some of the sexual relationships lasted barely two weeks; some extended a full two months. Gretchen was the exception. She lasted almost three months and she was the only woman to ever live with him in his aerie apartment. Except Jenny Stafford.

She could not make any sort of life for herself without him. She had tried. It didn't work. She spoke of nothing else to her shrink, her fixation on Quinlan. The shrink, a man named Greaves, said that what she needed was time. Six, seven more months and opening herself to others—and she would forget all about him.

Quinlan obviously didn't share the same opinion as his associate. Following one of her death-threat phone calls, Quinlan had Gretchen placed in the violent program in Building Two, where she remained for ten months. By pretending to be a good girl, by pretending that she was no longer interested in Quinlan, she won her freedom again. She was permitted to roam around the compound as long as she checked in five times a day. This meant reporting to the general staff office at each check time.

Gretchen managed to give the appearance of being a good and dutiful patient. But yesterday, she'd glimpsed Quinlan as he walked across the campus with a beautiful new patient. And Gretchen became enraged. The Tower had always intrigued her. Gaining entrance was no problem. She seduced a guard.

Now, she'd been caught.

"I know you're pissed off. And I don't blame you. I really don't."

"You crossed the line this time, Gretchen." He looked at her with the white rage she could see him struggling to control. "And now there's no way back. For either of us."

He came to her so quickly she didn't have time to move, even though she could see his right hand raising up and then chopping down to come crashing into the left side of her face.

"No way back at all," he said.

Then he went to the communicator built into the wall and instructed Barcroft to come get her and put her in the empty room down the hall. The soundproofed one.

Chapter Twelve

COFFEY started writing fiction after he read his first Joseph Wambaugh novel. That happened to a lot of cops. Half the homicide dicks in the country had to have partially finished book manuscripts in their desks, thanks to Mr. Wambaugh and the dreams of wealth and fame he inspired.

This morning, he was working on his second novel, about a cop who realizes his partner doubles as a mob hit man. But the longer he sat at his word processor, the more often he thought of the mystery woman. She was impossible to forget.

***

For lunch, he had a tuna fish sandwich and some potato chips. He decided it was time to change his writing T-shirt. He had two writing T-shirts and this one needed a washing. He checked the newspaper and watched the midday report on WGN. The TV station had a brief story about an as yet unidentified man who had been found stabbed to death at the Econo-Nite Motel. The police investigation was just getting underway. No other details.

He kept staring at the phone as if his gaze could make it ring. He wanted the woman to call and say that her memory came back and that she now knew she didn't have anything to do with the murder. And that, by the way, she wasn't married, engaged, or otherwise encumbered and would love to see him again, preferably in the next five minutes.

The phone rang, but it wasn't the woman. It was his sister Jan in Omaha. She was having her first baby in three weeks. They still hadn't come up with a name for the baby—they knew it was going to be a girl—and Jan was wondering if he'd heard anything from the realtor. Their Chicago house was still unsold and the double mortgage payments were getting to be a hassle. And then she got around to the subject she couldn't wait to get to: had he met anybody yet? "Anybody" meant, of course, a woman who looked like possible marriage material. Then her doorbell rang; it turned out to be a friend of hers she hadn't seen for a while, so she said good-bye.

He spent half an hour in the basement lifting weights, the same weights he'd had since he was fourteen years old. He'd been a skinny, gangly kid and the target of every bully in Chicago it seemed. Lifting weights hadn't actually made him any tougher, but had improved his self-confidence. All the time he worked out today, his mind went to the woman and where she was and what she was doing.

Dusk came around 5:30. He hated dusk. It affected him the way rain affected others. An almost paralyzing melancholy overcame him at dusk. He felt totally alone, and anxious for no reason that he'd ever been able to figure out.

He decided to start driving early, rather than sit around and stare at the phone. He took a shower and changed clothes, went out and got in his cab, and took off.

He wasn't usually much of a talker, but the first couple of fares he had tonight, he talked their heads off. Real nervous, almost manic talk. He wasn't sure why. But he couldn't shut up.

The night passed quickly. He had three different O'Hare fares, and one Schaumberg trip, which took a decent amount of time. He ran out of talk pretty early and went back to his familiar silences.

Around ten, he stopped off at a Pizza Hut and had a small cheese pizza and a large Coke. Watching all the young couples made him feel lonely. He wished the woman would call.

He kept wondering where she was and what she was doing.

Chapter Thirteen

AT the moment, a beautiful young woman named Jenny Stafford was sitting in her father's den with a slender, elegant psychiatrist named Priscilla Bowman. A fire glowed in the fireplace. They sat in facing leather chairs in front of the fireplace. Both of them sipped brandy from large snifters.

They had been at this for three hours now. Priscilla ran a little cassette recorder, set on a table next to Jenny.

Jenny was staring at her hands in her lap. She looked tired and sad.

Priscilla, a wan woman whose radiant blonde hair was pulled back into a fashionable but somehow prim chignon, leaned forward in her blue Armani suit and said, "I know it's frightening, Jenny. But we'll put it together. It just may take a little time is all. I'm going to start you on some new antidepressants tonight as well as a new kind of sleeping pill. The big thing you need now is rest—physically *and* mentally."

Then, "I've seen this happen a lot, Jenny. I really have. This kind of blackout, I mean."

Jenny looked up. "But for eight days?"

Priscilla said, "For much longer, actually. I once had a patient who lost an entire year of his life."

"Did he ever remember?"

"No. Not really. The most we were ever able to get him to remember were vague images."

"I don't even have those. At least not very many."

"You will," Priscilla said.

Jenny looked at her, smiled sadly. "Well, if anybody can help me, you can." She'd been seeing Priscilla for two years. At first, Molly and Tom had feared that their daughter was going through not only trauma but bulimia. She would vomit up most of the food she ate, then would go on wild binges. Then she would become so depressed that she would stay in bed for days. They certainly didn't want to send her back to Quinlan and his hospital, which she'd hated so much. Enter Priscilla, who had her office in the Loop near Tom. Jenny began seeing her twice a week. Improvement wasn't immediate—Priscilla had been careful not to promise any miracles—but gradually vestiges of the old Jenny slowly began to reappear. The biggest problem was that Priscilla couldn't find an anti-depressant that really worked for Jenny for any length of time. Recently, the bulimia-like symptoms had returned, too. Jenny lost twelve pounds off her already thin frame. And, depressed, she took to her room again. Eileen fixed a variety of sumptuous meals but none of them interested Jenny. She lost three more pounds. And then, eight days ago, she'd disappeared.

"I'm scared," Jenny said softly.

"Of not remembering?"

"That I did something terrible. You know, that I can't remember doing."

"That wouldn't be in character, Jenny. You doing something terrible. In the three years I've known you, I can't recall a single terrible thing you've ever done."

"I've been a lot of trouble for my parents."

"That's true. But I don't see that as 'terrible,' and I'm sure they don't, either. You've had a difficult time the last three or four years of your life. Most people wouldn't have handled it nearly as well as you have."

Jenny stared at her hands again. "I just feel this—dread. There's something right on the edge of my memory. I can't quite bring it back. But it's there and it won't go away."

"You're exhausted," Priscilla said. "I think that's your biggest problem right now. You need a lot of good old-fashioned REM sleep, and you need a regular diet of some very healthy food."

"You really think that'll do it?"

Priscilla smiled. "It sure won't hurt."

"I just want to get rid of this feeling—this dread."

"You will. A few days from now, you'll be feeling much better."

"Will I ever get the eight days back?"

"Maybe not all of them," Priscilla said, "but most of them."

"I didn't drink or take drugs. I don't know why I'd black out that way."

Priscilla said, "You were tired of who you were, tired of what you saw as all the hassles in your life. So you took a little vacation. You blacked out."

"That can happen?"

"Oh, yes. In fact, there's a theory that a lot of amnesia isn't caused by trauma at all but is largely self-willed. In other words, people feel they need an escape, and so they simply forget who they are and what they've been going through."

"Do you believe that?"

Priscilla smiled. "Well, psychiatry loves to toy with new theories and a lot of them—like some of Freud's pet theories—ultimately prove to be nothing but hot air. But this theory—Let's say that for right now, I'm intrigued by it. It would explain a lot about amnesia that we've never been able to explain before. Some psychiatrists are even starting to treat partial amnesia with psychoactive drugs, as if it's a mental illness rather than some kind of temporary fugue state or brain malfunction." She laughed. "Just what you needed, right? A documentary on amnesia."

"No, no," Jenny said quickly. "It's interesting. It really is."

"Well, in the next few days," Priscilla said, "why don't we start seeing each other twice a week in my office?"

"I'd appreciate that."

"And in the meantime, you relax and take your medication and give Eileen the opportunity to fatten you up. She's slicing me a big piece of her lemon meringue pie to take home."

"She's a great cook," Jenny said. "In fact, I may try some of that pie myself."

The two women ended up embracing. Then Jenny walked her to the door. "See you in a few days."

Priscilla nodded good night and left the den. She was supposed to stop in the living room and visit with Tom and Molly Stafford before she went home. She was tired and hoped she could keep the visit brief.

***

Tom and Molly Stafford sat on a long, gold-brocaded couch in the living room. Both looked anxious and drawn. "Well, how do you think she's doing?" Stafford asked as Eileen led Priscilla around a grand piano and then to a divan. He was so anxious he hadn't even waited until she was seated.

Priscilla said, "I could give you a lot of theories and conjecture. But I'll put it in English for you."

For all her poise and style, the psychiatrist looked nervous. Who enjoyed giving people bad news? She sat on the edge of her chair. "I've explained the 'fugue state' before. How trauma can erase memory." She hesitated. "I believe something may have happened to her during the eight days she was gone."

"Happened?" Molly Stafford asked. "I'm not sure what you mean."

"Unfortunately," the psychiatrist said, "neither am I."

"Well, maybe this will convince her to finally set a date with David," Stafford said, obviously trying to put some positive spin on the situation.

"Tom sees David as the white knight on the white steed," Molly said to Priscilla.

"Well, he's a hell of a lot better than that ballet dancer or whatever he was she was so crazy about," Stafford said.

"He wasn't a ballet dancer," Molly laughed. "He was a musical comedy stage actor."

"The first time he came here to pick up my daughter," Stafford said, "he was wearing makeup."

"He was late coming from the theater," Molly explained. "He still had some makeup on. He asked if he could use the bathroom to take it off. It wasn't any more sinister than that. And the reason, dear husband, he stopped coming around was because he went back to his wife. For what it's worth, he's very happily hetero."

Priscilla looked ready to cave in. She'd had a long day of appointments and tonight, without a break for dinner, had spent three hours with Jenny. "I'm afraid I need to go." She stood up.

Both the Staffords walked her to the door. On the front steps, Tom said, "You won't have to put her in the hospital again, will you? Those electroshock treatments—" He sighed. "The poor kid."

"We'll find an alternative," Priscilla smiled wearily. "Good night." And before they could start another conversation, she was walking briskly to her shiny black Lexus.

Chapter Fourteen

THE Windy City Cab Company had its offices in a deserted warehouse just off West Randolph Street. No attempt had ever been made to fix the place up. The lighting was murky, the toilets flushed when they felt like it, and the ground floor had so many cabs coming and going, it looked like a freeway. The air smelled of damp concrete, motor oil, cigarette smoke, overloaded dumpsters out in the alley, and the smell of rubber from the rack of new tires pushed up against the east wall. In the back was the auto repair shop. The noise was relentless, tools clanging on the concrete floor, mechanics shouting back and forth to each other, and one radio that played rap competing with another radio that played country western. Definitely a clash of cultures.

In the morning, after spending his time at the word processor, Coffey stopped in at the cab company offices. The city had some form for cabbies to fill out. It had to be notarized. Coffey could get both tasks taken care of here at the office. The day dispatcher was also a notary.

He finished with the form and then poured himself a cup of coffee. The mug had been washed around the last time the Cubs had won a pennant. He sat in the tiny lunchroom swapping cabbie stories with some of the other drivers. This was a whole subculture, the cabbie life. They tried to outdo each other with stories about fares who'd vomited, fares who'd been hostile, fares who had big boobs, fares who'd been great tippers. Every once in a while, one of the older drivers would look up at the walls of the lunchroom, and say, "Hey, what happened to the broads?" In the good old days, these venerable walls had provided a veritable art museum of *Playboy* and

Penthouse foldouts. But there was a new owner now—some leasing company out of Philadelphia—and a new attitude. The new company had sent one of their VPs out here to look things over, and she'd been horrified at sight of the foldouts.

Coffey enjoyed listening to the cabbies' stories. They were sarcastic and sardonic social commentators, and this included those who barely spoke English. The world was a different place when viewed through the eyes of a cabbie. He was about to leave when Benny Margolis came in. "Man, I sure hope I run into this chick. If I do, I won't turn her over to the cops, I'll head directly to a no-tell motel." He waved a police sketch at everybody.

Cabbies were always getting police sketches. Nobody got around the city as much as cabbies, so handing out sketches over here made sense.

The sketch made the rounds. Every man who looked at it had something to say about the person depicted on it.

"Hey," Margolis said, taking the sketch for a second look. "You know who I think this is?"

"Who?" somebody asked.

"Tom Stafford's daughter."

"Tom Stafford, the investment banker?" Coffey said. Stafford was one of the wealthiest men in the state.

"Yeah, and she's just the kind of chick the police would want for murder," one of the drivers said.

"They say they just want to talk to her because she may be a material witness," somebody said.

"They always say that bullshit," a third man argued. "It means that she's really their suspect."

"You really think it's her?" somebody asked Margolis.

"I'm sure of it." Margolis glanced at his watch. "I used to haul her around sometimes. Nice kid, actually. I've got to pick my wife up. She wants to take me out for my birthday lunch."

"You don't look a day over eighty-seven," one of the cabbies joked.

Margolis smiled. "And that's just how old I feel, too."

He handed Coffey the sketch. When Coffey looked at it, his entire body froze, as if it had just received a heart-searing jolt of electricity. His palms began to sweat and he felt dizzy, claustrophobic, unreal.

DAUGHTER OF DARKNESS 75

The sketch was clearly that of last night's dark-haired woman.

It took him a few minutes before he was able to function again. Meantime, the other drivers continued to make salacious remarks.

Margolis waved good-bye and left the coffee room.

Coffey walked out of the lunchroom with Margolis. "You really think that was Tom Stafford's daughter?"

Margolis shrugged. "Well, I wouldn't bet my nice little house in Hyde Park on it, but, yeah, I'm pretty sure it was. She was too beautiful to forget."

Coffey wished Margolis a happy birthday. "I'll walk out with you," Margolis said.

As they reached the parking lot, Margolis dug in the pocket of his green windbreaker and took out a business card. He handed it to Coffey. "This guy was asking questions about you this morning."

INTERNATIONAL INVESTIGATIONS, INC.
Ralph Cummings

Coffey looked it over. "What kind of questions?"

"Mostly, if any of us had seen you since last night and did we know if you had a girlfriend."

"Girlfriend?"

"That's what he asked."

"Thought I'd better tell you," Margolis said. He checked his wristwatch. "Well, time to meet my wife. Better get to it." He nodded to the card. "You can keep it." He grinned. "Pretty nice of me, huh?"

"Yeah," Coffey said. "Real nice."

Twenty-three minutes later, Coffey was in the library.

Chapter Fifteen

MOLLY always used to do this when Jenny was a little girl—sit on her bed with Jenny's head on her knee, and Jenny stretched out on the bed. They were in that position now in the big, bright bedroom.

Just after a late breakfast, Jenny had slumped into an anxiety state, the kind Priscilla Bowman had warned them to watch carefully. Jenny had been in this kind of mood when she'd left the house and not returned for eight days.

So Molly took Jenny upstairs and asked her to lie on the bed as they had in the old days. At first, they were both self-conscious about doing it—like trying to rekindle feelings and needs long dead—but after a few minutes of actually being on the bed, they both relaxed and began to enjoy themselves.

It was comfortable and private here. They couldn't hear sounds from anywhere else in the house and the warm sunlight through the windows made them feel as lazy as napping cats. The white drapes and furnishings and bedclothes gave the room a brilliance and cleanliness that automatically improved Jenny's mood. She felt safe and loved here. The darkness of her eight missing days no longer weighed on her mind. She had banished it, at least temporarily.

When Jenny was a little girl, Molly would always read to her. Jenny had two favorite stories that she liked to hear over and over again, "Cinderella" and "Hansel and Gretel," the first because it was so romantic—even rich little girls dreamed of being the princess—and the second because it was so terrifying.

Today, there were no stories. But there remained the old love and tenderness. And that was more than enough.

Molly wore a blue running suit. She ran two miles a day, always after lunch. Jenny's white blouse and fashionably knee-torn jeans gave her the look of a teenager. The back of her head rested on her mother's knee. Molly dragged a comb lazily through Jenny's lovely dark hair. She might have been a doll that Molly was grooming.

"David already called twice today," Molly said. "He practically lived here while you were gone. I don't have to tell you how much he loves you."

"I know he loves me," Jenny said. "I just wish I loved him. After he dumped me—I just don't feel the same way anymore."

"He'd like to take you to dinner tonight. That's what he said both times when he called this morning. I told him with all that's happened, I think you need your rest."

She reached up and touched her mother's hand. "I don't want to feel that I'm in a sickbed again, Mom. The way I was after—" Once again, the situation that had put her in the mental hospital came to mind—and she immediately pushed it away. "You know what I was thinking about doing today?" Jenny said, changing the subject.

"No, what?"

"Visiting Ted."

Molly hesitated. Then, "Well, that would be nice."

"God, I like him so much."

"And he certainly likes you."

Jenny rolled over so she could put her chin in her hands and face her mother. "You know what?"

"What?"

"I think he still has a crush on you."

"Oh, stop being silly."

"But you went out together for a long time."

"Not a 'long time.' Our sophomore year in college was all."

"Well, that's a long time."

Molly put her hand on the crown of Jenny's head and began stroking her hair. "I'm sure he'd be glad to see you."

"He always seems so lonely to me," Jenny said.

"I don't think I'll tell Daddy where I'm going," she added, and smiled. "He's still threatened by Ted, isn't he?"

"Well, I'd be threatened if the situation was reversed. Ted *is* a very good-looking man. And he's always being written up in the papers. And he's on TV a lot." Ted had been Molly's boyfriend before Tom Stafford met her. Tom wasn't crazy about the fact that Ted always sent them gifts and had befriended Jenny—but he'd learned to accept it.

"He told me he hates the publicity," Jenny said. "But that he doesn't have any choice. He has to do the publicity, or his paintings won't sell."

Jenny rolled over so that the back of her head was on her mother's knee again. "This room has more interesting ceiling patterns than mine does."

"Ceiling patterns?"

"You know. The patterns that sunlight makes through the trees."

"Oh."

"That's why I always used to come in here in the afternoons." Jenny laughed softly. "You always had a lot more going on on your ceiling than I did."

"Now there's a compliment if I ever heard one," Molly smiled.

"I used to do that in the psych hospital, too. My room had very interesting ceiling patterns, too."

Jenny's stay in the psych hospital was something rarely discussed in the Stafford house.

Molly put her hand on Jenny's head, as if she wanted to drive out all memories of that terrible time. And then—

They fell silent again, trying to just enjoy the moment here on the bed.

Jenny said, "When I got up this morning, I was afraid my period was starting. Thank God, I was wrong. I'm not ready for it yet."

Her mother stroked her hair some more. "You probably shouldn't go anywhere. You're exhausted. You should stay home." Then, "You always run to Ted when you have a problem, don't you?"

"Does that hurt your feelings?"

"No. Not really."

Jenny thought for a long moment. "I just like hanging out with him. He's fascinating. All the reading he does— He's always got some new passion. It's great spending a long afternoon with him. He'll start out talking about the current political scene and then end up telling you about how the gladiators prepared for battle. His mind's so full of information, and he's so enthusiastic about things. He's really alive."

"He certainly is that," Molly said.

Jenny said, "I'm trying not to think about it."

"I know, honey."

"Maybe I'll never know. Where I was for those eight days. When I was in the psych hospital, I met alcoholics like that. They'd lost days, even weeks, and they never got them back. I just don't want to think about it now. I just want to try and get my mind off it. So I thought I'd go see Ted."

"Then by all means, go see Ted."

"Just don't tell Daddy, all right?"

Molly laughed. "That's the first thing I'm going to do," she said, and then tickled Jenny under her arm. "Drive right over to his office and tell him where you're going."

Then she leaned over and kissed her daughter tenderly on her forehead.

Chapter Sixteen

THE library was crowded.

At the information desk, Coffey asked an attractive young woman if there was a section of books on Chicago society, and if it was kept up-to-date. Her answer was yes to both questions.

Coffey spent his first hour in the stacks, thumbing through books that referenced the Stafford family. In 1918, George Stafford, the founding father, brought a good deal of his oil money—he was a good friend of John D. Rockefeller's—back to Chicago. He had grown up here, one of six children born to an immigrant and impoverished family of Irish Catholics. Like many poor boys, he wanted to impress the city of his birth. He impressed them immediately. He went into investment banking with an almost religious zeal. He soon became great friends with the Wrigley folks.

His son Robert continued on in investment banking. Between world wars, Robert began to take great interest in European markets. He put the firm in a good position to take advantage of key European investments following World War II.

But it was Tom Stafford who brought the firm to true dominance. He took an early interest in computers. His roommate at Harvard, in fact, would become a major player in developing mainframe computers for IBM. This was at a time, the late fifties, when Wall Street and its allies in Chicago and Los Angeles still had doubts about the relevance of computers to their particular kind of work. Could you really trust computers? Tom Stafford believed you could, and this got him an extraordinary jump on his competitors. Stafford Investment Bankers became one of the most important players in contemporary investment banking.

Socially, Tom Stafford was also a noted figure. He spent his early twenties breaking the hearts of several beautiful debutantes. He also dated a few movie stars. Not many investment bankers found themselves in the pages of both *Esquire* and *GQ*. Stafford watchers were thus surprised when he settled his attention and fondness on a young woman he met working behind the counter of a small jewelry store near the Drake Hotel. Her name was Molly Davis and while her father, who owned the jewelry store, was a successful merchant, he certainly wasn't in the Stafford league. There was another unlikely aspect to the tale as well; though Stafford was handsome, charming, and rich, Molly Davis took no particular interest in him. She thought he was nice, she thought he was amusing, but when he asked her to marry him, she thought he was kidding. She said no. Nobody had ever said no to Tom Stafford. It was, at least to Tom Stafford, unthinkable. He redoubled his efforts. He courted her for nearly a year before she finally gave in. The wedding was one of the most lavish ever staged in Chicago. They day they married, Tom Stafford was thirty-eight (he'd had a long run as an eligible bachelor) and his Molly was twenty seven.

Seven months to the day of their wedding, Jenny came along. This was 1973. According to press reports, she was just about the perfect child—beautiful, joyful, and hypnotized by her parents, just as they were hypnotized by her. She spent seventh grade in Sweden, trying out a very tony private school. She didn't quite make it through the year. She was lonely for her parents, and they were miserable without her. She stayed in Chicago from then on, attending a private Catholic school and quite seriously studying ballet. The local press loved her as much as they'd loved her father. And she was even more photogenic than he'd been. She was an impossibly lovely seventeen-year-old when her Porsche convertible was back-ended by a truck and knocked down a steep ravine. The bets were she wouldn't make it. The Chicago news establishment held a death watch. The story had everything. People who didn't give a damn about high society—indeed, resented it—stayed fixed to their TV screens. Would the young heiress make it? Could the fates be so cruel as to snatch her life away?

She lived. But it was not easy. She spent two months in the hospital slowly and painfully learning to walk again. She had blinding headaches. And her memory was shaky. She'd lost long periods of time.

A year later, everything was fine. Her smashed leg had healed very well, the disk in her back was once again where it belonged, her memory had been fully restored and—if it was possible—she was even more beautiful than she'd been before the accident.

The press went right on loving her. For another whole year, she was their darling. She didn't want the attention—she was truly a shy person—but what choice did she have?

At about the time the press found a new life to suck dry—a dazzling young blonde skater who was, it seemed, headed for the Olympics and who had already been offered a modeling contract from the Ford Agency in New York—Jenny began to change.

All that anybody knew for sure—though it was the subject of much coy speculation in the local gossip columns—was that Jenny had suffered some kind of mental breakdown and was in a psychiatric hospital. One sympathetic gossip columnist noted that breakdowns were often a delayed reaction among people who suffered great physical traumas, such as Jenny had when her sports car had been knocked down a ravine.

This was where the story ended. There were no more references to Jenny in the books Coffey found. There had also been—for all the talk of her great good looks—no photograph of the young woman.

Coffey noted the approximate date when Jenny had been rumored to suffer a breakdown and then went over to the microfiche newspaper files.

Coffey was not a mechanical genius. Indeed, it took him a full ten minutes to string the microfiche roll into the machine properly. He did a fair amount of cursing which earned him a number of hostile glances from the people around him.

Then he got to work, and it didn't take long before he had his answer.

He stared at her photograph with an almost drugged expression. Not even the smudgy microfiche image could spoil her looks. He found himself drawn to her in a near-mystical way. He found himself longing to touch her, hold her, as he had last night. The longing was physically painful.

He had to see her. And soon. He had to find out how she was.

DAUGHTER OF DARKNESS 83

There was only one logical place to look for her. Her home, the Stafford mansion. But how could he ever approach them? What could he say? He'd sound like some kind of con artist, or a madman. Either way, they wouldn't take him seriously. They would most likely call the police. And what would he tell the police? He certainly couldn't tell them about last night, not without getting Jenny in a lot of trouble.

Jenny.

Did she even *know* she was Jenny?

And maybe she hadn't gone home. Maybe she was still wandering the streets, trying to reconstruct everything that had happened to her.

He rolled through several more feet of microfiche. He found two more pictures of her. They were as stunning as the first had been.

The second one was contained in a story about her going berserk in a posh pub on the Gold Coast. The story reported that she had slapped a woman and then proceeded to overturn several tables. She then began hurling glasses at the liquor bottles displayed behind the bar. The damage was estimated to be in the $5,000 range. She had been taken into custody and released two hours later to her attorney and her family. When she appeared in court the following morning, she claimed to have no memory of the entire incident. The judge set a trial date and suggested that Jenny look into Alcoholics Anonymous.

After this, there were no more stories about Jenny Stafford.

Coffey sat back in his chair. He knew what he had to do. Now he had to figure out the best way to do it, the best way to help Jenny.

As he sat there, he thought of several clever ways that he might get into the Stafford mansion. But that's all they were—clever. They wouldn't guarantee that he'd get to see her alone so that they could talk.

And that's what they badly needed to do. Talk. Alone. See if she'd had any luck puzzling through her loss of memory.

He checked his watch. Nearing noon now. He'd wait till dinnertime. It was more likely the family would be home then.

In the meantime, he'd buy the morning papers and see if there was any more information on the unidentified man they'd found dead in the motel room.

He rewound the microfiche, put it neatly back in its box, and left the library.

***

Jenny was on her way to Ted Hannigan's loft near the River North Gallery District when the news came on the radio. At first, she was tempted to change to another station. Unlike her parents, she had no interest in local politics, and with a city election coming up in six weeks, most of the local news concerned tracking polls and statements from candidates.

Then she heard, "The man found stabbed to death in the Econo-Nite Motel has now been identified as Earl Benedict of Skokie."

Her headache was instant and lacerating. She was afraid she might pass out. She gripped the steering wheel, not wanting to smash into the cars on either side of her. She was on the JFK Expressway, and it was extremely busy at the moment. There was no way she could drive in this condition.

The announcer went on: "A police spokesman said that Benedict was a salesman for a local radio station."

At the end of the exit ramp, Jenny shot across the street, pulling into the parking lot of an Arby's. The lunch crowd had descended on the place like a jungle predator on a carcass. Rock and roll and rap music boomed from two dozen cars with the windows rolled down.

Jenny sat in her car, trembling, and pressing delicate fingers to her temples. She felt suddenly dehydrated as well. She began licking her lips frantically.

Why would she respond to a news story this way? She didn't have anything to do with a dead man at some cheap motel, did she?

But she *was* missing eight days. . . .

She leaned her head back and closed her eyes. There was something in her mind . . . something slowly working its way to her consciousness . . . some ghostly image that she knew she didn't want to see . . . something that would perhaps explain the eight days she couldn't make register in her mind. . . .

And the story about the dead man in the motel had seemed to trigger it. But why?

Then she thought, *Maybe it's a coincidence. Maybe I just happened to react at the same time the story came on. Maybe any story would have triggered it.*

She sat in her car for several long minutes. She felt as if somebody had violently assaulted her. She felt isolated, the way she had in the psychiatric hospital.

It made no sense, responding to a news story like that. It *had* to be a coincidence. . . .

She walked unsteadily into Arby's and got herself a small Diet Pepsi. The smell of the meat made her sick. The psychiatric hospital at which she'd stayed had sat next to a farm. She'd frequently walked along the perimeter fence watching the cows go about their cowy business. And suddenly one day, it came to her that it was ridiculous—not to mention inhumane—to raise a breed of living beings for food.

The human faces about her looked grotesque suddenly. She remembered an old *Twilight Zone* episode about a party of upscale people drinking their martinis . . . and suddenly the hero sees them for what they are . . . pig-faced aliens.

Steady, she thought. This was the kind of mental self-indulgence she'd had to fight against after coming out of the hospital, these little excursions into phantasmagoria. She didn't tell anybody about them, of course. She didn't want to go back to the hospital. . . .

Then the people in Arby's were no longer monsters. They were just ordinary people—construction workers, salespeople, college students, mothers and their children—nice people for the most part, she was sure. People who wished her no harm, people who would help her if she asked. . . .

The spell, or whatever it had been, was starting to pass.

She sat in her car sipping at her soda. Her trembling had stopped. The worst of the headache had receded as well. It had been like a seizure, a great dark god holding her slender white body in his hand, and squeezing her until her life was almost snuffed out—

The sun had moved out from behind the clouds now. She rolled down her window. Even the air smelled fresh, and beautifully redolent of autumn—

She felt better. Even the dread associated with her eight missing days was gone.

She wanted to go see Ted. He always made her laugh, and she felt so secure in his strapping and powerful presence.

She started her car engine and headed back for the expressway.

***

Ted Hannigan's loft was located in the River North Gallery District, a section of the city Jenny loved. On a sunny day, it was great fun to stroll up and down the streets that were lined with art galleries. It was a little world unto itself, people here focused on art of every description. Sure, there were snobs and poseurs—a place like River North was bound to attract them—but most of the people were in equal parts enthusiastic, intelligent, and unpretentious.

Ted's loft was on the third floor of what had once been a warehouse. He often joked that this was the only place a man with three ex-wives could afford. Ted's interest in women was far more passionate than his interest in art. Ted had never kidded himself. He had adopted a Monet-like style of illustration and taken as his subjects the wealthy and arty set of Chicago. They loved his work, even if most of the major local artisans found it little more than clever commercial illustration and not in any way serious art. Ted had a Rolls Royce, a modest country estate, and spent at least two months of every year living well in Paris. He had made his peace with his own artistic limitations years ago.

While most of his art was for sale at the Harcourt Gallery right down the street, Ted did private portraits in his loft. Much as he hated such concessions, his portrait work required him to put a small business office in the front part of his loft. This meant a desk, a three-line phone system, two filing cabinets, a copying machine, a fax, and a leather couch and chair for his clients to sit in while they awaited the master. Ted always joked that the next thing you knew, he'd be joining the Chamber of Commerce and voting Republican. Oh, and one more thing came with the office—whatever stunning young thing Ted happened to be sleeping with at the moment. Ted's age range these days had gotten slightly older. The fetching short-haired blonde behind the desk this morning appeared to be at least in her late twenties—which was an improvement on the last one, who'd been a sophomore dropout from Northwestern. This one even dressed somewhat conservatively, in a nicely cut four-button jacket with casual white blouse and pleated blue slacks. Jenny could have lived without the nose ring and the butterfly tattoo on the top of the right hand, but then Jenny had never been much for fads or trends.

As soon as Jenny introduced herself, the blonde said, "Oh, yes, you're the one who walks on water." Before Jenny could say anything, the blonde stuck out a hand and said, "I'm Andi Teller. Ted's been telling me about you all morning. And I mean *all* morning. The way he was describing you, I thought walking on water was just one of your many talents."

Jenny smiled and shook Andi's hand. "Ted's sort of my unofficial uncle. I think he's slightly prejudiced."

"Well, he sure wasn't exaggerating about one thing, anyway," Andi said. "You're just as beautiful as he said you were."

Jenny blushed. She'd never been good at accepting compliments, and she didn't like being the center of attention. It put too much pressure on her. And, she was naturally shy. Good looks didn't necessarily make you gregarious.

"Like some coffee?" Andi said. "I made it, so it's safe to drink. Ted's is like car oil."

Jenny shook her head. "No, no thanks, I'll just sit down over here if you don't mind."

"Ted's running late with his sitting," Andi said. "I'll go tell him you're here. That'll hurry him along."

There was a door in the corner. Andi opened it and disappeared.

Instead of sitting down, Jenny walked around the reception area. The walls were filled with examples of his portraiture. He made things pretty, Ted did; too pretty, actually. But that was why people paid him so well, because he could deceive them into believing that they were something they were not. The overweight banker became the General Patton-like adventurer; the somewhat worn society matron became the ageless belle of whatever ball she attended. "I make them pay through the nose for their lies," Ted said mockingly to her once. It was the only side of him she didn't care for: the harsh, cynical side. She wasn't sure who he hated most—his clients or himself.

Fortunately, she rarely saw this side. Most of the time, Ted was the amusing, even dashing artiste who lived his life exactly as he wanted. He was her father-confessor. She'd told Ted things she hadn't even confided to her mother. He could bind you up with his tenderness. He could make you feel all right about yourself—something not even a long line of shrinks had been able to do most of the time.

The funny thing was, when she waited for him out in the reception area this way, she always got butterflies, as if she was about to have a date she didn't know very well. She knew why. She wanted him to like her, and she was afraid she'd disappoint him in some way.

Andi came back. "He said ten more minutes, max."

"Thanks."

She sat down next to a table filled with magazines about photography and art. A copy of this morning's newspaper lay across several magazines. She scanned the headlines above the fold. The phone rang. Andi answered it and began chatting with somebody. Jenny turned the newspaper over to see what was on the bottom of the fold.

DEAD MAN
DISCOVERED IN MOTEL

Jenny had an image of an ax being buried in the precise center of her forehead. The headache was that visceral. She grunted so sharply with the pain that Andi looked up, cupped the phone, and asked, "Are you all right?"

But instead of answering, Jenny staggered to her feet, grabbed her purse, and hurried to the front door. The bathroom was down the hall. It was a large room with a dusty skylight. The fixtures were new and the paint was fresh. She went into the first of the two stalls and threw up.

She was terrible at throwing up, and always had been. It terrified her. She felt she was going to choke and die. Her mother had always been there to hold her, to comfort her, to reassure her. But Jenny was too old for that now, of course.

It took two passes, kneeling next to the new white toilet bowl, to empty her stomach.

She stood up and walked shakily to the twin white sinks and the long mirror that stretched out above them. She opened her purse and took out a plastic toothbrush holder, a tube of Colgate white, a tiny vial of Chanel Number 5, and a bar of beauty soap. She spent ten minutes working on herself. She wanted to be perfectly fresh for Ted.

The headache had subsided but not her dread of what she'd read in the newspaper. Twice now a reference to the Econo-Nite Motel had made her head erupt with blinding pain. But why should it? What did she have to do with what had happened at the Econo-Nite Motel? Nothing.

But she couldn't recall eight days and nights of her life. . . .

She swallowed two aspirins, then hurried back to meet Ted.

Chapter Seventeen

QUINLAN drove his Mercedes sports coupe to the private airport where the hangar he leased housed his Lear jet. When people swooned at the extravagance of such a purchase, especially for a man whose business rarely took him out of the city, he pointed out that the Lear was nearly ten years old, and that he needed to escape from his work every now and then. He had been known to favor the Caribbean.

His pilot, a chunky thirty-seven-year-old redhead named McReady, was climbing out of the cargo hold when Quinlan arrived.

"You think there'll be room for everything?" Quinlan asked.

"Should be," McReady said. "I've never seen you take this much on a vacation before."

"Well, I'll probably be staying longer than usual."

Much longer, Quinlan thought. After McReady took him to London, Quinlan would disappear into a clinic where plastic surgery would turn him into a new man. "Quinlan" would never be seen or heard from again. As soon as his last task was finished in Chicago, which should be tomorrow, "Quinlan" would be gone forever.

"What're the weather people saying?"

McReady, wiping his hands on his gray overalls, said, "Some storms over the mid-Atlantic. But they don't look like much. Should be an easy go."

"Great." Then, "I've got something I want to load up myself."

McReady smiled. "Be my guest. My daughter's got a dental appointment. I'm supposed to pick her up at school and take her. I'll be back here in a couple of hours."

DAUGHTER OF DARKNESS   91

"No hurry. Everything looks like it's moving along fine."

McReady nodded and walked out of the hangar, his whistle echoing off the curved steel ceiling.

Quinlan moved quickly. He had a small gym-style leather bag that he wanted to put in the very back of the cargo hold. He climbed in and began rearranging trunks and bags. When he had cleared out a place against the rear wall of the hold, he slipped the bag in there, then covered it up with the trunks and other bags.

Eight million dollars in cash. It had taken him four years to accumulate it in various ways. About a third of it had come from his inheritance. His father had been a Los Angeles attorney who'd attached himself to some very powerful studio people. After he'd helped extricate one of them from a difficult—and potentially criminal—tax situation, they'd all pushed some very high-visibility WORK his way. He'd made a lot of money and had left half of it to Quinlan—the *only* thing he'd left Quinlan. He'd been a terrible, absent father. Quinlan hadn't thought much more of his mother, a very beautiful but strictly decorous woman who'd died of a brain tumor. He'd overhead one of the maids laugh one day, "I didn't know she *had* a brain." And cruel as the remark was, he had to agree with it. His mother had been a dope.

Eight million dollars in cash.

That was the best way to start a new life. And to inaugurate a new face. The very best way.

***

Most of the private investigators Coffey knew were jerks. They would literally do anything for a buck. Especially since the hi-tech revolution made spying a rather simple process. But the card Margolis had given him at the cab company led him to a surprising neighborhood.

He had low expectations of International Investigations, Inc. In spite of the imposing name, the place would be a dusty walk-up in an ancient four-story office building. There would be a pebbled-glass door with chipped black paint giving the name of the place. Inside, he'd find a waiting room with a few spindly chairs and some very old *Time* magazines on a scarred and wobbly table. Cummings himself—that was the name on the card—would be dumpy, vaguely unclean, and smell of beer or whiskey. Or both.

This was Coffey's composite sketch of private detectives.

So he was surprised when he found that International Investigations, Inc. shared a new one-story, concrete-and-glass office building in part of the city that was bouncing back from urban blight.

The cars parked in back of the building, in the International section of the lot, also surprised Coffey, a new Mercedes four-door sedan and a silver Jag. *The* silver Jag.

Coffey parked on the edge of the lot with his motor still running. Whoever had hired this firm to check him out had money. This was not a sleazy gumshoe operation. They probably had indoor plumbing and everything.

He sat there for ten minutes, trying to glimpse the clientele, when a young man in an Armani suit came out and walked over to the silver Jag. The man's hair was so sun-bleached it was almost white—just as it had been the other night when Coffey glimpsed him by the motel. The silver Jag was a prize, a collectible that could make people gasp. There had never been a car quite so dramatic in the sculpting of its body.

The young man looked dour. Whatever was troubling him had made him lose appreciation for the gorgeous machine he was driving.

He got in the silver car and drove away. He didn't even glance at Coffey.

After a few minutes, Coffey drove away, too.

Chapter Eighteen

COFFEY had just returned from the library—and was making a fresh pot of coffee—when the front doorbell rang.

He walked through the house, his cats Tasha, Crystal, and Tess trailing him, and went to the front door.

Takes one to know one, he thought, peering out at the woman who stood on his front porch.

It was easy to spot a male cop, that was for sure. It was the way they carried themselves, with a curious mixture of arrogance and humility—arrogance because they carried the badge, humility because police work was not easy. You failed a lot. Now even the women cops had started to look like cops. This one had curly red hair, wore gray slacks, a gray tweed sport coat, a crisp button-down blue shirt with a small scarf wrapped around her neck. She was looking around the porch and then at the adjacent yards. The combination of arrogance and humility was easy to see on her round, slightly snub nosed face. The hard blue eyes were especially coplike. He wondered what the hell she wanted.

He opened the door.

"Hi," she said, "are you Mr. Coffey?"

He nodded.

She reached into the left pocket of her tweed jacket and brought out her ID.

"Hey," he said, trying to act surprised, "you're a cop."

"Homicide detective, Mr. Coffey. Margie Ryan."

"Homicide? Wow." He intentionally tried to sound naïve and surprised. He was having a little fun with her. He wondered if she knew it.

"I'd like to speak to you for a few minutes if I could."

"My house is sort of a mess."

She smiled. "So's mine." She had a nice, girly smile. The kind that could trap bad guys into believing that she wasn't tough at all. That would be a fatal misperception on their part.

"I guess," he said, "we could have a game of house mess macho."

"House mess macho?"

"You know, whose house is a bigger mess."

"I'd win walking away, Mr. Coffey. I have a three-year-old and a five-year-old at home." She was obviously getting tired of his stalling. "So why don't we go inside and talk?"

He poured them fresh coffee. They sat at the kitchen table. The sun was out. In the window was a cardinal, which was soon replaced by a blue jay. There was an autumn haze over everything in the distance. The air would smell sweetly smoky. Coffey wanted to be outdoors. Today would be a good day to rake the leaves in the backyard.

He said, "I used to be a cop."

"That's what I understand." In the sunlight angling through the kitchen window, Margie Ryan looked especially vivid, with her red hair and freckles. She wasn't pretty, she wasn't even cute, but there was a vitality in her eyes and mouth that was erotic. At least for Coffey, it was. "I also understand your wife and daughter were murdered."

"Yeah."

"I'm sorry. And you drive a cab now?"

"Right."

"The cab is why I'm here, Mr. Coffey."

"God, couldn't we do better than 'Mr. Coffey?' I'm not a kitchen appliance."

She smiled. "I'll bet you've used that joke a thousand times."

"Two thousand is more like it."

She sipped her coffee. "This is good."

"Thanks. I combine three different kinds of coffee and then put a bit of mocha in it."

"It works." Then: "Windy City Cab 701."

"That's mine."

"A man saw it parked in the lot of the Econo-Nite Motel the night there was a murder. Last night."

"Yeah, I read about the murder."

"Were you there?"

"Yeah."

"About what time was this?" She'd already taken a pocket-sized tablet from her sport coat and put it on the table. Now she took a red ballpoint from her pocket and clicked the tip out.

He told her.

"You were alone?"

He looked at her. "I don't think you'd ask me that question unless you already knew the answer. Like a trial lawyer."

"Does that mean you were alone?"

"It means I *wasn't* alone."

She wrote a few words in her notebook then looked up at him again. "Good. Because that's what our eyewitnesses said. That you were with a dark-haired woman."

"Yes, I was."

"And you went into the room where this Earl Benedict was?"

"If that's his name, yes."

"That's his name. Or was. He's dead now. Stabbed to death. But you knew that already."

He nodded. "He was dead when we got into the room."

"And you didn't call Homicide?"

"I know I should've."

"Why didn't you?"

"I didn't want to get the woman involved."

"The woman is already involved. *Very* involved. She was seen entering and leaving Earl Benedict's room earlier that same evening. A couple staying in the next room said they heard a loud argument at one point between Benedict and this woman. So who is she?"

"I don't know."

"You didn't call the police and you don't know who the woman was."

"I'm afraid that's correct."

"And you expect me to believe that?"

"She was a fare. I don't usually ask my fares their names."

"She was more than a fare. She asked you to go into the room with her. At least I assume she did. Do you make a habit of going into motel rooms with your fares?"

"Not usually."

She made some more notes then looked up at him again. "Pardon my French, but your story sounds like bullshit."

"I'm sorry. It's the truth. She didn't tell me her name." And it *was* the truth. She hadn't *known* her name, so how could she give it to him?

"We'd like to talk to her."

"She's a suspect?"

"Right now, we're just treating her as a material witness. We'll worry about 'suspect' later." Her pen hovered above her tablet. "So why don't you tell me her name, so I can write it down here?"

"I don't know her name. And no matter how many times you ask me, I still won't know her name."

"Where did she go?"

"When?"

"After you left the motel where the body was."

"I don't know." It was the first real lie he'd told her and it made him uncomfortable. He wasn't a liar by nature or inclination. He hated lying.

"She just vanished?"

"I dropped her off."

"Where?"

Another lie. "Over near Wrigley."

"Any place in particular?"

"She didn't ask for any place in particular."

"The middle of the night and she's alone and she doesn't ask for any place in particular. Brave girl."

"She must be," he said.

"You wouldn't shit a shitter, now, would you, Coffey?"

He smiled. "I guess I might try. I mean, if I needed to."

She stared at him. She did not look happy. "A man's dead."

"I realize that."

"A man's dead and you've got information about him being dead and you're deliberately keeping it from me."

He didn't say anything.

"She must be quite a girl, Coffey."

He didn't say anything.

"She put out for you, did she?"

He'd used this technique himself. Getting people mad so they'd get riled and say something they didn't mean to.

He didn't say anything.

"Two people got a pretty good look at her," Margie Ryan said. "Dark-haired. Very good-looking. One of them even saw her car."

He didn't say anything.

She was watching him carefully. "Or did you know about her car? Somebody saw her drive in and park it earlier in the evening. The kind of car it is, there aren't that many to check out. She may not be as mysterious as you think, Coffey." Then, "How come you went over to the other side?"

"What other side?"

"The bad guys."

"I wasn't aware I had."

"You're lying to a homicide detective trying to conduct a murder investigation."

He went back to silence.

She stood up. She had a nice body. Young and firm. She was smart and, he suspected, probably a very nice woman under other circumstances.

She reached into the left pocket of her sport jacket and pulled out a white card. "Call me if you change your mind."

"Middle of the night all right?"

"Fine."

"I won't wake your kids up?"

She smiled. "I've deputized them. They're old hands at this homicide business already."

She sneezed. "Cats."

"Three of them."

"I'm allergic. And anyway, you look too big and mean to be a cat man."

"It's my sensitive nature that I keep concealed from everybody."

"You can really sling the bullshit, Coffey."

"So I've been told."

He walked her to the door.

"The car's a special edition," she said. "Vintage MG. Not that many of them on the road."

"I'll keep an eye out for it."

He opened the door and she stepped out on the porch. The afternoon had turned out beautifully. He was assaulted by the vigors of autumn, the colorful and resplendent trees, the melancholy smells. Soon there would be apple cider and Halloween pumpkins and little kids in spook costumes. He loved the fall.

"You're too smart to be a bad guy, Coffey," she said. "You'll come around."

And with that, she walked down the porch steps and headed for her discreet blue Ford sedan parked at the curb.

As he walked back inside, he hoped she was right. He hoped he really was too smart to be a bad guy.

Chapter Nineteen

THE only thing that kept Ted Hannigan from looking like an arrogant (and slightly aging) movie star was the vulnerability in his devoutly blue eyes. The face was as chiseled and handsome as a Greek bust; the six-three, one-hundred-eighty-pound body was kept hard by constant exercise and careful eating; and the swagger probably went back to the first day he was able to walk. He coupled all this with a dashing taste in attire. Today, for instance, he wore a loose silk white shirt with an outsize and open collar. It hinted nostalgically of pirate movies of the forties. His black jeans were almost illegally tight and his snakeskin cowboy boots as imposing as the rattlesnake itself had once been. Then there was his hair, a Byronic mop of black curls that at least half a dozen countesses had run their hands through down the years.

This was what Jenny saw when the door opened and Ted escorted an older and somewhat plump woman into the reception area. He was wiping red and blue paints off his hands with a white rag.

The woman, dressed in a regal purple suit, touched a delicate hand to her white hair and said, "You could have been a professional comedian, Ted."

He smiled. "Well, Agnes, I don't know if it's the same thing, but a lot of people already tell me that I'm a clown."

That was another thing about Ted. For all his self-drama, he had a good sense of humor about himself. He delighted in putting himself down.

Then he hooked a big arm around Jenny and pulled her to him. "This is my beautiful niece, Jenny."

"Oh, I recognized her right away," Agnes said. "She was a

debutante the year after my own Cindy. She was the most beautiful debutante of them all, too."

Jenny muttered a thank you, once more made uncomfortable by flattery.

"Well, I'll see you next week," Ted said. He took Agnes' hand and kissed it. Even though there was a hint of mockery in the gesture—most Americans not being great hand-kissers, thank God—it was easy to see that Agnes was charmed by the kiss.

"Next week, then."

When Agnes was gone, Ted turned to Andi and said, "Well, is she as gorgeous as I said?"

"More," Andi said.

Jenny's cheeks were hot.

"She hates compliments," Ted said. "She likes it better when you tell her that she's got a booger in her nose and that her breath is terrible."

Both Jenny and Andi giggled. Ted was suddenly the older brother teasing his little sisters.

Ted leaned his head back and stared at her face. "That's a very attractive booger, too, young lady. It almost matches your dress."

Jenny playfully swung at his stomach but he enveloped her little hand in his large one.

"No calls," Ted said, and led Jenny into his work space.

***

He had once been a happy little boy, Sean Gray. This was back when he and his mother and father had lived in Milwaukee. He went to school, he played with his friends, and in the summers he went on vacations with his parents, sometimes to places as faraway as Denver and Salt Lake City.

Then they moved to Chicago and everything changed. He wasn't sure why. It just—changed.

He was in seventh grade when it had happened, coming home early from school because he had been bitten by the same stomach bug that was felling people all over the city.

He let himself into the house with his key. As far as he knew, his mother and father were at work. She was an accountant and his father an attorney. He was so sick that all he wanted to do was get out of his school clothes and lie down on his bed. He had a special fat issue of *The X-Men* and a new issue of *Spawn* and he could take his mind off his churning stomach by reading them, and then dozing blissfully off to sleep.

He walked down the hallway to his bedroom. And then he heard it.

At first, it sounded like somebody in pain. And then he remembered. He'd caught his folks Doing It once and it had sounded just like this. His mom all grunts and groans and cries, as if she were being beaten or something. But it wasn't pain he'd been hearing, he'd learned. It was pleasure. It was weird that they would sound like one and the same thing but the world of adults was a pretty mysterious place anyway, so why *shouldn't* pleasure sound like pain?

He hadn't seen either his mom *or* dad's car in the drive, but maybe they'd parked at the curb as they sometimes did.

The closer he got, the louder the sounds of pleasure-pain became. There was a frantic, almost hysterical edge to them now. And then it was at an end. The crescendo could go no higher.

He was right up next to the door of his parents' bedroom. And then a male voice said, breathing hard, like a distance runner collapsing at the end of a long race, "Wow, that was some romp, huh?"

A male voice not his father's.

"Oh, God," said his mother's voice, "I really needed that." She was panting as hard as the man.

But who *was* the man and what was he doing in his parents' bedroom?

He felt sick to his stomach. And there was a wild panic in his chest—like a huge berserk flapping bird—as he thought of what this meant for his folks. Back in Milwaukee, a school friend of his told him how his folks had gotten a divorce because the mom walked in on the dad who was screwing his secretary in the middle of the day at home—when mom was supposed to be at work.

His mom and her lover hadn't heard Sean, so he hurried out of the house. He ran down the block to the small city park. He sat on a bench—he was miserable with flu, but he was even *more* miserable thinking about his mother screwing some stranger—and he remained there until it was time to come home from school.

When he got home, his mother explained that she'd decided to take the afternoon off just so she could get some house cleaning done. She had a lot of overtime coming, the income tax season having just ended, and it was either take it or lose it. Then she looked at him—really looked at him carefully—and said, "Oh, honey, you don't look good."

She got him in bed and took his temperature (101) and then brought him the stuff she always did when he had the flu, 7-Up and Pepto Bismal and Kleenex and Vicks (though why she brought him Vicks when he had the stomach flu, he didn't know).

She also touched him and kissed him a lot and for the first time in his life, he felt repelled by her. All he could think of was the bedroom and the man's voice he'd heard in there and the pain-pleasure cries of his mother. His own mother.

He changed, then. He was no longer a happy boy. His parents couldn't understand it. Neither could his home-room teacher. And it was worse than his simply being secretive and sullen. He started getting into fights, his grades dropped from a B+ to a C−. His dad got a call from the police station telling him to come down and get Sean. Sean had been arrested for shoplifting.

At the dinner table, he'd look with great contempt at his mother and great pity at his father.

His parents started having terrible arguments in the middle of the night. The arguments always woke him. While he couldn't understand the exact words, he sensed that somehow his father had learned about his mother. Michael certainly hadn't told him. He didn't want his parents to divorce. He was terrified they would split up. He prayed every night that they would stay together. And that somehow his mother would never be unfaithful again. And that his dad would see that his mom was a good woman, even though she'd been with that other man.

Sixteen months to the day after they'd moved to Chicago, their divorce was final. Sean stayed with his mother. His father saw him on weekends. Or "tried" to. It seemed that just about every weekend something "came up," and his father couldn't pick him up after all.

The man whose voice he'd heard in the bedroom that day,

his name turned out to be Pete Westbrook and he was at the house four, five nights a week. Mom and Pete always waited till they thought Sean was asleep before they did anything. But he could hear them because he didn't sleep well. He'd lie there in the dark and think about how his world had changed since the divorce. It was just about the only thing he thought about anymore.

***

While Jenny was visiting with Ted Hannigan, and Coffey was cleaning up after his visit with the homicide detective, Sean was walking into his last-hour seventh grade class. This being a rather tony private school—one conveniently located less than a mile from his house in Wilmette—the prospect of a student walking into class with a gun was never even considered. No metal detectors. No off-duty cops walking the halls.

Sean stepped across the threshold, looked at the four rows of desks filled with students, raised the .45 his mother kept in her nightstand drawer, and started firing immediately.

He killed three students before the teacher was finally able to wrestle him to the floor and take his gun away.

***

"No idea at all?" Ted asked.

"No idea at all," Jenny replied. "But as I said, I've developed these terrible headaches both times I heard about this murder at the motel the other night. I even threw up, I got so worked up."

Ted's studio ran the length of the building, which was considerable. The walls were brick, the floor hardwood. A few dozen completed canvases, of various sizes, were leaned against the walls. In the center of the studio was a stool where his subjects sat. The canvas he was working on sat on an easel, on either side of which were cabinets filled with tiny drawers which were, in turn, filled with tubes of paint, brushes, and other art supplies. A paint-spotted dropcloth covered the floor beneath the canvas. The painting of Agnes was a perfect example of Ted's masterful and deceitful work. He'd turned a rather plump, gray-haired society matron into a rather thin, silver-haired younger woman who bore a curious similarity to the older Grace Kelly. Jenny had smiled when she'd seen this.

She wasn't smiling now, though. For the past half hour she'd been telling Ted about her missing eight days. And how the murder at the Econo-Nite Motel upset her for no reason she could consciously construe.

"It could be a coincidence," Ted said. "Just because you happened to react twice to the same story isn't any kind of definitive proof."

"I know."

They were sitting on a large leather couch he had stuck over in a corner next to a radiator he'd painted a brilliant silver. On this section of wall he'd leaned several of his "serious" paintings, the ones he did for himself. Even though she didn't know all that much about art—she'd had an art minor in college, but that hardly made her an expert—she could easily see how derivative and empty they were. He had been greatly influenced by the French painters of the last century. He could steal their style for his commercial portraiture, but his thievery didn't work for real painting.

"Terrible stuff," he said, nodding to a painting of a young black girl running along the shores of Lake Michigan on a hot summer day.

"Oh, it's very good," she said. But they both knew she was just being nice.

He touched her hand. "I hate to say this but all you can do is wait and see what happens."

"That's all?" Jenny said.

"There was a segment on *60 Minutes* six or seven months ago. About various kinds of amnesia." He smiled. "That makes me an expert, doesn't it?"

"Are you ever able to fill in the missing time?"

He shrugged. "Sometimes. And sometimes not. Pretty helpful, aren't I?"

For all her consternation, she felt some peace sitting in Ted's presence. It was strange, not even her own parents could comfort her the way he did. This had been true since she was a small girl. There was always Uncle Ted.

Now, he took both her hands in his and leaned forward and

kissed her gently on the cheek. "I went through what you're going through now."

"You did?"

"Yes. I've never mentioned it. It—makes me uncomfortable." He paused. "I had a breakdown when I was about your age. I guess that was when I realized that I was never going to be anything more than a commercial artist. I'd done Paris and London and Rome, I'd won a few small awards, I'd even gotten written up in a few important magazines. But I realized that it was the force of my personality. A very bitchy woman critic wrote a line about me that really crushed me. 'If only his art were as seductive as he is.' I resented it because I knew it was the truth. Anyway, around that same time I went into this terrible depression. I left Paris and came back to Chicago, and my folks decided after a few months to send me to a shrink. I rarely left my room; I had no friends except for your mother. And I started having these very violent outbursts for no good reason at all. The shrink put me in a mental hospital." He laughed. But it was an angry laugh. "I even rode the lightning."

"You did?" Riding the lightning was what mental patients called electroshock treatments.

"Oh, yes. Sixteen times in three months." He withdrew his hands from hers. She sensed that he was withdrawing spiritually as well. The memories were sapping him. "I read once that Hemingway had sixty electroshock treatments the year before he died. I can't imagine that."

"God, I'm sorry, Ted."

He shrugged. "I couldn't face myself. That was the whole thing. All my life my teachers had told me what an artistic genius I was. And I believed them, of course. I *wanted* to believe that they knew what they were talking about. But then I got out in the real world. Paris and London—all I ran into was contempt. All I could do was keep collecting women. Rich, beautiful women. They were the only things I could put up against my disappointment." He looked at her with those shockingly blue eyes and that handsomely tortured face. "But you know what? Eventually, you don't give a damn. You make your peace; you settle. I'm happy now—at least as happy as I'll ever be—and I don't worry about not being a great artist anymore." He took her into his arms and held her. She slid her arms around him and held him, too. Home. That was how she always felt in his arms. It wasn't a romantic feeling—it was a childlike feeling, a *protected* feeling. He had been through so much in his life, but he had survived and now he was strong. She remembered a Leonard Cohen line from one of her poetry classes: "The simple life of heroes/the twisted life of saints." In his own way—and because of his suffering—he was a saint. Even if he did not have the skills of a great artist, he had the soul of one. He understood things—and felt things—that very few people ever did.

He let go of her then and smiled: "A friend of mine's opening a new pub over near the Talbott Hotel. What say we help him inaugurate it?"

She was caught up in his mood. "Now how could I refuse an offer like that?"

She needed to put her problems aside. He was always at his best in pubs. It was like watching a brilliant performance artist, with him getting half the people in the place to participate in his games and whimsies. She felt happy. She couldn't believe how quickly he'd changed her mood.

Five minutes later, they were in his elevator, heading for the street.

Chapter Twenty

COFFEY spent the rest of the afternoon writing. He was working on a scene where the hero heard a noise in the basement. It was near midnight. The hero lived alone. Heroes, being heroes, are supposed to be just as stupid as heroines. A noise in the basement? Think I'll go check it out. That's how a hero thinks. But not this hero. This hero crept outside and had a peek in the various basement windows, trying to determine if the wraith-like form had once again materialized in the basement. This was a lot better way to check things out than actually going down those dark steps and shining his flashlight around.

He was just peeking in a window, and just becoming aware of some kind of *presence* in the basement when—

—the phone rang.

"I just have a quick question for you," said his new friend Detective Margie Ryan.

"I'll answer if I can."

"Does the name Linda Fleming mean anything to you?"

"Linda Fleming?" he said, running it through the computer of his mind. "No, I don't think so. Any reason it should?"

"Just curious is all."

"I take it this has something to do with the murder at the motel the other night."

"You weren't real cooperative with me three hours ago," she said, "So I don't see why I should be cooperative with you. 'Bye, Mr. Coffey."

After he hung up, he glanced at the alarm clock he kept on his desk. He had to move Tess to read it. Tess guarded the clock face. She didn't want anybody to wear out the numerals by staring at them too often.

It was dinnertime.

He raised his eyes and looked out the window of the small bedroom he'd converted into an office. It was a brooding but handsome autumn dusk sky, clouds streaked with gold, clouds streaked with amber, clouds streaked with mauve, and a glowing brilliant silver quarter moon behind the city haze. That was one thing you had to give pollution. Ironically, it could be aesthetically pleasing to look upon.

He leaned back in his chair, stretched his arms, yawned. He had been able to totally escape into his writing, had given virtually no thought to mystery women or murdered men in motels. Most of the time, he had that ability. Writing was like being in a trance for him. But now it was back to reality, as if the magical spell had been broken.

Once again, he started thinking about mystery women and murdered men in motels.

He knew who she was, now. But how was he going to contact her?

Tasha climbed up on his lap. He sat there, staring at the darkening sky, petting Tasha and trying to convince himself that what he had in mind would work.

He'd go see her.

He'd drive right up to her mansion and ask to see her. That was the best way, the only way. Direct.

And she'd see him. She'd be too curious *not* to see him.

"You think I should go see her, Tash?" he asked his good and true and elegant friend Tasha the cat.

She looked up at him with eyes ancient as Egypt. She looked as if she understood exactly what he was talking about. And then she spoiled the effect somewhat by yawning. If she did understand, she found the subject awfully boring. He kissed her on the top of her head, set her gently on the desk, and then went into the bathroom to clean up.

A man wanted to look his best when he visited a mansion.

***

Coffey was approaching the Stafford estate, when he saw the dark Ford van. The lights were out. And it was parked on the shoulder of the asphalt road that ran past the estate. He wished there was time right now to check it out. He wondered again what the small box on the roof was. He definitely had to check out the van. But there wasn't time to worry about it now.

Coffey pulled his cab up in front of the iron security gates in front of the Stafford mansion. The mansion itself sat far back on the vast lawn, a huge Tudor that seemed to have light pouring from every window. The moonlight on the lawn cast everything into deep and graceful shadows. He thought of the parties Jay Gatsby gave in *The Great Gatsby*, one of his favorite novels, the parties that extended all the way across the silver midnight lawn to the edge of the ocean itself. But any romance he entertained about the Stafford estate soon vanished when he looked at the security fence surrounding the estate proper. A security camera pointed down from directly above the left side of the gates. A concrete wall, at the top of which would be glass and spikes in case you were foolish enough to consider climbing said wall. And should you somehow make it over the wall—despite the odds—then you would be immediately confronted by the dogs. Dobermans, no doubt (Coffey could hear them barking now). Merciless and angry Dobermans. Coffey left his headlights on, climbed out of the cab, and walked up to the small two-way communication box mounted inside the gate. All you needed to do was reach through and push the SPEAK button.

A male voice answered quickly. "May I help you?"

"I'd like to speak to Jenny Stafford, please."

"Are you a friend of hers, sir?"

"Yes." It was the simplest answer. An explanation, an elaboration, would be foolish and pointless.

"May I have your name, sir?"

"Michael Coffey."

"I'll be right back, sir. I need to find Jenny or her father."

"Thank you."

On the other side of the wall, the dogs sensed Coffey's presence. And were getting ready for him. Even from here he could hear the growling. They were waiting for him.

While he waited, a couple of cars flew past, headlights painting him yellow momentarily. He looked down the road at the van. He sensed eyes watching him.

The voice came back on. "Sir?"

"Yes."

"Jenny said that she isn't familiar with you."

"Tell her it's about the other night."

"I'm afraid she's getting ready to go out, sir. The family would appreciate it if you would leave the premises."

"All I need is a few minutes."

"You wouldn't be happy if we were forced to call the police. And neither would we. Good night, sir."

There was a clicking sound in the communication box.

And they would call the cops, too, Coffey thought. About that, he had no doubt.

Then he realized what the voice had just told him. That Jenny was getting ready to go out. If she was alone, it would be easy to follow her and then sit down and talk to her.

He had just started to back his car up, when he saw headlights lancing toward him. A car was moving quickly to the other side of the gate. Jenny.

At the prospect of seeing her again, he felt his heart begin to pound against his chest. He'd been in love a few times in his life. But never like his.

Then the gates were opening and a silver Jaguar pulled out on to the road.

PART TWO

Chapter Twenty-One

IF the man driving the Jag knew he was being followed, he didn't let on. He drove at a respectable speed and didn't try to initiate any sudden turns.

The dark countryside of hills and tall fir trees and farmland posted NO HUNTING soon gave way to the suburbs. Coffey missed the open land as soon as he was out of it. He loved seeing the moonlight paint cornfields and piney hills with its silver tones. Then came church spires, a Pizza Hut, a McDonald's, a Wendy's, a shopping mall. Suburbia. Everything neat and orderly. The train depot where commuters came and went. The small brick medical clinic where the earnest young doctor was eager to examine you and test his new skills. The football field ablaze on what had once been expensive pastureland, a Thursday night game pitting one suburban high school against another, the marching bands booming away in the stands. Coffey could almost smell the coffee—did it ever smell better than at a football game on a chilly night?—and taste the popcorn and feel the special thrill of glimpsing the girl you secretly had a crush on.

Then the Jag found the freeway entrance and shot far ahead of Coffey. Coffey sped up to keep pace. For some reason, the Dan Ryan was crowded tonight.

It was easy to slip into memory here, wife and daughter in the car as they were returning from a long weekend trip, the heater creating a soft, sleepy cocoon; the radio playing soft music low; the three of them luxuriously tired and ready for the warm, clean sheets of their own beds. The world had seemed so right, so *knowable* back then. Nothing could go wrong in such a realm. Nothing. . . .

Coffey had to do a little frantic driving to catch the Jag again, changing lanes abruptly, zipping in and out of car packs. He got a few horns honked at him, and a teenage girl gave him a double-whammy—her horn *and* her middle finger.

But he caught up with them, finally, keeping a two-car distance between himself and the sleek Jag. He tried to see if they were having a conversation or if Jenny was simply sitting there, staring out the window. But it was impossible to know from this distance. All he could think of was warning her, of getting her away from the blond man, whoever he was.

The Jag driver still seemed to have no idea that Coffey was following him. No idea at all.

***

The La Royale Restaurant was one of those places where the parking valets always put the Mercedes Benzes and BMWs in the back. They didn't want to give the place a bad name. The Rolls Royces went up front, where people driving by on the street could see them. Tonight, there were five. The valet had put them in a straight, gleaming line. The hoods and roofs reflected the purple tint of the sodium vapor security lights.

The Jag pulled up to the valet. He gave them a claim check for the car and then took it to the back of the small parking lot. The blond man and Jenny went inside. Coffey watched all this from down the street. He didn't like anything he was seeing. He particularly didn't like the way the blond man put a familiar and possessive arm around Jenny's shoulders as they walked to the formidable front door of the restaurant. Who the hell was this guy, anyway?

Coffey still had no idea what he was going to do. He'd just have to see what he found inside and play it from there.

The valet didn't need his lips to sneer. He could do it with his eyes. He looked monumentally superior when Coffey came up to the front door dressed in his blue suede jacket, white shirt, jeans, white socks, and penny loafers.

"The sock hop's down the street, mate," the valet said. He looked like a male model who might actually be able to take care of himself with his fists. He wore a mock-toreador outfit, snug red jacket, snug black pants.

"That isn't where I'm going, 'mate,' " Coffey said. "I'm going inside."

"Oh, yeah?"

"Yeah."

Coffey started to open the door, but the valet put a strong hand on his arm.

"You're not going in there dressed like that, mate," the valet said.

Coffey removed the valet's hand from his arm and then startled the young man by shoving him backward, shoving him hard enough to knock him up against a parked car.

Inside, the decor was solemn and reverent as a church. One did not come here merely to indulge the gross animal need for chow. One came here for—as the menu said—"the most unique dining experience in Chicago."

Coffey was reading the menu because there wasn't anything else to do. He sat in the bar, which was elevated a good five feet above the restaurant stretching out before it. You could see the restaurant through a long piece of plate glass. The bar was as dark as the restaurant, all leather and deep, dark pile carpeting and flickering candlelights. The catacombs had probably been better lit than this place.

Jenny and the blond man were sitting in the center of the restaurant. The wine waiter was taking their orders. In French, no doubt.

Every minute or so, Coffey looked up from the menu to check on Jenny. Still there. How was he going to warn her when the blond man was sitting there?

"The wild game in truffle broth comes with a pecan-dipped veal chop," the bartender said, nodding to the menu Coffey was holding. He was a stout man in a red brocaded vest, a white shirt and a string tie that was more Western than La Royale. Two of his front teeth were gold.

Coffey smiled. "You sound like a commercial."

"I'm not kidding. They always give the help a meal every night. It's usually whatever the special is. I had the wild game tonight, and it's sensational."

Coffey slid the menu back to him. Apparently, they left the menus on the bar so you could figure out what you wanted to eat while you were waiting to be seated. "I'd take another Diet Pepsi."

"Sure you can handle it?"

Coffey laughed. "Maybe if I pace myself, I'll be all right."

The bartender stared at Coffey for a time and then said, "We don't want any trouble."

"Trouble?"

The bartender leaned over, his elbows on the bar. "What's she doing, stepping out on you?"

"Who?" Coffey said, surprised.

"Look, friend, you obviously didn't come here to eat. Not dressed like that, you didn't. And you keep staring through the glass there at somebody in the restaurant. Last guy that did that, he sits here for an hour, hour-and-a-half really knocking back the martinis. I finally had to cut him off. Sonofabitch could barely walk. I'm getting ready to call him a cab and get him the hell out of here, but all of a sudden we get really busy, so I can't get to it right away. In the meantime, the guy sneaks off. He goes over to the restaurant part, walks straight over to this table where his wife is sitting with her boyfriend. He turns the table over, and then he starts working on the boyfriend. Mousy little guy, cheap suit, thick glasses. The boyfriend isn't any giant either, but he's a hell of a lot bigger than the husband. But the husband just starts stomping the guy. Nothing like a woman to make you crazy. Takes four busboys, me, and the maitre d' to pull the little guy off the boyfriend."

"And you think I'm going to do that?"

"I think it's at least a possibility, friend. You seem mighty interested in that one table down there."

"He's my cousin."

"Sure, he is."

"He's my cousin by marriage. My blood cousin asked me to check him out. Make sure he was being faithful. I guess I got the answer I didn't want."

The bartender looked at him skeptically. "So what're you going to do about it?"

"Nothing. I mean, nothing like start trouble. I'll just call Amy and tell her what I found out."

"She's going to be pissed, that's for sure." Then the bartender nodded to the table where Jenny and the blond man sat. "I got to give her husband one thing."

"What?"

"He's got great taste."

"You know who she is?"
"Huh-uh. But I sure know she's beautiful. Wow."
"How about the Diet Pepsi?"
"Just remember, no trouble."

Coffey nodded. He felt like a bad third grader the nuns were giving one last warning. "No trouble," he said, like a good little boy.

Chapter Twenty-Two

IT was another half hour before Coffey saw his chance.

By this time, the bar had filled up. The entire restaurant was starting to reach its maximum capacity. Places like this didn't really fill up till nine o'clock or so. The bartender had apparently decided that Coffey was harmless, after all. He scarcely looked at his ill-dressed customer any more.

The blond man got up and left the table, presumably to go to the men's room.

This was Coffey's chance.

He was down off the bar stool quickly. He worked his way through the crowded bar and started across an open space between the bar and the restaurant proper. The maitre d', a tuxedo'd man who looked like all the stuffy high-society men in Marx Brothers movies, lurched toward Coffey, clearly bent on stopping such a slovenly specimen from coming into *his* eatery.

Coffey just kept on walking. There were small knots of people here and there—all the pretty people drinking, thinking they'd got it made, as Bob Dylan had once sung—and Coffey used them as blockers as he headed for the goal line. The maitre d' didn't want a scene, God forbid. He fell back in place, up near the rostrumlike stand where he greeted customers. He stood there in his tuxedo and glowered with enough heat to go super nova.

Jenny's back was to him as he approached the table.

He hurried to her table and sat down in the blond man's chair.

Over her white turtleneck sweater, she now wore a navy blue blazer with a family crest on the breast pocket. With her dark hair, her seductive blue eyes, and her vivacious red lipstick, her beauty almost physically rocked him. He just wished he had time to sit here and appreciate.

"I think you have the wrong table," she said quietly.

He leaned toward her. "I don't look familiar?"

"Please," she said, "I'm really not in the mood for any games. My friend is here and—"

"Your friend?" he said. "How long have you known him?"

"That's none of your business. I really don't want you sitting here."

A huge Japanese man, also in a tuxedo, was now standing next to the maitre d' and the maitre d' was nodding in Coffey's direction. The Japanese man, who had to be six-seven or six-eight and two hundred and fifty pounds, started moving purposefully down the aisle between the tables. Right toward Coffey.

"I'm trying to help you," Coffey said. "The police are looking for you. Somebody's identified you—not by name but by description."

He saw that it was hopeless. She couldn't be a good enough actress to fake the blank look she gave him. She obviously saw this as a hustle of some kind—a romantic fool taking a desperate chance on meeting her. She didn't look troubled by anything he said—his words didn't seem to awaken any memories in her—she simply looked irritated.

"All I want is a quiet dinner," she said. "I really need to relax. And I can't relax when you're bothering me like this."

"I'm trying to help you," he said again. But he knew it was futile.

Then a hand the size of a catcher's mitt gripped his shoulder and began the slow but certain process of grinding his shoulder into a fine, powdery dust. The Japanese man no doubt spent a good deal of his time working out. He could probably bench press a Buick.

"Oh, thank you so much," Jenny said, looking up at the bouncer. "I wasn't sure what to do."

"You don't know him?" the bouncer said. He might be Japanese but he spoke perfect Chicago English, right down to the familiar nasality of tone.

She shook her head. "No. And I don't *want* to know him either."

That was all the bouncer needed to know. He doubled the strength of his grip on Coffey's shoulder and literally lifted Coffey to his feet. Coffey wasn't exactly a small man himself.

The blond man had just reappeared. "What's going on here?" he said, seeing the bouncer jerk Coffey from his chair.

"I'm just assisting the lady," the bouncer said.

"It's nothing to get upset about, David," Jenny said. "Anyway, it's over now."

"I'd still like to know what happened," David said, glancing at Jenny, then at Coffey. He wore a dark blue double-breasted suit, a buff blue shirt, a paisley blue silk necktie. All of them expensive.

Then Jenny looked overwhelmed by it all, her cool facade starting to crack. "I think I'll go to the ladies' room."

"It's all right, Jenny. It's all under control now." David's voice surprised Coffey. It was deep and masculine, but there was a gentleness to it that was comforting. Jenny brightened a bit at the sound of it.

"I'll be back, David. Don't worry."

She stood up, excused herself from the table, and walked away.

"Let's go," the bouncer said to Coffey.

"I want to talk to my friend here about International Investigations," Coffey said.

At the mention of the agency, David's eyes narrowed and he seemed to really look at Coffey for the first time. "Who *are* you?"

David wasn't what Coffey had expected. He seemed to be a decent guy.

"Why don't we talk a bit?" Coffey said.

"Yes. That'd probably be good." He told the bouncer that he would no longer be needed. The bouncer looked like a child whose favorite toy had been snatched from his hands. He frowned but walked away.

They sat down.

"Who are you?" David Foster said.

Coffey told him about how he'd met Jenny. He also told him that he'd once been a homicide detective. He didn't tell him about the motel room.

David Foster said, "Then we're on the same side?"

Coffey thought that was a strange thing to say.

Foster said, "The good guys."

"Meaning what exactly?" Coffey said.

"Meaning we both want to help Jenny." He looked sad. "I'm partly to blame for all this. I—sort of dumped her a while back. She might not be as messed up today if I hadn't—"

Coffey recognized the sound and look of guilt. Being out bowling while your wife and daughter were being murdered made him familiar with what Foster was going through. He surprised himself by actually liking Foster.

"I wish we had longer to talk," Foster said. "I've got International Investigations checking some things out for me about Jenny. I'd like to bring you up to date. Are you in the phone book?"

Coffey gave him his address.

"How about if I call you tomorrow sometime?"

"How about giving me a hint?" Coffey said. "I don't have any idea what you're talking about."

But just as Foster seemed on the verge of saying more, Jenny appeared. She was obviously surprised to still see Coffey here. Foster leaned over to Coffey and said, "I can't talk more now. Not with Jenny here."

Coffey stood up. "I'm sorry for any trouble. I guess I thought you were someone else."

She looked at him with eyes that reflected no comprehension of who he was or what he'd done for her.

"We appreciate the apology," David said heartily. "Now we'd like to get back to our dinner."

Coffey nodded and left.

Chapter Twenty-Three

DAVID kept suggesting places they might go. He loved nightclubs, loved sitting in a large booth with friends his own age, smoking expensive cigars and watching all the freaks on the dance floor. The fat kid still reveling in his new thin self. "Too noisy, too smoky, too freaky," Jenny always said. She rarely danced, and always got him to take her home early. He was trying to make up for what he'd done, of course.

They were in his Jag on Lake Shore Drive. The car heater made her drowsy. David had a Debussy tape in the deck. For her. He preferred rock. He'd been sweet and caring all night. She wished she'd been half as nice to him. She felt so badly about David lately. He worked so hard to get their relationship back on track. He'd wanted to run around some more, that's why he'd left her. He'd temporarily fallen for another girl, but what it was really all about was David getting to play the Neat Guy in all the trendy clubs. And that was hard to do when you had a steady woman in your life. But then he'd discovered—as in every romance novel ever written, and all too true nonetheless—that being the Neat Guy wasn't so neat after all. So, realizing his mistake, he'd come back to her. But it was too late. All she had for him now were excuses. I have a headache. I'm depressed. I'm tired. I thought I'd just stay in tonight and watch an old MGM musical on TV. All the excuses to lovers down all the ages. The black water of Lake Michigan to her right stretched all the way to where the moon hung low on the line of horizon. There was something pagan and cold about the moon tonight, and it unnerved her somehow. The building fronts—stores and condos alike—were bathed in a variety of electric colors, gold, mauve, light green.

He said, "Feel like driving around some more?"

"I think I'd like to go home."

His disappointment was obvious. She'd crushed his spirit. She didn't feel good about it.

"I'm sorry," she said. "You should go out and have fun, David. I'm just not in the mood."

"I'm worried about you, Jenny. I really am."

And she knew that was true. He really did regret walking out on her. And she believed that he really did love her. But she didn't love him anymore. Great fondness, yes. But love . . . no.

He looked over at her. "I love you. You're my life, Jenny. So we don't go dancing. So we don't hang out in nightclubs. I'd rather have you than any night spot in the world." He reached across the distance between them and touched her hand. "We're going to have a family together, Jenny. And a house on the hill. And we're going to be happy. We're going to forget everything bad in the past and just be very, very happy."

It all sounded so simple and sure. Two or three kids. A nice big white house overlooking a small ocean of green, green grass. A fireplace crackling with light and heat on Christmas Eve as they all sang carols together. . . .

So simple and sure.

But it was a dream long dead now.

"The man who came to our table tonight— Did you know him?" Jenny said.

"Know him? What do you mean?"

"You know, *know* him. Recognize him from somewhere."

"No. Why?"

"There was something—familiar about him. I'm not sure what."

She settled deeper into her seat, watched the panorama along the side of the freeway blur past.

The stranger who'd sat down . . . he'd looked familiar to *her*. Maybe that was why she'd also thought he might have looked familiar to David.

But why? Looked at objectively, he evoked no memories at all. Yet there was something in her mind . . . something about him.

She was beginning to think that her parents were right. She felt exhausted suddenly, physically *and* mentally. Maybe she should have stayed in tonight. Maybe she should even have scheduled another appointment with Priscilla for the evening . . . started right to work on the days and hours she'd lost.

David had a device that automatically opened the gates leading to her home. The Jag sedan was quick and sure on the winding road.

"Mind if I come in for a nightcap?" David said. He tried to sound jaunty, as if he didn't care one way or the other.

"I'm awfully tired, David. I'm sorry."

He smiled, but there was grief in it. "It isn't always easy, loving you."

"I'm sure it isn't, David."

She wanted to say, *So why don't we end it, then?* He'd parked the car, shut off the lights. Only a few feet separated them physically. Spiritually, it was another matter. Spiritually, thousands of miles separated them.

He started to say something. She quickly leaned over and drew his face to hers and kissed him. Kissing was easier than talking.

"Wow," he said when they broke apart. "You haven't kissed me like that in a long time."

"I know."

"That was like the old days."

Like all lovers, they'd spent their earlier times physically fixated on each other. Though she was a shy girl, David had made love to her in a number of semipublic places that now embarrassed her to think of.

"I needed that," he said.

"I did, too." She hated lying to him. She didn't know what else to do.

"It really gives me hope, a kiss like that. That it can be the way it used to be again."

He sounded like a very young boy who was both hopeful and frightened at the same time. In eleventh grade a boy had broken her heart—had kept on going with her long past the time when he really cared about her—and she could still remember the feeling of desperation she'd walked around with for weeks, months. She would have done virtually anything to get him back. But nothing worked. A new girl had come to school, and he and most of the other boys were bedazzled by her. She was a real femme fatale. Jenny had great looks, but she was no femme fatale. She lost weight, she started having headaches, she missed a couple of periods (thank God, she hadn't been pregnant), and she couldn't concentrate on anything except this terrible, overpowering need to see this boy again (Paul Denning was his name, not that that mattered). Her grades suffered; her mother and father canceled a European vacation because they were so worried about her.

It would be like this for David when they finally broke up. And she wouldn't wish that on anybody. David was too sweet to suffer that way. He didn't have it coming.

But she had decided at some unknown point tonight that it was over between them. Over. With no turning back.

"I really need to go in now, David."

"Just a few more minutes," he said, and she recognized the desperation in his voice. The same desperation that had been in *her* voice when Paul Denning had been breaking things off.

"All right," she said softly, "a few more minutes."

He didn't try to kiss her. He sat with his back to the driver's door, comfortable. "You know what my mother said at dinner the other night?"

"No, what?"

"That you and I would have beautiful children. And she's right."

"Oh, David, listen, please—"

"It'd be a great marriage, Jenny. It really would. I know you've been going through a lot of things lately. But don't you see? Our marriage could be your safe harbor. You'd be safe inside it. And loved. Oh, God, Jenny, I love you so much."

With a man as self-confident and sometimes ferocious as David, it was difficult to see and hear him cry. But cry he did. No big melodramatic moment. Just sort of silent tears that glistened in his eyes and made his voice raspy.

She couldn't stand to see him like this. She took him to her and held him. She felt embarrassed for him, and sorry for herself.

Finally he said, laughing harshly, "I'll give you a trip to London if you never tell anybody about this. You know, that I was crying."

She smiled. He'd always had a nice sense of humor about himself and his little joke now slightly redeemed the moment.

"How many days in Paris?" she said, sustaining the moment of humor.

"Six."

"Oh, it'd have to be at least seven."

He snuffled up tears. Sat back on his side of the car. Looked out at the night. "I pretty much had my life planned out. You know, where we'd live and how many kids we'd have and where we'd build our summer home." The humor was gone now. He sounded dismal. "I guess I got a little ahead of myself."

"I'm sorry, David."

He snuffled up some more tears. "That's something I was always afraid of."

"What?"

"Crying in front of you. I mean, I never even thought about it with any other girl. But we've always had so many ups and down. And sometimes, I'd get so sad—"

She reached over and put her hand on his shoulder. "I appreciate everything you've done for me, David."

He turned toward her. He looked both sad and angry. "But I guess it wasn't enough, huh?"

"Oh, David," she sighed, "don't make it any worse than it has to be."

"Maybe you'll change your mind."

"Maybe."

"I'm not really a bad guy," he said, "except that I cry sometimes."

She laughed. She could sense his shame. A big, proud man like David, the crying had to be very difficult for him to handle. "I cry all the time."

"Yeah, but you're a woman."

"Abraham Lincoln cried a lot, too," she said.

"Yeah, but look what happened to him. You think I want to get shot in some theater?"

The strained quality of the joke signaled that it was all over, at least for tonight. She leaned close enough to kiss him tenderly on the mouth. Then, "I'd better get inside."

"Yeah. I know you're tired." For the first time, he sounded bitter. "Tired of me."

"C'mon, David. Walk me to the door."

Hundreds of other nights he'd walked her to the door. But this was different. This was one of the last times he'd ever see her and they both knew it. Most nights, one of them would comment on the beautiful moon, or the sweet scent of the pine trees, or what tomorrow night would hold for them. But there was no such talk tonight. They didn't even hold hands. They just walked from the garage area up to the front of the mansion.

At the door, when he tried to put his arms around her, she slipped away from his embrace, and simply gave him another tender but very quick kiss on the mouth.

She would always remember the stricken look in his eyes here in the darkness; and he would always remember her scent and the way she could not quite meet his gaze.

"G'nite, David," she said softly, then hurried up the steps. She had to use her key, but that took only moments. Then she was inside, the door shut and locked behind her.

Molly hurried out of the living room to embrace her. "You're home early."

"I was just tired." She didn't want to get into the subject of David tonight.

Then her father came down the hall from the den. In his blue cardigan, white shirt, and dark slacks—his graying hair neatly combed and his handsome face the epitome of masculinity—he looked like an old-time sitcom dad. Father knows best.

He slid his arm around her, too. "You're home early."

Molly laughed. "I already pointed that out. And she said she was tired."

"You shouldn't have gone out in the first place, honey," he said. Father really *did* know best.

"I think I'll go up now," Jenny said, looking at the winding staircase.

"You don't want a snack?" her mother said. "Milk and cookies. Something like that."

She wondered if her parents would ever quit patronizing her. They'd treated her much more like an adult when she was in high school. Of course, she hadn't been a mental patient back then.

She gave her mother a kiss on the cheek. "I'm really exhausted."

"A warm bath and then a good night's sleep," her mother said. "That's what you need."

Her father kissed her on top of the head. "Good night, princess." "Princess" had been his nickname for her when she was a little girl. He only used it these days when he was feeling sentimental about her. He eased her to him, held her for a long and gentle moment. She liked the smell of his pipe tobacco—he smoked one pipeful a day—and his aftershave, the two scents she'd always associate with him. "We need to go out to the stables one of these days."

"Yes, we do," Jenny said. While she was growing up, she'd shared a great passion for horses with her father. They'd spent hundreds of hours out at a nearby stable. On her tenth birthday, her folks had given her a pony.

She could feel their eyes on her as she ascended the staircase, the huge chandelier ablaze above her. She knew they felt sorry for her, and their pity was the thing she wanted least. She'd been doing well, too, until eight days ago. What had happened to those days? What had brought it on?

She thought again of the stranger who'd appeared at her table tonight. The more she thought about him, the more familiar he seemed in some vague way. But why? Did he have anything to do with her missing eight days?

The dread was back. What could she have done during those times? She thought of the night they'd put her in the psychiatric hospital. Had she done anything like that again? Would the police come after her? She almost wished she'd talked to the stranger, asked him questions. Maybe he could help her reconstruct those lost hours.

She reached the top of the stairs, exhausted. Her mother's admonition—a hot bath and sleep—sounded wonderful at the moment.

***

David was still in his car. He had yet to leave the garage area and head away from the mansion.

He was using his cell phone. Punching in the same number again and again. And again and again getting a busy signal. David was not real long on patience.

Finally he made contact.

He said, "It's me."

"You sound pissed."

"I couldn't get through. Your line was busy."

"Believe it or not, David, I do have a life of my own. Now what can I do for you?"

"She dumped me tonight."

"I'm sorry."

"I still want to help her. And there may be someone who can help *us*. A guy I met tonight named Coffey." He briefly described his meeting with Coffey. And gave the other man all the particulars. "Will you check him out?"

"Sure. Now how about I go back to watching my Humphrey Bogart movie?"

"I thought you were on the phone."

"I was. But now the Bogie movie has started."

"Oh."

The man was not heartless or insensitive. He picked up on David's mood. "Maybe she'll come back to you. You came back to *her*, after all."

"I was so stupid to break up with her."

"We all do stupid things, David. It's just part of being human."

"I didn't know private eyes talked like that. You sound like a shrink."

"That's part of the job description," the man said. "Part shrink." Then he broke the connection. The line immediately began ringing busy again.

Chapter Twenty-Four

COFFEY woke up to find Crystal sleeping next to him. Every once in a while, one of the cats decided to come into his bedroom and bunk in. Crystal, who was black and white with a nose so cute only Disney could have designed it, yawned and looked up at Coffey. She knew the drill. He'd get up, pad to the bathroom, take care of his bladder, wash his hands, brush his teeth, pull on a pair of chinos, and then pad out to the kitchen where he'd start the coffee and give the three cats breakfast. Crystal looked awfully pleased at the prospect. She nuzzled him and scattered about a few extra meows.

As soon as he finished up with the cats, Coffey sat down and called a friend of his in Traffic. He gave the man the license numbers of the silver Jag and the van. The friend said he'd get back to him sometime this afternoon.

He worked out for half an hour, then wrote two pages.

He was just getting out of the shower, when his phone rang.

It was Sister Mary Agnes from the shelter. "There was a lady detective here this morning, Coffey. Margie Ryan, her name was."

"And she was asking about our mystery woman?"

"Right. Seems a couple of our men saw her come in here and told one of the cops who works this beat. Anyway all this got back to Detective Ryan, so she came over here this morning."

"She mention me?"

"Uh-huh. Same guys who saw her saw your cab here. They even remembered your cab number."

"I know who she is."

"The mystery woman?"

"Jenny Stafford."

"Not *the* Staffords."

"*The* Staffords."

"Wow," Sister Mary Agnes said.

He always smiled when she used vernacular.

"So what's next?" the nun said.

"I'm going to try and talk to her."

"Well, I'd better get back to work here, Coffey. I just thought I'd let you know."

"Thanks, Sister."

Coffey did a few more pages.

Then he had lunch, and sat on the sofa with the three cats watching the WGN noon news. There was another report on the man found dead in the motel room. Now there was also a police sketch of the dark-haired woman seen going in and out of the room. He was stunned by how much the sketch resembled Jenny.

At one o'clock, he still hadn't heard back from his buddy in Traffic. He decided he'd check his machine later with his remote.

He also decided it was time to do his least favorite thing of all—a butt-deadening stakeout.

He brought along a great old William P. McGivern heist novel called *Odds Against Tomorrow,* about a Southern bigot forced to work on a robbery with a black man. It had made a great movie, too, with Robert Ryan and Harry Belafonte.

***

Eileen, the Stafford maid, was eating a chicken-and-mayo sandwich on Wonder Bread (she'd loved this stuff since she was a kid) and watching the noon news on WGN.

The Staffords were, as usual, scattered, Tom to his business, Molly to her charities. Jenny was upstairs asleep—still. But after what she'd been through, she needed it.

Eileen had cleaned toilets this morning. There were eight johns in the place, only three of which ever got used regularly. She'd worn rubber gloves and now her fingertips were puckered, little white worms of flesh trailing down from the nails. She wondered vaguely if her whole body would look like this a few months after her burial.

She was just taking the last bite of her sandwich when she saw it. And when she saw it, she made a noise in her throat. And her bottom, which had just started to spread now that she had turned thirty-five, lifted a full inch-and-a-half off the kitchen stool she was sitting on. There on the screen of the 11" portable Molly Stafford like to keep on the kitchen counter—right there in front of her was a drawing of Jenny. No doubt about it. Jenny. Absolutely.

"Holy shit," she said. Or tried to say. Her mouth was still full with the last bite, so articulating her words wasn't easy.

The newscaster was saying, "Police insist that the woman is not a suspect but is considered a possible material witness. If you know this woman, call the police right away."

If you know this woman.

My God.

If you *know* this woman? She could just hear Tom Stafford. He could go from perfectly calm (which he was most of the time) to psychotic (though Eileen wasn't exactly sure what "psychotic" meant exactly) in under thirty seconds.

If you know this woman.

"Holy shit," she said, and this time, having swallowed her last bite, she managed the phrase very well.

She felt two conflicting emotions—excitement (sweet, quiet Jenny as a murderer was just the sort of thing *America's Most Wanted* loved to feature) and dread because Tom Stafford was no fun to be around when he was under stress. Molly was always buying him paperbacks on how to handle stress. Eileen had never seen him even pick one of them up. Lately, Molly had tried buying audio books. She didn't seem to be having any better luck with the tapes.

If you know this woman.

Eileen reached into the pocket of her gray uniform and took out a small beeper device. She punched 2-7 quickly.

"Yes?" Frank, her husband, was spending this week painting the Stafford garage.

"You'd better come in here, honey."

"Is something wrong?"

"I'm in the kitchen," she said. "Hurry, please."

Eileen loved crises and turmoil as much as Tom Stafford hated them.

DAUGHTER OF DARKNESS   133

If you know this woman.
Hard to get a bigger crisis than that.

***

Jenny Stafford pulled out of her father's estate at 12:58 p.m. that afternoon. She drove a green Oldsmobile convertible. The top was down, homage to the sunny and warm afternoon. She wore a white scarf that only enhanced the shape of her face and the midnight black quality of her hair.

Coffey let her get about an eighth of a mile ahead of him and then he went after her.

He had no idea where she was going.

An hour and a half later, he wondered if *she* had any idea where she was going. She had stopped at the cleaners but emerged with no clothes. She had stopped at the supermarket but emerged with no groceries. And she had stopped at a Barnes and Noble but had emerged with no book.

Then she pulled her car up to an outdoor telephone. It was too high for her to reach from her car. She got out. She wore a black sweater and jeans. She was so ethereal in Coffey's mind that he was startled by how gorgeous her body was. She was definitely an earthly creature and—for all the romance that bathed her in heavenly light—Coffey's desires were definitely earthly, too.

She didn't stay on the phone long.

A few minutes later, she was pulling away from the outdoor phone and getting back into the heavy flow of traffic.

Coffey stayed close by.

***

By three o'clock that afternoon, Jenny was starting to feel tired. It made no sense. She'd had plenty of sleep, plenty of good food. So why should she be so tired? Then she remembered something her shrink Priscilla had told her, that mental stress put more strain on the body than did most forms of physical labor.

She kept wondering about the eight days she'd lost. That was the stress. Where had she been? What had she done? How did you lose eight days? At a red light, she picked up her cell phone and punched in a number. She held the phone to her ear for a time, then broke the connection.

The headache arrived full-blown. No timid little mouse tracks across her forehead. The thing slammed instantly into complete and total war. She steered with her left hand as she pressed her eye with her right. The eye was throbbing with pain.

A few minutes later, she was taking an exit.

The thing was, she had no idea why. Or where she was going.

There was just the headache. And the disorientation. And this destination she had in mind.

What was going on?

She ended up over by DePaul University. This time of day, there were a lot of students on the streets, talking in small groups, lugging armloads of books back to stuffy little apartments and sleeping rooms, or scoring some drugs from the purveyors who roamed up and down the streets. You could tell the purveyors easily enough. They were the nervous-looking ones. The cops had been on their asses lately.

The place she went was one of the red brick apartment buildings constructed in the late fifties and early sixties, the notion being that brick would look better longer than any other type of building material. True, it would if it was kept up. But few landlords bothered to keep it up. By now, most of the red brick buildings looked as old and sooty as their wooden contemporaries.

She parked in back, next to a tan Pontiac sedan. There were no garages, just yellow lines on concrete. Rusted black fire escapes like giant roaches crawled up the backs of the buildings. She went in a rear door and vanished.

Coffey swept into the parking lot. He was out of his car and in the apartment house in moments. Once he was inside, he heard footsteps two floors above him. He hurried up the steps covered in faded green carpeting. A muddy transparent runner ran from the bottom step in the basement, where he was, to the third floor.

He came to the top of the steps on the highest floor and then stopped. She stood at a door near the far end of the hall. He took a couple of steps backward so he could peek around the edge of the stairway without her seeing him.

She got her purse open and started rummaging through it. She produced, finally, a golden key that she put into the lock on the door. The door opened. She pushed it inward. She glanced suspiciously down the hall. Coffey had time to duck back behind the edge of the staircase.

She went inside.

He gave her a few minutes then went up and checked out the apartment number. 3-C. Why would a woman who lived in a mansion keep an apartment like this in a lower white-collar place like this?

He went downstairs to check the number 3-C on the mailboxes. These were new boxes. Not a chip on them. Nobody as yet had had time to work them open with crowbars.

The name on 3-C was Linda Fleming. That was the name Detective Ryan had asked him about. Who was Linda Fleming? He went back to the third floor. The carpeting was dusty and made him sneeze. He also had to go to the john. He'd had three Diet Pepsis so far today.

He put his ear to 3-C. Listened.

What he heard mostly were the ghosts that lurk in all domiciles and disguise themselves as the idle noises of appliances and the gurgle of plumbing and the muffled cries of floor creaks and window rattlings.

He was just about to try the knob and see if it would turn when he heard the sound of labored breathing and heavy steps coming up the staircase at the other end of the hall.

She was at least sixty, she was scarecrow-skinny, she wore glasses so thick the people at Mt. Palomar would be envious. And she still smoked cigarettes.

Flowered, faded housedress. Two stained canvas grocery bags with handles. Industrial strength support hose. Floppy brown oxfords. Gray greasy hair worn like a helmet. And a cigarette that appeared to be at least a foot-and-a-half in length dangling from the right corner of her mouth. And the cough, of course. What could be more pleasant to have—or listen to—than a cigarette hack?

She studied him skeptically with watery blue-green eyes, coughing all the time, and then said, "She probably ain't home."

She was responding to the fact that Coffey had posed himself so that it appeared he was about to knock on Linda Fleming's door. By now, she was only three doors away. She set her groceries down and dug in the left pocket of her ratty blue cardigan for her apartment key.

"I just wondered if Linda was home."

"Uh-huh," she said, "she works all day." Then, "You sellin' something?"

He smiled. "No."

"You better not be because we got this place posted, front and back, NO SALESMEN. That gives us the right to call the law on you if you try to sell anybody anything on the premises here."

"I'm a college friend of hers."

"Oh, yeah? You went to the University of Illinois, too, huh?" She was hacking as she said this, hacking and dragging on the cigarette stuck in the corner of her mouth.

"Yep. I went there, too."

Great mischief came into her watery eyes and she smiled with tiny black teeth around her cigarette. "That's funny because she never went to the University of Illinois. She went to a girl's college named Clark over in Iowa."

She'd had her fun. She inserted her key, the door swung inward, she picked up her canvas grocery bags and she started to go inside. "The University of Illinois, huh?" she said. Then she was gone.

He stood there feeling tricked, foolish. She was a wily old bag, no doubt about that.

He went back to doing what he'd been doing, putting his ear to the door and trying to spy on the person or people inside. He was still rankled by the hag. On the other side of the apartment door, the phone rang. It was answered on the third ring. Far back in the apartment—the way he was visualizing it, she was in the bedroom—he could hear a female voice speaking. But it was so muffled, he didn't understand a single word.

His hand, almost as if it were spirit-guided, found the doorknob. Turned the doorknob. And found the door unlocked.

He eased the door open and stepped inside, closing the door quietly behind him.

The furniture was about what he'd expected. Clean, sturdy, unremarkable, dark blue couch, two matching armchairs, gray wall-to-wall carpeting, a kitchenette hidden behind two louvered doors, and three paintings that had been painted by artists who were not only starving but blind as well.

The bedroom door was open an inch. He could hear her more plainly now. She was saying, "Yes, I understand." Jenny's voice. She said good-bye and hung up. Moments later, Coffey heard a shower door being slid back. Then a blast of water. Then the shower door rattling some more as she stepped into the water stream.

He sat down and waited for her.

He could hear her in there, spritzing on perfume. The sound was oddly loud in the silence of Linda Fleming's apartment. He still wondered who Fleming was, and what her relationship to Jenny Stafford could be.

The spritzing stopped. A closet door was opened, then closed. And then her cell phone rang. But he noted the oddness of the ring sequence—two quick rings, then two long rings. He'd never heard a cell phone use this pattern before. The ringing stopped, then. He assumed she'd picked up. But she said nothing—or if she did, she whispered it very, very quietly. A strange moment, this. And for some reason he wasn't sure of, he thought of the vans that followed her around. And now, followed him around, too.

A minute later, the bedroom door opened all the way and she came out.

It was Jenny, and yet it was *not* Jenny.

Where Jenny usually dressed in expensive casual clothes, Linda Fleming favored a gaudy lemon-colored suit with a micro-mini skirt. There was a run in her dark stockings. The suit looked at least one size too small. Her makeup was as gaudy as her clothes. Too much blush; too much eyeshadow; too much lipstick. The only thing she wore that Jenny would have approved of was her modest one-inch black pumps.

It was a testament to the classic angles of her face that despite her best efforts to tart herself up, Linda Fleming remained a beauty.

"Who the hell are you?" she said, stunned and angry. While the timbre of her voice was Jenny's, there was a faint Southern accent to some of her words. Soft, the way Virginia accents are.

"C'mon Jenny," he said. "What's going on here?"

She strode across the room to where a white Princess telephone sat on top of a Zenith console model TV set. She picked up the receiver. "I'm calling the police. And my name's not Jenny. It's Linda." She started to punch in phone numbers.

"That wouldn't be too smart," he said, "since the police are looking for you."

She looked genuinely surprised. "Why would the police be looking for me?"

"The Econo-Nite Motel two nights ago," he said. "A dead man in Room 127."

He watched her face. She seemed to be battling certain memories. Her face showed confusion, then fear, then recognition. Then, "How you'd know about that?"

"It doesn't matter how I know about it. It matters how the *police* know about it."

He could see her pale even beneath the layers of her makeup, the weariness and wariness of her eyes.

She said, "I asked you who the hell you are."

"My name is Coffey."

She remained standing in the center of the floor and then she crossed to an overstuffed chair and sat down. She put one hand to her face and let the other one dangle off the side of the chair.

The silence of the place became overpowering once again. And then the silence was broken with her sharp, aggrieved tears.

Coffey stayed still. Letting her cry was the best thing he could do. He wanted to scrub her face. He wanted her to be Jenny. His Jenny.

Several times, her tears sounded as if they were trailing off. But then she'd get upset all over again and her tears would burst into violent new life.

After a time, he got up and went into the bathroom. He found a box of tissues and brought it out to her. She was at the sniffling stage, trying to shut her tears down. She muttered a tearful thank you.

He went back and sat across from her and didn't say anything.

By now, her too-heavy makeup was streaking, especially around the eyes, and her micro-mini skirt had pulled way up on her lovely thighs. He tried not to look. It wasn't easy.

He said, "I'd like to help you."

"Oh, right. How many men have I heard *that* from in my life."

"I'm serious."

"That's what they said, too." She waved a hand to indicate the apartment. "This is the kind've help they gave me. A dump like this." There was no point arguing with her. He sat back and looked at her. As he watched her, he realized that this was actually Jenny Stafford number two he was looking at. The plastic surgery following her car accident had changed her looks considerably. That was probably why more people hadn't recognized the police sketch of her. Not many people had seen the post-accident Jenny Stafford.

"Where'd you go to high school?" he said. He wanted to see how deep the Linda Fleming character ran. It was eerie, trying to think of her as both Jenny *and* Linda.

She looked suspicious. "Why do you want to know that?"

"I'm just curious."

"You seem curious about a whole *lot* of things."

He smiled. "Must be my nature. So where'd you go to school?"

"Kennedy."

"Any college?"

"One year. I dropped out."

"Where'd you go?"

She glared at him. "Man, you're really a pain in the ass, you know that?"

He probably was a pain in the ass. But he was working on a theory and he needed to know some things. "So where'd you go?"

"Clark College is where I went. God. No more questions."

"Just one."

She sighed, greatly put-upon. "All right. One more."

"How old is your father?"

"My father? He's dead, why?"

"When did he die?"

She shrugged. "Who cares? He never did much for me, anyway." Pause. "Eight, nine years ago, he had a heart attack."

"I see. And where had he worked most of his life?"

"At Motorola. Driving a delivery truck." She sighed. "I haven't done so good with my life. You know the funny thing? I was considered the smart one. I had two sisters. My folks couldn't really afford more than one, but my mom was a strict Catholic and wouldn't use any birth control. So they had three kids. And I was considered the smartest one. But that isn't the way things turned out. My youngest sister, she married this banker and they live out in Oak Park. And my oldest sister married this doctor and they've got this really beautiful house out in San Diego." Her head was still back, her eyes closed. It was almost like a therapy session.

"I've got this splitting headache."

"Why don't I get you a couple of aspirin?"

"Yeah, actually, that sounds good. You think you can find everything?"

"Sure."

Her bed was unmade. Three or four pairs of shoes were scattered across the floor. A bureau drawer was open, a pair of white panties hanging off the drawer edge.

The bathroom was no better. Myriad forms of makeup were strewn across the top of the toilet and the sink. The soap dish was encrusted with hardened soap residue. She hadn't bothered to put the new roll of toilet paper on the roller. It sat on the floor next to the john. The medicine cabinet above the sink was mirrored and probably hadn't been wiped clean for months. The mirror slid to the right to allow you access to the four rows of toothpaste, Vaseline, cold medications, combs, eyebrow tweezers, and cotton swabs that waited inside.

But what interested him most was the photo of the girl that had been taped to the far edge of the mirror. It was a society page item, a small story, the headline reading: DEBUTANTE OF YEAR NAMED TO ART MUSEUM BOARD. Four paragraphs detailed how the debutante would not only join the board but spearhead the next fund-raising job.

But the copy wasn't nearly as interesting as the photograph that accompanied it.

The photo showed a slightly posed but stunningly beautiful Jenny Stafford.

He spent the next minute searching through the medicine cabinet for aspirin. The clutter didn't make it easy. Finally, he found a small tin of Bayer. The tin was covered with some kind of sticky goop that had been spilled on it. He took the plastic glass on the sink and washed it out several times, then filled it up with fresh water. He carried this and the aspirin back to the living room.

She hadn't moved.

Her eyes were open, and she was staring at the ceiling.

"Here you go," he said.

She sat up straight and looked at him. "Well, I guess you're good for *some*thing."

"You're very kind."

She laughed. "You're a smart-ass, aren't you?"

"Sometimes."

He gave her the water and the aspirin.

"I'm sorry this place is such a pit."

"That's all right."

"I'm for shit as a housekeeper."

"Take your aspirin."

"Thanks." Ever mercurial, ever-changing moods, she said, "I probably look like hell."

"You look fine."

She looked at him. "How did you get in here? I just realized you never explained that."

"The door was open. I just walked in."

"God, I didn't lock it?"

"Apparently not." Then, "I want to help you, Linda."

"Help me with what?"

"With dealing with the police. I want you to see a friend of mine."

He showed her the police sketch that had been in the *Tribune* this morning.

"Hey, that looks a lot like me." Looks a lot like me? It clearly was her. At first, he thought she might be kidding. But then he saw she was serious.

He watched her somberly. The sketch had unnerved her. Anxiety played on her face.

"What sort of a friend are you talking about?" she said.

"A shrink."

She touched a hand to her head. "This headache is killing me."

"Then take the aspirin."

She took the aspirin. "I'll be honest with you. I don't remember much about that night." Her face tightened. "If the cops ask me—"

"That's where my friend can help. He's also a hypnotist."

"Oh, no. I hate booga-booga."

"It's not booga-booga. He can help you remember things under hypnosis. Do you even remember where you met the guy you were in Room 127 with."

She nodded. "Some bar. Arnie's, a sports bar or something like that."

"Is that some place you go very often?"

She shook her blonde head. "No. I'd never been there before."

"You've got a newspaper clipping in the bathroom."

Murky recognition shone in her eyes momentarily. "Oh, yeah."

"Do you know Jenny Stafford?"

She shook her head. "No. She just looked—pretty, I guess. I just clipped out her picture was all. No special reason."

A complete history, Coffey thought. Linda Fleming had a complete history, apparently down to the smallest detail.

He could already see her legal defense shaping up. He'd had a few experiences with multiple personalities before. He'd been skeptical of the whole multiple notion until he'd run into a black pimp who, by day, was a well-regarded bank clerk. In interrogating the man, Coffey had seen both personalities emerge strong and clear, shifting dominance in the man as his interrogation went on.

This would explain why she'd had no memory the other night. A small percentage of multiple personalities suffered acute memory loss following trauma. Finding yourself in a motel room with a dead man had to qualify as traumatic. Being a multiple also explained her temper. This was the temper that Jenny kept under control. Multiples were always expression of repressed impulses and needs and resentments.

He had all sorts of feelings for her as he sat there—desire, curiosity, protectiveness—but most of all he felt pity. There were few psychological burdens as difficult to bear as multiple personalities, both for the sufferer and all the people around her.

"How would you like to go to my place?" he said.

"I already told you," she said in her brassy Linda Fleming voice, "I gotta go to work."

"You go to work, the police could find you."

"Oh, I never thought of that."

"You could stay at my place tonight, and then we can figure out what to do."

Anger tightened her face. She was off again, mercurial. "You're pathetic, you know that? All this bullshit just to get laid. 'I'm really curious about you.' 'I really want to help you.' Guys sound so pathetic when they're sniffin' around a woman, and they don't even know it. Well, you're not *gonna* get laid. At least not by me."

"I still want you to come to my place."

"Even if I don't put out?"

"Even if you don't put out."

"You gay or something?"

"No."

"Then I don't get it."

"Maybe you remind me of my little sister. Maybe that's why I want to help you."

"Where's your little sister?"

"Omaha. She's about to have her third kid any day now."

"Man," Linda Fleming said, "no way I want a kid. Ball and chain is what a kid would be to me."

"Why don't we go?"

"Now?"

"Yeah."

She shrugged. "Give me a few minutes."

"Fine."

She got up and went into the bedroom. When she came out, she had even more makeup on. "I don't know about this shrink guy."

"You'll like him."

She rolled her eyes. Her beautiful eyes. "Oh, yeah. I'll probably fall in love."

Chapter Twenty-Five

ONE butterfly-summer afternoon at the northernmost edge of the compound, Gretchen found the dog. It was just a mutt, brown and white, with creek-dirty white paws and a thistle hanging off its tail. This was about three months after she arrived at the compound. One of Quinlan's favorite theories was that criminals, even double murderers such as Gretchen herself, could be rehabilitated through a combination of behavior modification, hypnosis, and drug treatment. He'd also done work creating multiple personalities, isolating the Bad Person from the Good Person. While no state legislature was likely to ever actually let any of his test-case people out of the hospital, they did look at his test results with curiosity and skeptical admiration. Three California psychiatrists who had evaluated three of Quinlan's most notorious patients for California murder trials—and found each of them hopelessly sociopathic—flew out to Chicago and spent a week evaluating those same three men again. The results stunned them. Under Quinlan's guiding hand, the three men exhibited a humanity the shrinks had never even glimpsed before. Gone were the violent impulses, the total self-absorption. They even had a limited sense of right and wrong. None of the men had become angels, true. But Quinlan's rehabilitative techniques were impressive and deserved further serious study and funding. Grant and foundation money poured into the compound.

If only Gretchen had been as malleable as those other three sociopaths. Her first month here she cut a female patient with her ballpoint pen, stabbing it into the woman's cheek and then ripping downward; her second month here, she set fire to the room they had put her in; and the third month she had seduced a guard and tried to get him to give her a gun. During all this time, she was sleeping with Quinlan, and spending many nights in his aerie. He'd been fascinated by her in those golden days. She interested him both as a case study and a seductress. She knew how to use her body and for the sexually adventurous, she could provide a memorable night's entertainment.

His pride was that he could bring her in line with everybody else. That through behavior modification he could help her unlearn her psychotic inclinations and rejoin society at large.

The night she tried to castrate him in his sleep, he decided she was hopeless. She'd walked in on him that afternoon. He'd been sleeping with the new nurse from Building One. A brunette she was, with breasts that owed far more to science than God. She'd made a scene. The nurse fled in terror. He calmed Gretchen down with sweet talk and drugs. She wouldn't leave. That night, in the darkness of his bedroom, she'd fallen asleep in his arms.

But something woke him a few hours later and when he looked up, he saw her straddling him, a pair of long scissors arcing toward his crotch. He rolled away just in time. Grabbed her, slapped her. She spent the night in a maximum-security room. He kept her there for three weeks.

And the day she got out, he told her she could walk around the compound and enjoy the spring day. But she had to check in every forty-five minutes or lose her freedom.

This was the day she found the dog.

He came timidly over to her outstretched hand. She petted him. And after he was no longer afraid of her, she hugged him. He had fleas, which pissed her off. She was fanatical about being clean.

Then she saw the rock, a jagged flinty piece that more than filled her hand. All the time she reached for the rock with her left hand, she continued to stroke the dog with her right. He was now whimpering, he was in such ecstasy from her touch. Her powers of seduction were apparently cross-species. What a goddess she was!

She had to club him four times before he was dead, before blood leaked from his nostrils, and he fouled himself all over his tail. Then she got to work.

Quinlan got the package next day. It was sitting on his desk waiting for him. It was gaily wrapped in expensive blue paper.

A lot of the women patients he slept with fell in love with him. Fortunately, this kind of transference was short-lived. They got over it. But while in its thrall, they were always sending him gifts.

He wondered who this one was from.

After he opened it, after he ran to his private john to wash his hands of the blood, after he began the useless process of trying to forget the sight of the dead dog's head in the box—after all this, he had no doubt who had sent the gift.

This time, he put her in maximum security for a month-and-a-half. He had even thought of requesting that another facility take her on. But that would make him look bad. She'd come here under splashy circumstances. Sending her away would make it look as if his methodology didn't work. Best to simply keep her locked up for a while.

She was thinking about the dog's head now, as she sat in the room where Barcroft had put her, right down the hall from Quinlan's lavish apartment. He'd wanted to put her in maximum security but there wouldn't be a room free till later in the day. And two other fully-secured rooms were filled as well, so he'd had to put her in what was almost like a hotel room. Sparse but decent furnishings—couch, table, magazines, TV—and even a tiny vertical window to look out of.

She walked over and turned on the TV. And a miracle happened. Jenny Stafford's face filled the screen.

There were points in her life when Gretchen felt as if her life was a dream—as if she were a disembodied psyche wandering in a world of ghosts and phantoms and other disembodied psyches—and at such times the faces of people she despised appeared to her. Sometimes, it was the mother who had picked on her twenty-four hours a day; other times, it was the father who'd shown no interest in her whatsoever. Now it was Jenny Stafford, and she was on TV.

What the hell was this all about?

She sank to her knees in front of the TV and listened as the announcer explained why the police were looking for the unnamed suspect who was clearly Jenny Stafford.

What the hell *was* this all about?

Then she thought of the videotape she'd made of Quinlan. The woman shooting the man. The woman under Quinlan's control.

... And then another image came to her, Jenny fading on the screen. Another, more disturbing image. Her mind sought to clarify the image ... find out what it had to do with Jenny.

The headache was so sharp and so sudden that she fell over backward from her kneeling position, clutching her face and screaming.

Chapter Twenty-Six

COFFEY called Hal Ford as soon as he got to his place. Jenny was using the john, so he could speak freely.

"I know you don't believe in multiple personalities," Coffey said. "But there's no other explanation for this."

Ford laughed. "Evil twin?"

"Yeah. That's it. Evil twin."

"Listen, it's not that I don't believe in multiples. It's just that I think they're relatively rare. I mean, you have all these TV stars and mass murderers claiming multiple personalities—no way. But I can be open-minded."

"I'd appreciate it if you could talk to somebody for me."

"Maybe it would be more relaxing over here."

"Some people are looking for her."

" 'Some people'?"

"That's about all I can tell you."

"Well, I'll be able to call you back in about an hour or so. How's that? I'll just chat with her on the phone."

"I really appreciate it."

Ford was one of the shrinks who had an arrangement with the police force. Officers could go in and see him whenever they wanted, and the city picked up the tab. Coffey had seen him a good deal following the murders of his wife and daughter.

"Now you've got me curious."

"Oh?"

"Maybe I'm about to talk to my first multiple."

"Maybe I can take your picture standing next to her, pointing at her. You know, the way men do when they've caught a big fish."

"You really are a wise-ass, Coffey."
"I just meant to puncture your lordly ego a bit."
Ford laughed. "Well, you did a good job, you sonofabitch."

***

He couldn't find her.
He'd heard the toilet flush several minutes ago. And her footsteps emerge from the john.
But where was she? Not in the living room, not in the dining room, not in his office.
She'd gotten scared and run.
That was all he could think of.
He started calling her name and retracing his steps through the house. Kitchen. Office. Living room. No woman. His friends the cats followed him room to room, meowing. They seemed to sense his fear.
He decided to try the bathroom. Maybe she'd gone back in there. His panic waned for a moment. That was it. The bathroom. She'd gone back there. Maybe she'd forgotten to clean up her makeup or something.
She wasn't in the bathroom. The door stood wide. The bathroom was empty.
He started back down the hall to the living room. He heard it faintly as he passed the bedroom. A soft, moist, almost purring sound.
The door was ajar but not by much. He pushed the door open.
She tossed restlessly on the bed, the way a child sleeps, limbs twisted every which way. She was completely dressed except for her shoes, which she'd kicked off her feet at the head of the bed. He smiled. He felt an almost painful tenderness for her. Then he felt the fear that had besieged him the past two days. He was so taken with her, what if she was put in prison? Or was somehow killed?
He closed the door quietly.

In the kitchen, he called his friend at the Traffic Bureau.
"Got something for you," the friend said.
"All right."
"David Alan Foster. 2245 Skyway Terrace. You know where that is?"

"I met him last night, actually. But I needed his address. Thanks."

"No problem."

"I appreciate it, Briney. You're not having any luck with the van?"

"It's a lease job. Imperial Leasing. That part's easy enough. But I haven't been able to find out who it's leased *to* yet."

"I'd appreciate it if you'd keep trying."

"My pleasure."

"I'm putting two fifties in an envelope as soon as I hang up."

"That's my pleasure, too," Briney laughed.

Coffey knew that he could probably have gotten Briney to cooperate free of charge. But this was more efficient. And it would incline Briney to help him again in the future.

"I'll keep trying on that lease job," Briney said.

He put on some fresh coffee. He found some sugar cookies up in the cupboard and set those out, too. They were a bit stale but edible.

He figured she wouldn't sleep long, and he was right. She lasted an hour, and then she got up and went to the john. She stayed in there ten minutes and came out. Her wig was gone. So was all her makeup.

When she came into the kitchen, she said, "It is you."

He just watched her.

"From the other night," she said. "The cabbie."

She walked over to the kitchen table. "How did I get here? The last thing I remember, I was home with my parents, and—" She looked around, her gaze lingering on various items. Then, "May I sit down?"

The correct usage of "May I" confirmed what he'd suspected the moment he'd seen her in the kitchen doorway just now. Linda Fleming was gone. She was once more Jenny Stafford.

"Sure," he said. "Sit down and I'll get you some coffee."

He took her cup to the counter, filled it, brought it back, sat down across from her.

"I had a blackout again, didn't I?"

"Well, not exactly a blackout. But something like it."

"I don't know what you mean."

DAUGHTER OF DARKNESS

"I'd better let my friend Hal Ford explain it. He'll be calling soon."

"Who's Hal Ford?"

"He's a psychologist."

"I'm already seeing a psychiatrist."

"Well, Hal practices hypnosis, too. He's very good at it."

She blew on her coffee. "Why would I need a hypnotist?"

"Does the name Linda Fleming mean anything to you?"

She didn't hesitate. "No. Who is she?"

He didn't answer her question directly. "Did you find a lot of makeup on your pillow this morning?"

"Yes, as a matter of fact." She set her cup down. Looked around some more. "I'm scared again. Just like the other night. I still don't know how I got here."

The phone rang. He was most appreciative. He didn't want to get into anything about multiple personalities until Hal Ford was here.

"Hello," Coffey said.

"This is your old friend Margie Ryan, Mr. Coffey."

"Oh. Hi."

"I just wondered if you'd heard anything from your friend."

"My friend?"

"I wouldn't be so coy, Mr. Coffey. I could still decide to tell the DA's office how you decided not to call the police when you found Mr. Benedict's body in the motel room. And how you just let the woman walk off."

"You really think they'd charge me?"

"They'd charge you in a minute, Mr. Coffey. In a minute. So why don't you knock off the crap and tell me if you know where your lady friend is?"

He looked straight across the table at Jenny Stafford. "No, I haven't seen her since that night."

Silence on the other end. "It's called aiding and abetting, Mr. Coffey. In case you're interested."

"If I see her, you'll be the first to know."

"You'd better. Because you'll be in a whole lot of trouble if I find out you didn't."

She hung up.

Jenny said, "You don't look happy."

"Just a little problem I have. No big deal."

She yawned. "Excuse me. I don't know why I'm so sleepy."

"It's not easy drinking coffee. Wears you out."
She said, "So how did I get here?"
"I think I'd rather wait till you've talked with Hal."
"That makes me nervous. That you won't tell me."
"It won't be long."
"Did I do something you're afraid to talk to me about?"
"I just think he can handle it a little better than I can, Jenny. Nothing sinister at all. I promise."
"Is my car here?"
"No," he said.
"Did I come here in a cab?"
"Jenny, look, I—"
The phone rang again.
"Just a minute," he told her.
He picked up the receiver from the wall phone. "Hello." Then, "It's Hal. He'd like to talk to you."
She got up and walked unsteadily over to the phone. "Hello."
Hal took over from there. They talked for nearly forty minutes.

Chapter Twenty-Seven

SKYWAY Terrace was a land of expensive, two-story brick homes set against a backdrop of forest and piney hills. The driveways were clogged with vans and Volvos. These were Mom's cars. Dad would have the more expensive one at work, unless he opted for the commuter train. Coffey noted a small depot on his way in. This wasn't a town. It was a small collection of new homes and nothing more. The closest Pizza Hut was five miles away, the closest mall ten. This was the veritable frontier.

His passage was noted by a few women out working on their yards. They leaned on their rakes and watched him with solemn curiosity. There was no thought of waving. Strangers were not welcome here. Strangers were house burglars and arsonists and child molesters. Given the way things had been going in this country, he didn't blame them for their fears.

He found the house he was looking for. He pulled in the driveway and stopped. David Foster lived in a Southern Traditional style home. The entrance was dramatic, flanked as it was by two brilliant white columns. There were gables and ornate moldings as well. The lawn was nicely landscaped. There was a bird fountain and a sundial and a gazebo. It was all a little cluttered, Coffey reasoned. But pleasantly so.

He got out of the car and walked up to the front door, past the two columns. Everything was new here. You could smell fresh paint. He pressed the bell. Inside, he could hear the bells peal forth a mini-symphony.

In all, he rang three times. There was no answer. He was about to give up when he heard a voice behind him say, "Something I can help you with?"

Coffey turned around. At the bottom of the steps stood David Foster. To celebrate the warm day, he wore chinos and a paint-splotched T-shirt and white tennis shoes without any socks. He was a good-looking young man, but there was an air of anxiety about him that made him seem very young and insecure. He wore mud-stained white work gloves. In his right hand he had a garden trowel. He held it like a weapon.

"Mr. Foster."

At first, Foster didn't seem to recognize who was talking. Just some stranger. But as Coffey walked out of the shadows of the narrow porch and into the sunlight, he saw recognition fill Foster's eyes.

"Hi," Foster said. "How'd you find me?"

"I used to find people for a living," Coffey said. "I was a homicide detective."

"Really?"

Coffey nodded. "In the restaurant, you made it sound as if you had something to tell me about Jenny. That's why I looked you up."

Foster pitched his trowel to the grass then slipped out of his gloves. "They say gardening relaxes you." He smiled sadly. "So far it hasn't done much for me. You like a beer or something?"

"No, thanks."

Foster stared off at the woods to the north. He didn't speak for a long moment. Then he turned his gaze back upon Coffey and said, "She tell you I dumped her?"

"No. I don't know much about her."

"Yeah. I just walked away one day. I'd met this woman. It didn't last long. Then I ran around a while. And then, finally, I realized that I was still in love with Jenny." Foster flung his gloves on top of the trowel. "Anyway, I've been trying to win her back. I see now that I still love her."

At first, Coffey didn't recognize the feeling for what it was. He felt irritated suddenly. But why? Foster was being nice enough. Jealousy. When he realized the feeling, he felt shocked. He was jealous of Foster. Felt possessive of Jenny. Didn't want anybody else to see her. Not even ex-boyfriends who'd been crazy enough to dump her. He changed the subject quickly. "The other night you said there were good guys and bad guys in Jenny's life. Who're the bad guys?"

"I'm not sure. Not yet. That's why I put off calling you."

"Maybe I could help you."

"Maybe. But not right now. I shouldn't have shot my mouth off the way I did."

"International Investigations helping you, are they?"

He was slow in reacting. He looked angry at first, but then his face broke into one of his melancholy smiles. "I guess you really were a homicide cop, huh?"

"Cummings made it easy for me. He left his card with a friend of mine."

"Maybe he's not such a good detective? That what you're saying?"

"That I couldn't say. I don't know the guy. But Jenny's in trouble, and if he knows anything that can help her, he should share it with me. Then we can take it to the police."

Inside the house, the phone started ringing. "I'd better get that. Then I've got to get ready to go into the city."

"What about Cummings?"

"Go talk to him, Mr. Coffey."

"Will you call him and tell him to cooperate with me?"

The phone was insistent now.

"I'll tell him."

Then Foster was running around to the back door of the small mansion, leaving Coffey to stand in the sunlight and look over the sweep of well-kept lawn. He was trying very hard not to think of the jealousy he'd felt just a few minutes ago. He was also trying very hard not to think about how much Jenny reminded him of Janice. With one exception—he'd never considered the possibility that Janice might be a killer.

***

The van was parked half a block away from where Foster's sweeping drive emptied out on to a tree-shaded, asphalt road.

For the first time, Coffey realized that there were at least two vans used in following him and Jenny around. This one had different license plates. And whitewalls. The other van had blackwalls. Otherwise, the exteriors were the same, including the same small black box on the roof.

The window of the van was empty as Coffey passed it. Presumably, the driver was in the cargo area of the vehicle. But not for long. Coffey had barely gone a block before the van swung into a U-turn and headed eastward to fall into place behind him.

They went fifteen minutes in this formation. The driver always stayed a sensible half block behind. Coffey pretended to be unaware of the van. But what he was really doing was setting up a maneuver that had worked for him a few times back in his cop days.

He drove a few more blocks then took an abrupt right into an alley that ran behind a shopping mall. They came right after him. He took seven blocks' worth of alleys and it was quite the ride. He was traveling at sixty mph. The car slammed into ruts, skidded into garbage cans and dumpsters, fishtailed on long patches of gravel. There was no reason for the van to come after him, but you could always count on a guy's sense of macho to make him do stupid things. The van driver was obviously not going to let himself be shown up by Coffey.

But was it going to work? Coffey needed a clear stretch of about a quarter block to pull his trick off. He also needed enough clear space to turn his car completely around. He drove two, three more blocks, the alley ruts seeming to grow deeper and deadlier, the bottom of the car banging against the ruts with mournful scraping-metal noises.

He lucked out. He found a small loading dock with a concrete apron just big enough for the maneuver. He gunned his car. When he was roughly a quarter block ahead of the van, he whipped into the loading area and spun his car around, accelerating in the turn, never once tapping the brakes. The screech of tires filled his ears and the surprise of the van driver's face filled his eyes. Coffey floored his car, driving straight for the front of the van. The van driver was good. He managed to brake the vehicle before slamming into Coffey, the van sliding and fishtailing on the gravel, the tires throwing gravel as far as twenty feet behind.

Coffey was already out of his car, running toward the passenger side of the van. His police revolver filled his right hand. There was a woman in some kind of uniform riding shotgun. She watched him coming then, as he got near, her window came down instantly. She had a harsh face with short, thatch-like gray hair. She took a small red plastic ball about the size of a lemon, ripped off the top grenade-style, and threw it at Coffey.

He was blinded and gagged instantly. She had loosed some kind of gas upon the air. A thick chemical-smelling fog encased Coffey and he dropped to his knees and then fell to his face on the gravel. Before he passed out, he could hear the van transmission whine in reverse. The van was escaping.

The van was . . .

and then there was . . .

nothing. . . .

***

The cancer scare had come right before Jenny had been put in the psychiatric hospital. Two aunts on her mother's side had died in their thirties of breast cancer. The day Jenny found the lump in her left breast—she wasn't very dutiful about self-exams while showering, always thinking, wrongly, that she was too young for such worries—that day she saw her mother and father dissolve into total terror. Her folks rushed her to the doctor as soon as possible. Then began the long wait for the biopoxy. Her mother put the best face on it she could. She was sure it was benign. She was sure it was nothing. But every evening during the three-day wait, she heard her mother crying late into the darkest hours of the night, Dad holding her and trying to comfort her. That was the great curse of the family, the genetic predisposition to breast cancer, and the women lived constantly under its shadow.

Jenny thought of this now as she lay in bed trying to nap after her session with Hal, Coffey's shrink friend. She had been afraid of the cancer, of course. During her visit to the doctor, she'd actually felt her knees buckle, she'd been so afraid. But given the car accident, the plastic surgery, and the profound depression that followed, she wondered if she truly had the will to live. In some ways, it seemed easier to just give in to the cancer.

And in some ways, now, as she lay on the guest room bed, she wondered if it wouldn't be easier to just give in now. The cancer had turned out to be a benign cyst. Maybe what she should do now—with her dread that she'd actually killed a man—maybe she should just turn herself over to the police and be done with it. Give in. And whatever happened, happened. She was sick of the headaches, sick of the way she had to grapple with her memory, sick of the notion that she might truly be this other person, this Linda woman. Hal had helped her escape from Linda. But now what was she left with? The prospect that she was a killer? Not very reassuring.

Finally, she drifted into an uneasy, sweaty sleep filled with quiet yet relentless demons.

***

Coffey didn't have any trouble getting into Linda Fleming's apartment. The lock on the door was a familiar style. All he needed was a credit card and the point of a pocketknife and he was in. He didn't even see the irritating old busybody down the hall. The only problem was that his sinuses and lungs were still responding to whatever kind of knockout gas the van people had used on him. He was coughing like a two-pack-a-day smoker.

Even with the place empty, he felt guilty about invading somebody's place. He'd arrested a burglar once who'd told him that the greatest thrill of all was going through the private belongings of somebody else. The man was now serving life for receiving his third felony conviction.

The place was noisy. Car doors slammed in the parking lot below. A TV blared above him, a radio below. People were talking in the hallway. The workday was over and folks were relaxing.

The living room air was thick with dust motes. He took an extended look at the shabby furniture, the water-stained walls, the cigarette-burned carpet. A few dozen quietly desperate lives had passed through this apartment, lives without enough money, without enough love, without enough hope. If you were lucky, this was the sort of place you started out in. And over the years, you worked your way up into something a lot better. But for too many people—especially in this era of corporate downsizing and part-time employees who got few raises and no benefits—this was not only where they started out but also where they ended up.

Coffey started in the living room. He had no idea what he

was looking for, just anything that would tell him something more about Linda Fleming.

He went through a stack of magazines, a three-tier bookcase, and a small, wobbly desk in a corner. He found nothing interesting or useful.

He tried the kitchen. There was a small wicker basket on the table filled with mail that mostly ran to coupons and fliers advertising discounts. Again, nothing useful or interesting, not unless you considered a dry cleaner changing its name a hot news item.

By this time, he held out little hope. Coming over here had probably been a waste of time.

He went into the bedroom. The scent of cheap perfume made him sneeze.

He started with the bureau, working quickly through the drawers with panties and bras so he wouldn't feel like a pervert. Nothing.

He next tried her nightstand. Nothing here either, other than a romance novel and some cough drops.

He didn't spend much time in the closet. There weren't many clothes to search through, for one thing, and he sensed instinctively that a closet wasn't going to yield much anyway.

Then across the room, on a window ledge, he saw a stack of six or seven paperbacks. Probably weren't worth looking through, though he decided he might as well glance at them.

More romance novels. The people on the covers were of a species superior to mere mortals. Nobody ever had breasts like these, or pectoral muscles for that matter; and nobody had ever posed so dramatically either, the wench caught up in the arms of the bad-boy hero. Mythic figures, not folks you were likely to run into in the supermarket.

One of the paperbacks had a small white envelope edge sticking out of it. He pulled the envelope free. It was a bill. The name on the return address was: Priscilla Bowman, MD, Psychiatric Services.

At first, the name meant nothing to him. But as he was sticking the envelope back in the book, he remembered that Jenny had told him about the shrink she was seeing. Priscilla Bowman had been her name. He was sure of it.

He took the envelope out again. Tugged out the bill inside. Read it.

On five occasions in the last month, Linda Fleming had seen Priscilla Bowman. Which meant that Dr. Bowman had to be aware of Jenny's two personalities. He wondered what else the good doctor knew about Jenny.

He put Bowman's bill in his jacket pocket.

He spent ten more minutes in the apartment, going back through the living room. Nothing else to be found.

He opened the door and peeked out. To his left, the hallway was empty. To his right—

The cranky woman was just going into her apartment. She was overburdened with three large grocery sacks. She wore the same faded housedress. Her knee-high hose had slipped down around her ankles. She'd be needing to get a new pair real real soon. The crowning touch in this portrait was, of course, the cigarette dangling from the corner of her mouth. She was having a hard time reaching past her grocery bags to slip the key in She had one knee against the door, supporting the groceries. But her cigarette was in place—the smoke, rising upward, causing her to blink and cough—and that was all that mattered.

He moved quickly. He was almost to the stairs at the opposite end of the hallway before she saw him.

"Hey! You! I seen you! I seen you!" she called after him. She had to stop every other word to cough.

What a lovely neighbor she'd make.

***

"There's a detective at the door, ma'am," Eileen said. She was dressed in her crisp gray maid's uniform. The end of the day like this, she looked tired. She worked very hard. The Staffords saw that she was well paid for her labors.

"A detective?" Molly said. She looked up from the Somerset Maugham collection she was reading. She preferred the writers of other eras to the writers of today. They were better storytellers, and the time of which they wrote seemed so much kinder and gentler than the world today. History made everything quaint, she remembered a history professor telling the class once. Even Caligula had a certain crazed romance about him viewed all these years later. Not to mention Vlad the Impaler, better known as Dracula. Reading Maugham was like looking at the French Impressionists of the 1880s and 1890s.

So soft and lovely, even when their material was coarse—a whorehouse or a working-class dance hall.

"She says she needs to talk to you, ma'am."

"I wonder what she wants," Molly said. She had her own little reading room, with a recliner in a small square room filled with built-in bookcases. There was good strong afternoon light in the window. She loved sitting in here and reading. It had the feel of a library.

"All she said was that she'd like to speak to you, ma'am."

Molly moved the recliner forward so she could more easily stand up. She wondered how she looked in her white turtleneck sweater and dark slacks.

"You look fine, ma'am," Eileen said.

Molly smiled. "I'm that vain, huh?"

"No. I just know that you worry about the impression you'll make. How you look and everything."

"I wonder what the proper attire is to meet a detective."

"You look fine, ma'am." Either Eileen hadn't gotten Molly's little joke, or she hadn't found it funny.

"Does she look mean?"

"No. She's very small and cute, actually."

"Good. Small and cute I can handle. Why don't you bring her into the study?"

"Yes, ma'am."

For all her banter, Molly was terrified that the detective was bringing some bad news about Jenny. She found herself wanting to run upstairs and take a cigarette from her secret pack. Five years ago, she'd promised both husband and daughter that she'd give up the devil weed. And, for the most part, she had. But every once in a while, especially when she sensed trouble coming— The secret pack was always upstairs. Her security blanket.

But she was being silly, she decided. For one thing, there wasn't *time* to run upstairs right now. And for another, she didn't even know what the detective was going to tell her. It certainly wouldn't be good news—but that didn't necessarily mean it would be terrible news, either.

The thing was to appear calm when she presented herself to the detective. Cops were probably like animals. When they sensed human fear, they probably got nasty.

The other thing to keep in mind was that the detective would very likely be intimidated by Molly and the mansion. That would give Molly the edge. It was the *detective* who should be anxious, not Molly.

As she left her reading room, Molly wished that she *felt* half as self-confident and poised as she looked. Everybody always remarked on how composed she was. But inside— Molly died a thousand deaths a day, wondering if she'd inadvertently hurt the bag boy's feelings, or reacted insensitively to something her hairdresser said.

She reached the study before the detective did.

She walked over to one of the mullioned windows and looked out on the grounds. Nature. That was her true solace. The beauty and grandeur of God. Nature was far more interesting to her than the human world, and its inhabitants far more trustworthy than the creatures who walked upright on two legs.

"Ma'am," Eileen said behind her. "This is Detective Margie Ryan."

When she turned and looked at Margie Ryan, Molly almost smiled. Eileen's description had been apt. Cute and small. Ryan came forward with her arm stiffly out, aiming herself at Molly like a hungry shark.

Some kind of body signal passed between the two women as they shook hands. And, for Molly, the signal was strong and clear.

She didn't like this little munchkin of a woman. And she certainly did not trust her.

Chapter Twenty-Eight

AS he pulled into his driveway, Coffey checked his rearview mirror for Hal's car. No sign of it.

He drove up the strip of concrete leading to the garage. Another melancholy dusk was falling, the stars already vivid in the night blue of the northern sky. The temperature had fallen six or seven degrees from the day. A fireplace and a good book and maybe a cup of hot cocoa. A simple yet satisfying need.

He went in through the kitchen door. At first, the house was quiet, which struck him as strange.

The phone rang. He picked up. Hal.

"I figured you'd want a report," the shrink said. "It was quite a session."

"Tell me about it."

"Definitely a multiple."

Coffey nodded. "That's what I thought."

"But it's not that easy."

"What's that mean?"

"The dividing line is too neat," Hal said.

"You're losing me."

"Look, multiple personalities reflect the repressed nature of the primary. If you're sexually repressed, one of your multiples may be sexually promiscuous."

"All right. I can see that."

"I spent two hours just talking to Jenny about her life before I hypnotized her. In other words, I got to know *Jenny* first. I like her. She's a nice, sensible young woman who's had a very difficult time in her life."

"Did she tell you about her breakdown?"

"Yes."

"Anything you can share with me?"

Hal coughed. "I promised I wouldn't tell you anything we discussed in our little therapy session. And I have to honor that."

"All right."

"I wouldn't be surprised if she voluntarily told you everything, though. She really likes you. And the way you sound now—pretty damned sappy, my friend—I can tell you feel the same way. In spades." He lifted his coffee cup and blew on the pool of the dark liquid. "But that's up to her. All I can tell you is what kind of conclusion I've come to."

"Fair enough."

"I don't think," he said, "that her Linda Fleming personality is a 'real' one."

"You're losing me again."

"I'm losing *me* again, too, my friend. As I said, most multiples are organic. The new personality reflects some need or repression in the primary personality. But from my conversations with Jenny, I can't see where Linda Fleming comes in. Linda isn't in any way a reflection of Jenny, if you see what I mean."

"And that leaves us where, exactly, Hal?"

"I'm not sure. But I've got some work I need to do tonight."

"Work?"

"I'm a very practical shrink. I tend to read only the new material that pertains to my practice. I don't get involved in a lot of abstract theoretical stuff, all that New Age psychobabble and all the super-drug therapies. I like to feel that it's mostly a waste of time for a hard-headed practical shrink like me. But tonight, I want to read up a little on brainwashing."

"Brainwashing?" Coffey said. The word startled him. His most immediate association with it was *The Manchurian Candidate*, one of his favorite suspense films, and the Korean War, during which the Chinese started to perfect brainwashing as a tool for both espionage and assassination. "You think she's been brainwashed?"

"Possibly. That's why I want to read up on it before I say anything else." He laughed. "Hard as it is to believe, Coffey, I could be wrong."

"Who the hell would want to brainwash her?"

"Somebody who hates her. Or who is jealous of her. Like a boyfriend who feels he's losing control of her."

"David Foster?"

"I'm just throwing out possibilities here."

"She sees a shrink. A Priscilla Bowman."

"Yes, she told me."

"You know Bowman?"

"Only by reputation. She's supposed to be very, very good. A lot of our peers knock her, but they're mostly jealous. She's got a firm grip on the millionaire business in the city. She makes a lot of money. And she's not known for being especially humble."

"Could Bowman brainwash her?"

"Could she? Probably. I mean, she has the opportunity certainly. She sees Jenny often, and sometimes hypnotizes her. Couple that with certain drugs, and she could probably mess with Jenny's mind pretty much as she wanted to. 'Mess with Jenny's mind' is technical jargon, by the way."

Coffey laughed. "You should write for Leno, the way you tell jokes all the time."

"There are some days I *wish* I wrote for Leno, believe me. Anything but sitting in my office being bombarded by people's problems."

"Like mine?"

"Oh, no. This is something real interesting. This'll get my shrink juices going again."

"Can you help her?" Coffey asked.

"I can help her if she wants me to."

"Meaning?"

"Meaning, she may be more comfortable with Priscilla Bowman."

"But what if Priscilla Bowman's behind this somehow."

"Jenny has a lot of faith in the woman. I don't have the professional or ethical right to shake that faith. I don't have any evidence that Bowman is being anything other than the first-rate shrink she's known to be. Therefore, I don't have any right to try and disrupt or alter their relationship." He grinned. "Plus, Priscilla is very litigious. She'd probably sue my ass if I took one of her clients away."

"God," Coffey said, "brainwashed."

"Listen to me, Coffey. I said that was a *possibility*. I didn't say it's what she's suffering from. There are all sorts of things she could be suffering from."

Coffey steadied himself for his next question. He didn't really want an answer. "Do you think she killed the guy in the motel?"

"I don't know. *She* doesn't know. Not for sure, anyway?"

"Not even under hypnosis?"

"Not even under hypnosis," Hal said. "That part of the evening is very vague to her."

"Do you think she'll ever remember?"

"Possibly," Hal said. "Possibly."

Coffey sat back in his chair. "David Foster had to be pretty desperate the other night. Following her to the motel."

"That sounds pretty desperate to me, yes."

"He was upset because he'd lost her. Meaning he'd been following her around all night. Meaning that he knew she'd gone into the motel room."

"Sounds plausible."

"Meaning that he might have gone into the room himself. After she left."

"And then *he* killed him?" Hal said. "That's awful neat and tidy, Coffey."

"Sometimes, it works out that way, neat and tidy."

"You've already got two suspects for brainwashing, and we don't even *know* that she's been brainwashed. I know you want her to be innocent, Coffey, but you've got to be open-minded about this."

"Open-minded?"

"She might actually have killed the guy."

"*She* actually killed the guy? I just can't believe that."

"Maybe you'll have to, Coffey."

"Gee, thanks, that's just what I need to hear."

"Coffey, look, I know how deep your feelings are for Jenny. I'm just trying to do what a good shrink does—warn you that this may not have the happy ending you want."

"I haven't even mentioned the van," Coffey said, desperate for Hal to believe in Jenny's innocence as much as he did. If Hal could only see how many suspects there were—

"The van?" Hal said.

"A Ford van," Jenny said from the doorway. "I've seen it, too."

Coffey looked over at her. She wore a pair of Coffey's pajamas. With her tousled hair and sleepy face, she looked like a little kid.

She came into the kitchen and said, "Hal is right, Coffey. We have to admit the possibility that I killed that man. I mean, I was the only one in the room with him as far as we know."

Bad enough, Coffey thought, that Hal held out the possibility that Jenny had killed the guy. Now, Jenny *herself* was saying the same thing.

He talked to Hal a few more minutes, and then hung up.

***

Margie Ryan said, "We got a phone tip, Mrs. Stafford, and we needed to check it out."

"A phone tip?"

Eileen had brought both of them coffee and set the cups on a shining sterling silver tray. She placed the tray between them at the small antique parquet-surface table by the study window. The window overlooked the northeast edge of the grounds. A gardener was at work on a tractor mower. The day was almost done now, but he seemed to have no trouble seeing. He used the lone headlight on the front of the tractor to illuminate his way.

Molly didn't like the detective. She was too forward, too cold. Molly wanted a smile or two and a gentler manner—and deference. Yes, a little deference. It probably wasn't very nice to admit—Molly really didn't like thinking of herself as a snob—but shouldn't the detective be at least a *little* intimidated coming into the Stafford house?

"Somebody said they saw your daughter at the Econo-Nite Motel the other night." "Perky" was the best way to describe the detective. She was just tall enough to have passed the police exam, and probably just heavy enough. She was finely boned, with a childlike face, and sharp, sudden movements, as if energy were overwhelming her. She wore a wine-colored blazer, a red-checked blouse, a dark skirt and one-inch black heels. She looked like a sales clerk in a medium-priced department store.

"I wish I knew what you were talking about," Molly said.

"Phone tips. Motels. We're talking about my daughter here, Jenny. She's a very proper girl."

"I'm sure she is."

"She's not a prude or anything like that. But a motel—I really doubt it. And even if she *was* at a motel, I don't see what the significance would be. She's over twenty-one. If she chooses to go to a motel, it's her business."

"There was a murder in this motel."

"Now you're telling me she had something to do with a murder?"

"No, Mrs. Stafford, I'm not. I'm simply following up on a phone tip. Do you know what time your daughter got home the night before last?"

"I'd have to think about it, I guess."

"We're not accusing her of anything, Mrs. Stafford. We just have to check this out."

"Who was murdered?"

"A sales rep named Benedict."

"A sales rep? But Jenny doesn't hang out with people like that."

As soon as she spoke, she knew she'd put her thought the wrong way. A tiny smirk appeared in the corners of Detective Ryan's mouth. "People like that." That phrase had identified Molly as the snob the detective had probably suspected. And now had confirmed.

"As I said, we're just checking things out, Mrs. Stafford."

"They used my daughter's name?"

"Yes, they did, if you mean the tipster, Mrs. Stafford."

"Jenny Stafford? The daughter of *Tom* Stafford?"

"Yes, Mrs. Stafford. Jenny Stafford, the daughter of Tom Stafford."

"I just don't understand why anybody would make a phone call like that."

Detective Ryan shrugged. "There are two possibilities. One, it was a prank, somebody who knows your daughter and wanted to have a little fun."

"Fun?"

"Fun as *they* saw it. Not fun for the police, and not fun for you and your family."

"And what's the other possibility?"

"The other possibility is that the tipster was somebody who

DAUGHTER OF DARKNESS

sincerely believed that he saw your daughter leaving the motel that night."

"If he was so sincere, why didn't he leave his name?"

"Tipsters rarely do. They don't want to get involved."

"He could've been wrong. Maybe it was just somebody who *looked* like Jenny."

"Very possibly, Mrs. Stafford. Eyewitnesses aren't all that reliable."

"See? You said it yourself. This must be a mistake."

"I'm sure it is, too, Mrs. Stafford. All I really need to know is where Jenny was the other night and what time she got in. And I *would* like to talk to her if I could." The detective reached inside her blazer and took out a standard business card. No fancy logo, no fancy script. Black type and white card. It identified her as a member of the Chicago PD, and listed her work phone and home phone. She set it in the middle of the table. "Tell her, I'd appreciate a call."

"I'm sure she was home by eleven," Molly said a little too quickly. "I just remembered."

"By eleven? You're sure?"

"Yes, positive." Molly wanted to clear the air. And she'd done it. Jenny *hadn't* come home until well into the night, but who was to know? Eileen would never tell. The only other person who knew was the cab driver who'd brought her home. And how would the police ever find out about *him?*

For the first time, the detective smiled. It was a coldly appraising smile. It was easy to see that she knew Molly was lying. She said again, "You're sure?"

"Oh, yes. Sure."

"Well, then, there we are."

"So you won't need to speak to Jenny?"

"Oh, just a quick phone call is all, Mrs. Stafford." She pointed to the business card that still sat between them on the table.

"But if I remember now, I don't see why you need to speak to Jenny."

"Just a formality," the detective said. "Just a quick call is all I need."

The cold smile remained on her lips all the way to the study door. "Just please be sure to have her call me."

Chapter Twenty-Nine

A panty-sniffer would be nice, Priscilla Bowman was thinking. Or a junkie. Or just a plain old garden variety bisexual. Or even a kleptomaniac.

But no. Today was divorce day in her office. And divorced people tended to say the same things over and over, an endless monotonous repetition of he said-she said, he did-she did. Gay couples were no different. Yada yada yada.

At least, she was winding up her day. Only five minutes to go with Heather Tompkins. And then freedom.

Heather was the spoiled daughter of inherited wealth, three generations of strapping Irishmen who'd cheated their way into dominant position on the docks of Chicago. Not that this background sullied Heather. She'd been sent to private school in Switzerland, and to Brown back here in the states. She was bright, polished, and relentlessly sexual. At age twenty-two—after an admittedly wild time as a single in LA—she'd married staid New England banking money and begun producing a brood of good-looking but intellectually dull children. She always said to Priscilla, and without a smidge of humility, they got my looks and their father's brains. And father's brains were largely the problem here. At thirty-five, (this being Heather's version), he'd become an old man. The only exercise he ever got, she once claimed, was passing gas after every meal. She also said that he'd flunked his bar exam four times before finally passing, which should have told her something. Because of his father's connections, the son had been made a partner in a most prestigious Gold Coast law firm, but he was never given anything more important than low-level trust funds to handle. He had lost interest in sex, in going out for fun weekends, and in bringing home all the neat surprise gifts he once lavished upon his "wifey" (as he always called her).

With all the money involved, with all the high society involved, you'd think this would be at least mildly titillating to Priscilla. But it wasn't. Because divorces, whether they involved the milkman or the governor of the state, were all pretty much the same. Cotton sheets from Penney's or silk sheets from Neiman Marcus, the tale was drearily similar.

Sex might be the thing Heather liked most, but talking uninterrupted came in a close second. She had spent her hour today reporting on one of her many infidelities, this at the country club the other night where she'd "done" a man and he'd "done" her in the back seat of his van while Don The Drone (as she frequently referred to her husband) was at the bar discussing the recent layoffs at J.P. Morgan and what they portended for the market in general. Like many men, Heather was of the mind that as long as there was no penetration, no actual sexual act had been committed.

Now she was winding down for the session, talking about her forthcoming high school reunion. She was trying to think of some way of keeping her husband at home. She'd have a lot more fun going by herself. They both understood what she meant by fun. What she wanted, in bringing up the subject of her going alone to the reunion, was Priscilla's approval. That was the big difference between going to confession and going to a shrink. Sometimes the shrink *approved* of you committing a sin.

But Priscilla didn't approve. All she said was, "You're the one who has to make that decision, Heather."

"Well, maybe I wouldn't be making decisions like this if he was a better husband."

"Maybe. Again, I can't decide for you."

"You don't approve, do you?"

"I'm not here to approve or disapprove."

"You know, that's such bullshit. I mean, I'm sorry for being so blunt. But it really *is* so much bullshit. You always say that, that you're not here to approve or disapprove, but I can always tell when when you like something and when you don't."

And then the time was up, Priscilla's small gold Bulova wristwatch chiming the hour discreetly.

"I hate that damned thing," Heather said.

"My watch?"

"Yes, your watch. I mean, if it's going to *ring,* it should *ring.* But it just make that tiny little noise. It's irritating is what it is. I'm sorry."

"No reason to be sorry."

"I'm starting my period."

"Really?" Priscilla said drolly. "I hadn't noticed." And then felt guilty. True, Heather was a lousy wife. But her husband was an equally lousy mate. She shouldn't be so judgmental when it came to Heather. Girls just want to have fun.

At the open door, Heather apologized three times and then gave Priscilla a Hollywood-style air kiss. "I'll be a lot nicer next week." Then she was gone.

In Priscilla's office, the phone rang. She prayed it wasn't an emergency, somebody with a slashed wrist, or a compulsion to jump off a tall building or swallow forty-seven Prozacs.

She went in and picked up. Glenda, her secretary-receptionist, would be gone by now. She didn't blame her. Glenda had three kids and tried very hard to be a good mother. She rarely got to leave at the appointed hour and frequently had to stay very late, letting her husband get the kids at the sitter and start dinner at home.

She picked up, and a familiar voice said, "She's all over the news."

"I noticed that."

"Every cop in Chicago is looking for her."

"Yes," Priscilla said. "Poor Jenny."

"Oh, yes," the voice responded. "Poor Jenny. Isn't it just terrible?"

"You're really enjoying this, aren't you?"

"Aren't you?"

Patricia smiled. "Yes; yes, I guess I am."

Chapter Thirty

IN the restaurant booth behind them, a woman who looked as if she would soon be a guest on one of the trashier talk shows ("My Hubby was Humpin' my Stepdaughter And Withinholdin' Hisself From Me!") was chastising her son for not eating all his food. "You don't eat that food, John Henry, Momma's gonna take you out to the car and slap you so hard your mouth'll start bleedin'." That had been the first threat. The second one had gone: "You know what yer gonna make yer Momma do, John Henry? Yer gonna make your Momma take you out to the car and use that switchblade Daddy keeps in the glove compartment." The latest, just now, ran: "John Henry, you're lucky I don't pour gasoline all over your arm and light it."

Jenny laughed. She had a nice, soft laugh and it was nice to hear it. "I think she should at least drown him."

"Or disembowel him."

"Or draw and quarter him."

"Or hang him."

"Or crucify him."

"You just got to teach these kids today a lesson," he said. Then, "Where's a social worker when you really need one?"

"God, don't mention social workers to my father. He hates them."

"Well, I'm not crazy about a lot of them," he said. "I had to work with some of them back in my cop days. Most of them were lazy and sanctimonious and didn't know what they were doing. The day I gave up was when a social worker recommended returning an eight-year-old girl to the same stepfather who'd been molesting her for two years. The social worker had interviewed the father twice and thought she'd 'changed' him."

Just then, the noise of a sharp slap overwhelmed all the other sounds in the family restaurant. The sound sickened both Coffey and Jenny. John Henry started to cry but Momma said, "You cry, and you get another one, y'hear me?" John Henry quit crying.

She loomed over their booth a few seconds later, Momma did, a chunky, unkempt woman with wild, graying hair and a soiled pink running suit so tight it show every ounce of excess flesh the woman carried. But it was the eyes that got Coffey. They should have been crazed, angry eyes. Instead, they were ineffably sad eyes, eyes that revealed that she had been raised just as brutally as she was now raising John Henry. Coffey didn't quite hate her anymore. He just wished there were some way of getting John Henry away from her.

She stuffed John Henry's arms into a tiny denim jacket—he couldn't have been more than two years old—and then yanked him savagely down the aisle, toward the front of the restaurant and the cash register.

When he looked over at Jenny, he saw that she was watching the John Henry episode with tears in her eyes.

"I'm sorry," Coffey said, "that kind of stuff can really get you down."

She shook her head. "It's not just that. It's memories of being in the psychiatric hospital. Some of the patients there. They were pretty sad."

Then she told him about Quinlan, her doctor, and how he'd fallen in love with her and pursued her romantically all the time she was hospitalized. When she told her parents, they thought she was just confusing professional concern for seduction.

"I've never met anybody like him," she said as they sat quietly, listening to the sounds of the restaurant winding down for the night, busboys loading up rubber tubs with dirty dishes, waitresses wiping down booths and tables, the cashier ringing up the last sales of the day. "First of all, he's one of the most handsome men I've ever seen. Sort of an Ivy League version of Warren Beatty. His charisma is really sexual as much as anything else and women fall in love with him instantly. Second of all, he's one of the smoothest talkers I've ever heard. He can

DAUGHTER OF DARKNESS

tell you very strange things and make them seem perfectly reasonable and sensible. He has that gift. And third of all, he's a very sympathetic listener. When he focuses on you, you feel completely flattered. And when he tries to help you with a problem you're struggling with, he offers you a little advice, and everything seems to be fine. At the time, anyway. He just seems so wise and—profound. There's no other way to say it."

"Sounds like he should run for President."

"This is all before you get to know him very well."

"I see."

"*After* you get to know him is a very different matter. He spends a good share of the day talking on the phone to his stockbroker, and the other part seducing all the pretty young things who come into the hospital. It's sort of an initiation rite, having a thing."

"You sound cynical."

"I am," she said, her voice steel. "Very cynical. I walked past his office one day and saw him making out with the one of the other patients."

She stared down at her cup. She'd passed on the last round of coffee the waitress offered. Too much coffee gave her gas and indigestion.

"I wouldn't sleep with him. As I said, I found him very appealing and seductive but I immediately felt that there was something wrong with all the women sleeping with him."

"He could be reported to the medical board and lose his license."

"I don't think so. He's *very* well connected. He's a good personal friend of the governor, for instance. He runs his place like a private domain. Plus, he's been very successful in treating criminally-insane patients. He's an important man."

"So Quinlan gave up on seducing you?"

She stared at her empty coffee cup for a silent time, then said slowly, "He could have drugged me. But that wouldn't have been good for his ego. He needed to feel he'd *conquered* me." She smiled. "He told people that I wouldn't sleep with him because I was insane. I'd made the mistake of telling him that I was hearing voices from time to time."

"Voices in your head?"

"Yes."

Coffey thought of what his shrink friend had said about

Jenny being a multiple. But how this multiple seemed artificially imposed somehow, like brainwashing.

"Any other symptoms?" he said.

"Symptoms?"

"Sounds like you were having a psychotic episode of some kind."

"I think he was putting something in my water or something like that."

"Possibly." He didn't want to tell her what Hal thought. Not yet, anyway. "So when did you leave the hospital?"

"After I'd been there ten months, I couldn't take it anymore. I started having blackouts."

"Blackouts?"

"You know how you get sometimes when you drink too much and can't quite remember the night before?"

"Uh-huh."

"Well, that was happening to me. And also these really terrible nightmares."

"What about?"

She hesitated. "About killing people."

"Anybody in particular?"

"A lot of people. People I loved, that was the strange thing."

"Your mother and father?"

"Yes, I'm ashamed to say."

"And David Foster?"

"Oh, yes, he was in there, too."

"So then you decided to leave."

She nodded. "Yes, my folks thought that I should stay. Quinlan insisted I wasn't 'complete' yet. But I finally pushed hard enough that my parents took me out of there and brought me back home."

She checked her wristwatch. "My mother is very worried about me these days. I really should call her."

"I'll be right here."

"I really appreciate all this, Coffey. I really do."

While she went off to call her mother, Coffey sat there and went through the conversation he'd had with Hal Ford about multiple personalities. He then thought for some time about Linda Fleming and how Ford thought she'd been "artificially imposed" on Jenny.

And then he thought about the dead man in the Econo-Nite Motel. Could you brainwash somebody into becoming a killer? The old answer was no.

Coffey wondered what the new, up-to-date answer was.

Chapter Thirty-One

DAVID Foster appreciated the pains Cummings took *not* to look like a private investigator.

Start with the office. It looked like a dentist worked here. Very bright reception area. A variety of family-oriented magazines on the coffee table, everything from *Time* to *TV Guide*. The walls covered with family-style framed paintings—a babbling brook, a Christmas scene, a football Saturday afternoon. The music was the same kind of stuff you heard on the elevators in the very best business centers. And the furnishings—a desk, six chairs, a coffee table and a small couch—had the professional impersonality of successful businesses everywhere.

Then there was Cummings himself. The carefully trimmed (if thinning) brown hair, the three-piece blue suit, the blue button-down shirt, the blue-yellow-white regimental striped tie, and the black wingtips all bespoke a successful businessman. Not a thug. Not a keyhole peeper. Not a shakedown artist.

Cummings had just poured them bourbon from an elegant, cut-glass decanter. He was just settling in behind his desk, as Foster was just settling in on the other side of the desk, when the phone rang.

Cummings picked up and said, "I'm a little busy right now, honey." Beat. "I know what day it is, sweetheart." Beat. "Of course our anniversary means something to me, darling." Beat. "As soon as I can, hon. And I'll pick up a good bottle of wine, too." Beat. "Love you, too. You know I do." He hung up and looked at Foster. "When she met me, I was just a cop. The investigative firm was her idea. We've had a hell of a good run, my wife and I."

Then, without changing his tone of voice or his position in

his chair, he said, "So I'm sorry about getting you over here so late tonight. But I thought you'd better see what I've come up with. I'm still having a hard time believing it myself."

So Cummings walked him through it. It was complicated and at several points, Foster wanted to stop him and say, "No, this is impossible." But he didn't. He listened. For one thing, Cummings had a very good reputation among Chicago's elite. You wanted a good private investigator, you hired Cummings. He was not only competent (ten years in Army Intelligence, ending his career when the Berlin Wall came down because Intelligence wasn't much fun without the Commies around), but he was also discreet (he served two months in jail for contempt rather than reveal the name of the man who'd hired him for a certain job) and relentless (two years ago, he literally blackmailed a key state senator into changing his vote on a certain issue). So when Cummings talked, people listened. And for a second thing, Foster was paying him a whole hell of a lot of money.

In all, Cummings spent thirty-five minutes laying it all out for Foster. And when he finished, he sat back in his leather, executive-style chair and said, "You don't believe it, do you?"

"It's mind-boggling."

"It sure is."

"How the hell did you find all this out?"

"It's what you pay me for, Mr. Foster. To find out."

"I'm going to need some time to—absorb this. Then I have to figure out what I'm going to do with it."

"I knew you'd be shocked. *I'd* certainly be shocked."

"I still have some doubts. I mean, what you were saying is—"

"I'd have doubts, too, Mr. Foster."

"Really?"

"Hell, yes, I'd have doubts. Somebody told me something as far-fetched as all this seems, I'd have *plenty* of doubts. But since I'm the investigator here, and since this is my work, I'm in the position of knowing it's true. Every word of it."

"Wow."

"Some more bourbon?"

"Please."

Cummings picked up the cut-glass decanter and poured them more bourbon. Then he settled back and said, "You're going to need some help figuring out how to handle this."

"I sure am."

"I can help you with that, too."

"Really?" He felt like a child in the presence of a wise man.

"But we'll have to be very careful."

"I know it," Foster said. "That's what scares me. I could lose everything here."

"Everything and *everybody*," Cummings said.

"God, yes, *everybody* for sure."

Cummings said, "What was that?"

"What was what?"

Cummings touched a finger to his lips. He reached over carefully and eased open the top right-hand drawer of the desk. He took out a small, silver-plated hand gun. Foster knew nothing about guns. This one looked fierce, a little angry bulldog of a weapon.

Cummings pushed back soundlessly from the desk. Stood up. He moved around the desk with grace and speed but absolute quiet. Not a sound.

He walked on tiptoe to the door leading to the reception room.

He put his ear to the door, listened. Then he waved for Foster to stand up, to move away from his direct line in front of the door.

Foster, starting to get scared now, did as Cummings wanted. He went over and stood by the window.

Cummings continued to listen with his ear to the door. Foster still couldn't hear anything more than the usual sounds of an office building at night, the whine of a distant elevator, a toilet flushing several offices away, a vacuum cleaner far down the hall.

Cummings reached over and clicked the lights off. Except for moonlight and some residual light from the office buildings surrounding this one, Cummings' office was completely dark.

Foster decided that standing next to the window probably wasn't a good idea. He tiptoed over to where a bank of three new four-door filing cabinets stood. He crouched down beside them.

He considered the possibility that Cummings was paranoid. Paranoia was probably an occupational hazard among private investigators. He could simply have gone to the door and said, "Who's out there?" couldn't he?

Foster was starting to feel ridiculous. It was like a child's game. Bad Guys vs. Good Guys. Crouch behind a tree and shoot Timmy or Billy or Bobby with your cap gun. As a kid, Foster had played shoot-'em-up a million times. You developed a fondness for it. Maybe Cummings had developed a fondness for it he couldn't shake. Maybe he took every opportunity to play it he saw. Such as tonight.

Maybe it was nobody more sinister in the outer office than a cleaning woman.

The lights came back on.

"What happened?" Foster said.

"He left."

"Who left?"

"The guy who came here to hurt us."

"The guy?"

"It could be a chick, I suppose. There are more and more hit chicks these days."

"Hit chicks?" Foster said.

All the care Cummings had taken to buff his image as a serious, honest, credible private investigator—the nice office, the expensive suits, the laid-back manner—had lost its luster over the past few minutes.

The guy was a nut case. At least that's how Foster saw things now. There hadn't *been* anybody in the outer office, at least not as far as Foster was concerned. And taking a gun. And hiding by the door. And turning out the lights. And talking about a "hit chick." Wow. The guy was a fruitcake.

Now, Foster didn't believe anything Cummings had told him tonight. Not a word. Cummings' tale was nothing more than the paranoid little-boy fantasies of a self-deluded Good Guy.

"Let's get out of here," Cummings said. The edge was still in his manner, in his speech. "He'll try for us again."

"I thought you said it was a chick."

"I said *maybe* it was a chick."

"I see."

"I know you're skeptical, Foster. But believe me, I know what I'm doing." He dropped the gun in the pocket of his suit coat. "Let's go."

Three minutes later, they were stepping aboard an elevator car. Seven minutes later, they were taking the walkway to the garage where their vehicles were parked. Ten minutes later, Cummings had reached his new Mercedes Benz sedan and was starting to say good night to Foster.

"You still look a little skeptical about this, my friend," Cummings said, as he put his hand on the door handle of his new Benz. "Believe me, given what we know now, both our lives are in danger. Both of them."

That's when the first shot was fired. It was explosive and loud in the echoing walls of the parking garage. One moment, Cummings was a composed if frightened businessman. The next, he was a frantic animal. When the bullet ripped into his head, he jerked to the right, eyes already rolling back into his head, and sent forth a pathetic little cry that was almost completely lost in the echoing gunshot. Then he spun around, and collapsed on his car, sliding down the door slowly, leaving a smear of blood in his wake.

Foster found himself processing a great deal of information over the next three seconds: so Cummings hadn't been paranoid, so everything Cummings had told him was true, so now there was a hit man—or a hit chick, in Cummings' ludicrous parlance—who meant to do Foster harm, too.

Should he run? Should he pitch himself under a car? Should he throw his arms up and shout that he'd cooperate?

The bullet made the decision for him.

The gun was raised, aimed, fired.

The bullet entered Foster's head a quarter-inch below the cerebral cortex and continued on from there, exploding silken tissue, cracking white bone.

Foster fell only a foot or so from where Cummings was sprawled, facedown, on the oil-stained concrete floor of the parking garage.

PART THREE

Chapter Thirty-Two

COFFEY knew right away something was wrong.

He'd been sitting there watching the staff put the restaurant back in order, remembering now that he'd promised his sister Jan he'd check out her house, when Jenny came back from calling her folks. She looked pale and shaken.

"The police found my car where I'd parked it near the motel. They took fingerprints off it and then compared them to the prints on the knife and in the room. Now, they want to talk to me. A homicide detective named Ryan."

"Good old Detective Ryan," Coffey said sourly.

"You know her?"

"I've talked to her a few times." He didn't elaborate.

Desperation had given her face taut angles. "They're going to arrest me, aren't they?"

"Possibly."

"My mother wants me to come home and have a talk with the family lawyer."

"That's something you should think about. Being on the run when the police are looking for you—"

She reached across the table and took his hand. "If I killed him, I'm willing to take my punishment. I won't have much choice. But what if I didn't kill him? The police'll convict me anyway. That's what's so scary about this."

"You need a place to hide," he said.

She nodded. "Maybe I could check into a motel someplace."

He shook his head. "This is a big news story. The police have probably issued a statement saying they'd like to talk to you as a material witness."

"What's a material witness?"

"It's usually a ruse. They use that term when they're looking for a suspect. They make it sound as friendly as possible, hoping he'll turn himself in."

Then he said, "Jan's."

"What?"

"My sister's. I told her on the phone the other day that I'd swing by her house. It's partially furnished. They had to move to Omaha. My brother-in-law got a better job there, and they had to leave in a hurry. They've been planning to have the rest of the furniture shipped to them, but they haven't gotten around to it yet. There's a bed and a couch, and the heat and lights are still on."

"That sounds great. I'd really appreciate it." She paused, then asked, "But how am I ever going to find out about what happened in the motel that night?"

"I'm going to help you."

She touched his hand again. "Oh, God, Coffey. I don't want to drag you into this. It's not fair to you."

"I'll get a novel out of it."

"You will, really?"

He smiled. "Sure. So this is kind of like doing research. Plus which, I get to see what life is like from the point of view of a hardened criminal."

He'd made a joke. All it produced was a wan and nervous expression in the tired eyes of Jenny Stafford.

"I guess that wasn't very funny," he said.

"I'm afraid I'm not very receptive right now." She made sudden fists of her hands. "After I saw Hal, I thought about just giving up. That's sort of what I've done all my life. Just given up—or given in. But this pisses me off. I want to find out what's going on here. I'm not going to give up this time."

She slid into his arms, and they held each other silently for several minutes. He liked her new resolve. He liked the side of Jenny he was seeing now.

Five minutes later, they were driving toward Kenwood, the neighborhood next to Hyde Park. In the old days, the mansions that lined several of the streets had been the bane of all Chicago society. Then affluence found other places to settle and the Kenwood area became less fashionable—or at least less sought after. But fifteen years ago, a measured urban renewal plan had been set in motion and today the old neighborhood was once again fresh, vital, and dignified. Jan had lived in one of the middle-class enclaves on the edges of Kenwood, a forty-year-old cottage-style house that she'd taken great pride in. She'd fixed it up beautifully.

And Jenny noted this fact as Coffey pulled into the driveway, headlights giving the small, tidy house a moment of snapshot illumination. He cut the headlights immediately.

The sound of the season's last crickets; the scent of newly mown grass from next door; the faint, throbbing pulse of a bass line in a rock and roll record from far down the block—all this data Coffey took in as he stood at the side door, inserting key into lock.

The house smelled fresh and clean. Moonlight painted the kitchen in deep, moon-shifting shadows. A faucet dripped, the sound hollow.

Coffey, feeling Jenny next to him, remembered what it was like to get home after a night at the movies, wife and daughter in tow, and that wonderful feeling of *belonging* to someone. He felt a little of that now. He wanted to hold Jenny, just hold her—he sensed that kissing her would spook her for now—just hold her, feel her warmth. But this wasn't the time. He showed her around the house. He'd brought a flashlight in from the car and, after his tour of Jan's place, handed the long, silver-handled flashlight over to her.

"The biggest problem is that the phone doesn't work," he said, "and you don't have a car. If you absolutely have to have a phone, go next door to the Carstairs. They're very nice people. Tell them you're doing a little housesitting for Jan. Tell them you knew her in college."

"You're not going to stay here?"

"I'll be back later. I want to talk to a reporter I know who did some stories on your guru friend. See what he's been up to lately—this reporter I know keeps pretty good track of him."

She looked around the house. "This is really a nice place."

"Jan loved it."

She surprised him not only by moving closer but by sliding her arms around his middle and hugging him. "I have a feeling we both need this right now."

"I charge by the hour."

"For hugging?"

"Yeah, but they're very reasonable rates."

They held each other, and it was wonderful.

They heard the car before they saw it. In the driveway. Pulling almost equal with the side door. Headlights ablaze.

Coffey, with great reluctance, moved from Jenny's arms to the kitchen window.

Just as he reached it, the car pulled out again. But it wasn't a car. It was a van. A dark green Ford van.

"Damn," he said.

"What?"

He told her who'd been in the drive. He stayed at the window until they backed out of the drive and pulled away from the house, disappearing into the night.

"Any word from the Traffic Bureau on the van?" she said.

"Only that it's a leased van. He's checking into who the lease was signed by." Coffey checked his watch. "I'm going to call him at home."

"This late?"

"It's just ten. That should be all right."

He reached behind his back and took the gun from his belt. "You keep this."

"God, Coffey, I don't know anything about guns."

"You will."

He gave her a good five-minute crash course on how to use this particular weapon. The lecture and demonstration were almost as simple as point and shoot. After he finished with the gun, he put on the alarm system he'd disarmed when they'd come in. He showed her how to activate it and told her to put it on the moment he left.

At the door, after finishing up with the alarm system, he found himself standing very close to her. He could no longer resist the impulse. He took her into his arms and kissed her. He felt her instant response, the open mouth, the soft fingers on his neck, the warm and supple feeling of her body pressed against his.

"Remember the gun," he said.

"Right."

"And the alarm."

"Uh-huh."

"And the Carstairs if you need—"

"—a phone. I liked that, by the way."

"Oh?"

"The kiss, I mean."

"Oh. Well, I liked it, too."

She slid her arms around him again and squeezed herself to him. "I just wanted to let you know that."

He held her for thirty seconds or so, then turned the knob on the side door. "I'll be back in a few hours."

He drove around a three-block area looking for the dark green Ford van. Not finding anything, he headed back toward the city.

Chapter Thirty-Three

HALLAHAN'S was a journalist's bar where such esteemed Chicago ink wretches as Ben Hecht and Charlie McArthur had all hoisted more than a few. With such a tradition, Ned Hallahan, III, grandson of the original owner, was able to argue that actually fixing up the dump would be to despoil history. So the john didn't work, the foot rail along the bottom of the bar had been wobbly for at least two decades, and the bar stools had holes in the seat padding that looked as if giant mutated rats had been munching on them all night. But the place had spirit and no amount of lousy decor, bad lighting, and numerous health code violations could take away from that.

Neely was late. But then Neely was *always* late. Coffey sat in a booth by himself, listening to the sixties songs on the jukebox ("Eve of Destruction" had been a piece of crap then and was a piece of crap now) and eavesdropping on the conversations all around him. Somewhere in Coffey's first novel was an ironic little paragraph about the topics of men's conversations as they progressed through their decades. In your twenties, you talked about getting laid. In your thirties, you talked about getting laid *and* getting a promotion. In your forties, you talked about getting a promotion *and* some of the health tests you were starting to have. In your fifties, you talked about some of the health tests you were starting to have *and* all the snot-nosed twenty-five-year-olds who were always talking about getting laid. And in your sixties you started talking about your grandkids and death. And not death in general, either. No death-as-an-abstraction, no death-comes-to-us-all. Real death. Specific death. *Your own* death, hard as that was to imagine, impossible as it was to accept. Extinction, was what you were really saying. What the hell had ever happened to that smart-ass twenty-year-old who used to think of nothing but getting laid? It had been a long, long time since you'd seen him in your mirror, that was for sure.

Neely arrived half an hour late. "Sorry."

"You always are."

Neely sat down and signaled across the shadowy bar to the bartender. After all these years, the man behind the bar was well-acquainted with Neely's needs, shot of rye with beer chaser. No doubt just what his granddad drank back in County Cork.

Neely kept up with the times. During the twenty years Coffey had known him, Neely had been, variously, a hippie, a disco lady killer, and was now something resembling a boomer, the expensive double-breasted suit, the hundred dollar haircut (sideburns shaved straight across far up on the ear) and the overwhelming aftershave. He'd always been one of those ridiculously good looking guys whose appearance misled many into thinking he was a creampuff. These days he looked like a suburban lothario who had spent one too many afternoons in a sleazy hotel with the wife of a close friend. Nothing is sadder to see than lover boys (or lover girls, for that matter) giving way to flesh and age. He had four kids by three wives and was always half a step ahead of all the loan companies he was in hock to. Anyway, not even the loan companies wanted his business, which was pretty sad given the fact that he was one of the city's ablest and best-known reporters. In the future, he'd probably have to start taking out juice loans. Someday, one of the juice loans would cost him his life. The mob loved to make examples of prominent people who didn't pay up.

"We had to tear out part of the front page," Neely said.

"Must be big."

"Very big. You know a private investigator named Cummings?"

"Sure. He's the one who works for all the rich people."

"Not anymore, he doesn't. Somebody killed him tonight. In a parking garage."

Coffey tensed.

"They killed a client, too. Guy named David Foster."

Coffey almost physically jerked at the mention of the name.

He could feel himself become colder, as if his body temperature was dropping quickly.

"You all right?" Neely said.

"Yeah."

"You look terrible."

"So do you."

"Yeah, but the difference is I cultivate it, Coffey. I'm too old to be the male ingenue anymore, so now I have to be the mysterious older man. It's sort of like changing from a young Robert Redford into an older Robert Mitchum. The ladies love it."

"How's Emily?"

For a minute, Neely forgot he was a lover boy, and that he'd almost won the Pulitzer twice, and that he was getting old and scared. He actually even forgot entirely about himself for this brief time. Emily was his daughter. She'd been born with cerebral palsy. Neely loved her with a ferocity and protectiveness that redeemed all the other bullshit in his soul. "She's getting along pretty good. They're making some progress, the scientists, I mean. People make fun of Jerry Lewis, but he does a damn good job for the cause. He really does." Then, and incredibly there were tears in his eyes, he reached inside his stylish suit coat and brought out a folded sheet of white paper. He opened it up. A pink crayon drawing of a birthday cake with the words HAPPY BIRTHDAY, DADDY! were scrawled across the face of the paper. "Emily drew it for me." His love for his eight-year-old daughter overwhelmed Coffey and for once, he actually felt a fondness for Neely.

Neely made a kind of sniffling sound, tears, and then reverently folded the paper and put it away. And then he went back to being the Neely everybody knew and hated. "So how come you wanted to see me, Coffey?"

At the moment, Coffey really wanted to talk about Cummings and his murder. But that wasn't why he was here. "Quinlan."

"The shrink slash ass-bandit."

"Yeah."

Neely smiled icily. "I wonder how much ass that guy has gotten in his lifetime. The word is he makes it with most of his female patients."

"That I've heard. Tell me something about him I *haven't* heard."

Neely told Coffey about Quinlan's CIA connections. How he did ground-breaking work with mind control and behavior modification. Then they fired Quinlan.

"Why?" Coffey asked.

"Well, as usual with the CIA, nobody knows for sure. But there were a lot of rumors that Quinlan was even more radical than the people before him. He started working with career criminals, trying to change their inclinations. And then— though there was never any proof of this—that he started doing the opposite, too."

"What's the opposite?"

"Demonstrating that he could take an average, decent person and make him capable of being a criminal."

"In other words, he could turn criminals into law-abiding people, and law-abiding people into criminals."

"Essentially, yes."

"Did it work?" Coffey said.

"Again, all I've got is rumors. The word is that he had some success, but that several of his patients ended up in mental institutions for the rest of their lives."

"Fortunes of war as the CIA sees it."

"Exactly."

Coffey thought instantly of what Hal had said about Jenny's two personalities, how one of them seemed artificially imposed. Mind-controlling drugs and psychotherapy would be one combined way to impose such a personality. As Hal had said, that sort of mental manipulation went back to at least the Korean War.

"Anyway, he came back to Chicago and set up a psychiatric practice. Strictly carriage trade. There used to be a joke about him that you had to bring your stock portfolio with you when you went for your first visit. His lifestyle got a lot better, too. He actually bought himself a Maserati, every boy's ultimate wet dream. He dated all the society women, too. If you remember the mid-eighties, there was kind of a trend back to the forties. Night clubs and dinner jackets and things like that. Well, our friend Quinlan reveled in all that stuff."

"Then he opened his psychiatric hospital?"

Neely laughed. "Better known as Joliet East." Joliet was the state prison. "If you were rich enough and in trouble enough, Quinlan could get you shunted into his hospital. Your trial would either be put off indefinitely or the state would just forget about you."

"You'd stay in the hospital?"

"Right. But unless you were completely uncontrollable—and some of them are—you could get used to life there real easily. It's the psychiatric equivalent of a country club prison. They even have weekly conjugal visits."

"A big family name like Stafford?"

Neely grinned. "Jenny Stafford was everything, man. Money and beauty. That's about the time I first started writing about him and his hospital. He was really smitten for a long time. The word I got from the hospital people inside was that Quinlan has sexual relationships with all the women when they come in. They usually don't last very long. He gets tired of them and then hands them off to one of his lieutenants. But I'm told that with Jenny Stafford it was different. He really seemed to be smitten for a time. He kept her for several months."

"Nice of him," Coffey said, trying to keep any bitterness from his voice.

"You ever see Jenny Stafford?"

"Once, I guess," Coffey lied.

"Well, I'd keep her for a lot longer than a few months. Or I think I would, anyway. I guess she's pretty screwed up." He tapped a finger against his skull to indicate crazy. "She convinced her parents to take her out of there. They found this other shrink."

"Priscilla Bowman?"

"Yeah, how'd you know that, Coffey?"

"I just picked it up somewhere, I guess."

"Well, do you get the irony?"

"What irony?"

"Don't you know who Priscilla Bowman is? Or was?"

"I guess not."

"She was Quinlan's old associate, the one he turned his psychiatric practice over to."

"And she took over Jenny Stafford?"

"Who better? Bowman had worked with Stafford for several years. She knew the various techniques he used. She'd even fallen under the sway of his CIA techniques for a while."

"So why was she helping the Stafford family?"

"L-o-v-e. She'd had this on-again off-again thing with our friendly guru Quinlan when they were still working together. I guess she seriously thought he was going to march her down the aisle someday. But his zipper problem got to be too much for her. So working on Jenny was a kind of spite. Rubbing his face in one of his failures."

"That's why they had the falling out?"

"I guess he's pretty hard to work with, too. She just got tired of being treated like a servant instead of an associate."

"I'll be damned," Coffey said.

The bartender automatically replenished their drinks.

"Think you can handle two Diet Pepsis in a row?" Neely said.

"I'll give it my best."

Neely knocked back his fresh shot of rye, shuddered orgasmically, and then said, "So what's your interest in all this?"

"My next novel."

"Say, that's right. I forgot. I keep thinking you're still a cop." A sip of beer. "By the way, I really liked your first novel except I guessed the killer about halfway through."

Coffey laughed. "I'll try harder next time." He checked his watch. "Well, I'd better go." He dropped a ten-dollar bill on the table. "Here's for the drinks."

"Hey, you don't need to do that," Neely said. But the hungry way he scooped the money up told Coffey how appreciative Neely was.

"Give your daughter a kiss for me," Coffey said.

"Thanks, Coffey."

Chapter Thirty-Four

THE Ford van had been parked across the street for forty-five minutes now, ever since Coffey had left. A couple of bored boys, ages eight and six respectively, thought of getting up on the bumper and trying to see past the dark-tinted windows. But there was something ominous about the van—what was the strange flat black box on its roof, and why did the van make that faint humming noise?—so they decided to work their way down the street to find something else to interest them.

***

The headache was so bad it woke her up. She lay, for a time, concerned only about her headache and how it might have gotten so bad.

Nothing to drink, that she could recall. No flu. Or any other kind of sickness. No special stress came to mind either.

So what was the headache all about?

She sat up in bed. Bra and panties were all she wore. The funny thing was, these didn't seem to be any bra and panties she'd ever *seen* before. These were almost comically sexy underthings. They made Victoria's Secret seem downright virginal.

She stood up. Walked over to a moonlit window.

Where the hell was she?

The window was filled with several backyards. Each with an outdoor grille, a clothesline, a garage. Suburbia.

But Linda Fleming didn't *belong* in suburbia. She was a city girl. And anyway, what was she doing in this strange house? She found a black sweater and black jeans and put them on.

Not hers either. But they fit well. She then put her feet into the black flats by the bed. Capezios. Not a brand she favored. Too expensive. Flats were flats. Why pay for a brand name?

On the bureau, she found the gun. The gun took her back to her small-town days. Growing up. Her father and brother had been gun nuts. When they weren't hunting, they were cleaning their guns, or hanging out at the gun store downtown where the owner was a member of the KKK and didn't care who knew it.

The gun felt good in her hand. She wondered who had left it behind, and why.

She had an easy time with the weapon, checking it for ammunition. She'd picked up a lot of pointers from the men in her family. She wasn't a gun nut exactly, but she liked the feel of a gun in her hand. No doubt about it.

The dark house would usually have scared her. But for some reason, tonight she liked the darkness.

She left the bedroom, groped her way along a dark hallway, and then came out into a living room. She kept a firm grip on the gun as she entered this new part of the house. She had no idea what she'd find.

After the living room came the tiny dining room and then the kitchen. No sign of anybody, anything. How the hell had she *gotten* here? She didn't panic too much because she'd had other nights like this. Had a little too much to drink—or, occasionally, a little too much dope to smoke—and would then find herself in some stranger's house, with said stranger gone.

But that was usually in the morning.

At night when she woke up in a strange house, the stranger was usually next to her in bed. Snoring drunkenly.

So where was the stranger who'd brought her here, anyway?

***

The Ford van was now fixing its infrared homing device on the house. The information it received: the sole inhabitant of the house was up and moving about.

***

Linda Fleming even went to the bathroom in the dark. She still felt comforted somehow by the shadows, a dark womb.

She realized, washing her hands and wanting some lotion to put on them, that she hadn't seen her purse since waking up.

She found a purse on the kitchen table. A small, black leather Gucci bag, which probably belonged to the woman whose clothes she was wearing. She opened it up and found three crisp hundred dollar bills inside.

She smiled and then shrugged. Since she had borrowed the woman's clothes, she might as well borrow her money, too.

In fact, she thought, she might as well take the *purse* while she was at it. She left the money in the purse and then slipped the small weapon in there, too.

She started out of the kitchen but then remembered that she'd forgotten something. The thought came so abruptly that it stirred her headache again. A bolt of pain struck her right eye as she stood there.

There was something she needed in this kitchen. . . .

Twenty minutes later, a Yellow Cab pulled up ahead of the Ford van.

Linda Fleming came running out of the house and up to the cab. When she opened the door, a blast of gangsta rap music assaulted her. The driver was a shrunken old man in his late sixties. A *white* man. Go figure.

Linda got in the cab. The gangsta geeza drove them away.

Chapter Thirty-Five

MARGIE Ryan started scratching herself almost right away.

She liked to think of herself as a tough-ass cop, and in most respects she certainly was. She'd seen—and effectively dealt with—every kind of bloodshed and carnage imaginable. She had been shot at, stabbed, and nearly drowned. One time when she was working undercover, she'd nearly been gang-raped by three men who looked as if they belonged at the Abominable Snowman's family reunion. She never had a single nightmare about any of this. Not once.

But put her in a room where somebody was sneezing . . .

Margie had always wondered where her hypochondria came from. Her parents were sane and sensible Irishers who felt ill only when they truly *were* ill. Nor had this psychological malady possessed any of her five brothers and sisters. Indeed, they used to take great delight in sneezing and coughing in little Margie's face just so they could watch her go crazy with hypochondrical symptoms.

So tonight at dinner, nine-year-old Brian said, "Sister Mary Ellen said that we should tell our parents there's a lot of measles going around the school."

At which, the dinner table noise came to a halt. No serving plates were passed. No silverware clanked against china. Nine-year-old Sam didn't make any of his armpit-farting noises (if armpit-farting was an Olympic event, Sam would win at least a half dozen gold medals). Neither of the twins exchanged one of their whispered private jokes. And Mike, Margie's stout insurance salesman husband, seemed to hold his breath. He looked at his beloved wife (sixteen years next month) and said, "You don't have the measles."

"Who said I have the measles?" Margie said defensively.

"Mommy's a handcriac," five-year-old Jason said.

All the other kids giggled.

"That's 'hypochondriac,' Jason," Mike said helpfully. "And yes, she is."

"Used to be," Margie said. "No more."

Mike loved to tease her. "Then you won't have measles by the time we go to bed tonight?"

"I read an article," she said.

"An article?" Mike said.

"In *Reader's Digest*."

"I thought our subscription expired."

"It did. I happened to read this in the dentist's office the other day."

"Good old Dr. Fitzpatrick," Mike said, "he still reminds me of the dentist in *The Marathon Man*."

"We were talking about *Reader's Digest*."

"Oh, yeah, right. Sorry."

"There was an article in there about hypchondria and it really helped me."

Mike shoveled food into his face, a half pound of mashed potatoes all mooshed up with green peas. "So what's it say?" His mouth was so full, Margie could barely understand him.

"It *said*, as if you're really listening anyway, that hypochondria is just a form of stress and depression that you develop when you're young, usually as the result of a trauma."

"Isn't that what they said about Ted Bundy, too?"

"Very funny. Anyway, it's pretty clear that I started in on hypochondria when my dad died. You know, when I was six, I mean. That's how I dealt with it . . . every time I got really lonely for him, I'd start feeling sick."

The phone rang.

"I'll bet it's Amy's boy friend, Brian," Sam said. He thought it was real, real weird that anybody would find anything appealing about his ten-year-old sister Amy. To him, she was just this skinny, gawky girl with no breasts (given the men's magazine Margie had found in his drawer, it was clear Sam was already and hopelessly a boob man), braces and a shy manner that was easy to make fun of. He didn't see any of the classic beauty or the gentle wisdom that Margie saw in her eldest— and that boys in Amy's class were also starting to see. Lately, a

DAUGHTER OF DARKNESS 201

public school boy named Brian Stoller had been calling her. Amy clearly liked the kid, though she was tongue-tied whenever he phoned.

Sam hopped up from the dinner table and plucked the receiver from the yellow wall phone. He looked instantly disappointed. It wasn't for Amy, after all. It was for Mom.

Margie took it in what they called "the den" but which was actually a room with an old couch, an old armchair, a twenty-year-old Zenith color TV console, and a bookcase filled with Mike's Louis L'Amour paperbacks.

"Hello," she said.

"Hello," said the voice. Male. Unfriendly. "I'm told you're a good officer."

"May I ask who this is?" All she knew for sure was that it was somebody official. That voice, it *had* to be official.

"Commissioner Scott."

"Commissioner *Ted* Scott?"

"One and the same, Detective Ryan."

My God, why would the police commissioner be calling *her?* The thing was, when Scott wanted to chew you out, he called your Commander and *he* chewed you out.

Scott was one of the first commissioners who had ever actually been a cop, though not a very good one according to locker room scuttlebutt. And even though he'd been a cop for a few years, he was still very much of the upper classes. Not many beat cops drove back and forth to work in a new Porsche. Nor did many beat cops number among their guests at Christmas time, the mayor and his wife. Scott was the son of a prominent architect and city planner. He clearly had political ambitions. First a cop, then a police commissioner, could the governor's mansion be far behind? He was mostly seen as ineffectual, which was fine with the rank-and-file. They'd had cop lovers, who invariably got in trouble with the press for excusing any kind of scum-bag police behavior; and they'd had cop-haters, who'd gotten in trouble with the cops themselves because they generally took the side of the citizens in any dispute. Scott spent most of his time at his country club, which seemed to make just about everybody happy. That's where police commissioners *should* spend most of their time.

"I understand," the Commissioner went on, "that you met some friends of mine."

"Friends of yours?"

"The Staffords."

"Oh, yes. I mean, yes, sir, I did." She sounded as nervous as poor Amy when she talked to Brian Stoller.

"And I further understand that you suggested that they might be impeding the police investigation to find their daughter."

"No, sir, I didn't."

"Well, that was the impression you gave Molly Stafford anyway. And she didn't like it."

"I was just doing my job, sir. Just asking the questions I'd ask anybody."

"These people aren't 'anybody,' Detective Ryan."

"I see, sir."

"They're friends of mine."

"Yes, sir."

"And they don't impede police investigations."

"No, sir."

"Not even when their own daughter is involved."

"I see, sir."

"I was in Los Angeles—there was a conference for police commissioners—when you started running Jenny Stafford's photo on the tube. This is ridiculous."

"What is, sir?"

"Jenny Stafford a murderer. Why in the hell are you looking for her, anyway? I've known her all her life. She isn't a killer. And she sure as hell doesn't spend her nights at the Econo-Nite Motel, I can tell you that."

"Sir?"

"Yes."

"We found her car parked half a block away. We took prints off the steering wheel, the dashboard, and the interior of the glove compartment. We compared them to the prints found on several surfaces at the crime scene."

"And you're telling me you got a match?"

"Yes, sir, we did. But that's not all."

"Oh?"

"We also got a match from the handle of the knife itself. The one in the dead man."

"Do you have any idea who Jenny Stafford *is*, Detective Ryan?"

"She's the daughter of Tom and Molly—"

"She's *my goddaughter.*"

"Oh."

"*Now* am I making myself clear?"

"Yes, sir."

"I want you to prosecute this just as hard as you can. But I want you to make it *fast*. You understand?"

"Yes, sir."

"There's got to be some kind of logical explanation for how her fingerprints got all over that motel room."

"Yessir."

"And I want you to find out what that explanation is."

"I understand, sir."

"And I don't want you hinting to the Staffords that they're not cooperating."

"I'll make sure there's no misunderstanding, sir."

"Good."

"I'm sorry to bother you at home."

"That's quite all right."

"Now, I'll let you get back to your family."

***

Later. The kids finally asleep. Mike lying next to her.

"Honey?" he whispered.

"Huh?"

"You think you could quit doing that?"

"Doing what?"

"You know, the scratching."

"I'm scratching?"

"Uh-huh. And it's pretty loud. I can't sleep."

"I must have dry skin or something."

"It must be the measles," he said.

"Very funny."

"It's subconscious. Why you're scratching, I mean. Deep down, you think you've got the measles."

She brought her hands up, prayerlike, and tucked them under her face as she lay on her side. She couldn't scratch with her hands in this position.

Then she said, "He really pisses me off."

Mike groaned. He just wanted to sleep. "Who?"

"The Commissioner."

"He's an asshole. Forget about him and just get to sleep."

"I just keep hearing his voice. Prep school."

"He went to prep school?"

"Uh-huh. Exeter."

"Well, if you gotta go to prep school, that's a pretty good place."

"Yeah, I suppose. He just sounds so—snotty."

"Night."

"You don't give a damn."

"Honey, I'm *tired*. The regional manager's coming in tomorrow. It's not easy kissing somebody's ass all day long. It takes a lot of strength."

She laughed. God, she loved him and that dorky sense of humor of his.

"She did it," she said.

"Huh?"

"Jenny Stafford. His goddaughter. She killed that guy."

"You really think so? A society girl like her?" He yawned.

"Now, you sound like him. And hell, yes, she did it. How else did her fingerprints get all over the place?"

She waited for an answer and after about a minute or so, she got it.

Mike started snoring.

Chapter Thirty-Six

AS Coffey pulled into Jan's drive, he knew that Jenny was gone. He had cop instincts, and they were rarely wrong.

He let himself inside and called her name and heard only his own echoes.

He went through the house, continuing to call her name, knowing how useless this all was.

Where the hell would she have gone?

He had to put a brief halt to his pointless search. He needed to pee.

While he was standing over the john, he happened to glance down at the wastebasket and see a mass of tissues.

After doing his business, he brought the wastebasket up and set it on the closed toilet lid. He started pulling the tissues apart and examining each piece.

A lot of foundation, mascara, eyeliner, eyeshadow, blush, lipstick and heavy layer of powder—all of which meant one thing. She hadn't gone out tonight as Jenny Stafford, she'd gone out as Linda Fleming.

He set the wastebasket back down, washed his hands, and then went back out to the living room. He'd go looking for her, but where would he even start? She'd probably taken a cab, but tracking the correct cab could literally take all night.

He thought about going back home. But maybe he should wait here. Maybe she'd come back here. But that was probably not the case. So he might as well go home. . . .

Headlights.

He ran to the window. He hadn't turned on any lights in here. He had a clear view of the street.

But it was just a passing car, silent and lonesome-looking in the late night.

He walked over to the phone, punched in the code for retrieving messages from his phone machine at home.

One guy wanted to sell him real estate, another guy wanted him to buy diamonds.

The third message was from Detective Ryan. "I'm getting heat about Jenny Stafford, Mr. Coffey. You know how heat works, don't you, Mr. Coffey? From your cop days? Well, since *I'm* getting heat, *you're* getting heat. I'm calling from my kitchen. My daughter's about ten feet away at the table doing her homework. Math. She gets straight As in everything except math. That's her downfall subject. So any time she has to work on her math, she's in a bad mood. Which puts me in a bad mood. And then I get heat from the police commissioner on top of it. I think you can see where I'm going with this, Mr. Coffey. There are all kinds of nasty words I'd like to dump on you tonight, but I can't because my daughter's sitting so close to me and I'm too lazy to walk into the little room we call our den. So, I'm just going to say this. Tomorrow, I'm going to come and see you and you had better, by God, be ready to cooperate. I need to find Jenny Stafford and get this whole case resolved. You understand me, Mr. Coffey? Good. Now you and Jenny have yourself a good night's sleep—wherever you're hiding out—and I'll get in touch with you in the morning. Sleep tight, Mr. Coffey."

Chapter Thirty-Seven

A lot of blacks came up by bus, though some traveled by train, and still others by cars a lot older than they were. The two biggest migrations from the South came right before and right after World War II. A black poet noted that many of these travelers carried only two things, "a clean change of underwear, and an absolute passion for the blues."

The blues flourished in Chicago until the seventies, when rock and roll took over. In the old days, hearing the blues meant going to the South Side, to mostly black clubs. Today, if you want to hear the blues, you go to the North Side. The musicians are still black, but the audiences are largely white. Working-class blacks, the people about whom the music was written, can't afford to come here. You see a lot of Volvos and Saabs and Mercedes Benz sedans in the parking lot. And inside, you see a lot of American Express Gold being handed over to the waitresses and the cashiers. The blues had originally been heard by cotton pickers and wandering ex-slaves and inner city menials and burned-out prisoners in southern jails. Now the only people who could afford to hear the blues live were white advertising people, doctors, stockbrokers and mid-level government bureaucrats. So how did the musicians feel about all this change? Bluesmen have to eat, too, you know.

Linda Fleming was working the blues bars tonight. And two hours after the cab dropped her off, she finally made what looked like a promising contact.

Accountant. That's what he looked like. Nervous little guy in a three-piece rack suit, glasses that kept slipping down his little nose, and sad sad Friday night eyes. He'd been dumped recently, or something like that. You didn't have to be telepathic to guess that. Siting alone at the bar, his silent suffering was louder than the music.

The bar ran along the left side. Small tables with glowing candles sitting in the center lined the right wall. A small stage was just big enough for the five-piece band, while the dance floor could probably hold six, seven couples. She didn't see a single black customer.

She sat down next to the guy at the bar.

"Hi," she said.

He didn't look at her. "Hi."

"Great music."

"Yeah."

"You like the blues?"

He still didn't look at her. "No, I drove all the way over here because I *hate* the blues."

"Maybe I'll just keep my mouth shut."

Still not looking at her. "Maybe that's a good idea."

The bartender came, then went away to get her a scotch on the rocks. She dug in her purse and took out a package of cigarettes. She tapped one free from the pack. Then she said, "I don't have any matches."

He sighed, greatly put upon. "Here."

He groped in the pocket of his cheap dark suit and found a book of matches. He tossed the matches on the bar in front of her. She lighted her smoke and then pushed the matches back to him.

He had yet to look at her. "You keep them. That way, you won't have to bother me again."

The bartender brought her scotch. He was a light-skinned black man with curly gray hair and a wide, friendly face. "Not none of my business, ma'am, but I don't think you'll be able to do it." He nodded to the man next to her.

She smiled. "I love a challenge. But I guess I don't know what the challenge is for sure."

"The challenge is Ron here."

"Shut up, Luther," Ron said.

"He got pissed on," Luther said, "and he don't deserve it because he's a nice guy. And I ain't sayin' that just because he's a regular in here. That gal of his pissed all over him."

DAUGHTER OF DARKNESS

"I told you, Luther, shut up," Ron said. Then, "Please, all right?"

"I won't say no more, Ron. But you know how I feel about it."

Luther went away.

Ron finally looked at her.

"You're pretty."

"Thank you."

"But you wear way too much makeup."

She was so startled, she laughed. "You this nice to all the girls?"

"All I meant was you're way too pretty to cover it up."

"Oh. I see. Well, then, thank you again."

"Carla isn't even all that good-looking."

"Carla?"

"The girl Luther was talking about."

"Oh."

"We've been living together a couple of years now. So I came home this afternoon and guess what I find?"

"She was in bed with somebody else?"

"Our own bed. Our own fucking bed. That's the worst thing of all. Even if we got back together, I'd never be able to sleep in that bed again. You know?"

"I couldn't either."

"Really?"

"Really," she said. "Every time I got into bed, all I'd be able to think of was them. You know, all they things they did with each other and said to each other and promised to each other. It'd be like sleeping with ghosts. There'd be no way I could handle it."

"God, that's such a good way of putting it. Ghosts. That's *exactly* what it'd be like. Sleeping with ghosts."

"I'm sorry you have to go through all this."

"*You're* sorry?" he snapped. "How the hell do you think *I* feel?"

Every few minutes, he seemed to explode like this.

She let him calm down again. Then, "That's kind of funny."

"What is?"

"That I should run into you."

"What's so funny about that?"

She shrugged. "Oh, because the same sort of thing happened to me a few weeks ago."

"Seriously?"

"Oh, not walking in on him, not the way you did. But he told me about it. Took me out and bought me a real nice dinner—and then he told me."

"That he went to bed with somebody else?"

She shook her head. "Oh, that was just the beginning. Not only did he go to *bed* with somebody else—and had been going to bed with her for nearly a year—he got her pregnant and now they're buying this house out in Niles and they're going to move in in a month."

"And you didn't have any warning?"

"None." She exhaled a beautiful blue trail of smoke. "Not a bit."

He looked at her for a time. Didn't look at her breasts or her hips or her legs. Just stared right at her face. This was a guy who really needed somebody and you could tell that because he concentrated on her face. On her eyes, especially. He needed company, he needed sympathy, he needed to talk. And then maybe he'd need a little sex. It probably wouldn't be very good; heartbroken guys were frequently impotent or at the least impaired. But she knew he'd certainly give it a try.

She put out a slender hand. "My name's Linda Fleming."

He shook her hand. "Ron. Ron Fitzgerald."

She'd found her next victim.

***

Ron Fitzgerald had an apartment near the Downtown South area, the top floor of what had probably once been a corner grocery store. The place was spacious and nicely decorated, with black, white, and gray furnishings and wall motifs lending a cautiously hip but still human air to the place.

He brought them wine, he put on some old Dave Brubeck (she didn't want to spoil his fun by telling him she'd never *heard* of Dave Brubeck before), but mostly he brought her himself and his griefs.

They spent the first hour perched on a white fabric sofa. Except for her excusing herself twice to go to the john, he talked incessantly. And always about the same thing—how his girlfriend, his *former* girlfriend, took advantage of his good nature, his innocence, his pure heart and his spectacular plans for their future together. He was, by turns, extravagantly angry, extravagantly sad, extravagantly forgiving, extravagantly vengeful. "She's so fucking worried about AIDS—she went through an AIDS scare once—let's see how she does whoring around the bars every night. I mean, I don't *want* to her to get AIDS, but—"

But of *course* he wanted her to get AIDS.

Would serve her right for dumping such a swell guy as himself.

Then he pounced on her. No warning whatsoever. Just pounced on her. Pinned her against one of the arms of the couch and insinuated himself on top of her and then began grinding his groin against her. It was like high school, the boys not quite knowing what to do so they just jumped on you.

His left hand cupped her left breast while his right hand wormed its way beneath her right buttock, while all the while he was rubbing his semi-erect self against her middle.

Then he rammed his tongue deep into her mouth.

She pushed him away as gently as possible.

"Wow," she said, "you don't waste any time."

"I thought that's why you came up here," he said, a most unpleasant whine in his voice.

"Maybe I did," she said. "But you think we could use your bedroom instead of this couch?"

"I'll never understand women."

No, you won't, she thought. But she said, "I just want to make it as nice as possible for both of us."

He rubbed a hand across his face. He was getting drunk. "You know what that bitch had the gall to say to me the night she left?"

Linda Fleming didn't have to acknowledge him. He'd tell her anyway.

"She said that we were sexually incompatible. It took her four years to find that out? And maybe it would've helped a little if she'd gotten that boob job. Hell, I was going to pay for it and everything. Wouldn't've cost her a dime. I mean, in the old days, a girl couldn't help it if she didn't have any boobs. But today, hell, there's no excuse." He glanced at her chest and said, "You don't have any problem, boob-wise. You've got some nice breasts."

"Thank you."

"Are they real?"

"Oh, yes."

"You'd get a boob job, wouldn't you, if you needed to, I mean?"

"Oh, I'd rush right out."

He didn't pick up on her sarcasm.

"Maybe I would've been better in the sack if she'd had a little more upstairs. I mean," he said, "I'm not blaming her."

Oh, no, of course not.

"But it couldn't have *hurt* if she'd had a little more boob-wise, could it?"

"No," she said, "no, it couldn't have."

He took her hand, then, staring greedily at her breasts all the time, and said, "Let's go have some fun, wench."

Wench? God, what a dipshit this guy was.

Twenty minutes later, wearing only her panties, she slid beneath the covers and lay there staring up at the ceiling. The streetlights made patterns on the ceiling, leaf patterns mostly, and it was relaxing to lie there and watch the patterns play and entwine. Mostly, it was a pleasure not to have the dipshit's voice pounding on her. He was in la toilette doing some damned thing or another. He'd been in there for some time.

Then her headache was back and she closed her eyes. She heard a voice. It was strange. The last couple hours she kept hearing this female voice she identified as "Jenny." It was very strange. Jenny was this cautionary voice. Telling her to get up and go—fast. . . .

He came out of the john wearing a pair of red bikini panties. He had hair in black silky thatches all over his body, little goatees of it. There was something ticking in his hand.

"What's the ticking?" she said.

"Stopwatch."

"Stopwatch? What for?"

"Make sure it's time."

"Time for what?"

"Well, you know. My erection."

"What, is somebody delivering it?"

He laughed and came over and sat on the edge of the bed. He didn't seem so self-confident now. "Viagra." He spoke the word with an almost mystical emphasis.

"I see."

"Ever since she dumped me, I've had erectile difficulties."

"Oh."

"I took the pill as we were leaving the club tonight. But we've been moving a lot faster than I thought we would." He gravely consulted the stopwatch in his hand. "We still have four-and-a-half minutes to go. It's always the same. Fifty-three minutes and bingo. I'm in business. I like to watch it come up. It's like a rocket at Cape Canaveral or something. You want to watch it?"

"No, I've already had enough fun for one night."

Four minutes and eight seconds later, he said, "Bingo!"

And with that, he pounced on her.

Chapter Thirty-Eight

THE first thing that Coffey did was roll over in bed and reach under the mattress where he kept his .357 Magnum.

The second thing he did was ease himself off the bed, trying to be as quiet as possible. He wore pajama bottoms, nothing else.

The third thing he did was make his way across the bedroom to the door. It was open an inch or so. He opened it another inch.

The solitude of the middle of the night. Thrum of kitchen appliances. City water gurgling in the pipes. A car passing in the street. The aches and groans of a fifty-six-year-old house.

And one more sound, one that shouldn't be part of this diminutive cacophony: an intruder.

To get in the house, the intruder had to know how to disarm a pretty darned good security system. Meaning the guy was a pro. And if he was a pro, it wasn't likely he was here to nab Coffey's piggy bank and collection of Travis McGee first edition hardcovers.

No, a pro would only enter a house like Coffey's this time of night if he was on a far more serious mission. Like murder.

Coffey listened intently. Whatever sound had awakened him was lost to him now. Or maybe he was imagining the whole thing. Maybe he'd been dreaming and simply dreamed a certain sound.

Then he heard it. Faint though it was.

The scrape of a shoe on the floor below. The basement.

Coffey's grip on the handle of the Magnum got a lot tighter. No dream. No imagined sound. Somebody was in the basement.

Coffey opened the door quarter-inch by quarter-inch. He

needed to be very, very quiet now. Then he went into his ballet-dancer routine, moving quickly across the hardwood floor to the end of the hall, and then to the living room. All on tippy-toes.

The kitchen was a pretty motif of shifting shadows. Everything was neat and clean. He imagined that the intruder would give him good marks for cleanliness.

He moved to the kitchen door. It was open a quarter-inch or so.

He had to make a decision. If he crept down the stairs, then he could possibly catch the intruder in the act. Whatever the act was. The downside here was that at any time in his slow descent to the basement floor, the intruder could glance up, see him, raise his weapon, and off him right there on the stairs.

He placed his ear to the open space between door and frame. Ambient sound overwhelmed him at first. He heard a dozen tiny sounds all at once. But eventually his ear focused on a single sound, a ratcheting kind of sound. Only after a time did he realized what he was listening to. Something metal was being dismantled. He could hear the sound of a wrench turning, he could hear the sound of a piece of metal being put quietly on the floor. Then more sounds of the wrench being used.

Even from here, he could approximate which part of the small basement the sound was coming from. The furnace, a new Lennox, was in the far west corner. He wouldn't have been able to hear it being taken apart, not that far away. Which meant the intruder was working on either the washer or drier, which were against the wall to the immediate right of the steps, or the gas water heater, which sat off to the left at the bottom of the steps.

As soon as he thought of the water heater, he came up with an idea about what was going on. One of the best ways to pass off arson as an accident—most cops knew their fair share of firefighters—was to tamper with the water heater or furnace. When the weather was hot like this, the arsonist wouldn't fool with the furnace. That would send up red flags immediately. Who'd be using the furnace on a night like this? But the water heater, yes. An expert could get past all the fail-safe mechanisms in the heater and make it look as if the heater had malfunctioned, thus setting fire to the house. It was well known among arson investigators that too few fire departments ever looked carefully enough at water heaters and were thus frequently deceived.

If that was the case, the next question was, who would want to kill him and why? His mind turned inevitably back to his wife and daughter. Another convict he'd helped to send up? Was that what was going on here? Somehow, he didn't think so. Somehow, he knew that this had something to do with Jenny.

He decided on a plan.

He tiptoed back to the butcher block island in the center of the kitchen. Pans hung from a rectangle above the island. This wouldn't be easy, getting three pans down without making any noise. As he worked, sweat began to chill him. He wished he had a shirt on. Once, he almost banged two pans together. Another time, he almost dropped a pan on the floor. Then there was the business of getting them over to the door without one pan nudging the other.

He reached the door, paused. If this didn't go right, the intruder would likely kill him. The intruder would have a clear shot at Coffey on the stairs. What Coffey hoped was that in the sudden clamor and confusion, the intruder would turn around and look for a place to hide. In that moment, Coffey would be able to snap on the basement light and shoot him.

He got the pans ready and pitched them down the steps. Moments after they started clanging down the stairs, Coffey fired two shots into the basement.

A curse, a cry. A man stumbling over some tools which made metallic sounds on the concrete floor. Another curse, sharp, angry, as the same man stumbled into the edge of the washing machine, scraping it several inches from its base.

Coffey descended the steps, snapping off two more shots as he did so.

Then the first shot came his way, a noisy, wood-eating crack that took a huge chunk from the wall just behind him.

Coffey reached over, clicked on the light and then threw himself to the floor, rolling across a stretch of new linoleum. He rolled behind the old sofa that the cats liked to sleep on during the hot summer. He lay there for long moments, getting his breath, listening. With the lights on, he could see the ceiling of the basement. They'd always been going to fix up the basement, cover up all the wiring in the ceiling. But somehow they'd never gotten around to it.

He sat up. Took another deep breath. Got ready to raise his head and peek over the top of the couch. Which he did. And that was when the intruder opened fire again. He put three bullets where Coffey's head had been only a millisecond before.

Coffey had already ducked back behind the couch. He still hadn't gotten a look at the intruder.

Then, something heavy being pushed aside. Then—footsteps, fast-running footsteps. The intruder making his break.

Coffey sprang up from behind the couch. There was no way he was going to catch the intruder before he got up the stairs and disappeared again into the night.

Now, for the first time, he saw the man. Dark blue zippered jumpsuit. A sinister, clear plastic mask that completely distorted the face it covered. A long-billed ball cap. Black leather gloves.

The man had no choice but to leave his tools behind, sprawled across the floor where he'd kicked them when he'd jumped up from the water heater.

He was running fast. No more than three steps away from the stairs. Firing wildly over his shoulder. Anything to keep Coffey off-balance. But his bullets weren't coming close enough to worry Coffey.

Once again, Coffey had to make a decision, but this one had to be decided instantly. He could easily shoot and kill the man. Or he could injure him and then try and find out where the man was from. Who he worked for.

Coffey needed information more than he needed proof of his machismo.

He shot the fleeing intruder right in the center of his left calf. It was a good clean shot, right into the meat of the leg, and the intruder had the grace to scream and clutch dramatically at his wound.

The thing was, the gunshot didn't slow him down. Or if it did, it was so slow a slowing down that it was imperceptible to Coffey. The sonofabitch in the zippered jumpsuit kept right on trucking up the steps.

Even in retreat, the intruder was a man of cunning. From the pocket of his jumpsuit he took the same kind of red plastic ball the woman in the van had used earlier on Coffey. He crushed the ball in his gloved hand and then flung it at Coffey.

The explosion was quick and sure. A heavy gray smoke instantly began to work its way through the basement in several simultaneous directions. But that wasn't all. This wasn't simple smoke. It was *corrosive* smoke as well. Even before the gray stuff had reached him, Coffey felt its invisible effects. His eyes itched, watered. He sneezed violently. His stomach began to wrench and lurch.

He dove through the smoke to the stairs. Just as he was scrambling up the steps, past the smoke, he was able to see, blearily, the back of the intruder as he reached the basement door.

Coffey fired again. He might well kill the man this time. He couldn't see. But he kept firing, anyway. Somehow, not one of the four shots hit the man as he lunged through the doorway at the top of the steps.

Coughing, rubbing his eyes with his left hand, then stumbling and banging his good knee one time, Coffey kept in pursuit of the intruder.

The house. Dark. Silent. The intruder knocking into furniture. Cursing on his headlong flight to the front door. Crystal the cat, sleeping somewhere in the living room, meowing in protest at the disturbance that had awakened her. Crystal didn't appreciate having her beauty sleep disturbed.

He got him in the hand.

The intruder was silhouetted against the square of beveled glass in the front door, the glass glowing with misty streetlight. Coffey saw his chance. Shot him in the hand.

Once again, the intruder gave Coffey the satisfaction of crying out. The impact of the bullet was sufficient to slam the man into the front door. His bloody glove fingers and palm left a red imprint on the glass. It was a dark symbol against the soft glow of the streetlight.

But the hand wound didn't slow the intruder down much either. He put his bloody hand on the knob and yanked the door back. He also turned an inch or two back toward Coffey. Coffey dove at him. The two men fell through the open door and on to the front porch. The man swung at Coffey, but Coffey blocked it and then grabbed the man's arm, ripping away the sleeve of the jumpsuit. And the man's wristwatch. The gold band broke, the watch flying across the porch.

A car went by, the driver startled by the silhouettes of two men fighting on the front porch. Nearby, a dog started barking. A light went on next door. Old Mr. Enright. Entertainment for the entire neighborhood.

The man used his bloody hand to dig into his jumpsuit pocket again. He brought forth another red ball and detonated it. Coffey was just bringing his Magnum up to the intruder's face when the smoke from the red capsule exploded into his face and left him gasping and gagging and groping his way around in the darkness.

A big engine starting. Van or truck. The only information Coffey received was auditory. He'd bet it was the van.

The vehicle screeching away. Brakes being applied at the far corner. The vehicle long gone now. The street sounds returning. Dogs and the early morning birds.

He staggered to his feet, found the door, and lumbered inside, bouncing off the doorframe once as he moved.

He felt his way into the bathroom. The stinging just grew worse.

Shower. Toilet. Sink. He was blind, groping. Ran water in the sink. Cool water. Opened the medicine cabinet and felt around—knocking innumerable jars, bottles and tubes over—until he found what *felt* like Visine.

Here goes, he thought, tilting his head back, opening his eyes. The Visine made him jerk, jump. It stung almost as badly as the stuff in the red ball. But after a few moments, the Visine cooled the stinging, and through the blur of his vision he was dimly able to make out his face in the mirror.

He worked on his eyes for nearly fifteen minutes. It took that long to get his vision back to something resembling normal. In the meantime, cats Tasha and Tess came in and stood on either side of him and rubbed up against his legs. They comforted him, he comforted them.

When he finished in the bathroom, he grabbed a flashlight from the kitchen and went down to the basement. He checked through the tools the intruder had left behind. A good detective should be able to find some distinguishing marks on the tools, something that would point in the direction of their owner. But the wrench and the screwdriver bore the stamp of True Value hardware. With a chain of stores that big, tracing these tools would be almost impossible. Hundreds if not thousands of these things were sold every day.

He next retraced the intruder's steps, trying to see if the man had dropped anything. Kitchen. Dining room. Living room. Nothing.

He took his flashlight and went out onto the porch. He liked this time of morning. The moon and stars, the hushed animal sounds of urban raccoons and possums as they foraged through yards, the soft sweet feel and tang of the fresh air.

He went back and forth over the front porch. He found nothing. Then he remembered the watch flying off the intruder's wrist. Apparently the watch had flown off the porch and landed in the shrubs planted along the side of the porch.

He went down the steps and along the side of the house. Just before she'd been killed, his wife had planted some Korean boxwood all the way around the house. It was a low-growing, hedgelike plant that kept its beauty for many long months a year.

He didn't have any luck at first.

The watch hadn't landed on top of the boxwood, nor had it fallen down and landed on the ground. Which meant that it was probably entangled in the hedge itself.

He took his flashlight and angled its beam through every inch of hedge from porch steps to where the house proper began. No way the watch could have gotten lost any farther back.

The search took ten minutes. He found nothing.

Crystal came out the front door and jumped up on the rail in back of the hedge. Tess was the most curious of the cats, but Crystal was the one most likely to stray out on the porch. They were all supposed to stay inside. They'd been spayed and declawed.

But here stood Crystal, looking down at her nice but dumb master. She wanted him, as always, to amuse her in some way.

"Go back inside," he said to her. "You know you're not supposed to be out here."

She just looked at him, a black and white and brown calico who could appear sweet and imperious at the same time, which wasn't easy to do.

Then Crystal made a decision. If *he* wasn't going to put on a show for her, *she'd* put on a show for him.

Crystal jumped on top of the hedge, instantly realizing that the surface of the hedge wasn't what it appeared to be. It was rough and prickly and she didn't like it.

She sprang from the hedge into Coffey's arms. She'd just landed when he heard the faint *thunk* of something hitting the ground.

He shone his light down on the black soil beneath the boxwood. There lay the intruder's watch.

He reached down, snatched it up, and then took himself, Crystal, and the watch back inside.

After giving Crystal a special treat of tuna fish, he sat down at the kitchen table and began going over the watch carefully.

The first thing he noticed was the strange symbol on the underside, a circle with a stylized S drawn inside.

And beneath that, in tiny script: SIGMA.

Chapter Thirty-Nine

SHE'S a little girl, and she's sick. The flu. The bad stomach has passed, at least. Now all that remains are the headache and the fever. The fever is especially bad for her. Even though she kicks the covers on to the floor, even though (against Mommy's wishes), she sneaks the bedroom window open, she is broiling hot.

And the nightmares. When she's sick like this, the nightmares are especially bad. Running down the long, dark tunnel. A hideous thing only partially human lumbering close behind her. Wanting her. She screams, but somehow she knows that the scream is only in her dream. Mommy can't actually hear the scream and neither can Daddy. She is trapped inside her nightmares, and nobody can get her out. Not ever.

And then she is awake. And she is not a little girl. And she is in a room not her own, a shadowy room.

She is Jenny. And Jenny is twenty-five. And Jenny should be home in her own bed this time of night. She has never been the type to sleep around and that's what this feels like. There's something *wrong* about being here.

She's Jenny Stafford. Age twenty-five. And she does not want to be here.

A soft mist-kissed breeze comes through the open window. It makes her feel better. Her anxiety flows away from her for a time. . . .

Her bladder is the real problem right now. She really needs to go. She looks around. Where is the bathroom? Then she sees it. The door open just a bit. No lights on. Presumably nobody in there.

She shivers, decides that the breeze isn't so nice after all.

She's getting cold. She starts to bring her left hand up to rub her chilly nose. The hand is stained with something dark and sticky. She brings up her other hand. Same thing, dark and sticky.

She is not an imbecile. She knows immediately what she's looking at. She feels overwhelmed by so many forces. Not knowing where she is or how she got here. Needing so badly to pee. And now, her hands streaked with what must be blood.

She stands up. Legs shaky. Body covered with rough goose bumps. She looks down at herself. Her thighs, her stomach, her breasts are also blood-splashed. What in God's name is going on here?

And then she remembers the other night. The motel room. The dead man. And her not being able to remember any of it. And then the stranger, Coffey, yes, that's his name. Can she really trust him? She has doubts.

It's now or never. Has to pee. Walks carefully across the hardwood floor, grateful for the occasional throw rug on the wood. The bottoms of her feet feel frozen.

When she reaches the bathroom door, she pauses. Force of habit. Good little Catholic girls always pause before bathroom doors. To make sure it's not being used. Someone might be sitting in there right now. In the dark. Some people probably *prefer* the dark.

She knocks. It's almost funny, knocking in this situation. But she knocks two times and then waits for an answer. When she doesn't get one, she pushes the door open, and that's when she sees the man lying face up on the bathroom floor.

There is a lot of blood in the crotch area. It has leaked on to the floor and has created a small river between his legs. The butcher knife, presumably the same one that claimed the man's masculinity, stands straight up in the man's throat. The eyes are difficult to look at. They are sorrowful eyes, probably a snapshot of the man's whole life. Difficult to imagine that a man would be *happy* that God or fate had dealt him such a hand.

She doesn't scream, run, get sick, or faint. She is still thinking back to the other night, to the dead man on the bed in the motel, dead also of a knife wound.

What other conclusion can there be? She very quietly goes back to bed and lies down and pulls the covers over her.

Two dead men. Her waking up in close proximity to them. Unable to remember much of anything on either occasion.

The electroshock treatments. The hint from the good gray doctors that Jenny, in certain circumstances, could possibly be dangerous to herself and others, Mrs. Stafford (with Jenny sitting right there next to her mother), and we certainly don't want that to happen, do we? The first thing we need to work on is the depression. I know you've heard a lot of negative things about electroshock, but believe me, it's going to make you feel very good about yourself for the first time in a long, long time, Jenny.

Could possibly be a danger to herself.

Or others.

In certain circumstances.

She thinks about calling Coffey. But can she really trust him? Wasn't it quite a coincidence that he just happened to be appear in that shelter the other night? He's so quiet, mysterious. . . .

And then a name—and a phone number—come to her as she lies there in the darkness. But, no, that's ridiculous. Why would she call him? But even as she thinks this, about him being her enemy, she has a sense that he'd be able to calm her down, walk her through her last week, help her come to terms with what's going on with her spiritually.

She wonders what time it is and then realizes that she doesn't *care* what time it is. She is too far gone to care. So scared. So disoriented. Is she muttering, or are her teeth merely chattering? She isn't sure. And then suddenly she realizes she hasn't peed. Didn't want to step over the body to sit down. Just too ghoulish. Still, her bladder can't hold out much longer.

She turns and stares at the phone on the nightstand. Even more pressing than her bladder is who she'll call.

Her mother is probably waiting by the phone, hoping to hear from her. The problem there is she'll be full of advice and lawyers and fear and anger and the whole thing will be a mess. Jenny needs time to sort things out. Figure out why she's killed two men. *If* she's killed two men. But if *she* hasn't, who has? And why blame it on her?

The more she thinks, the more she realizes that there really is only one person she can turn to for such enormous problems as hers.

A noise. Hushed voices in the hallway. Police sneaking up?

Beneath the covers, she tenses. What could she possibly say if they came in here? If they found the body (and why *wouldn't* they find the body), how could she possibly make them believe that she hadn't had anything to do with it?

Or hadn't she?

That was the most difficult problem of all to confront. Her anger toward men. Maybe, drunk, still slightly unhinged from her time in the psychiatric hospital, maybe she'd found a butcher knife and—

But it was hard to imagine herself, even in a frenzy, cutting off his—

It wasn't the cops. In the hallway. It was a man kissing his wife good-bye and whispering a few things to her. A lot of jobs started earlier these days, designed to let workers get off earlier. Then she heard the man's footsteps, retreating down the hall. Then there was car engine, firing up in the parking lot below.

And then in the silence, she started staring at the phone again. The headache was back. And with such force that she had to stab her fingers deep into her eyeballs to stop the pain.

And then a name filled her mind. Her entire consciousness enshrined the name.

My God, what a crazy, crazy thought, calling him. My God, he was the *last* person she would call, right?

The very last. . . .

She wondered what he'd say, being awakened at this hour, hearing her voice on the other end of the phone.

He'd been taken with her, no doubt about that. She believed that he sincerely, genuinely *liked* her for a time. And took a real interest in her. He even helped her in a lot of ways, showed her the things she did and felt that she should be proud of. Self-esteem. She hated that particular buzzword. It was so overused. But that, in effect, was what he'd given her—or, more importantly, shown her how to give herself.

Now it wasn't self-esteem she needed. Now it was sanity. Now it was somebody who could at least see the possibility that she hadn't committed these murders . . . even though most people would blame her absolutely.

She reached out to the phone. She picked up the receiver. She dialed the number. She knew it by heart.

A sleepy male voice answered. "Yes?"

She could picture him. He really was a striking man.

"It's Jenny Stafford," she said. "I need some help. Desperately."

She heard covers rustle. His voice being cleared. She could tell he was sitting up now.

"Where are you?" Quinlan said. "I'll come and get you personally and bring you back to the hospital."

"I'd really appreciate it," she said. "I really would."

Chapter Forty

WHEN the phone rang, Coffey sat up straight, like a comic version of Dracula in his coffin.

He was tired, exhausted really, so little sleep and so much stress, that he had to put himself in context before he could do anything.

Daylight. His bedroom. Bed. All three cats sprawled on the bed. Phone ringing. Phone on nightstand.

He reached over and picked up.

"Sigma Corporation," a male voice said, then continued, "it's your hard-working pal at the police department. Took me a while, but I found out who the lease company issued the van to."

"Sigma Corporation," Coffey said. He thought of the symbol on the underside of the watch the intruder had been wearing. The S shape inside the circle. "Did you get an address?"

"Not far from the Merchandise Mart." He then gave Coffey the address. Coffey kept a pad and pencil on the nightstand.

"I really appreciate this."

"No big deal. Just took a little persistence, is all."

As soon as Coffey hung up, the cats started meowing. Food time. They followed Coffey out to the kitchen. He put down three small plastic bowls on the floor and then put a small measuring cup of dry food in each bowl.

He spent the next fifteen minutes in the bathroom shaving and showering. In his bedroom, he put on black socks, black cordovan loafers, black slacks, white shirt, blue knit tie and tan summer-weight sport coat. This was one of those days when his cabbie attire wouldn't suffice.

He ate breakfast in a McDonald's parking lot and spilled a

smidge of coffee on his slacks. He spent half a foolish minute imagining the billions of dollars that would roll in when he sued McDonald's for scalding himself.

Then he was at the library, sitting in the section that had to do with local businesses. He felt like a genius when he came upon the Sigma Corporation logo and found that it matched the S inside the circle.

In the next twenty minutes he learned that Sigma had been incorporated five years ago with six board members and a mission statement that read, in part, "To expand the horizons of such controversial (but worthwhile) human endeavors as holistic healing, criminal rehabilitation through restructured thought processes, and the betterment of daily human life through a reordering of deviant impulses."

In a word (or two words, actually): mind control.

The most interesting name on the board of directors was Kenneth Bowman. He was listed as President and CEO. There was a brief bio of the man. Nothing in his background, with the possible exception of a four-year-stint as the sales manager of a pharmaceutical company, seemed to have any bearing on the stated goals of Sigma.

Coffey punched Kenneth Bowman up on the business computer. There were five such Bowmans in the Chicago area. One wholesaled fruits and vegetables, one had a discount TV and radio store, one owned six tire stores, and one owned three small pharmacies. The Bowman he wanted was listed as the President and CEO of Sigma—but was also listed as co-owner of three other small businesses (Orion, Ltd.; Stoneman Enterprises; and Walker Laboratories). What was even more interesting was the information about the other co-owner, Priscilla Bowman, a psychiatrist and Kenneth Bowman's wife.

And Jenny Stafford's shrink.

He knew where his next appointment would be.

Chapter Forty-One

SEVERAL times during the night, Quinlan had considered raping her. Easy enough to do with the drugs he'd given her. But these were light drugs. He needed her to look alert when he brought her in.

Of course, he'd considered raping her many times before. But he'd been reluctant. And he knew why. What would it prove if he had drug-induced sex with her? His pride was that he was able to seduce all his young women through the sheer power of his mind. Yes, he knew it was machismo. Yes, he knew it was vanity. Yes, he knew it was college-sophomore conquest. But he needed it. He was beyond money now; even beyond power in most respects. Power, especially, which brought so much responsibility with it. You constantly had to check on your power, make sure it was secure, and it got very, very tedious.

But sweet seduction. To take an intelligent young woman and to bring her completely under your sway through sheer willpower . . .

What could be better than that?

He stood now in the doorway of the bedroom he'd prepared for her. Beautiful Jenny, velvet hair a dark storm on the white pillow, eyes and nose and lips of such classical beauty that it made him oddly afraid of her. Beauty was true power, at least for Quinlan.

She stirred. It was time to wake her. Near noon.

She didn't seem to recognize him at first. Her eyes were briefly wild, afraid. And then she seemed to relax some.

He came over and sat on the edge of the bed. He'd slipped

her into a black strapless nightgown. Even her shoulders were lovely.

"Good morning," Quinlan said. "It's a beautiful autumn day."

He could barely stop himself from touching her. His fingers sensed the feel of her flesh; his ears anticipated the sound of her gentle voice; his eyes never wanted to close upon her beauty.

The only one he'd never seduced.

And now he would never get the chance.

He said, "Do you remember last night?"

"Last night?" Anxious; even afraid.

"Coming here."

"Yes. Coming here. Yes. I don't know why I came here, though." Her face pinched with disapproval. "You didn't treat me very well when I—was living here. So it doesn't make sense that I'd call you."

"But you did call me."

"Yes; yes, I did."

"And I picked you up and brought you here, and we talked."

"Talked about what?"

"You don't have any recollection?"

She watched his face carefully. "You're scaring me. If there's something you want to say, just say it."

"I'm not sure what to do now."

"About what?" she said.

He took his time answering. "You told me some things last night."

She brushed dark hair back from white skin. "Some things?"

He sighed and stood up and walked over to the window. This particular room was used for guests. The apartments were all decorated by those who lived in them. Guest rooms were as impersonal as most hotel rooms. Double bed, bureau, an easy chair, a bathroom.

In the warm sunlight, a lanky woman in a gray uniform steered a green riding mower around the grounds. At a nearby picnic table, one group of patients were having their lunch.

"What're you trying to tell me?" she said.

He came back over and sat next to her on the bed again. She had pulled the sheet up to her shoulders.

"I'm going to tell you something," he said. Then, "Remember how badly I treated you when you lived here with us."

"Of course I do."

"Do you know *why* I treated you like that?"

"No, why?"

"Because I was in love with you." Once again, he touched his hand to her cheek. "And I still am." He looked away from her. Nobody had ever accused him of underplaying a dramatic moment. "That's why it's so difficult."

"Why what's so difficult?"

A sigh. "I think you know, Jenny, what I'm talking about."

"No, I don't. I don't have any idea." Anxiety again. Slowly building fear.

He took her hand. "You killed those two men, Jenny. At least that's what you told me."

"No!" she said. "No, I didn't tell you that! I couldn't have! I wouldn't have!"

Another long sigh. "I have it on tape, Jenny."

She started to get up from the bed, gripping the front of the strapless gown so it wouldn't slide down.

But he pushed her back in bed. "Jenny, you have to stay calm. You know how you can get." She started to speak, but he stopped her. "Don't you see what you did? You called me because you wanted to confess. You knew I'd help you."

"I didn't kill those men!"

He stared at her. "I think you know better than that, don't you, Jenny? If you're really being honest with yourself?"

"No!" she said. "No, I didn't!"

She tried once more to get up. This time, she didn't let him stop her so easily. She pushed against him, raised her fists. He touched a button on the nightstand and Barcroft the security chief appeared.

"We need to get her to the police," Quinlan said. "And it seems she doesn't want to go."

***

Jenny wasn't sure what kind of injection they gave her. They had a lot of needles here at the compound. And a lot of different cutting-edge drugs, too.

Quinlan and his man got her down on the bed. Barcroft gave

her the injection. He was gentle, probably only because he didn't want there to be any bruising. How would it look to the police if you brought in a bruised-up woman?

The needle stung. Even when the tip of the hypodermic was penetrating her flesh, Jenny fought against the man.

The effect of the drug, whatever it was, was immediate. It was just a light supplement to the drug she'd already been given. Nothing heavy. She could feel a cold charge of serum coursing through blood. She expected the drug to drag her down, the way a pre-op injection would. But very quickly it became apparent that the drug was intended only to calm her, make her controllable for them.

She lay back on the bed and closed her eyes. There was no sense fighting the drug. There never was. Quinlan ran the hospital with drugs. He could set your mood according to his whim. All hail the hypodermic.

"We'll let you sleep a little while," Quinlan said. "Then we'll come back for you."

"Wear something nice," the man in the gray uniform said. "There'll be a lot of cameras at the police station. I already called the press and told them we'd be bringing you in."

She'd underestimated the effects of the drug. True, it didn't seem to be one of his killer drugs—one that would make you a zombie for days—but it wasn't quite as harmless as she'd first thought either.

It was putting her to sleep. . . .

And as she fell asleep . . . the man's words still in her ears . . . she saw the shape of it then. Like looking at a table full of pieces—and then suddenly seeing the shape of the whole puzzle.

Quinlan had killed those two men and then made it look as if she had. He had also—somehow—managed to manipulate her into calling him. And he had spent last night using drugs to get a taped "confession" out of her.

She remembered the long, sad days at the end of her hospital stay. How much he'd hated her. How many ways he'd tried to seduce her. In certain ways, it had almost been funny, the way a French sex farce is funny. And yet it was sad, too. For him, she'd come to symbolize some kind of acceptance. He needed to seduce her to prove this. And when she wouldn't comply . . .

he'd turn her over to the police. She could see him savoring the glory in the press. An insane girl (given her history, the press would have no problem casting her as a rich, spoiled, insane monster) that only a guru like Quinlan could deal with. Quinlan would be a hero. Even his numerous critics would have to walk more carefully around him. Most gurus didn't bother with civic responsibility, but here was Quinlan performing a service for the entire city. . . .

She slept. . . .

***

"You bitch! You think I don't know who you are!"

A nightmare. That was all Jenny could attribute it to. A young woman with a shaven head, a young woman who managed to be strikingly pretty even without hair, was slapping her, calling her names.

Jenny tasted hot blood. Her *own* hot blood. The inside of her cheek had been cut from one of the blows.

This was no nightmare.

Jenny rolled away from the arc of the young woman's slaps. Rolled away and then dove for the end of the bed so she could get to her feet. But the young woman was there, grabbing her hair. Jenny slapped her hard enough to move the young woman back a few inches. Jenny scrambled to her feet.

"Who *are* you?" she said.

"Gretchen," the young woman said. And for the first time, Jenny got a good enough look at the face to conclude that Gretchen was insane. The lovely dark eyes didn't quite focus upon Jenny but looked instead at some imaginary world that only Gretchen saw. The anger that tensed the face had an element of sadness about it, too. It wasn't righteous rage, the irrational moment of a rational person, but frenzy, the inchoate pain of the unbalanced.

"He loves me," Gretchen said. Then she touched her stomach. "I'm going to have his baby."

"Who?" Jenny said, still groggy from the medicine.

All sorts of questions flooded her mind. Who was Gretchen? Why did she hate Jenny so much? And how in God's name had she gotten through a security-safe door?

And who was the "he" she was talking about?

"Listen," Jenny said, taking deep breaths, forcing herself to calm down, "you need to explain what's going on here. I don't want either one of us to get hurt."

"He loves me," Gretchen said angrily.

"Who is 'he?' "

"Oh, c'mon. Don't be coy."

"You mean Quinlan?"

"Yes. Who else?"

"Well, then I'm glad he loves you. And I'm glad you're having his child."

"You lie," Gretchen said. "You want his baby. I know you do."

As strange and frustrating as the conversation was, Jenny more pitied Gretchen than feared her.

"Gretchen, listen, how did you get in here?"

Gretchen glanced around the room, as if electronic eavesdropping devices were everywhere. As perhaps they were. She then leaned forward and whispered in Jenny's ear. "I stole a pass card from the lock-up one night."

"The lock-up? How did you get in there?"

Gretchen smiled, then. Her smile was eerier than her frown. Scarier, too. "The little thing between my legs. A few of the guards find me attractive."

Jenny didn't have any doubt of that. Nor did she doubt that Gretchen got what she wanted as a result.

"That's how I found the tape, too," Gretchen said.

"What tape?"

Gretchen smiled again. For a moment, Jenny's compassion waned. This was like looking very, very deep into the pit. Once you looked down there, you were never the same again. . . . Perhaps Jenny feared that she would end up like Gretchen someday.

"Wouldn't you like to know?" The smile remained.

Jenny saw that here was a potentially useful confidante. Jenny needed any information she could get to fight Quinlan's story that she'd simply gone insane and killed those two men, then turned to Quinlan and asked him to hide her in the commune. It was clear that Gretchen didn't know about any of this. She was assuming that Jenny was here to stay.

"Gretchen?"

"Yes."

"If I left here and never came back, wouldn't that prove I wasn't trying to get Quinlan for myself?"

Gretchen hesitated, her small winsome face thoughtful. "I guess."

"You seem to know how to get around this place."

Gretchen smiled. "I know a lot more than people think I do."

"Could you help me get out of here?" The drugs were starting to wear off already. She was dizzy sometimes but kept forcing herself to focus on the moment.

Gretchen's brow furrowed. "You really mean that?"

"I really mean that."

Gretchen studied her some more. "You'd go and never come back?"

"Never."

"He used to talk about you sometimes. People always said you were the only one he couldn't get."

Gretchen's eyes glistened. Her hand covered her face. She began to weep. Jenny went to her—her head was clearing from the drugs already—slid her arm around her, held her. "I can't help how much I love him."

"I know, Gretchen. It's all right."

"And now with the baby and all—"

She continued to cry, her small body trembling in a kind of shattered rhythm. You could feel her grief in the little-girl way she clung to Jenny.

"And now he's mad because I stole the tape," she said. "He took it back from me."

The subject of the tape seemed to bring Gretchen back to this room and Jenny. "I guess I shouldn't talk about it." She was sniffling tears.

If the tape was something that made Quinlan angry, Jenny definitely wanted to hear about it.

"Maybe you need to lie down, Gretchen," Jenny said. "I'll get you some cold water. You feel very hot."

"I've just been so worried is all," Gretchen said, sounding weary and lost.

Jenny almost felt guilty, knowing she was going to use this

poor girl as a way of destroying Quinlan. But what choice did she have?

She got Gretchen on the bed and brought her some nice cold water. Then she sat on a chair right next to the bed and started asking Gretchen all her questions.

Chapter Forty-Two

YOU could tell a lot about a person by the type of receptionist she hired. Dr. Priscilla Bowman employed a rather severely pretty young woman with cold dark eyes and a terse, precise manner.

"May I help you?" she asked when Coffey came through the door. Her tone said that she doubted there was any way she could help or even *wanted* to help him. Even with a necktie and sport coat on, Coffey looked a bit on the rough side, the type of man this woman most devoutly disapproved of. The office furnishings reflected the same austerity, Nordic and stylish and cold as hell.

He glanced at the walls. Another way you could get a thumbnail sketch of someone's psyche was by looking at what kind of art they chose to be publicly associated with. Priscilla Bowman had covered her wall with the kind of bad imitation Picasso-style art that spoke of a profoundly neurotic universe from which there was no relief short of death. Just the thing to cheer up her patients.

He bearded the ice maiden. "I'd like to see Dr. Bowman, please."

"I'm afraid that's impossible. She's booked all day long."

"I'd only need a few minutes."

The ice maiden, a dark-haired woman with nice flesh and a coldly erotic mouth, shook her head and said, "I don't believe we've seen you before, have we?"

"No."

"Then it really is impossible today. The doctor must take care of her regular clients first."

"I'm here about her husband."

The ice maiden looked startled. "Kenneth?"

"Yes. Kenneth."

"But he's dead."

"That's why I'm here," Coffey said. "There's some new evidence."

The ice maiden's gaze now shifted from disapproval to distrust. "May I ask who you are?"

"My name's Coffey."

"And you're with—"

"Myself. I'm a private investigator."

He'd always wanted to say that line. He'd read it in scores of private eye novels and it always sounded so much more romantic than, "I'm with the police department." Anybody who was with any kind of department—fire department, streets department, sanitation department—always sounded like a bureaucrat. But a private eye . . . Maybe when he got done here, he'd go get himself a trench coat and fedora.

"I see." The disapproval was back in her voice. "Why don't you have a seat over there? I'll go speak with Dr. Bowman."

"I appreciate it."

She stood up. She was tall, with one of those slightly gangly bodies that was nonetheless girlishly appealing. A little long in the waist but nice hips and legs. He wondered if she was assessing him similarly—men forget that women judge men just as analytically as men judge women—and finding him wanting in a few areas himself. Movie star material, he wasn't.

He sat down and picked up *Psychology Today*. He read about the psychological components of impotence, spastic colons, migraine headaches, anal bleeding, headaches, shingles, cancer, psoriasis, and temporary blindness. It was all very uplifting stuff. He wondered if the good doctor might have a cyanide capsule he could bite down on. One thing an ex-cop and mystery writer didn't need to be reminded of was human mortality.

A man came in, looked around the office, then took a chair across the reception area from Coffey. He seemed nervous and embarrassed about being here. He kept straightening the jacket of his gray three-piece suit. Coffey felt compelled to tell the man that he, Coffey, wasn't a patient. *You're the one with problems, pal, not me*, Coffey wanted to say in defense of his own sanity, dignity, and masculinity. But he couldn't figure out any

DAUGHTER OF DARKNESS

way to do this. Will anybody who has psychological problems please raise his hand? He could try that old number, but the other guy probably wouldn't raise his hand, anyway.

The ice maiden was back. She looked at the man in the three-piece suit and smiled, careful not to say his name. Anonymity and expensive visits were the guiding principles in a shrink's office. She turned her reluctant attention to Coffey. "She'll give you ten minutes between appointments. In another five minutes.'

"Thank you."

Coffey felt the man in the suit staring at him. The man was probably thinking that Coffey was so desperately crazy, the good doctor had to squeeze him in immediately.

The good Dr. Bowman was prettier and more stylish than the ice maiden (Bowman probably had a plastic statue of Armani on her dashboard) but not one whit friendlier.

Her private office continued the Nordic motif of her reception area, blond, bold, barren. She opened a desk drawer, took out a package of cigarettes, and lit up.

"Bad habit," she said.

"Very."

She smiled icily. "Maybe I should see a shrink."

He smiled back. "Or a rabbi or a priest. They're cheaper."

She exhaled with great glee, and right in his direction. She'd probably put a voodoo curse on the secondhand smoke. She looked elegant and impressive in her blue linen suit and white scarf. "To what do I owe the pleasure of your visit?"

"I want you to tell me about Sigma."

Her gaze grew much colder. "What about Sigma?"

He took the wristwatch from his pocket and held it up for her to see. "I tore this from somebody's wrist last night."

He put it on the desk, slid it over to her. She picked it up, looked it over.

"We have forty-three employees at the moment," she said. "Some of them are young and occasionally do foolish things. I take it this altercation took place at a pub somewhere."

"No pub. My home."

She tried very hard to look startled but didn't quite make it. "Your home?"

He explained the break-in.

She pulled a classic defense lawyer's move. She immediately changed the subject. "I thought you were here to talk about Kenneth."

"Dear Kenneth."

"I don't like that tone. He was my husband."

"How did he die?"

"What the hell does that mean? I thought you were bringing me some new information."

"How did he die?"

She glared at him for a time, inhaled on her cigarette a few more times, and said, "Fire."

"House fire?"

"Yes. Why?"

"That's what your boy was doing at my place last night."

"I don't have any idea what you're talking about."

"I caught him in the middle of rigging up my water heater. Even a lot of big city fire investigators get faked out by water heater fires. They write them off as accidents when they're really arson."

"Well, he certainly wasn't there last night because Sigma wanted him there."

"No?"

"No," she said. "Absolutely not." She glanced at a slim, golden wristwatch. "You have four minutes left, Mr. Coffey."

"Do you still see Quinlan?"

She smiled. "Mr. Coffey, if you really are a private investigator, then you're a very incompetent one. Mr. Quinlan and I haven't been an item for years."

"What did Kenneth think about you and Quinlan being an 'item?' "

"Kenneth pursued his own leisure time activities. I didn't bother him, and he didn't bother me."

"Apparently. I mean, he agreed to front for Sigma when it opened up."

"Kenneth was an enthusiast, Mr. Coffey. That's why we used him. He looked good and sounded good."

"And he no doubt had a good memory."

"Memory?"

Coffey nodded. "For memorizing exactly what you told him to say."

"He was certainly useful. Starting a new company is a very dicey proposition these days."

"Especially when the product is mind control. That's a phrase that scares the hell out of most people."

She leaned forward and smiled at him. "It only scares stupid people, Mr. Coffey."

"I assume that would include me?"

She sat back. "Last year, we made the greatest strides in dealing with autism that anybody has in the past twenty years. This year, in addition to our research with autism, we're applying our 'mind-control' techniques as you call them to comatose severe trauma patients. We're trying to show that by communicating directly with a patient's subconscious, the patient can play a key and direct role in helping to heal himself. And at the same time, we've also been given a large federal grant to pursue ways of controlling schizophrenia through both drug therapy and hypnotherapy. There's your 'mind control' for you, Mr. Coffey."

"If you're so proud of your work, why don't you play a more public role in it."

She glanced again at her wristwatch. "I really do need to go, Mr. Coffey. But let me say this as my parting shot—you mentioned rabbis and priests. Well, that's how most of our clients like to see us. As doctors who've dedicated their lives to helping others. Even when you're involved in something as beneficial as Sigma, the press likes to play it as if you're this big, cold-hearted capitalist robber baron who has her hands in dozens of pies. Our clients like to think of us as rabbis and priests, Mr. Coffey. It's that simple." Another glance at her watch. "Now if you'll excuse me."

She stood up and started around the desk. She was going to hustle him right back into the arms of the ice maiden.

At the door, he said, "Was the fire marshal sure Kenneth's death was an accident?"

Dr. Priscilla Bowman said, "Have a nice day, Mr. Coffey."

***

Five minutes later, Coffey was in his car again, just wheeling out onto the street. He picked up his cell phone and dialed the number of his stockbroker. He'd invested most of his severance pay from the police force. It wasn't a lot, but it was something, anyway. He asked his stockbroker, Mallory, if he could get a profile of the Sigma Corporation, the board of directors, any heavy investors, etc. Mallory said he'd give it his best shot.

Then Coffey turned on the news.

He listened in disbelief to two stories: one about how Quinlan had called police and promised to deliver Jenny Stafford later this afternoon and the other about a double murder.

While he was sailing down the street, he reached over the seat and grabbed the phone book he kept back there. He put the book on the seat next to him and began searching through the pages for the letter C.

***

"You know who they were?"

"Huh-uh."

"You watch the news?"

"Sometimes."

"Well, a while back," Gretchen said, "this woman named Judith Carney and this young boy named Sean Gray . . . they killed a bunch of people."

"Oh?" Jenny said.

Gretchen nodded. "They were on the tape."

"What were they doing?"

"Shooting somebody."

"What?"

"Yeah. Some guy Quinlan had strapped into a chair."

"You sure it was Quinlan?"

"Positive. You could see him over in the corner of this room, giving them instructions."

"What kind of instructions?"

Gretchen shrugged. "Oh, you know. Do this and do that. At first, it was silly stuff. Lift your left leg. Or gallop like a horse. Or take a pin and prick yourself. Then he told them to take the guns from their pockets."

Jenny was beginning to see the situation clearly. "Did they looked drugged to you?"

Gretchen thought a long moment. "Yeah, I guess they did."

"Like they were moving slowly and weren't quite sure of what they were doing?"

"Yeah; yeah. Just like that."

"So what did they do then?"

"They shot him."

"The man tied in the chair?"

"Yeah."

"Did he bleed?"

"Oh, he bled, all right. I mean, it wasn't fake or anything." She paused. "Over in the warehouse, there's this big room they keep locked all the time. It has the word Sigma on it. I never knew what was in there until a couple of weeks ago when I snuck up to the Tower and found this tape."

She was beginning to see the relevance of the tape and why Quinlan had been so angry that Gretchen had taken it. Quinlan had long been obsessed with mind-altering and mind-controlling drugs. Like most sociopaths, he saw nothing wrong in devising ways to control people. He was much smarter than they were, wasn't he? And if he used his drugs and hypnotherapy to get them to do his bidding, what was the harm? Sometimes, you had to take extreme actions to get your way. And so be it.

Thinking about Judith Carney and Sean Gray, Jenny realized that Quinlan had achieved his dream. Persuading two people to go out and kill a number of other people for you . . . that was the ultimate expression of mind control. While the psychiatric establishment in the United States still considered that level of control a fantasy, most other major nations knew it could—and was being—done.

As she sat next to the bed where Gretchen lay, Jenny realized the implication of this. If he could get the woman and the boy to kill . . . then he obviously had gotten *her* to kill, too.

She had murdered those men, after all!

"What's the matter?" Gretchen said, sounding like a child.

"Nothing."

"You look—sad or something."

"I guess I just want to get out of here. When do you think's a good time?"

"Right after lunch."

"Good. The sooner the better."

Gretchen lay back and put her hand on her stomach and looked up at the ceiling. "I want him to be there for the birth."

"That'd be nice." Jenny was on autopilot, answering words that meant nothing to her. Her mind was still filled with the terrible realization that she really *was* a killer.

"I want him to see the baby coming out."

"That'd be great."

"And hold it before they wash the blood and the afterbirth off."

"Yeah. He'd always remember that."

"Then I want to streak his face all up with the blood and the afterbirth. You know, like an Indian warrior."

That brought Jenny back to the conversation. No more autopilot. It was hard to disregard what Gretchen had just said.

"Well, maybe that's going a little far, Gretchen."

"He's the father, isn't he?" She was angry that Jenny hadn't liked her idea. The insanity was back in her voice and eyes.

"Well, yes."

"Well, then why wouldn't he want to let me paint him up with the blood and the afterbirth?"

She needed Gretchen as an ally. "Maybe you're right, Gretchen."

Gretchen's gamine face turned toward Jenny. "Damn right, I'm right." The anger again. "He's the one who got me pregnant, the least he can do is show me he loves our child."

"Right."

"I mean, if he doesn't, I'll go to the police and tell them what he did with Judith Carney and that Gray kid. He'll be sorry then, believe me."

Jenny sat back in the chair. She needed for Gretchen to calm down. She needed Gretchen to be as rational as possible. Only Gretchen could lead her to an escape route. And if she displeased Gretchen in any way, Gretchen might very well turn her over to Quinlan.

She said, "I'm your friend, Gretchen. You know that, don't you?"

"You piss me off sometimes."

"I'm sorry if I do."

"He'd look real neat all painted up in blood and afterbirth."

"Yes, he would."

"You're not just saying that?"

"No, no, I'm not."

"He wants to fuck all these other girls."

"I'm sorry."

"I'm the only one he should want to fuck. I know tricks. Tricks other girls *don't* know. So why does he need other girls?"

"Maybe he'll change when the baby is born."

Gretchen turned her face back toward Jenny again. "You really think so?"

"Yes, yes, I do, Gretchen. I think he'll see that baby, and he'll realize that he should be true to you."

Gretchen's eyes gleamed with tears. "I just wish he knew how much I love him."

"Maybe he will when he sees the baby."

"He's all I think of."

Gretchen turned her head away. "Maybe he'll *hate* the baby."

"Why would he?"

"Some men do."

"He won't. I'm sure he won't."

"You promise?"

"Yes, I *promise* he won't."

"He'd better not, the sonofabitch." The anger, yet again. Then, "You know when I was in the mental hospital when I was ten?"

Jenny didn't know what Gretchen was talking about, but she went along anyway. "Yes."

"You know what a woman told me?"

"What?"

"She said that she loved her baby so much, she *ate* the afterbirth. You think that was true?"

"I suppose it could be."

"She said she paid the nurse to save the afterbirth."

"Wow."

"I don't think I could do that. I mean, even as much as I love this little baby inside me, I don't think I could do that. You think you could?"

"I don't think so."

Gretchen closed her eyes again. "He better not fuck anybody but me from now on."

"Gretchen."

"What?"

"Could we go?"

"I'm kind of tired. Maybe I should nap. Maybe it's because I'm pregnant."

"We really should go now."

"Right away?"

"I'm afraid so. All you need to do is get me to the fields, and I can go on alone from there. Then you can come back here and have yourself a nice, long nap."

"That does sound kind've good."

"Good. Then can we leave now?"

Gretchen went in to the bathroom and washed her face and dried her hands. She did all this with the bathroom door open. Then she came out and said, "You scared of tight spaces?"

"A little."

"Then you won't like this one. It's a tunnel, goes from the basement of this building all the way to the river."

"Have you ever taken it?"

"Oh, sure. A couple of times. But it's real scary. So narrow and all."

"I guess I don't have much choice, do I?"

Gretchen looked at her calmly. "I'm glad you're doin' this. Then you won't be around to tempt him. He can concentrate on the baby and me." Then, "You ready?"

"All set."

"Then let's go."

Chapter Forty-Three

COFFEY counted seven cars either in the driveway or out at the curb of the Cummings home. They were all new cars, mostly high-end Chryslers and Caddies, The B list of suburban wealth. The place was a large ranch with a terra-cotta roof and whitewashed stucco walls. It was well-kept, as was the landscaped lawn. Cummings had done pretty well for himself as a private operative. Coffey didn't see anything that looked like a police car. They'd probably finished questioning the widow until tomorrow or so. She'd be busy today with funeral arrangements and family.

He knocked on the front door, behind which he could hear the conversation of several people all, apparently, women.

The woman who came to the door was young and quite striking, mostly due to her almost unearthly blue eyes. She was blonde and slim and elegant in a country-club way, sandals and blue slacks and a tailored white blouse. Not a strand of polyester to be seen. Her hair was in a soft and somewhat loose chignon. Her eyes said that she'd been crying but she seemed utterly composed when she spoke. "May I help you?"

"I'm looking for Mrs. Cummings."

"*I'm* Mrs. Cummings."

"I guess I must mean your mother, ma'am."

"My mother lives in Connecticut and her last name is Walsh. Now, may I help you with something? This is a bad time. My husband was killed last night."

Cummings had done well for himself, indeed. The lovely lady had to be twenty years Cummings' junior and an unlikely mate for a smooth but hardass ex-cop like Cummings.

"That's why I'm here," he said. "About the murder."

"You know something about it?" she said. She sounded excited. Maybe she really had been in love with the guy. Anything was possible.

"Is there somewhere we could talk?"

"There's a patio?"

"That'd be great."

"You can walk around to the back. There's a gate. There's a big red dog back there. He looks fierce, but he won't hurt you unless I tell him to."

"Why don't you call him in advance, then?"

She smiled, tears collecting idly in the corners of her numbingly beautiful eyes. "You'll be fine." She turned an elegant wrist to the house behind her. "I'll go in and explain to the girls what's going on."

The dog turned out to be a retriever mix of some kind. He looked, as predicted, pretty fierce. Coffey opened the gate and let himself into a large backyard with a swimming pool, covered now for the coming cold months, and a large, screen-enclosed patio. Her dog followed him to the patio, growling all the way. He probably wouldn't get fed if he didn't act at least a little bit tough.

Coffey let himself into the patio and sat down on a rather slight-looking chair at the rather slight-looking garden table. The melancholy of autumn was in the air. Leaves fluttered from tree branches, and a high intoxicating scent of burning grass was on the air, the scent of nostalgia, the summer idyll gone now, the savagery of Midwestern winter just ahead. It was peaceful out here on the patio, almost its own little world. He could envision summer evenings here, the pool open, its icy blue depths perfect for swimming, and after swimming sitting here at the table talking softly against the background noise of crickets and the nightbirds, the dark air flickering with fireflies until, sleepy as children, you headed inside. There was only one suitable mate for such a moment, Jenny. And that was why he had to help her.

"My name's Rachel, by the way." She came out the back door quickly, carrying a small tray, efficient as a waitress.

"Nice to meet you, Rachel. My name's Michael Coffey."

"Are you a cop? You seem like a cop?"

"Ex-cop. Like your husband. Now I'm a mystery writer, and I own my own cab."

She set two glasses down in front of them. "I'm an iced tea nut. I just assume everybody else is, too."

"I like iced tea. Thanks."

She then emptied the tray of sugar, lemon slices, and napkins. "Help yourself." Then, "A mystery writer *and* a cabbie? Do you drive the cab to get ideas for stories?"

"I need to drive the cab to make a living."

"God, are you serious? Didn't Patricia Cornwell just get something like ten million a book?"

"Unfortunately, most of us never have that kind of luck."

She sat down, flicked her hair back with a model's panache, and then looked directly at him. For the first time, he noticed that for all her aggressive style and beauty, there was something a bit cold, distanced about her. She wore her looks the way she would wear a stunning new outfit, one she didn't quite feel comfortable with yet.

"I want to say two things," she said.

"Fine."

"First of all, I'm forty-two years old. My husband was only six years older than me. Just to put that thing to rest. He wasn't handsome, and he didn't have a very good formal education, but he was the gentlest and most tender man I've ever known. To me he was. To other people he could be a real prick. And I'd be lying if I said he didn't take some pride in *being* a prick to them. He was also the funniest guy I've ever been with. Had a real dry sense of humor. And he could actually do stuff. I'm an old-fashioned girl, Mr. Coffey. I can take care of myself, but I do like a husband who can fix a car or get the washing machine running again or who can climb up in the tree and get the cat down. There aren't a lot of men in our generation who can do stuff like that anymore. We've all become helpless little girls, men and women alike, I'm afraid, everything gets done for us by somebody else. He could build a passing fair cabinet and he could do some pretty complicated electrical rewiring when he needed to. And he could cook a mean steak dinner, too. And despite what you may have heard, I didn't marry him for *his* money—he didn't have much, not when I met him, anyway— if anything, he married me for *mine*. I came into quite an inheritance when I was thirty-six. He insisted on 'borrowing' the money from me. He didn't want a gift. We signed a contract and everything—bank-loan rates. His idea was to open up a private investigation agency for the wealthy. Most wealthy people are very wary of private cops. And understandably. There are a lot of sleazeballs in the trade. And secondly, I loved my husband very, very much. And I want the fucker who killed him. Because if he doesn't get executed by the court, then I'll kill the sonofabitch myself. And that's not just talk. If you can help me with that, great. If you can't, then please don't waste my time."

What a very different impression he had of her now from the one he'd formed when she'd been just another languid suburban beauty answering her door. She was a vital, impressive, grown-up woman.

"I think I can help you," he said. "And I think you can help me."

"Good," she said, and put forth a slender but muscular hand for him to shake.

"He was working on—"

"I have to be careful here, Mr. Coffey. I can't divulge the names of anybody he was working with. They deserve their privacy. I need to know if you're looking into the same case *I've* got in mind."

"How will you know that?"

"Give me a couple of names involved. Then I'll know."

He thought a moment. "Jenny Stafford is one."

Her face was unreadable. She watched him over the edge of her iced tea glass. She put the glass down and said, "Any others?"

"Quinlan."

"Any others?"

He smiled. "Do I win an appliance or anything if I come up with three names?"

"One more, Mr. Coffey."

"The obvious one. David Foster."

She nodded. "The same case."

"The police no doubt have his files by now."

"Yes. But my husband never wrote much down. Files are vulnerable. They can pretty easily fall into the wrong hands. He kept most of his information in his head. He had a great memory. He never forgot anything."

"Did he talk to you about cases?"

"Sometimes."

"About this case?"

"Yes," she said. "Yes, he talked to me quite a bit about this case, in fact."

"Anything you'd care to share with me?"

The anger was back in her eyes. He had no doubt that this woman would be able to kill the man who'd killed her husband. No doubt at all.

"There's a *lot* I'd care to share with you," she said. "Let me get rid of the girls—they've been very helpful all day long—and I'll be back."

She got up and went inside.

Coffey went back to his fantasy about sitting on a nighttime patio like this with Jenny Stafford.

Chapter Forty-Four

GRETCHEN had predicted that the tunnel was scary. She hadn't been exaggerating.

Even getting to the tunnel had been a problem, sneaking out of the apartment where Quinlan had confined Jenny, then waiting until they could get to the corridor leading to the basement. This time of day, there was a lot of foot traffic.

Gretchen seemed oblivious to being caught. She just assumed that they were going to make it, that there was nothing to worry about. Jenny also noted that Gretchen seemed much happier now that Jenny was actually leaving. She would have Quinlan all to herself, Jenny thought sadly. At least, that's what Gretchen thought. But no woman ever had Quinlan all to himself. He was fascinated with the notion of conquest, of defiling a woman. Then on to the next conquest . . . which, in Quinlan's case, would hopefully be prison.

For her part, Jenny would be glad to be out of here. Even this brief a stay brought back terrible and painful memories of her days here as a patient. She knew now that Quinlan had somehow "messaged" her to come here.

She followed two steps behind Gretchen. They took a long, empty corridor, then a short, empty corridor. The building was as quiet as a mid-morning five-star hotel. Baffling had been built into the walls to absorb loud noises. The quiet lent the place a certain unreality, though, as if they were moving across the bottom of a silent sea.

Finally, just as they reached the short corridor where they could see the steps leading to the basement, Quinlan's number two person Barcroft came out of a room several doors behind them.

"Say, where are you two going?" he snapped. In this kind of quiet, he didn't need to shout. His voice carried just fine.

Both women turned to look at him. Gretchen looked as if she was trying to concoct some logical-seeming lie. But no words came from her. And then she broke into a run.

Gretchen ran quickly and surely, taking the steps two, even three at a time, elfin and quick as an arrow.

Jenny should be so lucky. Not only did she stumble twice, she made the supremely stupid mistake of looking back over her shoulder. Barcroft was closing quickly on her, a big man with a loping run that reminded her of a bear closing on prey.

Gretchen disappeared around a right corner at the bottom of the stairs. She was now nothing more than sounds, foot-slaps against the tiled floor, breath-gasps as her burst of energy began to take its toll, then a metallic rattle as she pulled a large set of keys from the pocket of her drab uniform.

This was what Jenny saw, Gretchen with her keys, when she came around the same right corner Gretchen had taken a few moments earlier.

Gretchen got the door open and waved Jenny inside hurriedly.

The place was a large, square storage room. Large bags of everything from peat moss to dry puppy food to road salt were stacked ten high and five wide against one wall. Against another wall were boxes of everything from laundry soap to tampons to glassware. There were also new rakes, new sealed window frames, new toilet bowls. The hospital was a big operation.

Gretchen passed quickly through this room. Jenny followed her down a short, shadowy corridor to a second door. The jangle of keys again as Gretchen bent to match key to lock.

And that was when the alarm sounded.

It was an impressive alarm, whooping, looping, an audio spear jammed deep into the ear canal. It could reduce most people to quivering heaps in moments. It not only reached your hearing, it reached your *soul*. Jenny clamped her hands over her ears.

Gretchen pushed into the second room. A massive furnace

and air-conditioning unit crouched in the center of the concrete floor like a giant and obstinate alien machine.

Gretchen hurried past the equipment to a far wall where another door had been built into the wall.

Gretchen took from her pocket a device that looked like a phone beeper. She pointed it at the door and pressed one of four buttons on the device. The door swung slowly open. There was nothing beyond the door but more concrete wall. Which made no sense.

Jenny could hear them shouting. Barcroft and some others at the first door now. Like Gretchen, they'd have keys. It wouldn't take them long to get in here.

Jenny wondered if Gretchen had finally lost *all* her sanity. How could a blank wall be an escape route?

Gretchen pressed a button on the black device she held in her hand. At first, nothing happened. Then Jenny heard a noise, a rumble really, as something heavy—but what?—began to slowly move.

The wall began to move. To the right. And the more it moved, the faster it moved, revealing a small circular tunnel opening. The tunnel material seemed to be aluminum.

"I sure hope you're not real claustrophobic," Gretchen said over her shoulder, as she crawled into the dark tunnel.

"I'm *very* claustrophobic," Jenny said.

"Then this *really* isn't going to be any fun for you."

Then Gretchen was gone, swallowed up by the cold, grave-smelling gloom inside the tunnel.

Shouts now, closer. Barcroft and his men.

Jenny could hear them at the second door. It sounded like a large mob of them. Only moments away.

The tunnel opening was built low into the wall for easy access. She climbed inside. The darkness and the chill overwhelmed her. She could feel herself shrinking from the tomb-like passage that awaited her. Clawing, clawing to be set free. Getting lost in utter blackness. But she needed to escape Quinlan. Had to.

She crawled deeper inside. Far down the tunnel, she could hear Gretchen moving fast.

The second door burst open and the people rushed in. Only one door away now. She had to hurry. Gretchen must have been able to hear her, too. The door was beamed shut, apparently with Gretchen's remote device. The darkness was utter and complete now.

Jenny began to make her way through the grave-narrow tunnel.

Chapter Forty-Five

WHEN she was finished talking, Mrs. Cummings led Coffey back into the house from the patio, and to a small, nicely appointed room on the second floor. The windows had louvered shutters on them, the wine-red carpet was deep and plush, the desk was mahogany, and armchairs real leather. The walls were covered with various plaques and other mementos from Cummings' police years. He'd been a good cop.

She said, "The police went through his desk. They didn't find much. He wasn't a stupid man. He knew not to leave important things in a desk." She reached into the pocket of her slacks and took out a small, folded piece of white paper. "This is a combination to a safe. You'll find it on the floor of the closet over there. Covered by carpeting. The police didn't find it. Why don't you look through it?"

"I really appreciate this."

"It's for his sake." She looked wistful. "He was the only man who ever knew how to love me. He gave me my space, but he wasn't foolish enough to give me too much space because he'd knew I'd roam on him if he did." She was getting teary again. "There won't ever be another one like him, not in my life there won't, anyway. So I want them to pay for what they took from me. Understand?"

"Very well," he said, thinking of his wife and daughter. "Very well."

"Good," she said, "now I'm going to go downstairs and play some of the CDs he liked and start working on a good, hard drunk that'll take up most of the evening."

As soon as she turned and started to leave, he went to the

closet, and began to pull up the edges of the carpeting, looking for the safe.

***

Jenny wanted to go back. She hadn't gone more than four feet into the tunnel when she was overwhelmed with terror. She couldn't see anything, she was starting to have trouble breathing, and the space was so confining she could barely wriggle around. Somewhere in the distance, she could hear the steady progress being made by Gretchen. Not far behind her, she could hear the shouts of Barcroft and the others as they burst into the room where the tunnel opening was.

All sorts of fears played on her mind. What if the tunnel collapsed? What if Quinlan decided to block both ends of the tunnel and smother them to death? What if there were poisonous snakes or rabid rats in here? Thinking the latter, she again shrunk in upon herself. She could almost *feel* a snake, cold and slick, slithering over her hand and wrapping itself around her arm. She could almost *see* a rat, ruby eyes aglow in the gloom, approaching her, waiting to rip into her flesh with its filthy, ragged teeth. She was paralyzed here, her entire body filling with dread from some anticipated disaster that would end her life.

And then she got sick of it. Of her fear. Her whining. Her paralysis. She'd been given a chance to escape and here she was whimpering, indecisive. It was time to catch up with Gretchen, to take advantage of this opportunity.

She started moving again, slowly at first—she hadn't quite banished her notion of snakes and rats—but with ever-increasing speed.

She was even getting used to the feel of cold aluminum on the palms of her hands, and the grave-smell of the earth surrounding her.

She thought of Quinlan and how he'd set her up at the two motels. It was time for her to fight back. She'd been so weak all her life. But she would be weak no longer.

Just as long as there weren't any rats or snakes.

***

Coffey was sitting at Cummings' desk when Rachel came in.

"You've been up here over an hour," she said. "Thought I'd bring you a little refreshment." She waggled a fifth of Dewar's at him.

"Afraid I'm an alcoholic, Mrs. Cummings."

"Really? You don't look it."

"Been off the stuff for a while now. Don't look as bad as I used to."

"I just hope it isn't catching," she said, as she sat down in one of the leather armchairs, "your teetotaling, I mean. I'd never get through this without my friend here." She kissed the neck of the bottle with erotic fervor. Then she looked at him. She was a beautiful but sad lady, sad long before her husband was murdered. "I've got a drinking problem, too, I'm afraid. And someday I may get around to doing something about it." Then, "Did you find anything?"

"Yes," Coffey said. "I'm pretty sure I know who killed your husband and Foster and why."

"Really? Already?"

"Already," he said.

She sipped a drink from the glass she held. She'd set the scotch bottle on the deck. "It was Quinlan, wasn't it?"

"Did your husband tell you what he was working on?"

"A little. But that's who I figured it was. I've never seen him work harder on a case. He was obsessed with it. He thought that this was the case that would make him a national figure. He had a nice business here in Chicago, but he wanted to have offices in LA and New York. That was his ambition. He met a producer at ABC about a few weeks ago and told the guy what he was working on—no names of course, not breaking any confidences I mean—and the producer got very excited. He liked the hospital angle. He said he was sure he could get the case on one of their prime time news shows. My husband was real excited. *Real* excited. I think he worked harder on this case than any he ever had. And I think it was paying off."

"So do I," Coffey said, indicating the folder he'd found in the safe. The folder lay open, four neatly typed pages inside it. Coffey had been over the pages several times. He needed to familiarize himself with them, so when he called Detective Ryan, he'd sound as if he knew what he was talking about.

"Now what?"

"Now I call a homicide detective I know." Actually, he'd hoped to be alone when he made the call.

Rachel made it easy for him. "Maybe I'll make myself a ham sandwich. This booze is hitting me harder than I wanted it to. You want a sandwich?"

"No, thanks."

"It's very good ham."

"I appreciate the offer. But thanks, anyway."

As soon as she left, he picked up the phone and called Maggie Ryan.

***

Jenny was moving much faster now but still cautiously. A dark tunnel like this, you could run into practically anything.

She couldn't hear Gretchen any longer. She wondered if something was wrong. Could Gretchen already be out of the tunnel, waiting for her up top? Gretchen had given the impression that this was a long tunnel and would take some time to traverse.

So where was Gretchen? Jenny tried whispering for the other woman, but her whispers didn't seem to travel far. There was no way Gretchen could hear her.

The tunnel ran straight for quite a while. The first turn was actually a subtle curve. She had no problem making the turn. And a few moments later, she ran into the opening.

In the dark this way, she couldn't see the shape of the thing. She had to feel it, it was the only way she could get an impression of it. It was an opening in the side of the tunnel. She felt around it. Aluminum. Another aluminum offshoot off the tunnel.

But where did it lead?

She wasn't sure what to do. She wished she could see. She wished she could hear Gretchen. Had something happened to Gretchen? Was this some kind of trap? Then she remembered something Gretchen had said, something about a surprise. Was this the surprise?

She continued to grope inside the opening. She even poked her head into it an inch or two. The smell was different in the offshoot. It still smelled of grave, it still smelled of aluminum, and yet neither smell was quite so overpowering in the offshoot.

Should she enter it? Is this where Gretchen had gone? Why hadn't she let Jenny know what was going on?

There was only one way to find out.

A shard of headache stabbed into her right eye. She was so consumed by the tunnel and the offshoot that, for a time, she'd completely forgotten the events that led her to be in the tunnel. Quinlan. The mind control. The murders. The headaches. She could still very well be a murderer. The blood of two human lives on her hands . . . the grief she would have caused so many people. . . .

She took the offshoot. She moved very slowly. Somehow, the offshoot felt even more confining than the main escape tunnel. She had a moment of panic when claustrophobia overwhelmed her. She gasped two, three times trying to get her breath. She wondered where this led. What was she going to find when she got there? The river? Open forest? What?

Slowly, her pace increased. The darkness grew even darker. She had a moment when the whole situation struck her as dreamlike. Only a dream, and a terrible one at that, could duplicate this for its sustained menace.

She wanted to cry out Gretchen's name—the way she would in a nightmare—but she knew better.

All she could do was go ahead. Knees starting to ache very badly. Palms numb from the cold aluminum. Eyes useless.

Go on ahead and see what awaited her.

***

"I like the *X-Files*, too, Mr. Coffey. But that doesn't mean I believe in all that crap."

"Mind control isn't crap."

"I'm not a brain, Mr. Coffey. And I don't pretend to be. I'm a homicide detective. A good one. Not a great one. But a good one. And I'll tell you something, in order to keep my job, and do what the citizens of this city expect from me, I have to rely on evidence. Hard, clear evidence. And you know what, Mr. Coffey? You know the evidence I have? I have eyewitnesses who saw her at the murder scenes. I have her fingerprints all over the murder rooms and all over the murder knives. This is the kind of case I've prayed for ever since I became a detective, Mr. Coffey. Open and shut. Simple as hell. And that's what the jury is going to say, too."

"You're not even going to listen to me, are you?" he said.

"I already *have* listened to you, Mr. Coffey."

"Quinlan's job in the CIA was with a secret unit that worked with drugs and hypnotherapy to break down personalities and turn them into moles for various branches of the government. In other words, mind control."

"You can't hypnotize somebody into killing somebody else," she said. "I may be a dumb cop, but I know that much anyway."

"You can't turn them into killers with hypnosis alone," Coffey said, "but you can when you combine hypnotherapy and drugs. That's already been proved."

On the other end of the phone, Margie Ryan sighed. "What exactly do you want from me?"

"When Quinlan brings Jenny in, hold Quinlan, too. That's all I'm asking. I have a friend in the DA's office. I want him to question Quinlan."

"What do I hold him *for*, Mr. Coffey?"

"Just tell him there are a lot of unanswered questions that you'd like to go over with him. I'll have Dick Feldman there whenever you need him."

"Feldman, I like." She paused. A beeping sound. "There goes my beeper, Mr. Coffey. I have to go. I'll think about it. Get back to me in a couple of hours."

"I appreciate it," Coffey said.

But she'd already hung up.

***

Jenny sensed the wall before she actually saw it. If it *was* a wall. She couldn't be sure.

All she knew was that, not long after she took off the offshoot of the main tunnel, she encountered some sort of blockage.

Despite the darkness, she could sense a different texture to the thing that ended this part of the tunnel.

She put a hand out. Felt soil, and beneath the soil, metal. And behind the metal, very faintly, she heard a noise. She wasn't sure what the noise was. It was just a . . . noise.

She was ready to back up, which wouldn't be easy. Putting a car in reverse was simple; putting a human body in reverse was another matter. She was especially worried about getting around the corner of the offshoot.

A light appeared. She put a hand forward and pushed hard. The blockage gave way.

An electrical light. Revealing what appeared to be a concrete floor and a green-painted wall. Some sort of room, apparently. That's what had been on the other side of the metal sheath.

"C'mon in," a familiar voice said. Gretchen.

Jenny moved forward as quickly as she could. Crawling would never be her favorite method of traveling.

The room was long and narrow. There was a couch, chair, small bookcase crammed with paperbacks. There was a table covered with plastic quarts of bottled water. Nothing fancy, to be sure.

"There are a couple of people who know about the main tunnel," Gretchen explained, "but only Quinlan and I know about this little room."

"What's it for?" Jenny said, getting to her feet, brushing herself off.

"In case the place ever gets raided, you know, like in Waco."

"He hides in here?"

"Once in a while. He's real paranoid. See that door?" Another large door built into the wall. "There's a tunnel behind that door, too. It leads to another tunnel. It leads to a point in the woods. Quinlan figures if all else fails, he can escape through this one."

"That's where we're going?"

"Yes."

"Could we hurry, please? I just want to get out of here. I'm really getting claustrophobic."

Gretchen glanced around. "I sort of like it. It's so private. I hope I can get Quinlan to come back here with me someday."

Jenny walked over to the door, put a hand on the silver safety knob. She hoped to hurry Gretchen along.

Gretchen said, "I heard you had some very nice times together."

Her tone made Jenny nervous. Gretchen could sound just

fine for a time and then slip deeply into her Mad voice. She was there now, and it was eerie.

"I really want to get going, Gretchen."

"Is it true? You and Quinlan had some really nice times?"

Jenny sighed. "I thought we went through all this. He's all yours."

"People always talk about you. About how obsessed with you he was." She looked as if she wanted to cry. "He may still be."

Oh, I don't think so, Gretchen. I really don't."

Gretchen had been standing against the opposite wall. Now she started across the narrow room with its fluorescent light on the ceiling and its dust-laden, still air making Jenny feel dirty and raspy.

Gretchen put her hand on Jenny's shoulder. "I think he still loves you." The anxiety and sadness were back in Gretchen's eyes.

"He never loved me, Gretchen," she said softly. "He couldn't have me. And that hurt his ego. That's what it was all about."

"A smart girl," Gretchen said, leaving her hand on Jenny's shoulder, "that's how she'd play it with Quinlan. Hard to get. That's what I should've done, but I didn't have the strength. I never did, with guys, I mean. Any time I wanted a guy, I always went after him. And they don't like that, guys don't. Not guys worth having anyway. I always went right after them, and they weren't interested in me in the least."

Jenny realized that she would have to spend a few minutes here bringing Gretchen down from her perch. "But you're learning, Gretchen. That's the important thing. You're learning not to throw yourself at men."

"All they wanted was sex," Gretchen said. At least she took her hand away; took her hand away and walked back and leaned against the opposite wall. "I guess I'm pretty good at that. At sex, I mean. That's what the guys tell me, anyway. How about you? You good at sex?"

Jenny laughed softly. "Nobody's offered me any trophies, if that's what you mean." Then, "Gretchen, do you suppose we could go?"

"Quinlan's like that, too," Gretchen said, again giving an answer to a matter that had been raised several moments earlier.

"He likes them hard to get. And you know what? A real sharp gal, a gal who really knew how to play him, you know what a sharp gal would do?"

Jenny had never liked the term "gal." She associated it with the women in her mother's bridge club. But she decided now would not be a good time to bring up her aversion to the word.

She said, "Gretchen, could we please go now?"

"You know what a really sharp gal would do now if she really wanted Quinlan?"

Jenny knew she'd have to answer. "What would she do, Gretchen?"

"She'd run away. Make it look like she couldn't wait to get away. That'd make him really want her."

Jenny immediately saw where this was going, where Gretchen's constantly shifting paranoia was leading her. "This isn't a ruse, Gretchen. I really do want to get away from the compound."

Gretchen's eyes bloomed with sorrow. "You should hear him when he talks about you. He talks about you a lot." Her gaze met Jenny's. "A whole lot."

Jenny reached out, took Gretchen's arm. "He'll be all yours, Gretchen. I'll be gone. You'll have him all to yourself."

Gretchen said, "But you could always come back." Then, before Jenny could say anything, Gretchen said, "Nobody can find us."

"What?"

"You know the tunnel you came in to get to the room?"

"Yes," Jenny said, sensing that Gretchen was much wilier than she'd first given her credit for.

"Well, it fills in perfectly with aluminum, just like the rest of the tunnel wall. Unless you know exactly where to look, you go on right past it." Her eyes were once again on Jenny's face. "I wish you'd be honest with me, Jenny."

"I am being honest."

Gretchen sighed. "I try to be honest all the time. Even with Quinlan. Even when he hurts my feelings. You know, I saw this shrink on TV one time and he said that he never met a person who didn't lie. Well, then he never met me. Because I *never* lie. That's pretty good, isn't it?"

"That's very good."

Gretchen smiled. The Mad Smile that matched perfectly the Mad voice. "Though sometimes I deceive people. I mean, I don't *like* deceiving people but sometimes I have to. Like the way I deceived you."

Goose bumps coarsened Jenny's arms. In her quiet, sad way, Gretchen was one of the most terrifying people Jenny had ever known. "How did you deceive me, Gretchen?" Jenny said softly.

"Two ways, actually."

"Two ways."

"The tunnel." She smiled again, looking more crazed than ever. "Why I brought you here, I mean."

"You're going to help me escape."

"That's where I deceived you. I'm not going to help you escape. I'm going to kill you. And I'm very, very sorry about that. I really, really am." She paused. "And I killed those two men in the motel rooms."

Her words lacerated Jenny. "What are you talking about?"

"Quinlan had me go in and kill them after the microwaves from the van knocked you out. That way, when you woke up, you'd think *you'd* killed them."

She searched Gretchen's face. No smile. No coyness. No evidence of her little games. Gretchen *had* killed those men. She really had.

Gretchen walked over to the door and touched the knob. "The tunnel behind this door? It was never finished. Nobody could use it even if they wanted to. Quinlan gave it up. I guess he figured one tunnel was enough." Her small, white hand touched the center of the door. "Nobody ever comes here. After I kill you, that's where I'm going to put you. In the tunnel. Then I'm going to cover you up with dirt. Then nobody will *ever* find you. Not even Quinlan." The Mad voice was back, Madder than ever. "You might not think that he'd look for you even if he knew you were dead but you know what—I think that Quinlan's some kind of space alien and he's got these special powers. I think he can raise people from the dead if he wants to." Gretchen nodded her head vigorously, in agreement with herself. "People laugh when I tell them that, about him being a space alien and all. But I saw this show on TV—I mean, it wasn't fiction, it was the real thing—and they had this professor on and he told you how to recognize a space alien when you came across one."

Jenny was only half-listening. She was looking for an escape route. She kept trying to convince herself that if she only looked hard enough and long enough, she'd find an alternative escape to the tunnel.

"You know what an aura is?" Gretchen said, loony and sincere as ever.

"Around your head, you mean?" Jenny said.

"Uh-huh. Well, that's how this professor said you can recognize them, the space aliens. They have these really strange auras that kind of pulsate, like they're sending out a signal or something. Quinlan's got an aura like that."

"That's really interesting, Gretchen."

Gretchen said, "I'm sorry I'm putting you through this, Jenny. But I just know that if Quinlan ever finds your body, he'll raise you from the dead, and then where'll I be? Right back to square one. I had a shrink who always said that—right back to square one'—and I really like that expression."

"It's a great expression, no doubt about it," Jenny said, still uselessly looking around.

And then it was there. In her hand. Gretchen's hand. It wasn't all that much of a knife. A cheap paring knife with a plastic walnut handle. But plunged into the heart, or into an eye, it would certainly do its deed.

"I'm sorry about this, Jenny," Gretchen said, mad as ever. "I really am."

And it was then she lunged for Jenny.

***

The cab searched the dark, lonely road, its headlights fierce and angry as a jungle cat's. The only thing that spoiled the dramatic effect was the somewhat dorky insignia on the doors and trunk identifying it as a cab. Coffey's cab.

He was on his way to the Stafford mansion. He was preparing the little speech he'd give to the security microphone when he pulled up to the gate. Unless he gave a stellar performance, there was no way they were going to let him come inside. And he needed desperately to get inside.

He passed no other cars on the last stretch of road to the mansion.

As he approached the double iron gates, he was still trying out speeches in his mind. Toadying, pleading speeches. The trouble was, he was sick of giving toadying, pleading speeches. He was trying to save the life of their daughter and if they were too thick to understand that, the hell with them.

When he approached the closed double gate, he didn't even slow down. He just drove right on through, sending the gates flying low into the shrubbery on either side of the drive.

He drove fast up the long, curving drive. No doubt, somebody inside the mansion had already taken note of this sudden breach of security and was on the phone with the cops. The tearing sound of metal, and the crashing sound a piece of gate made hitting the drive, gave him a peculiar satisfaction.

The mansion still resembled a castle to him. All it needed was a moat, a drawbridge, and a guy in a Robin Hood costume walking the battlements. He pulled up directly in front of the main door, killed his engine, leaped from the car, and ran up the front steps.

The maid was just opening the door when he reached it—apparently and less-than-brilliantly, she wanted to peer out and see what was going on—but he only pushed past her and stormed into the house.

The living room with its massive chandelier and antique European furnishings was glitzy and empty.

He went directly down the hall, shouting their names all the while, his words echoing back at him from the splendid high ceilings.

They were in the den and there were three of them.

Tom Stafford said, "The police are on the way, whoever the hell you are." He wasn't going to be intimidated. He was Tom Stafford and he was rich and powerful, and so what if this young man had just driven through his front gates and confronted him in his own den? He *still* wasn't going to be intimidated.

Coffey could hear Eileen hurrying down the hall. "Ma'am, ma'am, are you all right?" she was yelling anxiously.

She looked in the den and went, "Oh."

"Don't worry," Coffey said. "Nobody's going to get hurt.

I'm here to try and save their daughter, whether they believe it or not."

A big, lanky man stepped forward and said, "My name's Ted Hannigan. I'm a friend of the family." He shot a sharp look at Stafford and smiled coldly. "Well, his wife likes me, even if he doesn't." He shook hands with Coffey. "Right now, I'm up to hearing anything that might help Jenny. If you were willing to put your ass in a sling by driving through the gates, then I guess you at least deserve a hearing."

Tom Stafford said, "I was under the impression that this was *my* house and that I did the inviting around here."

"Lighten up, for God's sake, Tom," Hannigan said. "Your daughter's life is at stake here."

Tom Stafford looked shamed when Hannigan reminded him of why they were all here. He waved his hand. "I guess you're right, Ted." Then, to Coffey, "Exactly why the hell did you come here, Mr. Coffey?"

"First, cancel the cops," Coffey said. "The cops," Coffey repeated. "We don't have time to do a lot of explaining to them."

"Please, Tom," Molly Stafford said. "You know they'll stop if you ask them to."

Tom Stafford considered a moment then went over to a phone, picked up, punched out a number and then said, "This is Tom Stafford, Mr. Mayor. I guess we won't need any officers here at the moment. I'll explain later." Beat. "Thank you."

"This had better be one hell of a story you've got to tell us, Coffey," Stafford said after he hung up.

***

The first knife-thrust caught Jenny on the side of the neck. It wasn't much more than a gash. But even this slight a cut startled Jenny, paralyzed her momentarily. There was pain and there was blood. It made everything—the knife, Gretchen, this smothering little room—real in a way it hadn't been before.

Gretchen was just getting started. She brought the knife down again, this time catching Jenny on the ear. Gretchen's aim had been true—she'd been going for the carotid artery—but Jenny had shoved her at the last moment, seriously altering the trajectory of the blade.

DAUGHTER OF DARKNESS

The slice on the ear was even more painful than the cut on the neck. But unlike the neck wound which had immobilized her with fear, the ear cut infuriated her. Maybe it was because the pain was twice as much. Or maybe it was simply because her survival instincts had cut in and she was really pissed.

Gretchen stepped back, making Jenny's grab for her knife hand useless.

The two women slowly began to circle each other. Gretchen looked Madder than ever. But she also looked more determined. She clenched the knife handle so tightly, you could see the veins in relief on top of her hand. She kept waving the knife, so that even if Jenny lunged for her again, it would be pointless. The knife would be in constant motion.

Jenny glanced around the room. There must be something here that would suffice as a weapon. But she didn't see anything. Gretchen watched her checking everything out. Gretchen smiled.

Jenny feinted a lunge a few times, but Gretchen could see that Jenny was just going through the motions. Gretchen kept both herself and her knife moving. Any minute now, she'd finish this.

That was when Jenny slipped the belt off her jeans. At first, Gretchen obviously didn't know what was going on. She watched, fascinated, as Jenny snaked the belt out of its loops. What was she doing, anyway? Gretchen's expression asked. But Gretchen was smart. She kept moving, and the knife kept moving, too, back and forth, forth and back, slicing the air, making it impossible for Jenny to grab the knife without cutting herself badly in the process.

It was a fashion belt, a Gucci, a slip of cordovan black leather. Gucci, God love him, did not design belts for combat. He designed them to adorn teensy-weensy little waists. If she got out of this alive, Jenny would have to write Gucci a note, thanking him for all the help his belt had been. Perhaps he'd run it in a testimonial advertisement in *Mirabella*—"I Kicked Ass With My Gucci Fashion Belt!"

Gretchen just now figured out what Jenny was doing. Her eyes got big and her mouth slackened.

Jenny cracked the belt like a whip. An impressive demonstration of the fate that was about to befall Gretchen.

"Why don't you put the knife down, Gretchen?" Jenny said.

She spoke gently, the way she would to a sick child. Her injuries still smarted, but she was no longer pissed. The woman was insane. It wasn't her fault.

"You planned this, didn't you?" Gretchen said.

Jenny had to stop herself from laughing out loud. "I didn't even know about this tunnel until ten minutes ago. How could I have planned it?"

"You read my mind," she said. She continued to circle, to wave the knife. "You're one of them. One of the people from the mother ship."

Jenny sighed. "Will you please just give me the damn knife, Gretchen?"

"So you can kill me with it and then have Quinlan all to yourself?"

"No—so you won't hurt me and you won't hurt yourself."

For the first time, Gretchen's determination seemed to wane. She looked from the knife point to Jenny then back to the knife point and then to Jenny. "Do you look like Casper inside?"

"Casper?"

"The friendly ghost. You know."

"Oh."

"I saw inside one of the people from the mother ship one time and that's what they looked like. Like little Caspers except with real big eyes."

Jenny struck then. She looped the Gucci belt over Gretchen's wrist and yanked. Gretchen was startled, and loosened her grip momentarily.

The knife dropped from Gretchen's stunned hand and skidded a few inches across the floor.

Jenny bent to pick it up. And then Gretchen flew into her with a flying tackle. Gretchen wanted her knife back. Perhaps she'd borrowed it from one of the people on the mother ship and needed to return it.

For such a slight woman, Gretchen felt like an NFL lineman. They were all arms and legs and sweaty grunts and groans as they wrestled on the floor for possession of the knife.

Gretchen was on top, then Jenny was on top, then Gretchen was on top, then Jenny was on top. Jenny punched her once in the jaw and Gretchen punched her back in the ear, the same ear her knife had nicked, and it hurt like hell.

Then, even though she was on the bottom, Jenny got the knife. Gretchen was busy trying to strangle her—while at the same time declaring her undying love for Quinlan—when Jenny saw the knife blade directly behind Gretchen's foot. Gretchen was too busy at this very moment being Mad to look for the knife. It took a few moments, but Jenny was able to reach down and reach the blade and get the knife in her hand. There were a few momentary delays, however, when Gretchen got serious about the strangling business and really bore down on Jenny's throat. Aside from a little occasional gasping, a little occasional gacking, and a little occasional gurgling, Jenny was doing pretty well.

She brought the knife up in a single swoop and placed the edge of the blade directly against Gretchen's throat.

"Nobody could ever love him as much as I do," Gretchen screamed, spewing spittle and crazed words everywhere.

"Gretchen, Gretchen," Jenny said in a strangling-raspy voice.

"What?"

"I'm holding a knife to your throat."

Gretchen looked down and saw the blade being held to her throat. "Shit, you found it." She sounded shocked, dazed.

"Yeah. Now kindly get up and get off me."

"Where'd you find it?"

"Gretchen, what's the difference? Now, just get up."

"I'm curious is all."

Jenny sighed. "Will you please take your hands off my throat?"

"Oh, yeah." She took her hands off. "So where'd you find the knife?"

"Will you please get up off me?"

"I'll get up off you when you tell me where you found the knife."

Jenny sighed. "It was behind your foot."

"Shit. And I missed it?"

"Yeah. You did. And now will you get up?"

Gretchen got up. "I like that belt of yours, by the way. Is that a Gucci?"

This, Jenny thought, was a nightmare created by the Marx Brothers. She stood up, folding the switchblade and dropping it in her pocket.

She brushed herself off and said, "Gretchen, I'm going to prove to you I want out of here—and you're going to help me, all right?"

"I am. How?"

"Well, listen. And I'll tell you."

Chapter Forty-Six

IT took Coffey about twenty minutes to lay it all out for them, and at first the three faces he was addressing looked alternately skeptical and irritated—skeptical that brainwashing of that sort could actually be accomplished; irritated that he was wasting their time with nonsense when Jenny was out there somewhere in desperate condition.

Only when he began to factor in the drug therapy did they start to look at least mildly interested. Using straight hypnosis as a way of creating a second and murderous personality in Jenny's mind sounded preposterous. No hypnotist had that power. But if the hypnotist used mind-altering drugs along with his hypnotic technique . . . that became much more believable. Both Molly and Tom Stafford even began asking him a few questions at this point. Ted Hannigan just sat there, looking anxious and vaguely angry. He was still pretty dubious.

Then Coffey got into the matter of pathological memory mechanisms. "I took Jenny back to the motel room where the dead man was. We must have spent twenty minutes there. Then I took her to my place. Sometime during the night, she got out of bed and snuck off. She then got into a cab and came home. Here. But she doesn't remember any of it. Her conscious memory kicked in only when she got home. When he was in the CIA working with creating assassins through hypnotherapy and drug experimentation, one thing Quinlan learned about was the pathological memory mechanism. He found it useful to keep his would-be assassins in an amnesiac state until they were home safely. Even if they were back in their primary personalities, they had no memory of anything related to the assassination. So Jenny didn't remember anything until she walked in this door. The next night, when I came up to her in a restaurant, she had no memory of me at all, even though she'd spent several hours with me."

"I just don't see how Quinlan could have done all this," Tom Stafford said, "when he hasn't seen her in at least two years."

Molly Stafford nodded. She had the same question.

"Maybe he *has* been seeing her," Ted said.

Coffey shook his head. "I don't think he's *needed* to see her. Because she's been seeing someone else."

"Who?" Stafford snapped.

"Priscilla Bowman," Coffey said.

"Her psychiatrist?" Molly Stafford said. "That's impossible. Priscilla is almost like part of the family. She's seen all of us through some pretty bad times."

"I don't have any doubt about that," Coffey said. "She's a good psychiatrist. One of the best in the city. She's also still in love with Quinlan and helping him with Jenny. Together, they've programmed Jenny into developing a second personality that they can dictate to."

"But Jenny's never said anything about Priscilla acting strangely or anything," Molly said.

"She frequently puts Jenny into a hypnotic state doesn't she?" Coffey said.

"Yes, but that's just part of her technique," Stafford said.

"When Jenny is suggestible like that, in a kind of trance," Coffey said, "that'd be a perfect time to manipulate her the way they want to, I'd say."

"These are just accusations," Ted said. "I mean, no offense, but where do you get the qualifications to be talking about any of this? What do you do for a living, anyway?"

Pulling rank, Coffey thought. When you don't want to believe someone, you find a way to belittle them. Put them so far below your station that you don't have to take them seriously.

"I drive a cab and I write mystery novels on the side," Coffey said quietly. "And I used to be a cop."

"Ever had any formal training in psychology?"

"No."

"Ever had any formal training in drug use or drug therapy?"

"No."

"But," Hannigan said, "you're standing here lecturing us."

"I'm repeating things I've read and heard and learned, Mr. Hannigan," Coffey said. "Nothing more, nothing less."

"It's possible that Jenny just had some kind of breakdown, isn't it?" he questioned. "And that the breakdown has nothing to do with hypnosis or drugs?"

"It's possible, yes."

"I resent that, Hannigan," Stafford snapped. "You're saying you actually believe that Jenny *committed* these murders?"

Ted sighed. The strain between the two men was easy to see, Hannigan, the rumpled but still-dashing artist, Stafford, the military-precise businessman. From time to time, Molly Stafford looked back and forth at them, as if she was trying to make some decision. They were both formidable men and it couldn't be much fun to get caught in the crossfire of their egos.

"I'm not saying anything about the murders, Tom," Hannigan snapped back. "I'm simply saying that Jenny may simply have had a breakdown. I spent a good share of the afternoon with her. I've never seen her this fragile. She looked extremely stressed." He paused. "She looked like she did the day she went into the hospital."

"She was getting better, Ted," Molly said. "She really was. Until this came up—this, these *murders*."

"She didn't commit them," Stafford said angrily. "We're all sitting around here and that's what's in the air. That she killed these men. But that's not true. It's impossible." He was glaring at all three of them now, his hand wrapped so tightly around his whiskey glass that his knuckles were white.

Chapter Forty-Seven

QUINLAN, who had once said, in his role as divine father figure for rich folks, "Guns shouldn't be a last resort. They shouldn't be any resort at all," Quinlan was packing a .45. Apparently, God had sent him a memo about guns being a last resort.

It hadn't taken long to figure out what Gretchen and Jenny were up to. Work their way through to the tunnel, out here to this grassy area, then hurry on down to the river. It was shallow and narrow at this point. They could easily swim across. There was a park area over there, and a pay phone.

Even in the heavy dusk, Quinlan could see exactly where the tunnel came out high on the face of a red clay cliff, hidden behind a stand of scrub pines.

Quinlan was alone because he didn't want any of the others to know where it came out. True, Barcroft and three of the others had seen the door that led to the tunnel, but they didn't know what was behind the door. This was an escape route Quinlan didn't want to share with anybody. Only a phantom like Gretchen could have revealed his secret.

Quinlan heard a sharp noise in the bush. He swung around, his .45 ready to fire.

A brown-and-white dog, that looked like a mutt with beagle blood in it, ran past him about four feet away. Quinlan followed the animal with his weapon. He'd never killed anything, and he wondered what the experience was like. Probably let him down; most experiences did. He'd experimented with everything at one point or another in his life—virtually every kind of drug, every kind of sex, every kind of mind game—but they all let him down in the end. He was stuck inside his own ego and couldn't get out and he knew it. Masturbation was still a better orgasm than any kind of humping; and controlling a person was far superior to any kind of friendship with that person. That was why Jenny had meant so much to him. Somehow, she'd made him respond differently. He had genuinely pursued her. Maybe there was something in her particular kind of pain that attracted him. Pain was sometimes the most interesting part of a person. And yet with Jenny the pain was balanced by an innocence that he found profoundly sexual. That she wouldn't sleep with him just made her all the more desirable. Yet, in the end, he knew there was no way he could ever have her. While she'd been attracted to him from afar, seeing him as an insatiable predator changed her mind about him. She was gone from him now, gone forever, and the only thing he could do now—the only kind of communication left to them—was for him to destroy her.

He looked back at the tunnel exit. Something there had just caught his attention. But in the dusk, it was hard to tell. Something he'd only imagined—or something he'd really seen?

He moved up closer, raising the aim of the gun as well.

At first, there was nothing, just the fuzzy gray half-light of dusk. Then—something.

A bald head stuck through the tunnel opening. Peered around. Like a nervous bird.

The head remained there for a couple of minutes, checking out everything spread before it.

Quinlan stayed in the shadow of a scrub pine. The ground here was sweet with the scent of pine cones and the heavy boughs promised comforting protection against the night winds. He wondered idly, as he watched Gretchen emerge like a struggling infant from the birth canal, what it would be like to sleep out under the stars the way the cowboys once had. He had all this money, all this power, and yet there was so much he hadn't gotten around to in his life.

When Gretchen had wriggled halfway out of the small tunnel opening, she made the mistake of trying to dive out the rest of the way. It didn't work. She came out about three-fourths of the way and just hung there, about four feet off the clay ground below, a trapeze artist awkwardly caught on her swing.

Quinlan made his move, came out of the shadows, started walking over to the clay cliff.

"Need some help?" he said.

"You bastard," Gretchen snapped.

He smiled and walked over to her, gallantly putting out his hand. "You've kept me waiting."

"You bastard."

"I believe you just said that, Gretchen."

"You don't give a damn about me at all, do you?"

She was still hanging from the tunnel exit. "Let me help you down."

"I don't need your help."

Then he said, "Where's Jenny?"

"Jenny? She was way ahead of me."

"What?"

"She was way ahead of me in the tunnel. She must've gotten away."

He reached up and grabbed one of her shoulders and yanked her entire body free of the tunnel exit. She landed facedown on the ground, landed pretty hard, in fact. Not that he cared.

He grabbed the other shoulder and yanked her around to face him. "Now tell me the truth."

"I *am* telling you the truth."

"You little bitch," he said, and slapped her hard. "Now where's Jenny?"

Gretchen started crying. "We went into that little room. You know the one I mean. She wanted to go first from there, she said. She said that we'd have a better chance if we came out of the tunnel one at a time. She said to give her a fifteen-minute head start. That's what I did. And that's the last I've seen of her."

He wanted to take the .45 and kill her with it. Not with bullets. With the butt and the barrel. Smash every delicate bone in her delicate face. And then crush a few ribs hard enough that blood was boiling up out of her mouth. Beating someone to death would give him far more tactile—and spiritual—satisfaction than would simply shooting somebody.

"So you're telling me she's gone?"

"As far as I know."

"Did she tell you where she was going?"

"No; she isn't much of a talker. At least, she wasn't with me."

Quinlan turned away and walked back toward the river. The streaked dusk sky was salmon and blue and mauve now. The moon was little more than an outline. In the distance, you could hear the cars and trucks on the Interstate. Closer by, it was owls and nightbirds.

"It's pretty, isn't it?" Gretchen said when she came down the slanting grassy terrain to stand next to him. "The river."

"At night it is," he said. "You don't see all the pollution."

Gretchen giggled. "You're so cynical. But I s'pose that's part of your wisdom." Then, "You know why I helped her?"

He just felt very tired. "I don't care why you helped her."

"For us."

"That's nice."

"Aren't you curious. Me saying 'for us?' "

"No."

"I love you, Quinlan. Can't you understand that. The other people all want something from you. I don't. I just want to be around you. I'd stay over in the corner and never say a word unless you wanted me to."

There had been a time in college—his last Romantic period—when a moment like this would have been as lovely and elegant as a sentence by his favorite writer, F. Scott Fitzgerald.

And here he was all these years later, with an undeniably attractive woman—even with her head shaved, Gretchen was beautiful—and the night was as wonderfully sad as the saddest song on the jukebox, that song that trails you all the way home and is still in your head when you awaken next morning, and yet he didn't give a damn at all. Would, in fact, kill this bitch if he thought it wouldn't create more problems than it solved. He wanted Jenny, and no one else. He'd just realized that all over again, and it was a terrible thing to realize.

Gretchen had slipped her arm through his, as they stood here looking down at this small Midwestern river that moved so slowly through the prairie night.

"I can make you happy, Quinlan," she said softly. "I really can."

And for a moment there—just a moment—he felt that, yes, it was true, she *could* make him happy. That the little-girl, totally-accepting way she loved him was just what he needed. A handmaiden, a sister, a mother, she would be all these things, and when he was lonely and depressed in the middle of the night, she would hold him and rock him as if he were her child, and she would give food when he needed it and sex when he needed it and companionship and solitude when he needed it.

And for a moment there—just a moment—he felt the swooning heady rush of escaping his ego, of turning himself over to someone else, "O Sisters, rock me on the waters and cool my fevered brow," as in the old Jackson Browne song, and, yes! It was so right! *Gretchen* was so right! And why hadn't he seen this earlier how right she was! And then—

And then the moment was gone, a firefly in a vast summer night. And Gretchen sensed it, too, the moment lost, because she clung to him as if he were drowning, holding him tight to her so that she could save him.

"I felt it, Quinlan," Gretchen said. "I *felt* what you were feeling. I really did. It was like telepathy, Quinlan. It really was."

But he took his arm from hers and walked along to the river by himself and looked downstream at the twisted turn of the river. A terrible emptiness filled him, a void of distance and melancholy, and he saw on the moon-washed river the outline of Jenny's face. And then even that was gone.

He reached in his back pocket and whipped out his cell phone. He punched several numbers quickly and said, "We've got a problem. She's gone."

He clicked off.

By the time he had replaced the cell phone in his back pocket, Gretchen was there. She grabbed the .45 before he could stop her—biting his hand until he gave it up. Then she knelt before him and undid his zipper. Holding the .45 on him all the while.

All the time it was going on, he stared up at the moon and stars. You would think that even a minor god like himself would find solace in the moon and stars. And yet he didn't. Not at all.

When she was done, he helped Gretchen to her feet, and she wiped her mouth on her sleeve, and together they walked back to the compound.

***

She couldn't really trust Gretchen. That was the trouble.

True, Gretchen had walked away with Quinlan. But what if

it was a trap? What if Quinlan was hiding just off to the side? Maybe Gretchen had reasoned that the only *final* way to deal with Jenny was to see that she was killed.

Jenny waited a few minutes, listened to the night right outside the tunnel exit, the slow-moving river, a nearby dog barking out of what sounded like boredom, and the wind in the scrub pines, the boughs bending with audible elegance. She was close enough to the end of the tunnel so that her claustrophobia wasn't so bad. She could think clearly now, without the frenzied need for escape.

It would all be over soon, and for the first time, she felt an almost joyous optimism. Quinlan was behind the murders, and the police would be able to understand that now. He had manipulated her. His long reach had extended from the time that she'd lived at the compound till the present time. But that long reach had now been stretched to its limit.

She listened to the falling darkness. Nothing untoward that she could hear. Maybe Gretchen really *had* kept her word to simply tell Quinlan that Jenny had already escaped, and to then lead Quinlan back to the hospital where, according to Gretchen's shabby fantasy, Quinlan would now be hers.

Now. Time to go. She'd find out soon enough if Gretchen had kept her word. If she hadn't, Quinlan would be standing out there with his gun.

She started to crawl to the edge of the tunnel. She didn't want to dangle from the edge the way Gretchen had, so she simply let herself drop head first to the ground. She had no trouble breaking her fall or getting to her feet.

When she looked around at the long grasses and the deep woods, it was hard to imagine that she was this close to the city. Commune land really did have the feel of a bucolic retreat.

The water would be cold. She had already steeled herself to that. She was a competent swimmer, no more, no less, and a reasonably good sport when it came to enduring unpleasantries. Jumping into the water this late at night, especially a river whose upstream tributaries were virtual toxic waste dumps, would put her endurance quotient to a severe test.

Under the spanning stars, in a darkness sweet with the smell of burning autumn leaves and a saucy chill nip of true fall on the air, she stood on the river bank, slipping off her small black heels. She knew that her Levis would be heavy in the water, but she also knew that she would freeze without them. And she'd certainly need them when she swam to shore somewhere downstream.

And that was when he said, "You look beautiful tonight, Jenny. But then you always do."

Quinlan had always been good at sneaking up on her. He was especially good when Jenny was preoccupied with getting her shoes off, and getting ready for the water.

He walked up and stood next to her now. "Smells good tonight. Can't smell all the pig shit from that hog farm."

The hospital was downwind from a nearby hog farm. The farm stench could get overwhelming sometimes. The last courtroom go-round, the judge had ordered the farm to install new equipment that would cut down on the smell considerably. Quinlan's first reaction was that the farm had gotten to the judge—paid him off or blackmailed him—and here was the judge ordering them to put a band-aid on a cancer. One thing was for sure, the stench reminded the commune people of how glad they were to be vegetarians.

He took her arm. "I could have my plane ready to go in two hours. We could be in Europe by tomorrow morning. They'd never find us."

She watched him for a time, amazed as always at the depth of his feeling for her—and yet frightened that he knew so little of the real Jenny. He'd concocted this princess fantasy about her—with himself as the white knight—and no matter what she did to convince him otherwise, she persisted as perfect in his mind. Her third or fourth week at the commune, when she was so desperate to be saved—she'd seen that with Quinlan it was the other way round—*she* was saving *him*. She represented something to him, some unfathomable Woman symbol that he felt could redeem him somehow. And when he learned that she wouldn't sleep with him, learned that she would never be his . . . he decided to destroy her by framing her for two murders.

He turned to take her in his arms.

"You're all that matters to me," he said.

"Is that why you wanted to send me to prison? Because I 'matter' to you so much?"

"We can get away, Jenny," he said. The desperation she always inspired in him was in his voice once again. "Nobody will ever be able to find us. I have plenty of assets. We can have a wonderful life together."

She slipped from his arms, then, and turned toward the river. He reached for her, grabbing the shoulder of her blouse, tearing the material, ripping downward, so that a large part of her blouse was torn all the way to the beltline. She just kept thinking about his inability to swim. He both hated and feared the water. She had to make it to the river. . . .

And then, from behind him, a voice said, "Stay right there."

Gretchen stood behind Quinlan, a .45, *his* .45, pointed directly at the back of his head.

"I want her to go," Gretchen said.

"What the hell're you doing here? I told you to go back to the commune."

"You don't really think that I believed you, did you?" Gretchen said. "That you just wanted to go for a walk by yourself? I knew you were coming back here." She looked at Jenny. "For the first time, I believe you, Jenny. That you don't want him for yourself. I see how it is now. How it *really* is." She waggled her weapon in a northerly direction. "There's a path over there. Take it and in about half a mile you'll see a highway leading to the city." She smiled. "Save you from swimming."

"Thanks, Gretchen."

Gretchen hit Quinlan on the side of the head with surprising force, enough force to drop the man to his knees. There in the dark, Quinlan held both sides of his head and moaned. The blow had been severe.

"Now, you're going to listen to me," Gretchen said. "And do just what I tell you. You understand me?"

And with that, she clubbed him again. He sank a little lower, shoulders dropping, knees sinking into the soft earth.

The whole thing was comic, really, a little girl scolding her bad brother—or her bad dog.

"And even if I have to get you saltpeter," Gretchen said, "you're going to give up having sex with anybody but me. I'm the only one who cares about you, and you can't see that. But you will." She stood over him. He was bent over, his arms covering his head.

She slammed the gun against his skull for the third time. He cried out and then moaned. And then he said, "You don't understand what's going on here. If you let her go, you'll destroy everything."

"You just want to keep her here for yourself," Gretchen said. "I'm trying to help you, can't you see that? Out of sight, out of mind. Now you start behaving yourself." She was using her bad-doggie tone. To her, Quinlan was as much as fantasy as Jenny was to Quinlan.

Gretchen looked up and saw Jenny still there. Jenny had been hoping she'd be able to get the gun from Gretchen and bring Quinlan in herself. But she could see that Gretchen was in control of things here. "Go on, Jenny. Get out of here."

Jenny took a final look at both of them, and then started walking quickly away.

Not long after, as she crested a hill, she got her first glimpse of a two-lane blacktop that stretched toward the city.

She needed to get to a phone. Fast.

Chapter Forty-Eight

THE Sigma Corporation was housed in a new two-story glass-and-rusted-steel building that looked almost gauche against its backdrop of forest and an artificial lake. Sodium vapor lights made the imposition of man upon nature even more ominous. Moonlight was much prettier than mauve electrical light. There was only one car in the small parking lot. No lights shone in any of the windows on the front or southern side of the building. Apparently Sigma lacked the Boomer spirit of eighteen-hour workdays a la Bill Gates. Probably all at home waxing and shining their family vans and Saabs.

He drove around the entire building. He still didn't see any lights. Surely, there was a security man in there. Most likely, he had a room where he stayed when he wasn't making his rounds. There was a good chance the room was windowless—like a large storage closet—and the light wouldn't show externally. There would also be a state-of-the-art security system in place. Sigma was all but impenetrable. He needed to get in there. He needed some evidence to link Sigma and Jenny together. He stood even less of a chance sneaking into the hospital grounds. He had to get his evidence here.

Then he got an idea. Shrinks always had answering services that could beep them in case of an emergency. Priscilla Bowman would be no different.

He used his cell phone to reach information and get Bowman's number. The answering service woman took his name and noted that this was an emergency and then took his number. She said, "May I tell her what this is about?"

"Just say it involves Sigma. She'll know what I mean."

"Sigma? S-i-g-m-a?"

"Right. And thank you."

Sigma sat on unspoiled land near Oak Park. A lot of aggressive new corporations were building out here. While he waited to hear from Bowman, he rolled down his window, closed his eyes, and took in the smells of autumn. He thought of his wife and daughter playing in piles of leaves, gold and russet and yellow leaves spraying up into the air like water in a pool. And the Saturday afternoon Northwestern games, their alma mater. And the Sunday afternoon drives over into Wisconsin to see the miles and miles of autumn foliage, God's own theme park.

He was drifting pleasantly on memories when the cell phone buzzed like an angry insect. He picked up, punched in.

"I wish you wouldn't use my service for something as inane as this," Priscilla Bowman snapped.

"How do you know it's inane? You don't even know what it is yet."

"Listen, Coffey. You've made the same mistake any number of other men have—they've fallen desperately in love with the beautiful, virginal Jenny Stafford. That's how she appears on the outside, anyway. But inside, she's not very beautiful and she's anything but virginal. She's sociopathic, Coffey. Totally. And she's killed at least two people that we know of. I'm sure she's killed even more. That's her real nature we're talking about. It's not something that I instilled in her—or anybody else, for that matter. She's like the woman in the east who has had this ongoing love affair with her fourteen-year-old student. You look at her and she looks like an angel. So much so that nobody wants to attach the word 'pedophile' to her. But that's what she is. Nothing more, nothing less. A pedophile. If she wasn't beautiful and elegant and the daughter of privilege, she would have been carted off to prison and nobody would have paid any attention to her. How could somebody with a face like that be a pedophile? Well, it happens, and it happens more frequently than we want to admit."

"That's a very nice speech."

She laughed. "I appreciate a good audience."

"But it's all bullshit. At least the part about Jenny."

"You're doing exactly what I said you were, Coffey. You're saying that nobody that seemingly sweet could possibly be a killer."

"I'm in a hurry, Priscilla. So I'm going to say this simply.

I'm out at Sigma Corporation. I need you to come out here and help me find proof of what you and your friend Quinlan have been doing to Jenny. There's still time to help yourself with the DA, Priscilla. But once I start talking to the cops, they won't be willing to cut any deals with you. They'll go after both of you."

There was a long silence. "I don't think you can prove anything."

"You know better than that. You know it's just a matter of time now."

Another silence. "How much do you know?"

"Not all I need to know. But one way or another, I'll find out. It's inevitable at this point."

"It would take me a while to get there."

"Leave now."

"I'll have to think about it, I guess."

"No, you won't." Then, "Leave now. Right now, Priscilla."

He broke the connection.

***

She wasn't going to come out here, of course. The pauses in her conversation were her trying to figure out how to handle this matter.

And she handled it just the way he'd thought she would.

He sat in his car and put together the scenario. Guard getting her phone call. Guard getting his shotgun. Guard taking a shadowy window spot to locate Coffey's car in the lot. Guard going out the opposite end of the building. Guard circling around through the woods, Coffey's car conveniently parked right up next to the line of forest. Guard in a crouched position sneaking up on Coffey's car and—

"Get out of the car." Guard standing on the other side of the passenger window.

Guard was white. And young. And big. And military-sharp in his dark blue uniform with the snappy zipper jacket and the wine-red beretlike headware. If they ever did another *Star Trek* spin-off, this guy was ready. On beret and jacket arms was sewn the distinctive Sigma logo. This was not a rent-a-cop. This was a full-time employee of Sigma. Which meant that he would probably do just about anything Priscilla Bowman told him to.

"One more time, pal, get out of the car."

He was a hard-ass, a real one, this lad. He looked as if he would take a genuine spiritual pleasure in carrying out Priscilla Bowman's orders.

Coffey had the small spray can ready in the palm of his right hand. It had been ready since he'd called Priscilla. He would have to be very, very quick. Guard was looking forward to World War III.

Coffey opened the door. The night air felt good, even if it was tainted by the coloring of the sodium vapor light.

"Turn around and spread 'em," Guard said. The way he savored these particular words told Coffey that he was probably a cop wanna-be who'd failed the psychological test. Under "Hobbies," the phrase "Killing people" almost always failed to impress.

This was Coffey's one and only chance and he took it. As he started to turn to his car so he could get himself in the position Guard wanted him in, Coffey raised his right hand and let Guard have some industrial-strength mace right in the face.

Guard screamed. Guard cursed. Guard started waving blindly with his formidable rifle.

Coffey kicked him in the nuts.

It was a good kick, too, a lot better than the kicks the Bears had been delivering these past two weeks.

Guard sank to his knees and as he sank, Coffey kicked him upside the head. This kick put Guard out.

Coffey opened the trunk, dragged Guard around, hefted him inside, and then bound and gagged him with various odds and ends and shut the trunk. But not before relieving Guard of all his keys.

Coffey got in the cab and drove to the far side of the building, the point from which the Guard had come. A few minutes later, Coffey was inside. He knew he didn't have long. Priscilla Bowman would be calling soon to see how Guard had done with Coffey.

The thing he hadn't counted on was how dissimilar all the keys looked to the lock in the door he'd chosen. It took him longer than he'd hoped to get inside, and then, once inside, he realized that he had no idea where he was going or what he was looking for.

The logical place to start, he figured, was the building maintenance staff supervisor. Guard'd have floor plans for the whole places plus the names belonging to the various offices. Priscilla's would probably be the best place to start.

He went looking for the building supervisor's office.

Chapter Forty-Nine

SHE used the john at a convenience store to clean herself up some. Finding the freeway hadn't been as easy as Gretchen had promised. A lot of brambly terrain had had to be traversed. Jenny was a sweaty mess.

The restroom was relatively clean as these places went. There were plenty of paper towels, the H faucet actually dispensed hot water, the air smelled pleasantly if artificially of pine-scented freshener, and no brown little things were to be found floating in the toilet bowl. Almost like home.

She stayed a long time in the john, just sitting on the closed toilet lid after doing all her business. Instead of a claustrophobic feeling, the john inspired a peaceful feeling. Nobody could get her in here. She was safe at last.

The knock on the door took her feeling of security away. "I got a little girl here, she really needs to use the can," a female voice said. "You been in there a long time."

Jenny felt guilty, embarrassed, keeping a little girl waiting. She got up, splashed cold water on her face and then went to the door.

She was all ready to say "Sorry," when the teenage clerk who'd given her the john key shouted, "That's her!"

In a moment, Jenny took it all in. The hefty woman in the Western clothes standing in front of her was a cohort of the clerk's. She looked very spiffy, the woman, in her white cowboy shirt with red piping, her white Stetson and her Levis and lizard cowboy boots. She'd lied about having a little girl in bad need of a john, just so she could lure Jenny out and the clerk could be satisfied that Jenny hadn't escaped out the john window or something.

"Grab her!" the clerk shouted.

The way her face had been on TV and in the newspapers, she was bound to be recognized eventually. And eventually was now.

The woman made a grab for Jenny. She had thick arms and thicker hands. She would have made a good professional wrestler. She gripped Jenny's arm and then slammed her back into the john.

She wanted to have a little fun, the lady wrestler. She slapped Jenny hard across the face a couple of times and then flung her into the wall. Jenny cracked the back of her head against a female napkin machine.

The clerk was in the doorway now. "Hey, take it easy, Merla! I already called the cops! They won't want you to rough her up!"

The cops, Jenny thought, as she ducked a slap. Everything pointed to her guilt. They wouldn't listen. Nor would the press. A rich girl made the best copy of all. Especially when two murders were attached to her name.

Then Jenny remembered Gretchen's knife in her pocket. At the same time she reached for it, she made a quick assessment of the two people in the john with her. The clerk was skinny and pale and looked extremely nervous about this whole thing. Not even the small gold rings he wore in his nostrils seemed to give him much courage. He'd be a lot easier to deal with than the lady wrestler.

Jenny subtly reversed positions, moving backward to the door. The woman put her arms out. Flexed her hands. "Rich bitch," she said. Then, to the clerk, "I spotted her, Mikey. That means I get seventy-five, you get twenty-five."

"Hell, the reward's only $10,000, Merla. My mom'll make me pay taxes on it, and I won't have hardly nothin' left." Mikey sounded as if he was about to cry.

She grabbed him. She felt a weird sort of pride. She just grabbed him, got him around the neck and dragged him half-out the door. She took Gretchen's knife out of her pocket and put it to the kid's throat.

"Do you have a car?"

"Oh, God, please put that knife away."

"Do you have a car, I said?"

"Yes'm."

"Good. Then take me to it."

"Yes'm."

"You leave that boy alone, you rich bitch," Merla said.

"C'mon, Merla," Mikey said. "Don't go pissin' her off."

"That's right, Merla," Jenny said. "Don't go pissin' me off."

In the distance, she could hear sirens. Mikey had said he'd called the cops. Apparently, he hadn't been lying.

She dragged him down an aisle. On one side were soaps and sundries. On the facing aisle were cookies and candies. She kept her arm good and tight around his neck. She also kept the knife point very close to his throat. Merla stalked them, three, four feet back, constantly looking for her chance to snatch Mikey away from Jenny. But Jenny didn't give her the chance.

As they came abreast of the cash register, Jenny said, "Grab me some money."

"The boss'll be real mad if I do, ma'am."

"I'll be real mad if you don't."

He managed to glance at her. "You're so pretty and high-class and all. I sure don't know why you're doin' this."

"The money, Mikey," she said, jabbing him a bit with the point of the knife. "The money."

When they got out on the drive, Mikey said, "It's over there."

Jenny almost laughed. This *would* have to be Mikey's car, a beat-up junker that had been painted a crude red with the word SATAN painted with equal crudity on the driver's door. There was also a small painting of a horned Satan on the back end of the car. Just in case you missed the point. "The keys," she said.

He gave her the keys.

Merla was still with them, standing nearby, glowering. She looked like the world's most forlorn cowgirl.

Jenny dragged Mikey back with her to the car. She had to move fast. The sirens were only a few blocks away now. And Merla would want one more shot at her.

Jenny moved. And at that instant, Merla moved, too.

Jenny pushed Mikey into Merla just as the cowgirl leaped for Jenny. This gave Jenny time to get into the car and get it started. It had a pair of thunderous mufflers.

Then, somehow, Merla's hands were on Jenny's throat and she was quickly choking Jenny into unconsciousness.

All Jenny's breeding, all Jenny's self-doubts, all Jenny's

temerity, said she shouldn't able to do it—too many social and psychological forces working against it.

Yet she did it. As soon as she saw that there was only one way she could escape, she raised the knife, the knife that Merla had apparently forgotten about, and dragged the point of it halfway down Merla's arm. Not enough to do any real damage. But enough to make a shocked and stung Merla jerk her hands away from Jenny's neck.

Jenny peeled backward at maybe fifty miles per hour, the smell of burning rubber tart on the chill night.

Merla flung herself at the car but missed by a half foot and went sprawling facedown onto the drive. Mikey bent over to help her up but Merla angrily refused his help.

Jenny knew she wouldn't get far driving a red car with SATAN painted on the door. People tend to notice cars like that. But she needed to escape the sirens. And then find a cab.

She took alleys. The cops were never far behind. Other cop cars joined in. The sounds of the sirens swelled. When she was halfway down one alley, she saw a cop car starting to turn in to the alley.

Fortunately, she found an ancient, open garage. She'd kept her lights off, so pulling inside wasn't exactly easy. As soon she was parked in the garage, she jumped out and dragged down the old-fashioned rope-pull door. The cop car was slowly working its way up the alley. The cop riding shotgun was flashing a big-beam flashlight on both sides of the alley. She crouched in a shadowy corner, hunched into herself, all sweat and fear and confusion and hope and despair and determination to persevere.

The cop car paused in front of the alley where Jenny hid, its big tires crunching gravel as it stopped.

The light played all over the face of the garage. Up, down, left, right. She kept waiting for the shotgun cop to get out and take a look inside. That would be the end. She might be able to get the jump on Mikey but never on an armed cop.

Then they drove on.

She sat there, shaking. For a moment, she seemed to lose all control of herself. And then the sharp, stabbing headache. The one she knew now that Quinlan and Priscilla Bowman had put there. The mind-control headache.

For a terrible moment, she thought she might lose it all, just collapse into a heap here until somebody found her and turned her over to the cops. It took so much to fight back sometimes. She knew why people just gave in. Because giving in was easier, even if it meant your own death.

Then, thank God, the anger came. The anger at Quinlan, mostly, his cynicism, his manipulative skills. She had to expose him, not just for her sake but for others. She'd seen so many sad and helpless people in the psychiatric hospital that time, just the sort of people Quinlan preyed on. She couldn't let him go on. *Wouldn't* let him go on.

After a time, when she hoped it was safe, she slipped out of the garage, and headed to a diner she knew of where cabbies drank coffee every night about this time.

She knew where she could hide now. She knew who would help her.

Chapter Fifty

COFFEY found the building supervisor's office in the basement. The trouble was getting in. Guard had carried at least twenty-five keys on his big silver ring. Coffey, like a manic quiz show contestant, had to try each one. Number seventeen did the trick.

In the soft light from the hallway, the supervisor's office looked small and tidy. A thermos and lunch pail stood on a table in the corner. A lot of supers worked their way up from janitorial ranks and never quite cut their blue-collar ties. But he couldn't have been too humble. He had his own little john. His desk was orderly. Coffey sat down in the tall leather chair behind the desk and went to work. He found the plans he wanted in a notebook in the second drawer on the left. Priscilla's office was on the second floor, 225-B as it was designated on the flooring plans.

He took the stairs instead of the elevator. The silence of the place unnerved him. He walked in and out of light, indirect ceiling light that didn't so much illuminate as glow. The second floor reminded him of the interior of a flying saucer as he'd always imagined one to be—vast, dark, mysterious, with subtle and strange noises playing constantly on the ear. A maze of hallways; heavy, plush carpeting the color of tarnished gold; and office furnishings half-glimpsed behind smoky glass. Easy to imagine ghostly Boomer executives sitting in their chairs all night, continuing their push, even beyond the grave, to take over the universe.

He went through the key routine again. This time, things went faster. The right key was number six.

Apparently what they did, the folks at Sigma, was have the

cleaning crew come in at night and throw everything on their desks away. If anything, Priscilla's desk was even *more* orderly and neat than the super's had been. Hers was also better appointed and far more expensively appointed, amber leather armchairs, amber leather couch, and an expansive glass desk. There was also a huge dark video viewing screen built into the paneled east wall.

He started going through the drawers. They were as barren as the surface of the desk. Nothing incriminating, nothing embarrassingly personal.

When he was finished, he sat in her chair and looked around the office. All her files were apparently kept elsewhere. He hadn't been able to find any here. He found himself continuing to stare at the viewing screen. There was a small door built into the paneled wall to the right of the screen. He decided to check it out.

It looked unpromising. There was a video player and stacks of VHS tapes in their cases. He was mindful of the time. It wouldn't take long for Priscilla to figure out that something had gone wrong out here, that the super was in some kind of trouble.

But for some reason—hunch—Coffey couldn't resist firing up the video player and sampling a few of the tapes.

He kept the sound low and watched as the screen began to fill up with human images.

***

A carload of black teenagers—slightly less frightening than gang-bangers, slightly more frightening than honor-roll students—offered to give Jenny a ride and waved a bottle of cheap wine at her as an inducement.

A white pimp, who looked at if he prayed every night to a poster of the Bee Gees—the guy was wearing an honest-to-God leisure suit—inquired if she had a "representative" and if not why not and if not, how about him?

And finally, a wobbling, weaving drunk came up to her and said that earlier tonight he'd seen a werewolf and if she didn't believe him, she could go fuck herself because she looked like such a stuck-up bitch anyway. He then proceeded to throw up in the gutter.

She hurried on.

She'd had the cabbie drop her four blocks from her destination. In case he suddenly remembered who she was, he wouldn't be of much help to the cops because he didn't know where she was really headed.

She had to smile when she saw the front of Sister Mary Agnes' homeless shelter. Jenny had been to Paris, London, and Rio many times over but no sight had ever thrilled her as much as this drab, rundown shelter in the midst of a depressed area right here in Chicago.

She hurried. She was exhausted, for one thing. And she needed a friendly face, for another.

Sister Mary Agnes would help her. She was sure of it.

***

The first tapes Coffey screened weren't all that interesting. They consisted mostly of Priscilla Bowman hypnotizing people. Fast forward. They were then given injections in their forearms. They were then asked to talk about their lives, from earliest childhood on. Fast forward. More of same. Coffey couldn't quite see what the point was of these exercises.

With tape five, he was ready to give up. Tape four had promised to be interesting because both Quinlan *and* Priscilla were conducting the hypnosis sessions. Still, after the initial excitement of seeing Quinlan on the tape, there was nothing. More people under hypnosis getting injections and talking about their lives. They weren't real interesting lives.

He was just about to shut off the whole set-up when he saw a lone tape sitting near the back of the video shelf. He'd give it a few minutes. If it didn't show him something really substantive—though showing Priscilla and Quinlan conducting the same hypnosis sessions was valuable, their "break up" being a sham—he'd shut everything down and leave.

He put the sixth tape in, not optimistic in the least. Color bars filled the screen; the tape (not a whole hell of a lot better than home video) broke up as the heads tried to lock in a good picture; and there began another hynpotherapy session. There was nothing special to see. They were in a small room, the walls a wine red. The subject sat in a straight-back chair.

Quinlan, in a suit and tie, stood next to Priscilla in front of the subject.

The subject was what kept him interested. Why did she look familiar to him? She was a rather nondescript woman with short hair going to gray. She wore a white blouse and a pair of blue slacks. After her injection, she began to talk about her life. Fast forward. Many minutes later, she was still talking about her life.

But then Quinlan stopped her. "Aren't you forgetting Alice?"

"Alice?" said the woman.

"Yes," Priscilla said. "Alice. That's who you really are. Alice."

The two shrinks then began to tell her about Alice. They had a whole history ready to go. The woman listened to them patiently and was then given a second injection. All the time this was going on, Coffey kept wondering who she was, why she was familiar?

Fast forward. The subject changed. A young boy. He, too, looked familiar. But why?

The room. The chair. The injections.

Quinlan: "Sean? Do you know a boy named Larry?"

Sean: "I don't think so."

Quinlan: "You should. He's your best friend."

Sean: "I don't know anybody named Larry."

Quinlan: "Think about it. Think about some of the photos we showed you the other day. Do you remember the photos?"

Sean: "Yes."

Priscilla: "Think about the photos, Sean. About the face in those photos."

Sean: "All right."

Why did this boy look so familiar, as familiar as the female subject had? Who were these people?

Priscilla: "Are you seeing the face?"

Sean: "Yes."

Priscilla: "Who does the face look like?"

Sean (hesitation): "Me."

Quinlan: "Yes. The face *does* look like you. Except it isn't you, is it?"

Sean: "No."

Quinlan: "Who is it, Sean?"

Sean: "Larry."

Priscilla: "Very good, Sean. Very good."

She leaned over and gave him a tender kiss on the cheek.

Coffey sat watching all this, stunned. He had finally figured out who the woman and the boy were—he now recalled their faces from a news story on WGN last week on how their respective trials were coming. They were the two who'd gone berserk and killed several other people, the woman in a mall food court, the boy in a classroom. Quinlan and Priscilla Bowman had given them the same sort of therapy they'd given Jenny Stafford.

He had just pressed fast word again when the sound of a ringing telephone startled him. His first impulse was to look around for a phone somewhere. A screening room like this one probably had one or two phones for the convenience of clients and staff alike. But he couldn't see any phone. And the phone kept ringing. Then he realized that the phone was in his pocket—his flip phone. He dug it out and answered it.

"Coffey? It's Sister Mary Agnes."

"You scared me. I wasn't expecting a call here."

"I just wanted you to know that Jenny's fine and she's with me. She's standing right here, as a matter of fact. Would you like to talk to her?"

"Very much."

"I sort of figured that."

When Jenny came on the phone, Coffey said, "I have to talk low. I'm somewhere I shouldn't be."

"They brainwashed me, Coffey. Quinlan and his people."

"I know. That's what I'm finding out, too. Quinlan and Priscilla Bowman."

"And I thought he was my friend."

"She and Quinlan go a long way back."

"Maybe it's time for me to go to the police."

"Not yet. Not until I've had a chance to go through a few more of these tapes."

"Tapes?"

"I'll explain later. In the meantime, why don't you do your folks a favor and go home?"

"That," Jenny said, "sounds like a great idea. It really does. I've had a chance to pull myself together, thanks to Sister Mary

Agnes, so I won't be too freaky when I get home. I think Quinlan gave me quite a few drugs when I was at his compound."

"I'll check in with you later at home. I need to wrap things up here. In the meantime, tell your folks to contact the lawyer they want. I'll turn these tapes over to him and then explain what they are."

"I really appreciate this, Coffey."

"My pleasure."

Coffey flipped the phone off and went back to work, hurriedly running through videotapes.

***

The Stafford mansion was quiet. Eileen and her husband had the night off. They'd gone to a Neil Diamond concert in the city and were staying at a posh hotel overnight. Tom was in the den, working. Molly had elected to leave him alone. Not only was he upset about Jenny, having Ted Hannigan in his home bothered him, too. She'd never realized before tonight how deeply Tom disliked Ted. Even mouthing the most rote of social pleasantries had taken a huge effort on Tom's part. Most of the evening, he looked as if he simply wanted to smack him—and then kick him out.

Now, Molly was in the upstairs TV room watching a movie musical from the forties. Even though all the great musicals had been written and filmed long before she was born—her generation, alas, had only the melodramatic clamor of Andrew Lloyd Weber to boast of—she felt very close to them, as if they'd been the pictures of *her* childhood. She loved the Ginger Rogers and Fred Astaire movies especially. It was a fantasy world she longed to escape into. Too bad you couldn't buy a time-travel ticket or an other-dimension ticket and go to the world depicted in these wonderful old films.

The movie was ending when she saw the red light go on. This meant that somebody was at the gate. She got up and walked over to the wall with the small black communicator box. She punched a button and the blinking red light went off.

"Yes?"

"Mom, it's me, Jenny. I'm at the gate. In a cab again."

Molly felt giddy. Jenny was home. Whatever else might befall them, for now, they were a family again. Jenny was home.

She pressed the button allowing the cab through the gates, then she hurried down the stairs to the den to tell Tom.

***

There was a back way into the commune. This was the way Priscilla always used. She had a remote device that allowed her instant entrance. She parked and then walked amidst the dark buildings. My brave new world, Quinlan had always called it sarcastically. He was right. Thanks to a combination of hypnotherapy and drug therapy, and thanks to various predispositions that left them in need of a guru-type leader, the souls who lived in the commune followed orders without fail. They were already in bed, for instance, the four dormitory-style red brick buildings dark against the frosty night sky. There was great prairie quiet here, too, a rushing distant train and her footsteps across the damp grass being the loudest sounds.

She felt relief and fear—relief that she felt that she and Quinlan would be leaving the country together within the next eighteen hours; fear that something would go wrong. Despite all the "optimistic" speeches she was always giving her clients, she was a profoundly pessimistic person. Anything she'd ever really wanted—certain men, positions, awards, the favor of certain powerful people on the psychiatric governance board—she'd never been able to have. She would never love anyone as she loved Quinlan. Would their escape together fail, too?

She hurried on to his building. Even from here she could see that the light was on in his nicely-appointed apartment.

***

Gretchen would never have seen her if the drier had been working properly.

Each dormitory had its own washer-drier set up in the basement. After returning from the tunnel, and from Jenny's departure, Gretchen had felt confident enough about her relationship with Quinlan to let him go. She'd go about her business, he'd go about his. Later tonight sometime, she'd said, drawing him to her, they'd get together. She'd sleep with him all night.

But first she had some things she needed to get done, laundry chief among them.

So, of course, the drier stopped working, which was the fourth time in two weeks it had stopped working, which was why she'd argued with McGivern, the man who always bought supplies, about buying things at Sears. Their stuff just wasn't what it used to be, Gretchen had argued. (She'd heard that on TV on a consumer complaints show and it had stuck in her mind. Not what it used to be.)

So, of course, here she was lugging her laundry basket across to the next dormitory, the one where Quinlan had his apartment, and that's when she saw her.

Priscilla Bowman. Ever sleek in one of her Armani suits. Coldly beautiful and regal in the way of a statue. Far more poised, intelligent, erotic and mercenary than Gretchen would ever be. A woman who no doubt got everything she wanted.

Gretchen had a Thought. In her mind, there were thoughts and then there were Thoughts. This definitely belonged in the latter category. She'd been so paranoid about Jenny—Jenny this, Jenny that, Jenny Jenny Jenny—that she'd failed to identify her *real* competition for Quinlan's heart and soul . . . Priscilla Bowman. Wasn't Priscilla always sneaking out here late at night? Didn't Quinlan spend a lot of time talking to Priscilla on the phone? Wasn't Priscilla exactly the kind of woman a handsome, powerful man like Quinlan would *want?*

She ducked behind the corner of a building, watching Priscilla make her way to Quinlan's dorm. Her mind exploded with sexual images—images of Priscilla and Quinlan in the most intimate of moments. She couldn't let this happen. Not after all the work she'd put into getting rid of Jenny. And it wasn't fair. What chance did a young woman like Gretchen stand against a wily older woman like Priscilla? The type of woman who could convince Quinlan that she was the right woman for him?

Gretchen set down her laundry basket. A great and terrible frenzy overcame her. These were her most painful moments, when the panic took control. At such times, she always saw control slipping away from her. She was at the mercy of forces that overwhelmed her, like the huge forest trees that night she'd run away as fourteen-year-old, and gotten lost in the woods, rain and lightning lashing the big trees and turning them into looming, stalking giants who planned to snatch up little girls and eat them.

Well, this time, she wouldn't let herself be at the mercy of overwhelming forces. She could be strong, too, couldn't she? She could fight back, too, couldn't she? Of course, she could.

She picked up her laundry basket. Might as well take it back to her room. That's where she needed to go, anyway. There was something in her bottom drawer she needed to get.

No, she wasn't going to be her usual helpless self. Not this time. She truly loved Quinlan and she believed that, whether he wanted to admit it or not, he loved her, too.

She walked quickly now. It was nice to have a purpose. She'd spent so many years just drifting on her pain. Now she had a purpose and soon enough there would be no pain. None at all. She was sure of it.

Chapter Fifty-One

HOME.

It had never looked better, felt better, sounded better, smelled better.

Home.

Jenny's entire life was reflected within these walls, from the framed baby pictures on her mother's dressing table to the high school clothes packed and stored in the attics, clothes her mother held on to as if they were religious relics.

Home.

Her parents stood in front of her now, gleeful and rosy as actors in a TV commercial about how cameras capture those perfect family moments.

She barely heard them. Her mind was comfortably collapsing amidst the familiar setting. She didn't have to be on guard, she didn't have to be suspicious, she didn't have to be afraid.

Home. Safety. Security. Peace.

Molly heated up apple cider in the microwave, explaining that just today Eileen had bought two gallons of fresh Wisconsin cider from a roadstand. She put cinnamon sticks in the cider, too, just the way Jenny had liked it since she was a little girl.

They sat in the breakfast nook. Jenny told them everything that had happened tonight. She spent a great deal of time discussing what she'd learned at the hospital, including how Gretchen had actually killed the two men.

"But why did you go out there in the first place?" her father said.

"Don't you see, Dad? He'd planted all these commands in my head. That's what those vans were doing. One of them was to return to the hospital."

"Well, if you'll remember," Tom Stafford said. "I warned you about him a long time ago."

"We're just glad you're home," Molly said, obviously wanting to steer clear of blame and recrimination.

Tom smiled, reached across the table and took his daughter's hands. "Your mom's right. We're just glad you're home and that's all that matters. The police'll take care of the rest."

"I think you've got an admirer in Mr. Coffey," her mother said. "He looks quite smitten."

"He's a very nice guy," Jenny said. "And I'm smitten with him, too." She told them about Coffey's novels, and what had happened to his wife and daughter.

Molly smiled. "I think you've finally met somebody your Dad will approve of."

"He's certainly a step in the right direction," Tom Stafford said. "He doesn't like ballet, does he? Or modern art?"

"Ballet, I doubt. Modern art, I'd have to ask him."

They both looked so healthy and handsome sitting across from her in their pajamas and silk paisley robes. Her father looked so *Forbes*-magazine distinguished with his clean white mane of hair. Her mother looked so young and vital.

"We're going to get this thing over with," Molly said, "and then we're going to take a nice family vacation."

"Paris," Tom Stafford said.

"I was thinking more Rome," Molly said. They both looked at Jenny.

Jenny said, "Do you really have to ask?"

"Oh, God, not London again," Molly said.

London was not only Jenny's favorite city but also her obsession. She liked the sense of history the city gave her. Plus she enjoyed the culture. She was an incipient anglophile, no doubt about it.

"Well," Tom Stafford said. "I think I'll go back to my office a little while. I've still got some work to do on the Japanese project." His handsome faced grew taut with pain. "What a time to invest in Japanese retail. Their whole economy is collapsing over there."

Jenny wasn't much for the financial world, but she knew enough to be stunned by the Japanese economy starting to collapse so quickly. The term "house of cards" had never been more appropriate than in this matter. Once one of the great Japanese financial houses had imploded, others started falling down like dominoes. Less than a year ago, the venture capital side of her father's signature corporation had started investing heavily in retail outlets over there.

Tom Stafford stood up, walked over to his daughter and kissed her on the cheek. "It hasn't felt right in a long time in this house, honey. Now, all of a sudden, it feels right again."

She wished that some of his critics could see him now. They were always talking about what a cold and hard-assed businessman he was. But right now, tears silvered his eyes and his voice trembled with powerful emotions.

"Oh, Daddy," she said, and hugged him tight around the neck. They stayed like that for well over a minute. Watching them hug seemed to overwhelm Molly. She started crying, too.

"It really does feel good again in this house," Molly said after Tom was standing straight up again, looking very whiskey-ad sophisticated with his hands stuffed into the pockets of his silk robe and a pipe tucked into the right corner of his mouth.

"Well, I'd better go call my Japanese friends," he said.

"He works so hard," Jenny said, watching her father leave the kitchen. "I'll be glad when he retires."

Molly laughed. "Retire? Oh, he makes noises sometimes, but honey, can you imagine your father actually *doing* it? I can't. He'll have them put a flip phone in his coffin so he can keep on giving orders." Then, "More coffee?"

"No, thanks, Mom. And speaking of coffee, I'm hoping my own Coffey will call pretty soon. Let me know what's going on. In the meantime, I'd like to take a quick shower and change into some clean clothes."

"Sure. If he calls, I'll tell you right away."

She looked across the table at her mother. "God, I've screwed up so many things! I never should've given myself into Quinlan's power."

"Quinlan fell in love with you," Molly said. "He apparently decided to destroy you. Since he couldn't have you, I mean." She touched her daughter's hands again. "But all we have to concern ourselves with now is planning that vacation I was talking about. The courts and the lawyers will take care of everything else."

"I sure hope you're right, Mom."

"I *am* right," Molly Stafford said, lazily yawning. "Just wait and see."

She exulted in the shower. The warmth. The cleansing. The relaxing effect it had on her entire body and mind.

At one point, Jenny leaned back against the tiled wall and simply let the shower have at her. She felt as if every pore in her body were receiving individual treatment, being purged of dirt and grime.

Washing her hair felt especially good. She'd cut it very short, back in her commune days. She knew why Quinlan had insisted on this. Demonstrated his command over her. Demonstrated that she was more concerned with obedience than vanity. But she still wouldn't sleep with him. And that, apparently, had driven him quietly crazy. Why else would he focus all this murderous attention on her, enlisting her own shrink to help destroy her?

She wondered where Coffey was at this very moment. Her feelings for him had changed so quickly. She felt attached to him in a way she'd never felt attached to anybody. She liked him and maybe it was as simple as that. He wasn't perfect or ideal in any way. But she liked him and trusted him and depended on him—and in turn she allowed herself to be trusted and depended upon by him. She'd never extended herself to a man this way before. And she liked it. It was different from simple romantic love—it was romantic love but a lot more, too.

She wondered where Coffey was at this very moment.

***

There is a weariness now. Panic, too, of course. But the weariness is predominant. He is headed for the den. His retreat. He locks the door. But turns on no lights.

He is familiar with everything in the den, Tom Stafford. Why does he need lights? He sits in the Louis XIV chair at the desk and stares at the phone. Momentarily, he feels too weary to even lift the receiver.

He was this weary when he learned that Jenny was not his daughter. A harmless annual physical report mixed in with some of her other insurance papers. Five years ago. A blood test listing her type of blood. She could not possibly be his daughter. Hiring a private investigator. Checking up on the most likely father. Ted Hannigan. Suspicion confirmed. Jenny and Ted share the same rare blood type. Plotting his revenge. As a secret stockholder in Sigma, he asks Quinlan to help him. And Priscilla. They start feeding Jenny drugs that destroy her sanity. Lead to depression. And hospitalization. Inch by inch her mother and she suffer. His pleasure. The doting father. Watching Jenny destroyed. But even that isn't enough. His rage has taken him over and there is something dead in him now. His only pleasure is their pain. How could Molly deceive him this way? Jenny not his daughter.

He picks up the phone.

"I knew it would be you," Quinlan says.

"She's here."

"I figured that."

"It's coming apart. Everything is coming apart."

"Cummings and Coffey figured it out, my friend. I suggest you do what I'm doing."

"And that would be what, exactly?"

"Leave the country. I wanted to end on a high note here—turn her over to the police. But now the police'll be looking for *me*."

"Where're you planning to go?"

Quinlan laughed. "You don't really expect me to answer that, do you?"

Stafford wants to say more. Much more. He's never much cared for the crazed, arrogant Quinlan and now is his last chance to express his feelings.

But Quinlan doesn't give him the opportunity.

He hangs up.

Leaving Stafford in the den. In the darkness. In his own dead dazed mind.

***

She had just started running the hair drier when she heard it. She disliked hair driers—and ceiling intake fans—for this reason. They distorted all sound. You could never be sure what you were hearing outside the bathroom.

But she'd heard *some*thing. At least, she was pretty sure she had.

She clipped off the drier, standing at the double sink in a nubby pink cotton robe, bra and panties underneath. Hair still very wet.

So what *had* she heard? She heard nothing now, that was for sure.

That was another thing she hated about hair driers. Sometimes, they made you think you'd heard something when you hadn't. The roaring of the drier motor played tricks on you.

She listened a bit longer, then went back to drying her hair. This time, the motor sounded louder than ever, gave her an unnerving sense that all sorts of terrible things were going on in the house—that the white noise of the motor was keeping from her.

And then she heard it again. Or thought she did. A sound that should not be in this house. A sound that was being hidden from her by the sinister, isolating roar of the drier.

She put down the drier, clicked it off, and went to the door. Out into the hallway.

The hallway went dark as she stepped out. The hallway was never dark. The hallway was not *supposed* to be dark.

Then she noticed that there was no light shining from downstairs up the grand staircase.

Was the entire house dark?

And what was the sound she'd heard behind the roar of the hair drier?

She got her answer quickly. For now—with no drier to muffle it—the sound came quite clearly to her.

The sound was a scream.

***

This time of night at the hospital always reminded Gretchen of summer camp. People winding down for the day, talking softly against the night, sleepy and idle talk mostly, and a sense of peace everywhere. She'd liked camp. Well, her *first* year there she'd liked camp. Her second year, she'd been with the marijuana. Just two joints, but the counselor had acted as if Gretchen were the biggest dealer outside Colombia for God's sake. They wouldn't let her come back the following year, but by then Gretchen didn't care anyway. She'd met Earl at the mall, and her life had never been the same since meeting Earl. But as much as she'd loved Earl, she didn't love him half as much, not even a quarter as much, as she loved Quinlan.

She worked her way between the dormitories. She would have preferred a moonless night. Lights were going off in various rooms. Breakfast was at 6:05 a.m. Even on Sundays. With the keys she'd had duplicated, she had no trouble getting in the front door, no trouble getting on the elevator, no trouble getting on his floor.

She kept the .45 pushed deep down in the pocket of her gray uniform trousers. She was going to surprise them completely.

The entire floor being Quinlan's, Gretchen had to look around to find which room he was actually in. He had a nice spread up here.

She wandered through the library, the viewing room, the living room, the room where he kept his scientific equipment including his telescopes. Nothing, no sign of them.

She next tried the master bedroom. She was convinced that she'd find them there. She was ready, too. The gun in her hand. She put her ear to the closed door. Nothing. Not a whisper of a sound on the other side of the door.

Maybe they were gone. The sudden thought chilled her. She felt a swirl of overwhelming emotions—loss that he might have deserted her, wild terror that she would be left to make her own decisions in a life without him, and rage that Priscilla had come between them, had somehow stolen him.

She raced around the same places she'd covered only minutes before—bedroom, library, the room with the telescopes. Nothing—no Quinlan.

And then she heard them. Far, far back she heard them. She tried to imagine what room they were in but couldn't. She began to slowly move toward their voices, drawn like a wild animal to a campfire on a cold night. Shelter and protection was what she needed. And only Quinlan could give her those things.

She followed a long, carpeted corridor that moved toward a large window at the far end of the building. Through the window she could see the front of the commune, gates and guards and fencing that gave the commune the feel of a military outpost.

The conversation grew louder. It wasn't conversation she wanted to hear.

Priscilla was saying, "We have to face it, sweetheart. We need to move on and very quickly. The police'll be here by tomorrow asking questions. Everything would have been fine if that Coffey character hadn't gotten involved. But it's all coming apart and you know it. We can be in Paris by tomorrow night—way ahead of the cops."

"I suppose you're right," Quinlan said.

Gretchen was trying to read his mood by the tone of his voice. She couldn't. He sounded simply businesslike.

"We'll be free, darling," Priscilla said. "No more of the commune bullshit keeping you tied down here. No more hiding our experiments. The Germans and the Russians'll be much more accommdating." There was a pause and then a long silence accompanied by a rustle of clothes. Kissing. They were kissing. Gretchen made a face and then tightened her small hand into a fist. *Bitch. You bitch.* No wonder Quinlan was always cheating on Gretchen. It wasn't his fault. She could see that now. Not his fault at all. Not with all these women throwing themselves at him. Deep down, Quinlan was probably a very faithful man. But how could he help himself? You couldn't hold men responsible, you really couldn't. Men were weak. They thought with their crotches. They could easily be led astray. No, this wasn't *his* fault at all.

They were in the small office that Quinlan used late at night. For some reason, he liked the little hutchlike place. He only reluctantly let anybody in there. That's another reason Gretchen resented Priscilla. What right had she to be in here when Quinlan kept even Gretchen out? Pushy, that's what she was in there. Priscilla was one of those people who pushed and pushed and pushed until you finally had to give in and let her have her way.

No more. That was going to end tonight. Indeed, that was going to end right now.

Filling her hand with the .45, Gretchen kicked the partially open door so hard that it slammed backward against the wall.

Then she went in, swearing at Priscilla and waving her gun around.

***

There were no more screams.

And there was no light either.

Jenny stood in the doorway of the bathroom, trying to adjust her vision to the darkness. She knew the house very well, of course, and had a good sense of where things were. But still, between the screams and the loss of electricity, she was disoriented and frightened.

She didn't call out. She knew instinctively that she needed to move away from the bathroom without giving away her position. She didn't know who had managed to get into the house—or what they'd managed to do once they'd *gotten* in here—but she decided to move about as quietly as possible.

She moved down the hall toward the staircase, passing a grandfather clock that chimed the quarter hour. The sound was both familiar and alien. As she neared the staircase, she paused. Her parents' room was on her left. She had to look in there. She had just realized that she hadn't heard her parents' voices since before taking her shower. Which made the scream and the lights going off all the more sinister.

She tiptoed across the hall. The door was closed but not locked. She opened it silently and peered in. In the pale moonlight, everything looked perfectly ordinary. The canopy bed, the huge European furnishings, the Chagall prints, the built-in giant-sized TV screen, the bathroom off the bedroom . . . This was how the master bedroom always looked. Then her eyes lingered for a time on the partially open door leading to the master bedroom toilet. Could somebody be in there?

She didn't want to check, but she knew she had to. She crossed the master bedroom and stood before the bathroom door. She listened. A dripping sound from inside. The sink. A steady drip. Any other sound? She listened even more intently. No, no other sound.

Of course, if someone were lying dead in there, they wouldn't make any sound at all.

She put a tentative finger to the door and eased it inward. She peered inside. There were shadows that revealed only parts of the interior, like a modern painting—angle of cabinet mirror above sink, one water faucet, half of toilet, angle of towel rack. She saved the tiled floor till last and when she looked down she made a sick, sobbing sob in her throat.

There were just drops of the stuff, and not very big drops at all, but she knew just what they were, the drops. And just what they signified.

She pushed the door further inward and walked into the bathroom. Under other circumstances, going into the bathroom this way would have scared her. She would have been waiting for somebody to jump out from behind the door. But not now. Not since seeing the drops on the floor. She thought of her mother, her father. Wounded. Or dead.

To make absolutely sure she was right, she bent down and touched a fingertip to the tiled floor. The stuff was still warm, smooth and warm between her fingertips.

Then she saw the mirror. A bloody handprint. And then the walls. Bloody handprints all over, streaked down the buff-colored walls. She felt sick. Mother. Father.

Then she saw the sink. Heavy swaths of blood on the white double-basins.

Then the shower. This was the worst of all the places in the bathroom to confront. The shower door was opaque. It could be hiding anything. She could open the shower door and—

She tried seeing through the opaque door but couldn't. A body could be lying dead on the floor of the shower and she wasn't sure she'd be able to see it. She became aware of blood smells now, tart, metallic, stomach-turning. Whose blood?

She extended a hand to the shower door handle. Took a deep breath. Wished there were light. Wished she already knew what was waiting for her in the shower stall.

She felt as if a trick had been played on her. That was her feeling when she opened the shower door and looked inside. Even cast in deep shadow as it was, the shower stall was clearly empty.

* * *

All her fear, all her anxiety and—nothing. She was relieved, and yet vexed, too, because she still had no answer for the blood smears everywhere.

She withdrew from the shower, withdrew from the bathroom, withdrew from the master bedroom. Stood now in the hall, looking around, listening. Nothing to see *or* hear. Her eyes settled briefly on the bay window at the far end of the hall. It had a window seat. As a small girl, she'd liked to sit there and watch the clouds and refashion them into different shapes—angels and sailing ships and big white fluffy dogs.

Since she could find nothing helpful *inside,* maybe she could find something helpful outside.

She wanted to change clothes, though. She didn't feel ready for a situation like this dressed in a robe and silk pajamas. She returned silently to her room, changed quickly into a blouse, jeans, and loafers.

She was just leaving her room when she saw the shape in the shadows at the top of the stairs. Human shape. Could be man or woman. Impossible to tell from here. The shape was as dark and sinister as the shadows themselves. And then the shape was moving down the stairs. She thought of calling out, but she sensed that the shape hadn't seen her. So why give her position away?

She hurried to the far end of the hall and the window seat. She looked out the window and what she saw made no sense at first.

What was Ted doing here? There in the turn-around area in front of the garages was Ted's vintage red MG. He hadn't been there when she was downstairs talking to her parents. He must have arrived as she was taking her shower. Maybe they'd called and invited him out because she was home again and he'd been so worried. But, no. He couldn't have made it out here that quickly. And anyway, she couldn't believe that Dad would have let him in his house twice in just a few days. Even Jenny had to admit, for all his charm, Ted's self-absorption could get to you after a while.

So what was he doing here?

And then the significance of his car being here struck her.

What if it was Ted responsible for the scream? For the blood all over the master bedroom?

Ted had been in love with Molly for many, many years, and

always would be. And Ted and Dad loathed each other. And always would. What if Ted simply snapped, couldn't take it any longer?

The electrical lines had been cut. So had the phone lines. Ted was somewhere in the house, she realized—and then thought of the shape at the top of the staircase.

If he had been up here—

She needed to check the rooms at the other end of this floor.

On her way, she stopped into the second floor den and picked up a bottle of brandy. Not because she needed a drink but because she needed a weapon. She was angry now, resentful of all of them, Ted and Quinlan and Priscilla. It was time she fought back, *really* fought back, and if that meant violence, so be it. She was tired of being a helpless girl woman. She had a need to be an adult. And to be treated like an adult. And that meant fending for herself. If she found out that Ted had hurt her folks in any way—

She clutched the brandy bottle tightly and hurried down the hallway, slowing only when she reached the first guest room. The door was ajar. Moonlight traced the edge of the open door. She tried to peer inside without opening the door, but all she could see was angle of bed and bureau and window. No sign that anybody was in there.

She pushed open the door. Before her lay the large canopy bed and the heavy last-century European furnishings that her parents had brought back from a trip a few years ago. Castle Dracula, her Mom had called this room. And it *was* an appropriate name. The whole room had that feel.

She was three feet into the room before she noticed the dark drops on the tan carpeting. She watched where they led— directly to the bed. But they still didn't tell her much because the drapes on the bed were closed. It was impossible to see what was on the bed.

She'd have to draw the drapes aside. Anxiety filled her chest. Heart racing. A skin of cold sweat on her face, arms and back. She did not want to open the drapes. What if—

All she could think of was the red MG by the garage. Ted. She'd thought he was such a good friend and—

She crept closer to the bed, almost unaware of moving at all.

Being an adult. Taking responsibility for herself. That meant opening the curtains. Looking inside. Now.

A few more steps, avoiding the drops of blood on the carpet, that chain of stains that foretold a terrible tale.

Two more steps. Three more steps. Moonbeams through the mullioned windows. And the absolute stillness of this night. Two more steps. Three more steps. She reached the bed.

Her hand reached out for the dark drape—when you slept with the drapes closed, you were halfway to a sensory deprivation chamber—and came away with something sticky and wet clinging to her palm. She had no doubt what it was as she held it up to the moonlight for inspection. All she wanted to know was to whom the blood belonged. And she knew she was about to find out.

She reached out again for the drape. Her fingers anticipated the sticky feel of blood. She reached out for the drape and—

That was when the scream came. At first, Jenny couldn't be sure from what part of the mansion the scream had come. But she quickly realized that the sound was fairly close by.

Her impulse was to run toward the scream, see if she could help the person in danger.

But she was here at the bed, the drape in her hand. If she hurried.

She ripped the drape back and looked inside. A dark figure—almost a silhouette, a shadow—lay on the bed. She pulled the drape back even farther, so that moonlight exposed the interior of the canopy bed. She could not tell in that first awful moment who it was. But she could tell what it was sticking out of his forehead. A butcher knife. The one with the gently curved Scandinavian bone handle her mother had had made specially for the family.

Only then was Jenny able to focus on the face of Ted Hannigan.... The eyes were open in shock; blood from his forehead trickled down into his right eye. His mouth was wide open in a scream that would never be fulfilled. His hands were oddly peaceful, lying at his sides, fingers partly splayed. She took all this in within seconds of throwing back the drapes—

And then the scream came again.

She dropped the drape, letting Ted rest in peace. She felt terrible that she had suspected him of being the killer—

She ran out of the room and down the hallway.

There on the top of the steps stood a bloody figure she did not recognize at first, a figure whose clothes hung in blood-soaked rags, whose white body was scarred with long knife slashes and smeared with blood. The blood made the naked breasts and the exposed genitals obscene—they should have been beautiful and clean as they ordinarily were.

This was her mother.

Jenny cried out several things but had no idea what she was saying. She was simply reacting to the vulnerable sight of her mother who was now starting to fall facedown upon the hardwood floor at the top of the stairs.

Jenny lurched forward, getting her arms under her mother before the woman reached the floor. She held her with great tenderness, getting her under the arms so she could half-lift her and get her into the nearest bedroom.

Molly was sobbing and babbling. She was clearly in clinical shock. There was a guest room with two single beds. In the moonlight, the white chenille spreads seemed to glow. She stretched her mother out on the bed. The white chenille became instantly red.

"Who did this?" Jenny kept asking uselessly, over and over.

She hurried to the closet and got a heavy blanket and covered her mother with it. Then she knelt next to her, checking her mother's wrist pulse, taking the blanket edge and wiping sweat and blood from her face.

It took her a few minutes but she was finally able to calm her mother. Beneath the blanket, Molly curled in upon herself fetus-style. She seemed oblivious to her knife wounds. Her eyes were as haunted as Ted's had been in death. Her teeth made clicking sounds as they grated upon each other.

"Oh, Mom, Mom," Jenny said, brushing sweat from her mother's forehead with her hand. She kissed her mother's cheek, terrified at the notion that Molly was slipping into death.

Then he was there in the doorway. She heard him before she saw him.

"Dad!" she cried, looking up.

But this man with the bloody butcher knife and the blood-dripping hands and the bloodstained white shirt was an imposter. Her father could never look like this—especially not with the fierce, crazed, protuberant eyes and the blood-spattered forehead and cheeks.

"I'm afraid I'm not your dad," he said with eerie calmness from the guest room doorway. "That was an honor that belonged to Ted Hannigan. They deceived me just as much as they deceived you."

Chapter Fifty-Two

THEY'D been embracing.

They were still in each other's arms when Gretchen came through the door she'd just kicked in. The weird thing was, at least for Gretchen, neither Priscilla nor Quinlan showed any fear at the sight of her *or* her .45.

All they showed was irritation. Like parents really annoyed that their child had come back down the stairs after being put to bed.

"You couldn't even be faithful for a *night,* could you?" Gretchen said, looking sorrowfully at Quinlan.

He wore a banded-collar blue shirt, chinos, and white Nikes. He always looked handsome in casual clothes and he looked so handsome at this moment that Gretchen profoundly resented his looks. It wasn't fair he should look so good; it made not loving him all the more impossible.

As for Priscilla ... She was at last beginning to show the proper respectful attitude—fear. "Gretchen, you really shouldn't be carrying that thing around. You don't want it to go off, do you?"

Gretchen smiled bitterly. "You should be wearing your white uniform before you sound like that."

Priscilla looked confused—and frightened.

"That's how you all sound," Gretchen said, "all you 'mental health professionals' when you're talking to crazy people like me. Like I don't know what this is or something, Priscilla? Like I'm so crazy, it might go off all by itself. Well, I've got some fucking news for you, bitch. It'll never go off accidentally because that'd spoil all my fun. And that's all I can get from this touching little scene here, Priscilla—fun. Seeing two of my favorite 'mental health professionals' bite the big one."

"Do something, Quinlan," Priscilla said. "Talk to her."

Quinlan still didn't look scared. He looked irritated, maybe even a little bored, but not scared. "She loves melodrama, our little Gretchen. So she's staging a psychodrama for us. What is this, Gretchen, the fifth or sixth time you've pulled a gun on me?"

"I'm not kidding this time, Quinlan," Gretchen said angrily.

"I believe that's what you said the last three or four times," Quinlan said. "Now be a good girl and put the gun down on the table over here and get your ass back to your room. We can get together in the morning and discuss whatever needs to be discussed. But for right now, Priscilla and I have some business to discuss." He smiled. "Grown-up stuff, Gretchen."

"I'm not going anywhere," Gretchen said, "and neither are you."

Priscilla was showing signs of panic. This was wonderful for Gretchen to see. She'd been seeing shrinks since she was eight years old but she'd never seen one give in to panic. But she had the feeling she was about to.

Quinlan walked over to her. Put his hand out. Turned his hand palm up. "Why don't you give me the gun so Priscilla can relax a little?"

"Why don't you give her one of your famous injections?" Gretchen said. "The kind you gave poor Jenny Stafford."

"What does she know about Jenny Stafford?" Priscilla said, anxiety growing constantly in her voice and expression.

"She found some tapes," Quinlan said, not willing to admit that Gretchen had been instrumental in Jenny's escape.

"What kind of tapes?" Priscilla snapped.

Quinlan frowned. "Priscilla, will you just please calm down? She found some tapes and I took them back from her. Nothing more to it than that."

"Kiss her," Gretchen said to Quinlan.

"Just give me the gun," Quinlan said, putting his hand out again.

"Kiss her," Gretchen said. "Just the way you were when I broke in here. You would've ended up fucking her over there on the bed. And that's what I want you to do now. I want you to kiss her and then I want you to fuck her. Put on a little show for me."

Quinlan got another panic-tight glance from Priscilla.

"I always knew you were a voyeur, Gretchen," Quinlan said calmly. "It was just a matter of time till it came out."

Gretchen stepped over to Priscilla and put the gun against her temple. "Take him in your arms, Priscilla. Right now."

"I really don't want to do this," Priscilla said, trying to summon at least a modicum of self-respect.

"I really don't care," Gretchen said. "You're going to do it anyway."

Priscilla sighed. Anger was winning out over fear. She put her arms out. Quinlan looked more irritated than ever. But he came over and slid into her embrace.

"Now kiss her, Quinlan."

"I'm really getting sick of this bullshit," Quinlan said.

"Kiss her."

He kissed her.

"More passion," Gretchen said.

They put more passion into it.

"Now start taking her clothes off."

"No," Priscilla said. "No, I won't do this. I refuse to."

Gretchen put the gun to her head again. "Then I'll kill you."

Quinlan nodded for her to comply. He was starting to show some concern himself. He no longer looked quite so complacent.

Priscilla took off her Armani jacket.

"Now the skirt."

She slipped off her skirt. She stood in a wine-red bra and very skimpy matching panties. She had a very nice body.

"Now take the rest of her clothes off, Quinlan."

"Are you just going to stand there?" Priscilla said to Quinlan. "Talk to her."

Gretchen said, "He's getting scared, Priscilla. He doesn't know what to say to me. He's starting to sense that this is different from the other times. He's thinking that maybe I really will kill him this time—and you know what? Maybe I will. Maybe I really will."

***

Coffey had known a couple of cabbies who'd souped their engines up. He'd always thought that was a pretty useless idea. Hit the kind of speeds those cabbies did, you'd inevitably lose your driver's license.

He was wishing now that he had a souped-up cab. He was moving so slowly on the freeway. Every few minutes, he'd punch in the same number on his cell phone—Jenny's parents. He needed to warn Jenny about her father. But he always got the same response from the operator. The phone was out of order. All kinds of terrible images played at the edges of his mind, the worst being those involving her father. Or her *presumptive* father, as the lawyers liked to say. On one of the tapes that showed Quinlan and Priscilla using both drugs and hypnotherapy, Tom Stafford had also put in an appearance. He was the man paying for all this.

He wished again that he had one of those exotic, souped-up cabs, one of those cars that would leave a half-block of rubber when it peeled out.

Unfortunately, he had to contend with a nice, dependable, drag-ass car that rarely went more than seventy miles per hour.

He frantically punched in Jenny's phone number again.

***

"Leave her alone, Jenny. I want her to die." Tom Stafford spoke very quietly.

Her father—or the man she'd always *assumed* was her father—came into the guest room not with great rage or drama but with a kind of weariness, a kind of sadness.

He came over, stood by the bed. In the moonlight, the blood that covered his body in splashes and smears and spatters gleamed wetly. The gleaming butcher knife remained in his right hand, though it seemed to dangle there, forgotten.

She looked up at him from where she knelt next to her mother. "I wish I could feel sorry for you but I can't. You've killed Ted and tried to kill my mother."

"She deceived me," he said, the sorrow and exhaustion still evident in his voice. "Our entire life was a lie."

"She shouldn't have done that," Jenny said softly. "But you shouldn't have done this either." Jenny looked at her mother, at the faint rise and fall of her chest. Her breathing was slowing all the time. Death wasn't far away.

"Oh, Mom," Jenny said. And then leaned forward and kissed her again on the forehead. And took one of her hands and held it gently. Why would her Mom hide such a secret all her life? Why hadn't she been honest with Tom?

She was so engrossed in her thoughts that she momentarily forgot about Tom behind her—

She was stroking her mother's cheek with the back of her hand when her mother's eyes opened suddenly, and she looked up at a point directly above and behind Jenny—

And screamed.

Jenny looked up just in time to see Tom bringing the bloody butcher knife straight down to plunge it into her neck—

Chapter Fifty-Three

"TAKE her bra off, Quinlan."

"This has gone far enough, Gretchen. It really has."

Gretchen smiled. "You're scared now, aren't you?"

She went over to him, pushed the gun in his face. "admit it, you're scared."

"This isn't a pleasant experience for any of us," Quinlan said.

Gretchen smirked. "I love it when you get stuffy, Quinlan. It turns me on." She looked at Priscilla, who stood there in her wine-red bra and skimpy panties.

Gretchen had never seen Quinlan acting shy before and, she had to admit, there was something pretty sweet about it.

"Take her clothes off, Quinlan,"

"Don't do it, Quinlan," Priscilla said. "Give in to her once, and she'll just want more."

"Sort of like you and Quinlan here?" Gretchen said. "Wanting more all the time?" She turned back to Quinlan. Her voice softened; tears trembled in her voice. "All I ever wanted was for him to love me. And to be faithful. My father wasn't faithful to my mother, none of my boyfriends were ever faithful to *me*—I just wanted Quinlan to be different. And I thought he'd understand that. You know, because he had all this superior wisdom and superior insight." She put the gun to Quinlan's temple. "But you're just another con artist, aren't you, Quinlan?"

"Please put the gun down," he said quietly.

She smiled. "Can you see him start to sweat, Priscilla? See up here? On the forehead? He's really starting to get scared now. And it's embarrassing. Because he's a total control freak, aren't you, sweetie?"

"This isn't helping anybody, Gretchen," Quinlan said, still speaking quietly. "Now please put the gun down, and I'll send Priscilla away and we'll talk."

"Send Priscilla away?" Gretchen said. "Before you've serviced her? I'll bet Priscilla wouldn't appreciate that, now, would she?"

"Please, just let me go," Priscilla said. "Then you and Quinlan can resolve your differences. Please."

But Gretchen still wanted to have some fun. "Now, how can you stand there, Quinlan, and not want to put your hands all over her? This is a very, very nice body here. Prime meat, as one of the boys in the psychiatric hospital used to call it. And he should know—he used to cut up women with knives. And I'll bet he'd love to get you alone, Priscilla, a body like this." She looked back at Quinlan. "So c'mon. Get these clothes off her and take her over there and service her. Because if you don't, you're going to start pissing me off. And I don't think you want to do that, Quinlan. I really don't."

But Quinlan didn't make a move or say anything. He just stood there, looking depleted. All his powers to dominate situations had left him. He looked weak and confused.

"Please," Priscilla said again. But to whom was she speaking? She didn't seem to know. She was just mouthing a word. Please and thank you. Weren't those the *magic* words?

"Well, boy," Gretchen said, "you're really letting me down, you know that? A beautiful woman standing here without many clothes on—and you're too shy to do anything about it. You're starting to slip, Quinlan. You really are. But luckily, I'm here to help you."

She walked over behind Priscilla and put the gun to the back of her head. "One false move, babe, and I kill you on the spot. You understand?"

Priscilla, whose eyes suddenly filled with tears, nodded slowly.

Gretchen started undoing Priscilla's bra straps. Priscilla had a straight, lean back. "I can see why teenage boys have trouble with these things. They're not easy when you're in a hurry." Then she got the hooks undone and slid the straps off Priscilla's shoulders. Gretchen stepped back and looked at

Priscilla's large, well-shaped breasts. "Oh-oh. Store-boughts, Quinlan. Or hadn't you ever noticed that before. You used to be as flat as I am, weren't you, Priscilla? You got your money's worth, though. Those are nice tits. They really are."

She was starting to feel the frenzy, that strange tornado of emotions that was rage, fear, shame, self-loathing, and arrogance all at the same time.

"Get over here, Quinlan," she snapped. "Get over here and take her panties off."

"Please," Priscilla said again. "Please, just let me go."

"Shut up, Priscilla," Quinlan said.

Gretchen made a clucking sound. "If there's one thing I hate to hear, it's two lovers having a spat." She shook her head in mock grief. "It's just so sad."

Then the frenzy overtook her. She grabbed Priscilla by the arm and yanked her across the room to the bed. She threw her on the bed face-up and then reached down and ripped her panties away. "Now get over here and service her, Quinlan. And I mean right now."

"I won't do it," he said.

"Sure you will," she said. And shot him in the right thigh.

He cried out, as did Priscilla. Gretchen knew she wouldn't have long now. Barcroft and the other guards would come lumbering down here any moment now, after the gunshot.

"Service her, Quinlan," Gretchen said. "Or I shoot your other leg."

What choice did he have? He looked pale, pasty, profoundly confused. He did not enjoy being treated like this at all. But his terror overcame even his pride and, clutching the leg wound that was already starting to saturate his trouser leg, he began hobbling toward the king-sized waterbed.

Gretchen followed right behind him, prodding him with the gun. How many times she'd wanted to do this within the walls of the psychiatric hospital. Wipe away all the superiority and pity and amusement on the faces of all those doctors.

"Now, take care of her, Quinlan," Gretchen said. "Give her a real ride."

Quinlan eased himself down upon the bed. Priscilla reached out and touched the leg wound. "He's bleeding pretty badly, Gretchen. He really needs to see a doctor."

"Is he now?" Gretchen said. "The poor thing. Bleeding like that."

And then it was there, bigger than her will to fight it back, bigger than her self-control to keep it at bay temporarily.

"Hold her, Quinlan," Gretchen said, barely whispering, "hold her the way you held me and tell her all the things you told me. She'll like that, Quinlan." She leaned over the bed where Quinlan and Priscilla clung to each other like frightened children.

Then she could hear them coming. Heavy footsteps, hurrying, hurrying down the hall. Coming here. Barcroft bellowing.

"C'mon, now," Gretchen said. "We don't have much time. I want to hear you tell her you love her, Quinlan. Tell her that. She'll love it."

He glared up at her. Barcroft or one of his guards began pounding on the door.

"I told you we didn't have much time," Gretchen said. "Now go ahead and tell her."

He looked at her and started to say something but then stopped himself. How could you possibly argue rationally with anybody as far gone as Gretchen?

He turned his attention back to Priscilla. "I love you."

The pounding grew louder. "That's nice, Quinlan. That's very nice. Just the kind of note I'd want to go out on."

She shot Quinlan three times in the head. Even as meaty chunks of his brain were sticking themselves to the wall next to the waterbed, Priscilla was trying to roll away from him. But it was too late. Way too late.

Gretchen put three bullets in her face. There was some writhing—and the blood on her naked body gleamed with rubylike beauty—and then the air was fouled by Quinlan's bodily fluids.

And then Barcroft and three guards were smashing through the door with a red fire ax.

She acted quickly. Had to. Otherwise she would have been at their mercy, and she did not want the Barcrofts of this life—stolid, unimaginative, cynical—to control her anymore. She wanted all decisions to be her own. She wanted dignity, if nothing else.

They were rushing at her—the scene had assumed certain surreal aspects, not the least being the dreamlike haze which seemed to be rolling through this apartment like a fog . . . and somewhere in the fog somebody shouting, "She's got a gun! She's got a gun!"

And then the bullets ripping into her. There was a strange beauty in the pain. That was the thing uppermost in her mind . . . the beautiful and painful *inevitability* of all this . . . as if her entire life had been a joke and this room the punchline that tied all the stray moments of her life together.

She fell backward onto the bodies on the bed, the gun dropping from her hand and landing on the floor.

And then they were all over her, a circle of the guards, peering down at her and cursing her because of what she'd done to the father they'd all adopted. What would become of them now, Quinlan's children?

One of them, so overwhelmed with anger he couldn't help himself, came over to her and spit down into her face.

She was only vaguely aware of this. It was a sunny day and she was in a park at a duck pond and she and Quinlan were throwing the ducks pieces of bread. Gretchen was five months pregnant and positively gorgeous. And every few minutes, Quinlan would put his hand on the curve of her belly and listen to the child inside. And oh, how he'd smile. The perfect husband. The perfect mate. Here in this sunny, perfect world inside Gretchen's perfect mind.

"Bitch," one of the guards said.

That was the last thing Gretchen heard, and then she was dead.

Chapter Fifty-Four

. . . ROLLING away from the knife that was coming straight down toward her neck, Jenny angled herself so that she could get to her feet before Stafford could slash at her again.

But he didn't give her much time. She reached out and grabbed on to the edge of the nightstand so she could push herself to her feet. But by the time she did this, he was already lunging at her. Fortunately, she was able to step aside. He stumbled onward, slamming into the nightstand in the deep shadows of the bedroom. When he jerked his head around to look at her, his face was an angry silver mask that the moonlight had painted on him. Spittle ran from the left corner of his mouth. His teeth looked huge, predatory.

She had to get out of this room. Not only did he have a knife, he was strong and fast. She needed to get downstairs, outdoors. She felt guilty leaving her mother . . . but her mother was dead. Now she had to worry about herself.

But as she turned to the door, Stafford righted himself and leaped on her, tangling his fingers in her hair, yanking her to her knees.

The pain was blinding. She could feel hair being torn from her head. And then she could feel the blade of the butcher knife at her throat. *This is where I'll die,* she thought. She'd always wondered about that, where and when death would come to her. She hadn't seen this as morbid, just simply a natural curiosity about her time on the planet, and when it would end.

Here's where it would end.

"She betrayed me," he said. "Our whole life together was a lie."

She could almost feel sorry for him. She had no idea why her mother had kept the identity of her real father a secret, but whatever the reason, her mother had been wrong. She'd owed Stafford the truth.

"I—I'm sorry, Tom," she said.

That was when she bit him. His forearm was directly in front of her mouth. She knew that he could react by slashing her throat—if there was time, if the bite didn't weaken his grip—or he would give in, at least momentarily, to his pain.

She bit hard enough to draw blood. He cursed her, tried to rip his arm away from her teeth. She raised her hands and clamped on to his arm, enough to push the knife blade away from her, enough to let her get to her feet and run, stumbling, sobbing, to the guest room doorway and the hall.

Darkness. The staircase. If she could reach the front door, and outside . . .

"Make it easy for both of us," Stafford said, emerging from the bedroom. "Just stop running, Jenny. You know I'm going to catch you."

The stairs . . . clinging to the banister . . . if she stumbled, he'd leap on her and kill her . . . halfway down now . . . and then turning around . . . seeing him at the top of the stairs . . . his chalk-white face streaked with blood . . . his hands gleaming in the moonlight with blood . . . like a surgeon right after a particularly gory operation . . . coming down the steps one at a time, not hurrying at all, as if he knew for sure that he would catch her, kill her . . . as if he was the messenger of death, inevitable, inexorable.

She started to move again, but stumbled. He grabbed her, the man who used to be her father . . . the man who was now her enemy.

She started to get up, but then he was there, grabbing her by the shoulder, jerking her to her feet. He pushed her back against a wall. Moonlight through the front windows once more made a silver mask of his face. "Be a good girl now, Jenny," he said, his voice startlingly gentle. "Just give me a little bit of help here, and I promise you it won't hurt you. I'll do it very, very fast."

He raised his hand and gently touched her face. "I hope you understand that I really do love you, Jenny. It's just that I need

DAUGHTER OF DARKNESS 331

to destroy everybody involved in the lie—Ted and your mother and . . . you. I'm sorry, Jenny. I really am."

He raised the bloody knife once again.

***

Coffey used his two-way to phone for police help. He gave the address of the Stafford mansion and told them that he thought the place had been taken over by burglars. He also threw in the fact that he used to be on the force. That could play either way. Either the dispatcher would glow warmly in the light of police brotherhood and sisterhood or he'd do the verbal equivalent of rolling his eyes, and let you know that just because you *used* to be a cop didn't do diddly-squat for him, and in fact he was embarrassed for you that you'd even brought it up, like listening to some old fart brag about what a stud he'd been in his youth. This dispatcher just said, "Oh."

He was just now pulling into the mansion's drive, passing the smashed gates that looked like the broken wings of angels.

***

This time, Stafford didn't try to stab her. He just studied the knife in the moonlight—as if it was an object he'd never seen before.

He'd already told her all the things he'd done to her over the past five years with Quinlan.

He brought the knife to her face. She kept trying to ease her way out of his grasp. But how?

"You're still my father," she said. "Blood doesn't matter, Tom. You were the one who raised me. You were the one who loved me. And who *I* loved."

He smiled sadly, the blood streaks blending with the moon-silver of his mask. "I'll bet you don't love me very much right now."

She reached out and touched his face. "That's the strange thing, Tom. I still do. I really do."

Then, from the bottom of the stairs, a voice said, "It's time to put the knife down, Tom."

Both of them stared down at Coffey. He stood there with a gun in his hand. His police training had included talking to hostage takers. Calm. Friendly. "Nobody else has to get hurt, Tom. Just put the knife down on the step."

Stafford pulled Jenny even closer now, the knife at her throat. "We're coming down the stairs and walking to my car. Just stay back, and I won't kill her."

Coffey was still out of breath from running inside. All he could do now was watch.

"You need to calm down," Coffey said as gently as possible.

"You heard what I said," Stafford said. "I'm going to kill her soon—but it doesn't have to be right now."

Coffey knew he had just one opportunity. He couldn't take the chance of shooting Stafford. In a moment of panic, Jenny might get in the way. All he could do was hope to scare Stafford—and give Jenny her chance to escape.

He fired two bullets into the wall to the side of Stafford.

Stafford, startled, instinctively loosened his grip on Jenny. And then—just as instinctively—he started to tighten it again. But it was too late. Jenny worked herself free, pushing Stafford against the banister with such force that he screamed and pitched over the side, falling four feet to the floor.

His cry told Coffey immediately what had happened. Coffey ran to him. In the shadows, Stafford lay facedown. Coffey knelt and rolled him over. Stafford had fallen on his knife, the blade piercing his heart and killing him almost instantly.

Jenny ran up the stairs, crying out her mother's name. She knelt next to Molly, hearing the dreadful death rattle in her mother's throat as she tried to speak.

Sirens. "It's an ambulance, Mother. You're going to be all right."

Her mother's face seemed to have lost detail in the moonlight. The only clear aspect were the lovely, dark eyes that glistened with tears.

Jenny felt her die. It wasn't dramatic. No shudder, no spasms, no last gasped words. Rather, she felt her mother's body simply and quietly *stop*. All the busy circuits, all the highways and byways of the physical self, simply ceased.

There was a moment of aching silence that Jenny knew would never be filled again by the tender and winsome voice of her mother.

She became aware of the sirens again. She'd somehow

DAUGHTER OF DARKNESS

blocked them out. But they filled her ears now. So many of them.

She gently straightened her mother's body on the bed and then stood up. Her father lay on the floor below her, a sad marionette whose strings had been cut, and whose limbs were all sharp unnatural angles.

She had loved them both so much. So much.

The nightmare was over, she realized as she walked to the front door, leaning on Coffey for strength. But so was the dream, the earnest dream of her youth when people were just what they seemed to be, and sadness was never more serious than losing at puppy love.

She walked out the front door of the mansion to see ten police cars ringing the front of the drive, all headlights pointed right at her, all emergency lights saturating the night sky with blood red.

She wouldn't find any comfort until much, much later when, near dawn, she would fall asleep in Coffey's arms.

Elizabeth Forrest

☐ **DEATH WATCH** UE2648—$5.99
McKenzie Smith has been targeted by a mastermind of evil who can make virtual reality into the ultimate tool of destructive power. Stalked in both the real and virtual worlds, can McKenzie defeat an assassin who can strike out anywhere, at any time?

☐ **KILLJOY** UE2695—$5.99
Given experimental VR treatments, Brand must fight a constant battle against the persona of a serial killer now implanted in his brain. But Brand would soon learn that there were even worse things in the world—like the unstoppable force of evil and destruction called KillJoy.

☐ **BRIGHT SHADOW** UE2695—$5.99
When a clandestie FBI invasion of a cult ranch blows up, Vernon Spense manages to rescue one little girl, Jennifer. Though Spense finds what he thinks is a safe haven for her, to one man she's far too important to let go. Either he will get her back or he'll make sure she's beyond everyone's reach. And to that end, he will eliminate Spense or anyone who gets in his way. . . .

☐ **RETRIBUTION** UE779—$6.99
A former child art prodigy, Charlie has begun to paint again. But now her vibrant paintings bring to life a shocking revelation of undiscovered murders and the killer whose identity would soon become clear—unless Charlie herself becomes the stalker's next victim. . . .

Prices slightly higher in Canada. **DAW 134X**

Buy them at your local bookstore or use this convenient coupon for ordering.

PENGUIN USA P.O. Box 999—Dep. #17109, Bergenfield, New Jersey 07621

Please send me the DAW BOOKS I have checked above, for which I am enclosing $_____ (please add $2.00 to cover postage and handling). Send check or money order (no cash or C.O.D.'s) or charge by Mastercard or VISA (with a $15.00 minimum). Prices and numbers are subject to change without notice.

Card #_____ Exp. Date _____
Signature_____
Name_____
Address_____
City _____ State _____ Zip Code _____

For faster service when ordering by credit card call **1-800-253-6476**

Allow a minimum of 4-6 weeks for delivery. This offer is subject to change without notice.

Vampiric Thrillers from
S. A. SWINIARSKI

THE FLESH, THE BLOOD AND THE FIRE
During the Kingsbury Run murders over a dozen bodies—mutilated, decapitated, and drained of blood—were found along the railroad tracks and waterways of Cleveland, Ohio. With the whole city gripped by terror, safety director Eliot Ness instituted the largest manhunt in Cleveland's history, one that would eventually involve the entire police force. Despite these efforts, only two of the bodies were ever identified and the killer was never found—or was he? For one member of Cleveland's finest, Detective Stefan Ryzard, refused to give up the case. And his search for the truth would send him down a bloody trail that led from the depths of the city's shantytowns to the inner citadels of industrial power to the darkest parts of the human soul.
☐UE2879—$5.99

RAVEN
He awoke in a culvert, with no memory and no knowledge of how he had gotten there. The only thing he knew for sure was that he had become a vampire. . . .
☐UE2725—$5.99

Prices slightly higher in Canada.   **DAW 213X**

Buy them at your local bookstore or use this convenient coupon for ordering.

PENGUIN USA   P.O. Box 999—Dep. #17109, Bergenfield, New Jersey 07621

Please send me the DAW BOOKS I have checked above, for which I am enclosing
$_____ (please add $2.00 to cover postage and handling). Send check or money order (no cash or C.O.D.'s) or charge by Mastercard or VISA (with a $15.00 minimum). Prices and numbers are subject to change without notice.

Card #_____ Exp. Date _____
Signature_____
Name_____
Address_____
City _____ State _____ Zip Code _____

For faster service when ordering by credit card call **1-800-253-6476**
Allow a minimum of 4-6 weeks for delivery. This offer is subject to change without notice.

OTHERLAND
TAD WILLIAMS

Otherland. A perilous and seductive realm of the imagination where any fantasy—whether cherished dream or dreaded nightmare—can be made shockingly real. Incredible amounts of money have been lavished on it. The best minds of two generations have labored to build it. And, somehow, bit by bit, it is claiming Earth's most valuable resource—its children. It is up to a small band of adventures to take up the challenge of Otherland in order to reveal the truth to the people of Earth. But they are split by mistrust, thrown into different worlds, and stalked at every turn by the sociopathic killer Dread and the mysterious Nemesis. . . .

☐ **VOLUME ONE: CITY OF GOLDEN SHADOW** UE2763—$6.99
☐ **VOLUME TWO: RIVER OF BLUE FIRE** UE2777—$24.95

Prices slightly higher in Canada. **DAW 214X**

Buy them at your local bookstore or use this convenient coupon for ordering.

PENGUIN USA P.O. Box 999—Dep. #17109, Bergenfield, New Jersey 07621

Please send me the DAW BOOKS I have checked above, for which I am enclosing $_____ (please add $2.00 to cover postage and handling). Send check or money order (no cash or C.O.D.'s) or charge by Mastercard or VISA (with a $15.00 minimum). Prices and numbers are subject to change without notice.

Card #_____ Exp. Date _____
Signature_____
Name_____
Address_____
City _____ State _____ Zip Code _____

For faster service when ordering by credit card call **1-800-253-6476**

Allow a minimum of 4-6 weeks for delivery. This offer is subject to change without notice.